CHAPTER ONE

Their in-car computer screen lit up with a whoosh just as her partner was shouting their orders into the speaker at the Tim Hortons drive-through. A BLT and medium double double for her, and a crispy chicken combo with a large double double for him. Another awesome dinner on the job.

Hannah read the alert. "Unit 3206A, 10-55 at 26 Lake Point Road. Two-person call."

"Ah-ha," Rick said, "10-55. What's that?"

"Domestic disturbance." Hannah leaned forward to type a reply just as a large black F-150 pulled into line behind them.

"Tell them we'll be a moment."

She glanced across at him in surprise. At 8:58 on a sticky evening in late May, dusk was just leaching colour from the sky. The street lights had come on in the parking lot, splashing puddles of light into the gloom and carving sharp angles into his tired face. Rick was a cop with twenty-six years on the street, assigned as her coach officer to teach her the ropes. Twenty-six years of responding to calls like this day in and day out. Were they just a number to him now?

He flicked his hand at the line ahead. "We're not going anywhere. Plus, we need to eat or we'll be no good for the rest of the shift. Lesson number one, Pollack, take care of yourself first."

"We could jump the curb."

He gave her a slow smile, that annoying one he saved for special moments when he was sharing his superior wisdom. His superior experience. "Tell them we're blocked in a line at Tim Hortons so we'll be a couple of minutes."

"It's a domestic," she said.

"Five minutes tops. Ask Dispatch if anyone else is available."

Hannah cringed but did as she was told. She kept her mouth shut as they crawled forward in the line, just handed over her ten-dollar bill and took the sandwich he passed to her. Barely a spare word had passed between them all shift. Maybe if she'd been one of his buddies, they would have talked about the NHL playoffs, but the twenty-five-year age gap between them, not to mention the gender gap, was too big for him to leap.

The screen lit again, asking if they were on their way. Rick took a swig of his coffee and shut his eyes. "Tell her we're responding. What was that address again?"

"It's 26 Lake Point Road." Hannah scrolled through the details. "It's a detached residence owned by Edward McAuley; report of screaming called in by a neighbour, Philip Walker, at 24 Lake Point."

With a sigh, Rick put the cruiser in gear and accelerated out of the parking lot.

"Lights?" Hannah asked.

He shook his head as he pulled onto Carling Avenue and stomped on the accelerator. "That's a quiet, high-end neighbourhood. Low crime. No need to go in with sirens and lights blazing. But check out the owner while we're en route. Domestics can be tricky, and his name rings a bell."

Hannah was already pulling Edward McAuley up on their internal database. "He's pretty clean," she said as she scanned. "He called 911 once when his daughter broke her arm, another time he was witness to an MVA, two noise complaints against him by a neighbour for loud parties —"

"Same neighbour?"

Hannah nodded. "Philip Walker. And another complaint from Walker about destruction of property." She tried to make sense of the brief note. "Looks like McAuley cut down his tree."

Rick grunted. He was shooting down Carling Avenue, wide open at that time of the evening. On his right, the broad Ottawa River sparkled in the emerging moonlight as they passed the sailing club. Hannah loved the many faces of the legendary river that began far to the north and coursed through the city on toward the St. Lawrence. At some points of the city, it hurtled through rapids, but here it spread out as wide and gentle as a lake.

Rick slowed briefly to glance at the GPS. "Run the neighbour's name. He may be a chronic complainer."

Hannah entered the new name. "Not much. The same complaint entries, plus a 911 call on December thirty-first last year — his wife collapsed. Paramedics treated on scene, deceased." She stopped as the human story behind the cold, sparse notes sank in. She thought of her grandfather, who had never recovered his joy after his wife's death years earlier. This man's wife had died in their home on New Year's Eve, not even six months ago.

Rick eased his foot off the gas as he turned off Carling Avenue onto a narrow residential street. In the growing darkness, the houses were barely visible on spacious lots behind tall, lush trees.

"So he's grieving," he said. "He may be extra sensitive. We'll check out the McAuley house before we talk to him."

As they rounded a bend, 26 Lake Point Road loomed ahead in a blaze of lights on the quiet street. There were security lights at every corner that cast the shrubs into eerie webs on the fieldstone walls, and a porch light burnished the expensive columns on either side of the front stoop. Hannah wondered if they were marble. Even by the standards of the street, it was a huge house. A silver Lexus SUV and a blood-red Mercedes coupe sat in front of the two-car garage, and at the edge of the drive was a speedboat on a boat trailer. Behind the trailer were several pallets of patio stones and a pile of crushed stone. The fancy house was about to get fancier.

They climbed out of the cruiser and stood a moment. "What do you see here, Pollack?"

Hannah took stock. "Blinds are drawn on all the windows. Huge windows but you can't see inside. Security lights everywhere." *Someone hiding from prying eyes*, she thought, but kept the speculation to herself. Rick was a "just the facts, ma'am" kind of guy. She listened for screams but heard nothing but the chirp of crickets and frogs. Through the trees, she caught the shimmer of the river behind the house. "No sound of fighting. Some serious money here, though."

He nodded and pulled on his mask as he started up the drive. "I'll handle the beginning, and you take the wife. Okay?"

The bell rang through the house, setting up a high-pitched yapping inside. A man shouted at the dog, to no avail. After a delay, during which Hannah suspected they were being sized up on video cam, the door opened to reveal a man dressed in shorts, T-shirt, and flip-flops. He'd made no effort to put on a mask. Although he wasn't tall, he was well muscled and reeked of confidence — the kind of confidence that comes with owning a two-million-dollar waterfront home and tooling around in a Mercedes coupe. A few strands of gray at his temples lent an air of dignity to his blond, boyish good looks, and his blue eyes were sharp.

Rick sucked in his gut. Somewhere inside, the dog continued to yap.

"Good evening, Officers," the man said with an easy smile. "What brings you out to our quiet neck of the woods?"

Rick introduced himself. "Mr. Edward McAuley?"

"Guilty. What can I do for you?"

"We received a call —" Rick began but was drowned out by the barking.

The man's blue eyes flickered, and with a sigh, he turned back inside. "Krissy, honey, could you quiet the dog? The police are here about something."

There was no reply from inside, but the barking stopped. Hannah strained to see past the man into the hall, but he was blocking her view. "Sorry about that, Constable ... Geneva, was it? Your name's familiar."

"Geneva, yes, and this is Constable Pollack. We're responding to a complaint about a disturbance at this address."

"Disturbance? What kind of disturbance?"

"Shouting, screaming, sounds of things breaking. This occurred about eight fifty p.m."

"Well, I can't think ..." He snapped his fingers. "I know you! Constable Geneva. Rick, right? You investigated a traffic injury case I was handling for one of the parties. You did a good job, if I recall. A very thorough report." He chuckled. "It helped my client win a lot of money."

Rick smiled. "Right, I recognize you now. I hope that poor man is recovering."

"Well, he'll never be the same, but the money helps. Now, about this shouting and screaming. I mean, my wife and I had a bit of an argument over doing the dishes. We probably raised our voices. That's what happens when two excitable people marry — I'm Irish and she's Latina, so ..." He shrugged and ran his hand through his hair. "We forget that we're not really out in the country here, and with the windows open ..."

"So everything is all right, Mr. McAuley?"

"Ted, for God's sake. Yeah, yeah."

"Who lives here in the house with you?"

"My wife, Kristina, and my two children. Daughter is seventeen, and she's always in her room with her headphones on, so she wouldn't hear a thing. And my son is only three. He's fallen asleep watching TV in the family room. In fact, there might have been screaming on the TV, too. You know how these shows are." Ted peered past them into the drive. He still hadn't invited them in, and the humid outside air was drifting into the house. "I'm guessing it was my neighbour who complained. Philip Walker? What exactly did he say?"

"We'll be interviewing him next."

"Oh. Well, go easy on him. He's really a very nice man, but he's going through a rough time right now. His wife died suddenly this winter of a brain aneurysm, and he's in the place alone. It's probably too much for him — too empty, too many memories. I don't appreciate him calling you guys on me, but I guess he …" He trailed off, his voice tinged with regret, his hand already on the doorknob.

Rick made no move. "So everything is okay here?"

"Yes. You're welcome to come in to see."

Rick cocked his head at Hannah, her cue to take over. Taking in a breath, she stepped forward. "I'd like to speak to your wife, please. Protocol, to confirm her side?"

He gave her a faint smile and turned back. "Krissy, have you got a minute to talk to the police?"

A woman's voice could be heard in the distance, and a few seconds later, a tall woman glided down the hall, cradling a little mop of a dog in her arms. The dog growled, and she quieted it with a soft whisper.

Kristina had a messy tangle of black curls piled on her head and a ragged caftan robe that covered her from her neck to her toes. The elegant diamond ring looked oddly out of place. Her face betrayed no emotion as she met her husband's eyes.

"It seems Philip called the police again," Ted said, reaching out to stroke the dog.

"Oh."

The dog growled again, and as Ted withdrew his hand, Hannah noticed a scratch on his arm.

"Nasty scratch," she said. "How did you get it?"

Beside her, Rick shifted but didn't interrupt. She knew it was off script but appropriate. Ted glanced at his arm as if he was surprised to see the scratch. Droplets of blood had beaded along the wound. "Oh, it opened up again. I scratched it on some branches biking home from the office. They really ought to trim the brush along the river path."

Rick grinned. "Not our department."

Hannah ignored the banter. "Can you confirm that, Mrs. McAuley?"

The woman's face remained expressionless. "Yes. I mean, I didn't see the accident, but that's what he said when he got home."

"Can I have a few words inside, Mrs. McAuley?"

"No." Kristina glanced quickly back down the hall. "I mean … I don't want to upset my son. He's having trouble settling for the night."

"Then can we step outside for a moment?" When Kristina glanced at her husband, Hannah touched her elbow. "Just while Rick and your husband finish up the formalities."

Kristina was already backing up inside, pressing the dog close. "No, that's not necessary. Everything is fine. I shouldn't leave Peter...."

Hannah studied Kristina carefully. There were no bruises or red marks, no sign of recent tears, but the damn caftan hid almost everything. She was refusing to talk to them, and they had nothing to go on.

Except Philip Walker's word.

Rick was already thanking them for their time and preparing to leave. On the doorstep, standing in the harsh porch light, Ted called out, "What happens now?"

"After we take Mr. Walker's statement, we'll write it up. Don't worry, we'll go easy on him."

Ted nodded. "Thank you."

Philip Walker had an older, smaller house that was barely visible through the jungle of shrubbery. An archway through the cedar hedge led them to an inner yard exploding with plants. The sweet scent of lilacs filled the air. A dim porch sconce cast a weak light on the flagstone path, but Hannah turned on her flashlight to get a sense of their surroundings. It was chaos. Tall trees spread their boughs overhead, filtering the sprinkle of stars. Bird feeders swayed from the lower limbs, and lilac bushes heavy with flowers arched over flower beds bright with irises and bleeding hearts. Blue forget-me-nots popped up everywhere.

Sharon would love this, she thought. Her father didn't know a cactus from a tulip, but her stepmother painstakingly coaxed beautiful flowers out of every corner of their garden.

"You coming?" Rick was already on the doorstep, ringing the bell. Hannah switched off her flashlight and scurried up. "This time just take notes and let me do the talking unless I give you the nod," he muttered.

She bit back a retort. It wasn't her fault Kristina had refused to co-operate. Her quick temper had landed her in trouble lots of times in the past, and she was determined not to screw up this job. Rick was always hinting that she'd got the job only because she was a woman and her father was a senior officer. Much as she hated it, if she wanted to prove herself, she had to follow his rules, even when they were dumb. She'd be free of him in a few weeks when the coaching period was over.

The door opened, and the man who greeted them looked concerned but unafraid. Hannah had been expecting an elderly man sapped of strength and will, but Philip Walker looked surprisingly young to be a widower. He stood straight and strong, his dark salt-and-pepper hair cut short and his brown eyes steady. His nod was firm and confident when Rick introduced them.

"Please come in, Officers. I assume you cops are all vaccinated? Can I get you a cold drink? Perrier, ice tea?" He chuckled. "Nothing stronger, I guess."

He was already heading down the hall. Rick declined and hesitated on the threshold, about to take off his shoes.

"Oh, don't worry about that," Walker said. "I'm in and out of the garden all the time. If my furniture can't take a little dirt, it's not worth having."

In the living room, Hannah could see his point. Everything was old, frayed, and battered. There were water rings on the tables and mismatched throws to cover the worn spots on the couch. China figurines and photographs cluttered the tables, collecting dust.

"I don't believe in throwing things out as long as they work," he said, tossing aside a cushion so they could sit. "Our landfills are piled high with perfectly serviceable possessions discarded just because we want something new. Most of this is from my wife's childhood home, so it harbours memories." He took a deep breath. "But enough of that. You're here about the 911 call, I assume. Is she all right?"

Rick kept his face deadpan. "Can you take me through it, Mr. Walker? What you saw and heard?"

Hannah took out her notebook.

"I didn't *see* anything. Their blinds are always drawn, and in any case I have too many bushes in the way. But I heard them. I keep my windows open when it's warm like this. I love the breeze off the Ottawa River and the sound of crickets and frogs."

"What did you hear?"

"Screaming. Swearing, shouting."

"Him or her?"

"Both. Well, her more than him. Her voice is shrill when she's angry."

"Could you make out anything they said?"

"I heard him say 'useless' —" He paused and glanced at Hannah.

"We've heard it all, Mr. Walker," Hannah said. *And used it even more*, she thought but kept her eyes on her notebook.

He tightened his lips. "He called her a useless cunt. Sick, crazy, always going off like a fucking volcano. I'm sorry, I hate vulgar language. He said she couldn't even run a house properly, and she was messing up their son. Although he said 'fucking up.'"

"Anything else?"

"She was so loud and shrill, it was hard to make out what she said. I did hear her say 'I hate you, don't you dare,' lots of disjointed nonsense. 'No. Stop.' And then a really loud crash."

"Like what?"

"Something heavy hitting the wall? A pot or a lamp, maybe? I think they were in the kitchen, which is on this side of the house."

"Did the fight continue after the crash?"

"Yes. I heard screaming and thumping."

Rick paused to study him. "Did it sound like screams of pain?"

"That's difficult to tell, isn't it? Pain, fear? Maybe even rage." He looked down at his hands, which had formed fists. "I'm sorry, that's not very helpful."

"It's all helpful, Mr. Walker," Rick said with surprising softness. "His screams or hers?"

"Hers. Then a door slammed, and that was the end of it. I thought it was too quiet. I even went outside to check if I could hear or see anything else. Nothing. I got worried. That's when I called 911."

Rick stood up. "Can you show me where you were in the house when you heard the fight?"

They followed Philip into the kitchen, which was clean except for a small pile of dishes in soapy water in the sink and a single empty wineglass on the counter. He stood at the open window over the sink and pointed outside. "I was just starting my cleanup. When I turned off the tap, I heard it."

Hannah peered out the window. Philip was right; the thick cedar hedge blocked his view of the McAuley property. She could see the bright security lights through the hedge but no details.

Rick returned to the living room. "Mr. Walker, why did you call 911?" When the man looked baffled, he added, "Was it the noise? I know it's a quiet neighbourhood."

Philip's brows pinched together in an irritated frown. "No. I didn't like the noise, but I called because I was worried about her."

"Had you any other reason for that worry? Had she confided in you? Had you ever witnessed any violence before or seen any suspicious injuries?"

Philip hesitated. He seemed to be sizing Rick up, taking in the wide cop stance and the implacable set of his jaw. "Nothing I can swear to. But they fight a lot. I don't think it's a happy marriage." He paused. "When they first moved here, my wife and I tried to be friendly. It's a very secluded community — just a few streets along the river — and everybody has always stood together. But Kristina kept to herself. He was friendly enough at first, but then they started renovating and building that huge addition. It's way too big for the property. They took down all the beautiful old trees and ploughed the gardens under. We tried to protest, all the neighbours did. The house blocked the light, the sunset, and our view of the river. But we lost. He's a lawyer, you know, and he knew all the ins and outs. After that, it's been much less cordial."

"With everyone or just you?"

He flushed. "Well, I'm the one most affected. That monster is right on my doorstep!"

Rick studied him thoughtfully for a few seconds. Hannah could almost see him putting the pieces together to form a picture that discounted Philip Walker completely. Sure enough, he rose to his feet, thanked him, and headed for the door.

Back outside in the cruiser, she flipped through her notes. "Should I write it up for Partner Assault?"

He shook his head. "No, I'll do it, but it won't be a priority for them. There's nothing there."

"There was a violent fight, and the neighbour obviously thinks something is going on."

"That neighbour is biased. His conclusions would be laughed out of court."

"But the couple are secretive. Every window is covered."

"Maybe that's because nobody likes them in the neighbourhood."

"But —"

"Look what we have. It doesn't even come close to reasonable grounds. Shouting, mostly her. Screams, mostly hers. One visible injury, and that's to *him*. If anything, we could be charging *her* with assault."

Hannah turned her impressions over in her mind. The husband's aw-shucks, buddy-buddy explanations, the caftan that covered everything, the wife's expressionless face. The dog.

"There's the dog."

Rick snorted. "What about the dog?"

"I have a dog. I mean there's a dog at my parents'. She was a rescue who'd been traumatized. Dogs don't hide their feelings. That dog wasn't friendly, especially to the husband. It was tense and fearful. It was quiet in the wife's arms, but when the husband went to pet it, it snarled."

Rick buckled up and started the cruiser. "Seriously? You want me to push a case based on a dog? The Partner Assault Unit is swamped. They review literally thousands of cases a year. Cases with merit."

Hannah's temper flared. Always a bad idea when you're a rookie policewoman still on probation. "We don't need certainty. We don't even need reasonable grounds. If it's a domestic disturbance, it goes to Partner Assault."

"And it will. Don't tell me what procedure is, Hannah. This is our job every day — messy, contradictory statements, hunches, always the danger of being wrong. We're talking about Edward T. McAuley, personal injury lawyer. I've seen him in court. You don't want to be wrong."

CHAPTER TWO

Inspector Michael Green glanced at the clock on his dashboard as he accelerated up the ramp out of the parking lot below the Ottawa Courthouse. He was going to be late. In his frustration, he barely registered the glorious blue sky and spring sunshine. Instead, he pictured his son staring out the front window, or worse, sitting on the front stoop, his soccer bag at his side and a familiar look of resignation on his face.

Sharon would have fed him supper before taking their daughter to the sitter and going to an evening meeting. But she would have left him to do his homework with the promise that Dad would be home any minute to take him to his soccer practice.

Soccer was Tony's passion, and he was good at it, to the surprise of his father, who'd grown up playing pick-up ball hockey in the dusty back alleys of his inner city neighbourhood and who had never owned a pair of soccer cleats, or much of anything else, growing up. And whose own father had never had the least idea what he did with his time. Fortunately.

Now it was his job to be the cheerleader dad, sitting with the other parents in folding chairs on the sidelines of the grassy field and watching the nimble slip of a twelve-year-old dribble a determined path toward the opposing goal.

Soccer kept the high-energy boy out of trouble, Sharon said, pointing out the tumultuous, hair-trigger teenage years they'd had to navigate with Hannah. It didn't matter that Hannah had spent her first sixteen years living with her utterly self-absorbed mother on the other side of the continent and had arrived on their doorstep as a bundle of rage and mistrust. Due more to Sharon's persistence, patience, and wisdom than his own, she had grown up. Now that quirky, rebellious kid with the black lipstick and the multiple body piercings had become a cop!

Green felt his blood pressure ease as he thought of her. He'd caught a glimpse of her in bail court today as she conferred with the Crown attorney. She'd looked calm and demure, her hair now a sedate brown and pulled back into a ponytail that hid the secret green streak underneath. He hadn't wanted to embarrass her by speaking to her. He'd been standing at the back of the room, ostensibly making sure that everything was running smoothly, from the court security to the flow of documents to the Crown and the judge.

This was actually his staff sergeant's job, but Green often used the excuse to escape the dull confines of his office and the tedious paperwork that piled up on his desk. Being down in the busiest courts made him feel in the thick of police work again, alive and connected to the daily drama that had been his passion for nearly thirty-five years.

Over four years! Four years since he'd been shuffled out of Criminal Investigations and into this stifling, paper-choked tomb of court security. He didn't even have an office at the main police headquarters anymore but was stuck in the courthouse a kilometre away. Green called the job the three *P*s — procedure, protection, and paperwork — and someone had to do it. Without it, the entire system of justice was in jeopardy from a misplaced court document to a gun smuggled into the courtroom. But it was a repetitive and never-ending tedium of dotting *i*'s and crossing *t*'s, broken only by his forays down into the courtrooms, where he could still feed by proxy his addiction to the messy thrill of catching bad guys.

Every year, he applied for a transfer out, only to be overlooked, but now, as the five-year mark approached, he was clinging to hope. Any other department would do, even an assignment to a task force or a secondment to the OPP. Another year of this exile from the only kind of police work he was any good at — solving major crimes — and he'd be ticking the time off to retirement. With a son still several years from university and a younger daughter who'd just turned six, that was unthinkable.

He drove as fast as he dared along Queen Elizabeth Drive, enjoying the welcome shade of the leafy trees, the grand old houses on the bluff, and the occasional glimpse of kayaks on the Rideau Canal. Once through the Experimental Farm, he entered his home territory of Westboro, only fifteen minutes late. If Tony was ready at the curb, he might still make the opening whistle.

He turned the corner onto his street, and sure enough, there was Tony, still a little boy but beginning to lose his round edges. He wasn't scanning the street impatiently but was instead talking excitedly to a young woman leaning on her motorcycle. As Green pulled up to the curb, Hannah turned to him with a smile.

"I saw you in court today," she said. "Checking up on me?"

He sidestepped the challenge. With Hannah, even after all these years, there was always a challenge. "I didn't even know you'd be there. But you looked good." He paused, longing to ask more, to get a small taste of life on the streets, but didn't want to get her back up. "Interesting case?" he ventured.

She shook her head. "Not that one. But there is something …"

"Put your bike in the drive and hop in. We can talk once I get Tony to his practice."

Hannah's story came out slowly as they stood slightly apart from the crowd, occasionally distracted by a rush up the field. She spoke softly so as not to be overheard as she described a routine call two days earlier. A fight reported by a neighbour who suspected domestic violence, although the couple denied it.

"I know women deny it sometimes dozens of times, even when they've made the call themselves," she said. "I know they recant in court. But it doesn't mean it didn't happen. But my partner thought there was no credible evidence, and he was all buddy-buddy with the man. The questions he asked, the way he wrote it up, it'll just be buried."

"Rick Geneva is old-school," Green said. "A good cop, an experienced cop who's seen a lot of these and probably has a nose for them. But yeah, he's going to look at this through the lens of 'Can we make a charge and can we make it stick?'"

"But I studied a lot about domestic violence in my criminology courses. The actual chargeable offences — the bruises, threats, hospital trips — are just the tip of the iceberg. The violence goes on day after day in private, in everything from monitoring her phone texts to giving her the 'look' when she crosses him. In fact, even when she doesn't, just to remind her what he can do. What else is she going to do but deny it with him standing right beside her?"

"I know, honey. It's the hardest thing about policing: knowing bad things are happening but not being able to prove it. The same thing happens in gang-controlled neighbourhoods. People are too afraid to co-operate with police because they don't trust us to protect them. With good reason, I'm afraid."

"Rick told me to handle the wife's interview, but she refused to co-operate. I think … I should have pushed harder to get her alone."

He longed to give her a hug but didn't dare. "That might have made things worse."

She watched Tony for a moment, looking sad, and to Green's eyes, very young. "Should I go over my partner? Talk to the Partner Assault Unit in person?"

"You could," he said carefully, "if you're prepared for the consequences with Geneva."

She scowled. "Fucking Force, controlled by blind old white guys."

"Or you could look into it a little more. Do some background checking. Maybe visit the woman when the husband is out. You have to be careful, though. You don't want to put her at risk."

She shot him a small grin. "You want me to play detective?"

He shrugged, trying to look casual. "It's a thought." He didn't add *it's probably what I'd do*. That would guarantee her doing the opposite.

"Are you kidding me?"

Green paused, his wineglass suspended in midair, and looked at Sharon in surprise. "What?"

"You sent her back into an abusive situation with no backup?"

"She's just going to poke around to get some background. On her own time. She doesn't think her partner was thorough enough."

He and Sharon were sitting on their patio as the late-evening sun sank through the trees. The mosquitoes had not yet descended, and they were enjoying a rare moment of catch-up in their busy lives.

It was not going well. Sharon had abandoned her wineglass on the side table, and even through the deepening shadows, Green could see the dangerous flash in her eyes. "You know better than me that domestic violence cases are among the most volatile and unpredictable that an officer can face."

"She's not going anywhere near the guy, Sharon. I told her to make sure she only talks to the woman when he's away."

"That doesn't mean he won't find out. If he really is abusive, he'll be monitoring her, checking the security cameras and her phone, asking neighbours. And who's to say the woman won't throw Hannah under a bus if it comes to protecting herself?"

Not for the first time since he'd told Hannah to investigate further, he felt a niggle of unease. "Hannah's smart, and she's seen more of the seedy side than most cops her age."

"She's twenty-three years old! She's been on the Force four months!"

"She's got good instincts, Sharon. The kind of instincts and curiosity that make a good detective."

"Oh no, you don't! She's not you, Mike. Don't push her just so you can live vicariously through her."

He was shocked. The problem with having a psychiatric nurse for a wife was that she often saw right through him. Saw things even he didn't. He turned the idea over in his mind. Yes, he hated his current post. Yes, he longed to be back in the thick of criminal investigation, piecing together clues, picking apart evidence, and chasing down bad guys. Could that really be at play here?

He took a slow, deliberate sip of wine. "That's not fair, Sharon. I'm just trying to encourage her. She has investigative instincts, but there's little chance to use them on patrol. All the big stuff is referred on up the line while you're on to another service call. It took her a long time to find a job she really wanted. I didn't want her to be a cop, but now that she is, I want her to thrive. I want her to follow as far as her instincts take her. She's asking exactly the questions I would have asked."

Sharon sat in silence, twirling her wineglass. The last shafts of sunlight had faded from the treetops, and the crickets had started their song. Green couldn't see her expression but sensed she was softening.

"Okay," she said eventually. "I know she's a restless spirit, and she's going to find it hard to stick to the daily procedures and monotony of most police work." She chuckled. "Just like her father. But she's not you, honey. You've had over thirty years of police experience. You know the danger signs and the lines in the sand. And even apart from all that, do you want to create a rift between her and her coach officer? He made the call, and she's second-guessing him. That won't go over well. You of all people shouldn't be encouraging her to go rogue."

He bristled. "It's hardly rogue. It's simply follow-up. We cops are not robots; we're allowed to exercise our discretion. She's just thinking a little outside the box."

"Which could earn her a reprimand or at least a note on her file if Rick Geneva feels like it." Sharon reached out and caught his fingers in hers. "She's a rebel, Mike, just like you. And she's trying to be just like you. But it's up to you to be a steadying influence. She's twenty-three. Remember what you were like at twenty-three."

He did remember. And it was thanks to that cocky, impatient young officer that he was now out of Criminal Investigations and serving time in the Siberia of career postings. "I was just pleased she asked for my opinion. She never talks to me about her job. You know Hannah and her ten-foot wall."

CHAPTER THREE

Philip Walker was surrounded by bags of mulch and compost as he knelt over his rose gardens. He looked up in surprise as Hannah walked under the cedar arch and up the path. She had dressed in torn jeans, tight T-shirt, and Ottawa Senators ball cap to look as little like a police officer as possible, and Philip seemed to take a few seconds to recognize her.

"Hello, Mr. Walker," Hannah said.

"Officer? Is something wrong?"

"No. Just routine follow-up on the call."

Philip grinned. He was wearing a large Tilley hat and sunglasses to ward off the early-June sun. "Are you undercover or something?" he asked in a low voice.

Hannah laughed. "No, just passing through."

Philip glanced past her into the narrow street, looking puzzled. The man didn't miss much, Hannah thought.

"I parked around the corner." She didn't elaborate. She had timed her visit carefully, assuming most of the neighbourhood would be at work at noon on a weekday. The red Mercedes was gone from the drive, but a pick-up truck had taken its place, and she could hear male and female voices next door. She knew both she and Philip would be visible from the upper windows of the McAuley house.

"Can we sit in the shade, Mr. Walker? Maybe on the porch?"

Without question, Philip led Hannah to a pair of creaky old wicker chairs on the front porch. "How can I help?" he asked as he pulled off his gardening gloves. "And please call me Phil."

"Have you remembered anything more about the incident that night? Or other incidents?"

"They fight a lot. The poor woman has no friends, and I don't think she's happy. I wouldn't be either, married to him."

"Why?"

"He's full of himself. He built the biggest house on the block and bought himself every expensive toy a man could dream of." He gestured through the shrubs. "Just look at that huge boat. Noisy, smelly, gas-guzzling. I have to look at it every day, blocking my view of the trees down the street. And he has his fancy Mercedes."

"I guess he makes a good living."

"He's a lawyer. I've got nothing against lawyers, but when his clients get a settlement from an accident case or something, I'm sure he takes most of it."

"How do you know that?"

"How else can he afford all this? His wife doesn't work."

"So she's home?"

"Most days. She doesn't go out much. She has the little one at home...." He paused. "He's a handful. Tantrums, crying. Like I said, not a happy home."

"How long have they lived here?"

"Four years. It used to be a nice bungalow like mine, with lovely trees and a deck overlooking the river. Like everywhere else around here, these older homes are being torn down, and people are building these huge boxes that take up almost all the lot. It means they're right next door to me, and when the windows are open, I can hear everything."

She grinned. "You probably learn way more about their marriage than you want to."

Phil glanced at her and laughed. "Well, yes, they're pretty noisy about that, too, and it doesn't sound like much fun for her. And I know he's a stickler for detail. I've heard them arguing about bills — how much she spends on groceries or vet bills or the little boy's music lessons. Ted can have all the luxuries in the world, but ..." He paused. "I know it's all little things, but I'm a social worker, on disability at the moment, and so I guess I have a radar for the little things."

"There's a teenage daughter, too, right?"

"You'd never know it. I hardly see her. She catches the bus to school early in the morning and comes back late in the evening. I only see her when she goes jogging or biking, but she barely says boo to me, always has those earphones on and her nose in her phone. Apparently she plays competitive soccer at school. He's a fitness buff, too, cycling and kayaking, but beyond that he hardly goes outside. He hires her brother to care for the lawn, such as it is." He paused, his lips tightening. "It looks like the brother is about to rip up even that postage stamp and lay down an ugly concrete patio."

Hannah perked up. Here was a possible source of support. "Oh, she has family in the city?"

"I mostly see her brother and her father. They've done a lot of the reno work, and they usually come when Ted is out. Avoiding him, I'm sure. He's such a nitpicker." He nodded toward the McAuley house. "That's the brother over there now. She doesn't get many friends visiting. Another little red flag that bothers me."

"Is there a mother? Are they close?"

Phil seemed to weigh his words carefully. "I wouldn't say close. She tries to help out, comes to the house sometimes to do cleaning and laundry or bring food. But I think she's very religious. Old-school, if you know what I mean. They're new Canadians from Latin America, so she's …" He shrugged. "Well, the man's the head of the house, and it's the wife's job to keep the family happy."

"Okay, so not someone Kristina could turn to for support. Any other incidents that made you worried, like the other evening?"

Phil sat forward and cast a wary glance toward the bushes. "Once this winter I heard a lot of screaming and crashing. The windows were closed, so I couldn't make out what was being said, but it sounded nasty. I was a bit embarrassed for them, actually. I mean, no one wants to have their fights overheard. So the next day I waited until he drove off, and I went over there with the excuse of offering them a bottle of Christmas peach brandy. I make it every year. She didn't answer the door for the longest time, and when she did, she looked like she'd been crying. I asked if she was all right, and she said yes, just tired because her little boy was up most of the night. It was the middle of the pandemic, so she didn't invite me in, and I couldn't see inside the house. I got bold and told her I'd heard something break, and I asked if she needed help fixing it. I'm pretty handy with a hammer and saw. She said she'd dropped a plate and was sorry it had disturbed me, and then she couldn't get rid of me fast enough." Phil paused. "She was wearing a thick turtleneck sweater so you could hardly see it, but it looked like red marks on her neck. Like she'd been choked. That's not such a little thing."

"You didn't report that."

He averted his gaze and reached up to pick a dead bloom from a hanging vine. "I couldn't be sure, and she was denying everything. I didn't want to make things worse. Ted is a lawyer, and he'd go after me with both barrels. And to be honest, my wife died shortly after, and it all kind of went out of my mind. I don't feel good about that, so recently I've been keeping an eye out more."

Hannah worked hard to hide her dismay. Even though Phil couldn't be sure, this was the first real hint that maybe Ted McAuley was not just mean and controlling, but also dangerous.

Phil seemed eager for the company and the chance to talk, but figuring she'd got all the information she could, Hannah thanked him soon after and walked back out to the street. Standing behind the protection of Phil's hedge, she studied the McAuley house. The dusty white truck parked in the drive had *RR Contracting* written on its door and a jumble of rope and tools in its bed, but no sign of the brother. Even at the height of the day, the blinds in the house were drawn, but Kristina could still be watching the street through a crack in the blind.

Putting on her mask and pulling her baseball cap low, she circled the block and approached the houses across the street from the opposite direction. There was no one home at the first two, but the third door opened to reveal a pregnant woman with a toddler propped on her hip, peanut butter in her hair, and a harried scowl on her face.

Hannah identified herself as Constable Pollack and explained that she was off duty but doing routine follow-up on a call for service she'd made a few days earlier at the McAuleys'.

"I didn't hear anything," the woman said, trying to fend off the toddler's sticky fingers. "I'm asleep by nine o'clock, and a bomb could go off without waking me. My husband mentioned he saw a police car in the driveway, but honestly, we don't know what it was about."

"What can you tell me about the McAuleys?"

The woman frowned. "Why? What have they done?"

Hannah shook her head, frustrated at her clumsy question. "Sorry. Probably nothing. Let me ask, have you ever witnessed anything between them that caused you concern?"

The toddler had begun to squirm, and the woman's frown became edged with impatience. "What? Witnessed what?"

Hannah gave up. "We had a report of a disturbance."

"Oh, the fights. Yes, we do hear arguments. Mostly her. She's a screamer. My husband's friendly with Ted — they both love boats — and he complains about the pressure at home. He says his wife had a breakdown after her last kid, and she can hardly manage the house. Their little boy has something wrong with him — I think he's on the spectrum — and the mother spends her whole time trying to deal with his issues."

As if on cue, her own toddler began to scream and throw himself out of his mother's arms. She put him down hastily. "I'm sorry, that's all I can tell you. I don't know anything about the disturbance, but it was probably someone in the house having a meltdown. The kid or the mother, take your pick."

Afterward, Hannah stood on the curb, eyeing the McAuley house. There was no sign of the Mercedes, but the brother's pickup was still there, and now the blinds were open on the downstairs windows. The garage door was open, and Hannah saw several kayaks and high-end bicycles on wall racks inside. Another bike with a child trailer attached was parked outside.

All looked peaceful. Was a visit even necessary? She didn't want Kristina complaining to her husband and her husband complaining to Rick. From the neighbours, two very different pictures of life at 26 Lake Point Road had emerged. Phil's opinion was clearly skewed by his dislike of Ted and his lifestyle and the pregnant mother's by her husband's friendship with Ted.

But except for the one hint of possible choking, neither picture seemed to point toward outright abuse. No matter how dysfunctional the home life was, no matter how much Kristina and her son were struggling, Ted did not appear to be the whole reason.

But she was here, less than a hundred feet from the front door. A simple follow-up inquiry would seem totally normal.

The dog barked as soon as she rang the doorbell, and Hannah heard some sharp words before the door opened and a man peered out. He was tall and slim, with rich black curls and deep-brown puppy-dog eyes you could drown in.

He smiled. "Well, hello there. Who are you?"

Hannah felt colour rush to her cheeks, and for an instant she forgot why she was there. She drew herself up. "Constable Pollack of the Ottawa Police. Is Kristina McAuley here?"

At the mention of the Ottawa Police, alarm flickered in his eyes, so briefly that she wondered if she'd imagined it. An instant later, his smile was back, broader than ever. "You don't look like a Constable Pollack. Is there something wrong, Constable?"

"Nothing's wrong. Would you tell her I'm here, please."

"But … I don't … What do you want with her?"

She made a soothing gesture. "Nothing's wrong, sir."

"Fine. Wait here." He turned and sauntered down the hall out of sight. She heard the murmur of voices, and after a few seconds, Kristina came down the hall with her brother hot on her heels. Seen together, the family resemblance was obvious in the oval brown eyes and high cheekbones. She was wearing ratty old shorts, tank top, and bare feet, and carried the dog in her arms.

Her frown gave way to surprise. "Oh, it's you. You look different out of uniform."

"Yes, I was biking in the neighbourhood and thought I'd stop by. A courtesy call, just to follow up on the other night."

"Is that usual?"

Hannah shrugged. "Our new police chief is restoring an emphasis on ongoing community policing rather than just responding to calls. I'll only take a minute of your time." She was surprised how easily the explanation popped into her head and relieved that Kristina seemed to accept it.

"Well, everything is fine." Kristina turned to hand the dog to her brother. "Can you take her out back for me while I deal with this?"

The brother looked about to protest but finally stepped back. "You call me if you need me," he shot over his shoulder.

Kristina took a minute to gather herself before turning back to Hannah. "I have nothing to add about the other night. Phil blew this whole thing out of proportion, as he often does. Sometimes I have to keep my blinds shut just so he can't spy inside. I don't even like to go out in our yard if I know he's watching."

"I'm sorry. I think he's just concerned," Hannah said, wondering where to go from here. What was she doing here? Everyone here was messed up, but none of it was a police matter.

"He's got too much time on his hands, what with being off work. But Ted has more of an issue with him than I do," Kristina was saying. "I don't like to get in the middle of it."

Hannah heard a child scream inside, and Kristina glanced at her FitBit in dismay. "Oh, damn. My son's TV show is over. Look, if there's nothing else ..."

Hannah thanked her for her time and as an afterthought held out her card. "My cell number is on here. In case anything else comes up." Startled, Kristina took it before almost slamming the door on her.

Neighbours, Hannah thought as she retreated down the walk. Such a beautiful neighbourhood and all the money in the world, but people still found stuff to fight about. She walked around the corner to her motorcycle and was just unlocking her helmet when a metallic-red Mercedes coupe rumbled down the street and braked at the corner. She caught a brief glimpse of the driver as he craned his neck to look at her.

Shit, she thought.

CHAPTER FOUR

Green had been looking for a pretext to bump into Hannah casually, hoping to raise the issue of her domestic violence case without appearing to meddle. Hannah had exquisitely tuned antennae for meddling, honed no doubt by the hysterical helicopter parenting her mother had specialized in.

With a generous contribution from his genes as well.

But two days of trying had yielded nothing. She had not been to the courthouse, and when he came up with an excuse to check on the holding cells at police headquarters, she was nowhere to be seen. In the end, he turned to Sharon as she was preparing dinner.

"Can you invite her to Shabbat dinner this Friday?"

"Why don't you invite her?"

"Well …"

"Ah." Sharon laughed. "She'll see through that ruse, you know."

Admitting defeat, he phoned and left a message on her voice mail. "Text her," Sharon said. "She might not listen to her messages for days."

"Young people today," he muttered as he texted.

Hannah texted back within two minutes. *Zaydie's chicken?*

Green felt a warm glow. His father had been dead for almost five years, but during his last years few things had brought him as much joy as his relationship with Hannah and Sharon's Friday night Shabbat chicken. The classic Yiddish dish was one of the few reminders the old man tolerated of his life in Poland before the Holocaust. Whenever the family served it, it felt as if he was still at the table.

When the dinner was over and Sharon had discreetly spirited the two younger children away, Hannah sipped the last of her wine and smiled at Green. "So. You invited me here to find out what I did about the case."

It was a statement, not a question, but it was on the tip of Green's tongue to protest. To say, *Of course we wanted you here at Shabbat, how can you think such a thing?* But he merely inclined his head.

"I did what you suggested. Low-key, civilian clothes. I interviewed two neighbours and the wife. A classic case of 'it depends who you ask.'"

He wanted to say, *Welcome to police work*, but decided that might not be wise. In the silence, the Shabbat candles flickered as they burned low.

"The bottom line," she said slowly, "is I'm still not comfortable, but I've got nothing to go on."

"So case closed."

"I gave her my card." She shrugged. "It's not like I don't have other people needing my help, right?"

He wanted to hug her, to tell her there would always be more people needing her help and she had to preserve her sanity. But he sensed she wasn't ready to let go. "But?"

"But as I was getting on my bike, the husband drove by. He saw me. He recognized me."

Green kept his expression blank. "That might not be a bad thing," he said carefully. "If there is something going on and the husband thinks we're watching him, it might be a deterrent. He's a member of the Bar. He's not going to want a police investigation or a charge on his record. For some reason, the Bar doesn't think that's acceptable behaviour for a lawyer."

"That's what I'm afraid of."

"What do you mean?"

"It might make him double down on her even more, to make sure she keeps quiet."

That had been exactly his concern, but he didn't voice it. "Not likely, sweetheart. You did what you could. You reached out to her and gave her your card. That's all you can do."

He could tell she was still unhappy, but she accepted his reassurance and headed out into the night. He hoped she'd learn to put it, and other troubling cases, behind her for the sake of her own mental health. *A neat trick if you can pull it off*, he thought as he lay awake deep into the night.

The email appeared on Green's computer screen so briefly that he barely noticed it. He was scrolling through the routine daily reports and notices in his inbox, most of which were irrelevant to him, stuck as he was out in Siberia, and the name registered after the fact. He stopped and backed up to double-check. The notice was a missing persons report filed that morning by a Joan McAuley regarding her son, Edward.

He read the report carefully as he pieced the story together. The mother, who lived alone in a high-rise condo on Richmond Road, had not seen or heard from her son in ten days. This was not usual for him; he always phoned her at least once a week, usually on Sunday. When he failed to phone the first Sunday, she left phone and email messages but got no response. His personal assistant at the office had seemed evasive but said he might be away on business, which the mother disputed. Her son always informed her of his travel plans. Because of her health problems, she had to be able to reach him at all times.

When the son had not called by the second Sunday, the mother phoned her daughter-in-law, Kristina McAuley. They weren't close, and she had wanted to avoid a family dispute. The daughter-in-law expressed surprise that Edward had not contacted his mother but told her he was supposedly away on business. The wife had not tried to reach him, but according to the mother, she wasn't concerned. Mrs. Joan McAuley, a widow, then phoned her granddaughter and Edward McAuley's partner in the law firm, neither of whom had heard from him. However, his law partner, Roland Featherstone, said he knew nothing about a business trip.

The report was filed by Missing Persons detective Meredith Johnson. Having never heard of her, Green assumed she was new to the division, and once again he cursed how out of touch he'd become. He did know the inspector in charge of the overall division, because that had once been his own job, but probably by design, a more different administrator could hardly be imagined. With his gaze fixed firmly on the upper rungs of the ladder, Inspector Fanel excelled at balanced budgets and cliché-ridden reports but left the actual policing to those below him. *It's a wise man who knows his limits*, Green thought, but it meant that Inspector Fanel would know fuck-all about any missing persons inquiry.

Green was just going through a mental checklist of his contacts when a soft knock sounded on his door. He looked up to see Hannah standing with one foot in the doorway, as if unsure she really wanted to be there.

He gestured her inside to a chair, but she chose to stand.

"There's a missing persons report," she began.

"I saw it."

"It makes no sense!"

He frowned. "How so? Have you had any further involvement in the case?"

"No. I figured I'd gone far enough. But why would *he* disappear? It should have been her, not him."

"You mean her going into hiding?"

"Or dead. Isn't that what happens? The husband murders her, dumps the body somewhere, and then reports her missing?"

He came to her side. "Don't get way ahead of yourself, honey. We don't yet know what's going on here. We have to let the officer assigned to the case do her job."

"But she's been in Missing Persons for only two weeks!"

"She has a sergeant. He'll help."

"I know. But I have a bad feeling. He *saw* me!"

"Did you tell Rick Geneva you did a follow-up visit?"

She whipped her head back and forth. "Are you kidding? He already thinks I'm a ditz."

"Are you going to tell this Detective Johnson?"

"I don't know. You think I should?"

He nodded. "This is where you have to trust your fellow officers. She needs to know. But it can be an informal chat."

She was staring at the ground, clasping her hands together as if to keep them still. Hannah was tough, and rarely had he seen her so upset.

"You won't get into trouble, honey. You didn't do anything wrong. You just did some routine follow-up."

"But it looks like he disappeared right after my visit. What if … what if something happened to him, and it was because of me?"

Hannah had to wait until the end of her shift the next day to meet with Meredith Johnson. She found the detective at her desk, resting her chin in her hand as she listened on the phone. Johnson was older than Hannah had expected, with frizzy grey hair, thick jowls, and too many pounds.

She managed a weary smile as she hung up and looked at Hannah.

"I know you're on the McAuley missing persons," Hannah began after introducing herself. "My partner and I responded to a call at his home a couple of weeks ago."

"I know. I already talked to your partner. Marital dispute. Looks like the guy got fed up with his wife and his family responsibilities."

"Is that how it looks? He disappeared on purpose?"

Johnson nodded. "There had been a big fight about her dog the night before. McAuley owes a lot of money. He said he'd been called away suddenly on business and wasn't sure when he'd be back, but that's bull. His partner says there was no business trip, he had no out-of-town clients, and he hasn't touched his corporate bank account in two weeks."

Hannah eased into the seat beside the desk. "It was his mother that reported him missing, not his wife. He's been gone ten days. Wasn't she worried?"

"She claims he sent her a couple of emails that he was going away on business."

Hannah got a sinking feeling. "So there's only her word for it."

Johnson puckered up her jowls into a scowl. "Look, I saw the emails. They look legit. I talked to his business partner and a couple of his neighbours. They all said there were a lot of pressures in the marriage. Money problems — he was overextended at the bank because of his house reno — the pandemic lockdown hit his practice hard, and one of his big cases didn't settle the way he expected. They have a kid who needs all this expensive therapy you hear about and a wife who can't go back to work because of it. And because of her own problems. Plus, he might have had a bit on the side. He's a good-looking high flyer, and I've seen his wife. She has other priorities than her appearance."

"So he packed a bag, grabbed his two-hundred-thousand-dollar car, and took off?" Hannah tried to think what her father would do. "What about other bank activity since he left?"

"A disappearance is not a crime. No crime, no warrant. No warrant, no access."

"But —"

Johnson gave her a humourless smile. "I've got this, Constable."

Hannah's temper flared. "His wife will be stuck without money. Isn't she worried about that?"

"Some of the stuff is in her name. Of course, it's mostly a pile of debts. But she has a credit card and a debit card to at least one of his accounts, so she says she's doing fine. She's just waiting for him to get tired of his girlfriend and come home."

"That's her theory?"

"That's what she says. She doesn't seem to miss him much." Johnson cocked her head. "Look, I'm just being nice here. You and Rick both thought this was a marital dispute. In fact, Rick lays it mostly at her feet. So what are you doing here?"

Hannah studied her hands. It was now or never. "I wasn't so sure. I know something about abuse. I have friends who were on the street because of it. The couple's behaviour rang some alarm bells, so I went back a few days later to talk to the wife. Routine follow-up. I was just checking how things were."

"Rick didn't mention that."

"I … haven't reported it yet."

Johnson stiffened, and her scowl returned. "Oka-ay, and?"

"And nothing. The wife stuck to her story and said the neighbour was too nosy. Another neighbour across the street said basically the husband had a lot on his plate."

"Okay then, why are we talking?"

"Because the one neighbour, Philip Walker, mentioned another incident where he thought there were red marks on the wife's neck."

"Did he report that one?"

"No. But if Ted McAuley did choke her, that's a huge red flag for greater violence. Plus I know these things are mostly underground. I know how much incredible danger there can be in the home that no one on the outside ever sees. Until it blows."

Johnson sighed and gave Hannah another annoyingly patient smile. "It can happen, and if we were investigating the wife's disappearance, yeah, I'd be a lot more worried. By the way, the mother got an email from her son, too, saying he was away on business, but she doesn't believe it's from him."

"Why?"

Johnson shrugged. "Just a feeling, she said. He's an only child, and they always had their own secret style. In my opinion, this is a waste of police time and resources, brought on by an overprotective mother who never liked her daughter-in-law in the first place."

"So you're closing the file?"

"I have no reason to suspect a crime has been committed or that the individual's safety is at risk. Partner Assault didn't even follow up on the original complaint. We have an alert out on the car, and maybe I can convince the bank and telephone company to give me a peek at his records. But I'm not holding my breath, and, of course, if he's as smart as he seems, he won't use either because he won't want to be traced. If I get no more leads in a couple of days, I'll tell the mother to hire a PI."

Hannah stewed as she changed out of uniform and headed down to the parking garage. She was looking forward to getting on her motorcycle, bombing down the Queensway, and letting her frustration fly away in the wind. Her little blue Honda wasn't much by motorcycle standards, but it had been her dream for years, and now it was all hers, bought as soon as she got her first paycheque. Lightweight and nimble, it deked in and out of city traffic like an elite slalom skier but still hummed effortlessly on the open road.

Her spirits lifted the minute she spotted it. Crouched beside it with his head bent intently over his own bike was another officer. He straightened when he heard her and gave her his most charming grin.

"I bet that little sweetheart is yours."

He was cute, she'd give him that. Thick black hair, forest-green eyes with a fringe of lashes to die for, and skin a warm, velvet brown. "It is. And that little sweetheart packs a lot of power."

"I bet it does. It suits you." He studied her. "I saw you up on the third floor earlier. Are you a detective?"

"Not yet," she replied. He waited, but she let him dangle.

"Any girl who rides a motorcycle already has my attention," he said, holding out his hand. "I'm Josh Kanner."

She let the *girl* comment slide. He *was* cute, even if he knew it. "Hannah Pollack," she said, returning his handshake after a split second's hesitation. His hand was warm and dry.

He slid her a sideways glance. "Inspector Green's daughter?"

She'd chosen her mother's name — her actual official name — to avoid just such a connection. "What makes you think that?"

He held up his hands in mock surrender. "Word gets around. I've just got an assignment to Major Crimes, and his name is still legend around there."

"Congratulations. That's a cool gig."

"It's temporary, for the summer. But I hope if I do well, they'll keep me on."

Suspicion flashed through her. Had he set up this encounter on purpose, or was she just being paranoid? Muttering, "Good luck," she pulled on her helmet and prepared to roll her bike out. He stepped in front of her and put his hand on her handlebars.

"Any tips?"

"Well, for one, don't assume you can go through me."

He jerked his hand away. His handsome face flushed. "Sorry, I didn't mean … I was just being friendly. I really do want to do well. This is my dream job. I have a good record, but so do a dozen other guys."

"Then I'll give you one more tip. The only one that matters. The one my father would give. Do your job better than them."

He lowered his gaze and laughed. "Looks like you're a chip off the old block, Hannah. I hope I haven't screwed up my first impression."

"Step out of my way, and maybe I'll forgive you," she shot back, smiling at how fast he leaped back. She fought the urge to look back as she pushed her bike toward the exit, but she wondered if he was giving her the finger. He was cute, but she'd met dozens of guys like him. They were always more trouble than they were worth.

CHAPTER FIVE

Four days later, Hannah was parked in her cruiser in a Loblaws parking lot. It was nearing the end of her shift, and she was typing up notes while Rick dropped into the grocery store to pick up dinner supplies. His teenagers were eating him out of house and home, he said.

Her cellphone rang, and she glanced at it. An unknown number with a local area code. She hesitated, because cleverly disguised spam calls were becoming a huge pain in the ass, but after five rings, she answered it.

Silence. Breathing. *Damn.* She was about to hang up when a hesitant voice spoke. "Constable Pollack?"

"Speaking."

"It's … it's Kristina McAuley. You gave me your number a couple of weeks ago? Said I could call?"

Hannah glanced out the window at the Loblaws exit doors. No sign of Rick. "Yes, Mrs. McAuley."

"I don't know if you know my husband has disappeared?"

"I saw the notice, yes."

"Well, he's still missing. I — I thought he'd just run off, you know? He said it was a business trip, but the firm says it wasn't. So I thought, well, he's been under a lot of pressure —"

Hannah spotted Rick coming out of the store, bags in hand. "Mrs. McAuley, can we meet? I'm on shift, but I can be there in an hour and a half."

She hung up just as Rick slid back into his seat. She was glad that he'd barely glanced in her direction before starting the car. She felt flustered and caught off guard as she wondered whether she'd overstepped her bounds by arranging an off-duty meeting alone.

She worried over the problem all the way to the station. Should she call Meredith Johnson? Should she call her father? But this was her problem. Her contact. Kristina had not called Johnson, or general inquiries, or even Rick. She had something to say and had chosen Hannah.

By the time she arrived at 26 Lake Point Road, she was calmer. She had the whole Ottawa Police Service to back her up if she got out of her depth. She was just about to ring the bell when the door flew open and Kristina drew her inside with her finger pressed to her lips.

"Peter is asleep, finally, so we have to talk quietly." Tonight, instead of her shapeless caftan, Kristina was wearing jeans and a T-shirt. She seemed less agitated than earlier, but she had deep circles under her eyes, and Hannah thought she'd lost weight. She led Hannah into the living room, which looked like it was out of a fashion magazine. Everything was black, white, and glass. Hannah chose the white leather sofa, which was as smooth as butter but hard as a rock.

The house was very quiet, although somewhere in the distance a radio played soft music. Soothing music to sleep by.

"I guess this isn't a thing for the police," Kristina began. "I feel silly for calling you, but I want to know what's going on and what I can expect. The other cop told me even if they found Ted, if he didn't want me to know where he was, they would respect his privacy."

"That's true."

"But have they found him? Am I worrying for nothing?"

"They would tell you that much."

"They would tell his mother, because she made the report. She might not tell me."

Hannah had encountered some seriously messed-up families in her life — her own mother topped the list — but even that sounded far-fetched. "They haven't found him. I think they suggested to your mother-in-law that she should hire a private investigator."

Kristina twisted her wedding ring. Hannah noticed the diamond rock beside it was missing. "I didn't tell that cop, but I'm broke. I don't know where to turn. The bank keeps taking off the mortgage payments and the car payments, and my overdraft is building up. Credit companies are sending letters about loans I didn't even know we had! There's no money coming in, and I can't access the money he has in his own accounts. I don't even know how much money is there."

She hung her head like she was ashamed. "Ted always said he'd take care of everything and I shouldn't worry about it. He's … I know he's a big spender. Money's always been important to him. No matter how much money his father made, he was still working class, so it's like Ted has to prove ..." She broke off, shaking her head angrily.

Hannah jumped in to steer her back on track. "You can't access anything? Or sell anything?"

"I've tried to guess his bank passwords to get online, but he must have changed them all, and now I'm blocked. The Lexus and the boat are in his name, so I can't sell those. I can sell off my jewellery and some of our art, but most of this stuff looks more expensive than it is. I thought one set of earrings were diamonds — he makes me wear them to law firm parties — but it turns out they're crystal." She splayed her fingers, her chin trembling. "I already sold my engagement ring. Got a fraction of what it's worth, but I paid off my son's therapist. Now I can't afford to take him anymore."

She broke off, tears gathering in her eyes. "How can he do this to us? As mean as he could be sometimes, I never thought he'd do this to me."

Hannah tried to divert a second rant. "What do you think has happened to him?"

"I thought he'd just run off. I didn't report him missing because I was ashamed. My mother warned me if I didn't make an effort, he'd get tired of me someday. I tried!" She took a deep, ragged breath. "That night, after you came, we had another huge fight —"

"About what?"

"My dog!" she wailed. "Ted never liked Toto. He hated the mess she made, the fur, the mud she tracked in, the barking. It was raining that night, and Toto came in all wet and dirty. She jumped on the sofa — that sofa you're on — and Ted freaked out. He said she had to go. We were all screaming at each other, my daughter included. My son, Peter, woke up and started head-banging, which he does when he gets overwhelmed. Ted snatched up the dog and left the house."

She pressed her fingers to her lips. Hannah glanced around the room and out into the hall, noting for the first time that there was no dog. She felt a chill.

"He sent me a text saying he was taking her to the Humane Society. I called the Humane Society but got no answer. Of course, it was nearly midnight. I thought maybe they had an emergency area, so I grabbed Peter and drove there. But the place was closed, and there was no sign of her. I was frantic. Peter loves that dog, and sometimes she's the only one that can calm him. But I couldn't show how scared I was in front of Peter. I told him Daddy was just playing a game, and we went home. Ted wasn't there, so I sent him a text asking where Toto was. He said, 'Oh, I tied her up outside. They'll find her first thing in the morning.'"

"Jesus," Hannah muttered before she could stop herself.

"I guess someone stole her. What a thing to do! I searched for her for days. I put signs up, I advertised on lost dog websites. My brother, my father, and my daughter, Justine, combed the whole area around the Humane Society, calling her name and showing people her photo. Nothing."

"What did Ted do?"

"I never saw him again. That night, he blamed me for letting the dog out in the rain in the first place, and he got mad at Peter for freaking out. 'It's just a dog,' he said. But looking back on it, I think he was ashamed. He realized he'd snapped and gone too far. He gets like that when he feels guilty. That's why he took off and sent me a text saying he was going away on business."

"Did he have any luggage, like an overnight bag?"

"Not when he took the dog. But after I got that last text, his bag was gone. Phil Walker says he came back for it in the morning while I was out looking for the dog."

"Did anyone else in the family talk to him? Your daughter, maybe?"

"No. Justine was in her room, I guess, or maybe at school. I ... I wasn't paying attention. My mother came by to get some laundry, but she says she didn't see him."

"What did he pack?"

"Only enough for a few days. His shaving kit, a suit, and a couple of golf shirts and jeans." She shrugged. "He didn't even take his sandals. I've been waiting for him to cool down and come back. That's what he usually does."

"Wait. He's done this before?"

She nodded. "When he's mad at me or needs to blow off steam. He checks into a hotel for a bit —"

"What hotel?"

"I never know. That's the point. But he's never been gone this long."

"Do you know if your mother-in-law hired a PI?"

52

"She wouldn't tell me. To her, this is all my fault. Even having a son with autism is my fault. Like I ruined her perfect family."

As she had when she first met the family, Hannah felt overwhelmed by the quagmire of bitterness. She couldn't think of a single thing she could do except listen.

"I feel for you, Mrs. McAuley, but there's not much I can do. It doesn't seem like a police matter."

Kristina looked at her through bleak, haggard eyes, her anger spent and fear creeping in. "What if it is? What if my mother-in-law is right and something has happened to him? What if his car is down a cliff somewhere or at the bottom of a river?"

Maybe this was at the heart of it all — a tattered remnant of the love she had once felt for the man. Hannah sighed. "What do you want me to do?"

"Talk to my mother-in-law. Find out if she hired a private eye. Find out if they've discovered anything. And please, if the police learn anything, can you let me know? I'd rather talk to you than to that cop who came before. It felt like she was just going through the motions."

What a mess I'm getting myself into, Hannah thought as she parked her motorcycle outside the high-rise on Richmond Road. It was one of the new wave of luxury condos sandwiched between the Ottawa River and the upscale shops and restaurants of Westboro. Hannah knew from her own hunt for an affordable apartment that a shoebox unit could cost over half a million dollars, while a river-view penthouse could run over three million.

Old Lady McAuley was not hurting.

Old Lady McAuley could also get her in serious trouble. She was way out on a limb with no official authority and no safety net. Neither Rick nor Detective Johnson knew what she was up to. Not even her father did. She could — should — just walk away. But something about Kristina's desperate sadness troubled her. The woman was on the brink of losing everything — her home, her possessions, even her children's well-being — whereas all Hannah risked was a probable slap on the wrist for insubordination.

Then there was the dog.

She finger-combed her hair, put on her mask, and marched up to the imposing glass doors. When she rang the unit, a querulous voice came through right away.

"I have nothing to say to you."

Hannah was thrown off. Was there a video feed somewhere? "Mrs. McAuley, I'm Constable Pollack of the Ottawa Police."

Silence, followed by mumbling that might have been an apology before Joan McAuley buzzed her through. Just as she was entering, a dumpy, middle-aged woman bustled out of the elevator, her face red and her brows drawn in a scowl. Hannah had to leap aside as she pushed past and flung open the heavy glass door.

"You're welcome," Hannah muttered at her retreating back before crossing the marble lobby to the elevators.

The woman who opened the door to unit 802 was a surprise. She wasn't dressed in silk and dripping with jewels, but instead stood in the doorway bracing herself with her walker and dressed in pull-on cotton clothes and Velcro slippers. Her face was a mass of crags and crevices, but her blond hair was just beginning to grey and above her mask, her blue eyes sized Hannah up sharply. Hannah suspected she was younger than she looked.

Since she was on her own time, Hannah wore her only pantsuit instead of her uniform, but she showed her badge wallet ID. Joan peered at it closely before handing it back with a grunt. Hannah noticed a faint tremor that shook not only her hand but her whole body.

"You better come in. I'm sorry about … I thought you were someone else."

The apartment opened almost immediately into a large, bright living room with pale watercolours and delicate cream furniture. A solid wall of windows looked out on the glistening river, treetops, and the blue outline of the Gatineau Hills in the distance. Joan chose a wing chair by the window and took some time to settle herself before turning her attention to Hannah.

"So they're sending an underling now."

"I'm sorry?"

"Last time it was a middle-aged woman. Not very bright, so no big loss. What have you found?"

Hannah had worked out a half-assed cover story but now figured Joan would see right through it. She decided on a more direct approach. "Have you been in touch with your daughter-in-law, Mrs. McAuley?"

Joan stiffened. "Why? What's happened?"

"She's heard nothing, and she's becoming a little desperate."

"The woman is always desperate. What is it this time?"

"She's running out of money, and she can't do anything with the assets that are in your son's name."

"Ah-ha. Showing her true colours, finally."

Hannah persisted. "She's as anxious as you are to find out where your son is."

"Oh, no she isn't. She doesn't want him found. She even sent her mother to tell me to withdraw the missing persons report."

Hannah thought about the woman who had just barged out of the building. "Did she just leave?"

"Yes, that's who I thought you were."

"Why did she want you to withdraw the report?"

"She said it was a private marital matter. She's more worried about the embarrassment and shame it would bring to the family to have the police poking around. None of them, not even you police, care at all about what's happened to Ted."

Hannah sidestepped the accusation. "Did you hire the private investigator as the police suggested?"

Joan leaned forward. "Private investigators cost money. I pay taxes. I expect you police to do your job."

"When there is no foul play suspected —"

"Of course there's foul play. There has to be. This is completely uncharacteristic of my son. He's left not only his family and me high and dry, but his clients as well."

Hannah hid her surprise. Johnson had not mentioned that. "In Detective Johnson's assessment —"

"The woman barely investigated! She talked to his friends, his wife, and asked me if he had a history of depression, which is an insult. She asked his law colleagues if he'd made any enemies, and they all said what a great guy he was. But of course he's made enemies! He's a lawyer, and a damn good one. He took people to court and cost them millions when he won. But did she ask me questions about that?"

Hannah's curiosity was piqued. It was a possibility that hadn't occurred to her. Perhaps this whole family dispute was irrelevant. She chose her words carefully, aware she might screw up future lines of inquiry. In her interview training, "don't lead the witness" had been drummed into her.

"What do you think happened to your son?"

"I don't know. But don't you think it strange that I had to report him? That his wife wasn't worried when he didn't come home for ten days? Even though his law partner said there was no business trip? She was happy enough to be rid of him."

Hannah was still mulling over that idea, which had already occurred to her, and trying to figure out another non-leading question when Joan gripped the arms of her chair and took a deep, tremulous breath. "I'm frightened. I don't know anything for sure, but I have a bad feeling. I never liked her or her family. They're from El Salvador and had a rough start in a terrible part of the world. Her parents learned how to survive, and I don't think it was always legal. My husband ran a construction business and hired the father when they first came to Canada. When Kristina finished high school, my husband took her on in the office, too, to help out the family. She set her sights on my son from the first day she spotted him. Ted was no match for that hot-blooded Latina. I'm sure it was her mother's idea. That woman knew a good thing when she saw it."

Joan stopped, flushed at the memory, and cleared her throat. Fascinated by this glimpse into the family relationships, Hannah waited.

"Ted was a fool. Pregnancy, you think that was an accident? I tried to warn him, but who listens to a mother? Kristina's mother wanted an extravagant wedding at the Château Laurier, and what she wants, she gets. We paid for it. My husband set her father up in his own carpentry business and lent him loan after loan, which he frittered away on God knows what. It nearly put my husband under, and the business never really recovered before he died. But do you think she cares? Ted gave her father a mortgage for his little house when the banks wouldn't, and he paid for this condo. I bet she doesn't even know. He has to hide things from her."

Hannah finally found an innocent question. "Does this condo have a mortgage?"

"Apparently, according to the bank, which has been calling me. Ted never told me he had to borrow for it. He just said he was giving it to me. That's Ted, a big heart." Joan looked at her grimly. "There, my dear. Now you have my secret. I couldn't pay for a private investigator even if I wanted to, so you officers just have to up your game and find my son."

Hannah hovered at the edge of the room, scanning the cubicles for Meredith Johnson. A few officers were hunched over their desks, talking on the phone or staring at computers. She braced herself. When she'd phoned to ask for a meeting, she knew she had no choice, but the detective was going to be seriously pissed. It wasn't a rookie patrol officer's job to be traipsing all over a more senior officer's investigation.

Even if that officer was being an idiot.

"Okay, what's up, Constable Pollack?"

She jumped. Detective Johnson had sneaked up behind her and stood with her hands on her hips, expressionless.

"It's about the McAuley case," Hannah said.

Johnson said nothing, merely pointed to her desk and led the way, her jaw set. Hannah perched on the edge of the chair, feeling like a kid again. She'd been in trouble often enough that she knew that feeling. Equal parts fear, excitement, and defiance.

As then, she had her story ready. "I didn't plan to have any more involvement with the case. I was going about my regular patrol when Kristina McAuley phoned me. She wanted to know if we'd made any progress finding her husband because she'd heard nothing —"

"She had my number. Why call you?"

Hannah shrugged. Johnson leaned forward. "I'll tell you why. Because she knew you were young and inexperienced and she could manipulate you more easily."

Hannah looked at her. The defiance kicked in. "Maybe I'm young, maybe I'm inexperienced, but I don't manipulate easily."

Johnson held her gaze and smiled faintly. "Sure. What did she get out of you?"

"Mostly a friendly ear. She wanted to talk. She told me about the incident leading up to the disappearance — the dog — and that story bothers me. She told me her husband has never been gone this long, and she's running out of money —"

"Uh-huh. I figured that was coming next. The squeeze is on."

Hannah ignored her. "I told her it wasn't our job, and her mother-in-law should hire a PI. She asked me to ask her mother-in-law if she had."

Johnson rolled her eyes. "Jesus, Pollack. And you did?"

Hannah clenched her fists in her lap. "To be honest, I was curious. Kristina made out like her mother-in-law hated her, and I wanted to see for myself."

"That's not your job, Pollack, and you're messing up mine. You don't get to decide what you're curious about."

"The mother-in-law doesn't have the money for a private eye either. It turns out they all rely on Edward McAuley. The mother is convinced something's happened to him."

"Mothers don't usually know half of what their precious sons are up to."

"But she did tell me one interesting thing, and that's what I really came to tell you." She waited until Johnson leaned in. "She said he's made enemies, because when he wins in court, people lose lots of money."

Detective Johnson sat back with a snort. "Believe it or not, Pollack, I thought of that. And dismissed it just as fast after talking to his associates. The people he sues are businesses and insurance companies, not the mob. If I tell you exactly what happened to Edward McAuley, will you go back to your patrol car and leave my job to me?"

Hannah scowled at her, prickling at her tone.

"Edward McAuley's earnings have fallen by half during this pandemic. Fewer accidents, so fewer clients. Cases postponed. Whatever. He found himself with a mountain of debt he couldn't repay, a lifestyle and image he couldn't maintain, a whole lot of people sucking the life out of him, so he took off. He walked out of his life, and he's never looking back. And since that's not a crime, that's the end of the story."

Right on cue, Johnson's phone rang. She answered, listened for a moment, and then flicked a glance at Hannah. "I'll be right over." As she hung up, she gave Hannah a huge, triumphant grin. "Well, well. Edward McAuley's red Mercedes has turned up. Guess where. In long-term parking at the Ottawa airport."

CHAPTER SIX

Before signing off for the day, Green checked his calendar for the next day's meetings and court cases. His gaze drifted to the following weeks. Only two weeks before the vacation time he had booked off. In the old days, the anticipation of time off would not have been cause for such celebration, but that was when he had cases on the go, crimes to solve, and bad guys to catch. That was before Siberia. Now the workdays stretched endlessly ahead of him, full of briefings, schedules, reports, spreadsheets, and Zoom meetings, without a single moment of drama.

The school year was almost over, which meant nine long weeks when Tony and Aviva would need entertaining and supervision. He and Sharon had planned their weeks off to cover some of it and enrolled Tony in soccer camp and Aviva in day camp. Tony had argued that he was old enough to be home on his own, and although Green conceded that in theory that was true, he remembered how much trouble he and his friends had got up to when left to their own devices at the age of twelve.

He was wondering whether he should use up more of his vacation time so that the whole family could go on a road trip when his phone rang.

"Hey," Hannah said.

"Hey back," he replied, recovering from his surprise. Hannah wasn't big on staying in touch. There was silence. "What's up?"

"They found his car." Her voice gathered momentum. "Edward McAuley's car. At the airport."

"Oh. How long has it been there?"

"Since the day he supposedly disappeared. The day after my last visit."

"So what's the theory? He's taken off?"

"That's the Missing Persons detective's theory. She's basically shut the investigation down."

Green could hear the *but* in his daughter's tone and suspected she had more on her mind. "I'm almost done for the day. Do you want to meet for a coffee?"

"No, I have to go on shift. I just wondered … is there other stuff the detective would check to make sure he really took off?"

"Of course there is. She'd check passenger flight manifests for that day, she'd check border security. She could even check the CCTV cameras in the parking lot, if they keep the files that long. Did she do that?"

"She's not going to tell me fuck-all, Dad." Silence again. "You have access to everything, right? Do you think you could access the file?"

"I don't have access to everything, especially not the details of her ongoing investigation."

"But you know how to get it, right? You know lots of ways around the rules?"

He was about to protest but stopped himself. Hannah guarded her independence fiercely, a habit she'd cultivated from living with her erratic mother. Trust did not come easily to her, and he knew what it cost her to ask for his help.

"Well …" he began, inwardly exploring possibilities. But she was already moving on.

"Never mind. Rick's here. Gotta go."

After two years of construction, noise, and dust, Elgin Street had emerged from behind its barricades to celebrate its elegant new look of cobblestone sidewalks and fashionable street lamps. Some shops were shuttered, but those that had survived the chaos and the pandemic sported shiny new signs, and on this warm, sunny June afternoon, the sidewalks bustled with tourists and locals.

Patios were busy, a welcome sight after the pandemic lockdown and the difficult winter, but Green saw that Brian Sullivan had snagged a prime table in the back corner of the Lieutenant's Pump. It paid to have done a few favours for the pub's owner. With a pint of golden ale on the table before him, Sullivan was casually scanning the street from behind his trademark mirrored sunglasses. A grin spread across his freckled face when he spotted Green.

Green felt a rush of affection. They were textbook opposites, Sullivan the large, brawny farmer's son and

Green the skinny immigrant kid from the back alleys of the inner city. But their friendship went back over thirty years to their rookie days together on patrol, and only Green's recent posting had separated them. Sullivan had remained in Major Crimes, now as staff sergeant.

Throwing caution to the wind, Green enveloped him in a big hug. For a minute, his voice failed him. *Fuck, I miss the old days!* He laughed and patted Sullivan's stomach.

"What's this? Your new boss not keeping you busy enough?"

Sullivan sat back down with a grimace. "He's keeping me behind a desk is what it is. What about you? You're wasting away!"

"That's what the gulag does to you."

A waiter was threading through the tables and Plexiglas dividers toward them, and Green gestured for two more beers. Then he leaned in. "And I'll tell you a secret. I'm so bored, I'm going to the gym."

Sullivan threw his head back in a laugh. "Jesus, Mary, and Joseph! Hell will be freezing over next!"

"Don't let the word out. It may not last. But it wouldn't hurt you to join me. How's Mary? The kids?"

"Mary's good. Cashing in on the real estate boom, which is a good thing because the kids' university bills are bleeding us dry. What about you? How's that little heartbreaker Avie?"

"More and more like Sharon every day."

"That's a good thing."

The two men chatted about families, colleagues, and the pandemic, but once their beers arrived, Sullivan pointed at Green. "You've got that look, so we might as well get it over with."

"What do you know about Meredith Johnson?"

Sullivan's eyebrows shot up. He waited a beat for an explanation before shrugging. "She's not in my section. Missing Persons."

"I know that. But she's on the floor; you must bump into her. Is she any good?"

"You don't learn much about someone by bumping into them."

Green glared at him. "You know what I mean. You hear things."

"About her? Not much. She's new. She does her job, ticks all the boxes, but …"

"But what?"

Sullivan wagged his finger at him. "Are you nosing around in something that's none of your business? That's a surprise."

"It's Hannah's business. A missing persons case she doesn't think Johnson is handling all that well."

"If I know Hannah, she may not be too happy with you sticking your nose in."

"She asked me to."

"Really?" Sullivan broke off to take a long, thoughtful sip. His brow furrowed. "Johnson's by the book. Competent but not very imaginative. She was assigned to us for a bit, until I told the inspector she'd be better suited to Missing Persons. What's the case?"

"The McAuley disappearance. You heard of it?"

Sullivan's eyes lit up with excitement. "Are you kidding? It's the talk of the town. Several of our guys have had run-ins with him. Hot-shot new gun in town, did a short stint as a Provincial Crown down in the Toronto area, so he knows his way around cross-examination. Cops have to have every fucking *i* dotted and *t* crossed. Leave a small hole in the case and he'd barrel right through it."

"So he's aggressive?"

"Cool as a cucumber. Just deadly."

"You think he made enemies?"

"You mean the concrete shoe kind of enemy?" Sullivan shrugged. "He certainly pissed people off, but he's not in criminal law anymore, so unless someone has a long memory ... What does Johnson say?"

"She thinks he's done a runner. They found his car at the airport. Supposedly he had huge debts and an unhappy marriage, but he could also be running from someone. Some people do have long memories."

Sullivan smiled. "Same old Mike, same old imagination. What do you want me to do?"

Green returned the smile. "Same old Brian, too. Find out what Johnson's done about the car. Flight manifests, border services, CCTV."

"Missing Persons is under a lot of financial pressure. The new emphasis from the top is frontline officers, beefed-up community policing, prevention, gun violence — you know the story. Unless it's a high-profile, high-risk disappearance, Missing Persons is under pressure to check it out, close it, and move on."

"But she should at least have done those checks before putting the case on the back burner. That's basic investigation."

"What does Hannah think happened?"

"She doesn't say exactly. She took the original domestic disturbance call, and she's worried she missed an important sign or made things worse."

Sullivan drained his beer and stood up. "Okay. I'll nose around. For that amazing girl, anything."

Two days later, Sullivan dropped by his office. He was there to watch the trial of a murder suspect they had taken years to bring to trial, but on the day jury selection was to begin, the defence had requested yet another postponement.

"Story of my life," he muttered, dropping into a chair that squawked beneath his weight. "This is where the money is wasted! Not on investigations but on playing the system."

"Ours not to question why."

"Yeah, yeah. I talked to Johnson. She shut the investigation down when the car turned up at the airport, which confirmed her theory. 'If new information comes to light, blah, blah, blah.'"

Green scowled. "Seems to me this is new information that merits at least a question or two."

"For a private investigator." Sullivan grinned. "Or … if you're really bored, you've got a friend in the airport policing section."

"Who?"

"Sue Peters. She's just got an acting sergeant's posting."

A smile spread through Green. Sue Peters had been a brash, charge-through-the-mountain kid when she'd first arrived in Major Crimes ten years earlier. She was a rebel after his own heart, stubborn, curious, and undeterred by the fine print in procedural manuals. "Good for her. A loss for Major Crimes, though."

, "Yeah, well, your replacement has been busy cleaning house. He thought we needed new blood and a new attitude. But Sue would be happy to see you, and I bet by now she's pretty bored with arranging security for bigwigs and confiscating nail clippers."

Sullivan's prediction turned out to be accurate, but he'd always had an uncanny insight into his officers. Green waited until the next evening, when Peters was on shift. After the usual greetings and teasing, he explained the situation and asked if she could get access to the passenger lists for June 2 and a few days since, as well as passport control. Without missing a beat, she led him into the border security office. It took them less than ten minutes on the computer to check and double-check the lists.

"Nothing, sir." Her eyes danced with curiosity. Marriage and motherhood had tempered her impatience and softened her rough angles, but she still had that gnawing drive for answers that makes a good investigator. "He didn't get out this way, unless he used a fake passport."

"That would suggest a whole new level of subterfuge. Ordinary people don't get a forged passport on a whim. It requires serious intent, planning, and criminal contacts that even a personal injury lawyer probably wouldn't have. It's possible, but it's more likely he parked at the airport in order to misdirect us while he left by another means. Can we —?"

"Check the parking lot CCTV? Yeah, it has a feed in here. They don't keep it forever, but we should be okay." She led him next door to the video room, where officers sat in front of banks of screens showing every inch of the airport area. Peters entered the date and time, pulled up the file, and ran it on fast-forward. Together they peered at the dizzying comings and goings of hundreds of cars, passengers getting in and out, scampering across the parking lot and clambering on and off shuttle buses. Finally, the distinctive Mercedes appeared and pulled into a spot in the middle of the lot. Peters slowed the feed as the driver climbed out and strode out of the frame. Before Green could even ask, she rewound and zoomed in, capturing a figure wearing what looked like casual pants, a leather jacket, large sunglasses, and a baseball cap and mask that hid most of his face. It was impossible even to distinguish the gender, let alone identify McAuley.

"Take a screenshot and email it to me," Green said. "And then let's see where he goes."

Peters tracked the figure through several cameras as he wove through the parked cars until he climbed onto the airport shuttle bus. Not once did he look toward the camera.

"Looks like he was trying to stay out of view as much as possible," she said. "It could be just dumb luck."

"I don't think so. It looks as if he'd scoped out the cameras beforehand."

"But at least we know he did go to the airport. That shuttle bus doesn't stop anywhere else."

"Yeah, but he would, because he knows we can track him. But he could have got off the shuttle at the airport and grabbed a cab anywhere, and we'd have lost him. Can you email me that video of him walking? It and the close-up might help with an ID."

Peters didn't ask questions; she just sent him the files. As he was leaving, she looked up at him with a glint in her eye. "Anything else you need, any other way I can help, boss, you just ask."

Once the rush of being back in the hunt faded, Green wasn't sure what to do with the files. If it was a major crime investigation and he was still in charge, he would have shown the photos to the wife and mother to get an identification. But as it was, with the investigation closed and him way out of his jurisdiction, not to mention well above the appropriate rank, that could blow up in his face and bring the wrath of the senior brass down not only on his own head but also on Sue Peters's and Hannah's. He couldn't hand the files over to Hannah for the same reason.

He could hand them to Johnson directly without mentioning Peters and suggest she take the small extra step of asking the family to identify the figure. But if Johnson were as rule-bound and unimaginative as she seemed, she'd simply betray him to her boss, and the same wrath would cascade down.

The proper route would be from one inspector to another. He knew his replacement, under whom the Missing Persons Unit fell, had spent years trying to purge his influence from the division and would not take kindly to being undercut once again. Hannah and Peters could still be hurt in the crossfire.

He tossed and turned most of the night, but by morning he'd come up with the only solution he could comfortably live with. It would probably cause him some grief, but he was used to that, and if he handled it right, Hannah and Peters might be spared.

Moreover, if he were honest, he couldn't ignore that special thrill he'd felt at being out in the field again.

He opted to tackle the wife first. The Lake Point house was extravagant, even by the standards of the neighbourhood. Just as he approached the house, a man in rough work clothes emerged and climbed into the dusty pickup parked in the drive. He glanced briefly at Green's Subaru as he backed out, and something in his look rang a bell. Green tried to grab the memory, but it drifted out of reach. When he climbed out of his car, he took a minute to study the house. Tasteful, minimalist, but strangely soulless. Sunlight poured into the yard, but there were no other cars in the drive and no answer to the doorbell. Disappointed, he was about to leave when he heard music and laughter from the back of the house. Skirting the stack of patio stones by the front gate, he took the path around the side and stopped short at the stunning river view that lay beyond the yard. Small sailboats danced on the water, and farther along, a red kayak hugged the shore.

A woman and small boy were playing with LEGO on the half-finished stone patio, and dump trucks and other toys were lined up along the edge. A collection of dusty tools and a wheelbarrow full of gravel sat on the grass. At the sight of him, the woman scrambled to her feet in alarm, her laughter cut short. She stepped in front of the child, spread her arms, and faced him with wide eyes. He'd met women like her before, always on guard, easily spooked, although to be fair, any woman would be spooked by a strange man walking into her backyard.

He held out a soothing hand. He'd dressed in casual slacks and T-shirt, and now he adopted his most easygoing tone. "Mrs. McAuley, I'm sorry. I didn't mean to scare you. I heard voices, so I …" He flashed his badge wallet. "I'm Mike Green of the Ottawa Police. I won't trouble you for long."

Her jaw dropped. "Oh! Have you found him?"

"Not yet. Have you heard from him?"

She shook her head. "They told me they were closing the investigation and I should hire a PI. Which I can't afford. I can't afford anything! I'm planning to sell my Lexus, which might buy me some time, but I need some answers soon. We all do. My mother-in-law thinks I killed him. That's ridiculous. The police found his car, so he's obviously taken off. Are you the new detective on the case?"

He dodged deftly. "I'm just clearing up a couple of loose ends. Can you look at a couple of photos and tell me if you recognize them?"

She approached, took his phone, and carried it into the shadow of the house. Her son had stopped lining up his LEGO and was watching with silent, baleful eyes. "What are these?" she asked.

"Routine CCTV."

"Of a parking lot?"

"Do you recognize the person?" He studied her face carefully for signs of alarm or relief but could only see puzzlement.

"I don't know. I can't see the face well enough."

"What about the clothes?"

"Well … I mean, it could be him. He does have a leather jacket like that, and he has lots of baseball caps. He buys them as souvenirs wherever we go. This one looks like a Senators cap, and he has a couple of those."

"Are they still in the house? The jacket and hat?"

She shrugged. Her eyes were wide, and the phone trembled in her hand.

"Can we go and check?" he asked gently.

Inside, the house was immaculate and almost institutionally bland. It had a faint floral scent, and soothing classical music filled the rooms through invisible speakers. *There's no life in here*, Green thought.

"He always hangs that jacket in his bedroom closet," she said as she headed upstairs with her son in tow. The boy had been laughing while they played LEGO, but now he crept along like his mother's shadow.

Upstairs, the bedroom seemed almost as big as Green's entire house. The two walk-in closets could have doubled as bedrooms themselves, and the ensuite bathroom reminded Green of a Roman spa.

Kristina pawed through the racks of expensive suits, perfectly ironed dress shirts, golf shirts, windbreakers, and jean jackets. On hooks up above hung an array of hats, from cocky fedoras to leather cowboy hats to battered old ball caps. He'd never seen so many clothes.

Kristina's voice interrupted his amazement. "The jacket is not here. I didn't think it was."

"What about the hat?"

She studied the hats and shook her head helplessly. "I can't tell if one is missing. He has so many."

"Okay, don't worry." He led her out into the natural light of the room while her son stayed behind, hiding behind suits. "Can you take a look at this video and tell me if it looks like your husband?"

Dutifully, she studied the video. This time, an emotion flickered across her face, unreadable and quickly suppressed. "This picture is no better," she said, thrusting the phone toward him.

"Take your time. Watch it a couple of times. People have distinctive walks."

She looked a second time and a third before frowning with dissatisfaction. "I can't be sure, but I think it's him."

Curiously, she didn't look relieved or even angry. She looked bewildered and possibly a little afraid.

CHAPTER SEVEN

Sullivan phoned him the next morning. "The shit is about to hit the fan, buddy. Apparently McAuley's wife told her mother-in-law about your visit, and the mother-in-law phoned Meredith Johnson, furious she hadn't been contacted since she was the one who reported him missing. She wanted to know who the hell this scruffy old man Mike Green was. Johnson told her sergeant, who told his staff sergeant." Sullivan chuckled. "Luckily, we're old friends and he knew exactly who scruffy old Mike Green was. He asked me what he should do about it."

Once Green recovered from the scruffy old man insult, his thoughts raced ahead to damage control. "Tell him to keep a lid on it, don't say anything. I'll handle it."

"Dare I ask how?"

"Mano a mano."

The scene was so familiar that Green felt a pang of longing. The buzz in the squad room, the phones, the murmur of voices, and the shuffle of feet. Even though there wasn't a familiar face in the room, it felt as if nothing had changed, from the smell of old coffee cups and the row of offices along the outside edge to the door to the corner office.

His door.

It was ajar, but he stood in front of it for a second, collecting himself for the battle. Looking at the name.

Inspector Paul Fanel.

He'd told the man he was coming but not why. He didn't want a cascade of repercussions until he had laid out all the facts and protected Hannah as best he could. When he finally knocked and nudged open the door, Fanel conjured up a smile as he came around his desk. He didn't offer a handshake, but Green would live with that. Even with the vaccines, the pandemic still cast a shadow of unease.

"Let's go grab a coffee," Fanel said. "I could use a break."

Green wondered briefly whether Fanel was deliberately taking him out of his former stomping ground, but he sensed the man was nervous and didn't want witnesses. He chattered about inconsequential things until they were both sitting over coffee in the police cafeteria. To show he came in peace, Green picked up the tab. Once Fanel had run out of small talk, Green leaned forward and looked him in the eye.

"I won't beat around the bush. This is about the Edward McAuley disappearance. I want to hand over some evidence I acquired. It probably makes no material difference to the case, and it may not need to go any further than you and me, but it should be in the record."

Fanel stiffened. "What evidence?"

"Are you familiar with the case?"

Fanel's lips tightened. "Not the details."

Green sketched out the details about the initial disturbance call, the man's subsequent disappearance, and the eventual conclusion that the disappearance was voluntary to escape problems at home. His vehicle had been found at the airport. At that point, Green paused to choose his words carefully. "You may be aware my daughter is a patrol officer. She and her partner took that initial domestic call. She was concerned that there was violence in the home, so she took an interest in the case."

"What do you mean, an interest?"

"She spoke to the assigned Missing Persons detective a couple of times, including just before the vehicle was found."

"And?"

"And this is where I thought you needed to be informed, to make sure the investigation was as thorough as it should be. Before the case was closed, the flight manifests should have been checked at the very least, right?"

He held Fanel's gaze while he waited. To his credit, the man seemed to sense he was being led toward a trap, for he shrugged. "That would have been the staff sergeant's call."

"Whosever it was, it should have been done, but it wasn't. So informally, on my own, I did it."

"You? You …?" Fanel sputtered as he tried to figure out how to respond.

Green smiled sheepishly. "I admit I was out of line. Old investigative habits die hard. I wanted to make sure it was necessary before I brought it up officially. If he was on a flight to the Cayman Islands or something, case closed, and your Missing Persons detective and NCOs would be as clean as a whistle."

"And was he? On a flight somewhere?"

"No. So I had to go one step further. I showed parking lot CCTV footage to the wife to ask her to ID her husband. She was pretty sure it was him. Pretty sure isn't perfect, but it's all I was prepared to do."

Fanel was beginning to relax, no doubt less worried about his exemplary record going up in smoke. "So if you hand that evidence over to me, I will see it gets into the file. Discreetly. And I will have a quiet word with my staff."

"There's a slight glitch. The wife told her mother-in-law about my visit, and she phoned Detective Johnson demanding to see the footage."

Fanel looked alarmed. "You aren't going to show it to her, are you?"

"No, no. It's Johnson's case. Your case. I'm happy to hand it all over. But it would be a good idea to show the footage to the mother-in-law so we can get from pretty sure to very sure. And to satisfy the person who actually made the missing persons report in the first place."

"Agreed, agreed." Fanel bobbed his head up and down. "I'd like a full report on this from you. For the file."

"Sure. If you think that's wise. But Johnson should get the wife and mother-in-law in for proper ID statements, anyway, so the official record is all in order. That might be better than a report from me."

"Yes, a good idea. That's the way to go."

"Good enough. And she should probably get an official copy of the CCTV footage, so all the *t*'s are crossed." Green pushed back his chair. "No harm done, and it's a good learning experience for her."

Two days passed. Surely enough time for Detective Johnson to get all her proper paperwork in order and to have the two McAuley women in for official IDs. Despite himself, Green was starting to feel the pull of the hunt. As an antidote to the dreary succession of court requirements, the case had begun to capture his interest.

By the morning of the third day, he could stand the suspense no longer and phoned Brian Sullivan. "I don't suppose you've heard any more about the McAuley case from your friend over in Missing Persons."

Sullivan chuckled. "We had a good laugh about Fanel. He said since he was going to be signing off on their work, he'd like to keep a close eye on high-profile cases like McAuley from now on. He didn't say how he'd learned any of this, just that it had come to his attention that a few leads should have been better followed up. No mention of you, so Rolly didn't say a word. Just 'Yes, sir.' You still have a lot of friends over here, you know."

"Well played. So ... anything?"

"What? Oh, you want to know what they found out? Is that why you're calling?"

"Well, I'd like to reassure Hannah it's all solved and she doesn't have to worry."

"Sure, Mike."

"Brian!"

Sullivan laughed. "As it turns out, it's not all solved. The wife gave pretty much the same statement she gave you, but the mother-in-law insists the person in the photos is not her son. The walk is completely different."

Green felt a surge of excitement. Was there more to this case than everyone thought? "So now what?"

"So now we have possible evidence of a crime — the theft of the car — to hang a warrant on. That should be enough to get access to his phone, internet, and financial records. And we'll see if this guy really has flown the coop or if Mom is right and something has happened to him."

CHAPTER EIGHT

Lillian Chang tilted her head back to feel the glorious early-morning sun on her face. Warm, but not yet sweltering. Her favourite time for a dog walk. Ducks and Canada geese flapped toward the shoreline, a Cooper's hawk patrolled high overhead, and delicate chickadees flitted from tree to tree, chirping warnings as she drew near. She felt as if she were miles from the bustle of the city. The gravel path was flat and wide, but on either side the thick brush and tall grasses pressed in. Somewhere in there, invisible, she heard her Lab Collie mix crashing through the underbrush, nose to the ground on the trail of a rabbit or groundhog. Hopefully not a skunk or coyote.

The Shirley's Bay nature trail was one of her favourites. It was off the beaten track and too flat to challenge serious cycling and hiking enthusiasts. The birdwatching was spectacular, however, and the views where the path skirted the broad Ottawa River were stunning. As with all National Capital Commission trails, it was against the law to walk dogs off-leash, but it was a law Lillian happily ignored. She had yet to encounter an

NCC officer, and her lumbering, oversized pup needed all the exercise he could get.

As she walked, she trained her binoculars on birds. She carried a bird book in her fanny pack and was teaching herself to identify as many birds as she could. She was busy focusing on a bluebird in a distant buckthorn tree when Titan crashed out of the bush and trotted toward her, trailing something in his mouth. He was generally no match for the agile prey he chased, but now she sucked in her breath. *Please don't let it be an animal.*

Proudly, he dropped the object at her feet, not an animal at all but a dog leash attached to a collar. She bent to pick it up. It was dirty but expensive looking, with a pattern of pumpkins along it but no identity tags. Not even a rabies tag. Dogs wriggled out of their collars all the time, so she didn't think much of it until she noticed the dark red stains on the collar. There were more on the leash, all of them dry and crusty.

Alarm shot through her. This dog had been injured, badly. A coyote? The collar size suggested a little dog that would have been easy prey for a coyote or possibly even a fisher. Perhaps it was lying in the bush somewhere, bleeding but still alive.

Titan was not the best trained of dogs. Lillian had never taught him to retrieve or track. All she needed was a loveable, goofy companion who usually came when she called. But now she waved the leash in front of his nose and plunged into the bush in the direction he'd come from.

"Titan, come! Fetch!"

The dog looked bemused. Lillian continued into the bush along a barely visible deer track. Perhaps the injured dog had been following this trail as well. As she plunged deeper and deeper into the undergrowth, fighting with twigs and branches that clawed at her, she began to doubt her mission. She knew that somewhere ahead, perhaps half a kilometre away, was civilization in the form of houses along the river, but there was no hint of that through the willows and buckthorn that choked everything. This area was part of the river floodplain that often flooded in the spring, but in late June the ground was spongy with leaf mulch and woody debris. A fetid stench like mossy rot filled the air.

As she tried to make out the trail, Titan was following at her heels, uncharacteristically shy. Suddenly, he bounded ahead and veered off the trail into the deeper brush. She was about to call him back when he barked and ran farther. *Something he wants me to see.* The smell grew stronger. *Please don't let it be a dead dog.*

She clutched the leash tightly as she fought through the brush. Up ahead she spotted a small clearing, some trampled grasses, and Titan pawing furiously. She held her nose and peered around cautiously. The ground was chewed up, but there was no sign of an injured dog. No tufts of fur or blood to indicate a fight. She allowed a sense of relief to creep in until she saw the bone lying half chewed against a fallen tree. Then another and another.

Tears filled her eyes. She rushed over toward the hole Titan was digging. "Leave it, boy. The poor little —"

The rest of the words stopped in her throat as she saw what Titan had uncovered: a ball cap and the first hint of the head on which it had once sat.

Green was plodding through yet another internal memo on proposed Covid changes when his phone rang. Gratefully he snatched it up. Sue Peters's voice came through, tense and excited.

"Sue, what's up? More news on McAuley's whereabouts?"

"Possibly, sir. It's still early, but I thought you'd want to know. At nine oh-three this morning a 911 call came in from a woman walking her dog in Shirley's Bay —"

Green sucked in his breath.

"Reporting a possible dead body found in a wooded area off the trail. It's a slow day here, and I was lucky enough to be on my computer, so the call for service caught my eye. There have been a bunch of follow-ups, and it's definitely human remains."

Green glanced at the time: 10:48. Major Crimes would be there by now, along with Ident. "Any further details on the ID?"

"Not yet, sir. But the thing I thought you should know? The first officers on the scene were Rick Geneva and Hannah Pollack."

Green was off the phone and out the door in less than thirty seconds after a quick word with his staff sergeant. Luckily, his staff ran the section far better than he could and needed no handholding, but he was less sure about Hannah. She'd never dealt with a case like this. Human remains in the secluded bush would be quite an awakening. Why the hell hadn't Sullivan alerted him?

Ten minutes later, he was barrelling west along the Queensway. It felt like old times, that peculiar mix of apprehension and sorrow that accompanied the beginning of every death investigation. It was too early to tell whether it was murder yet, or indeed whether it was Edward McAuley, but his instincts were humming.

When he arrived at the trailhead parking lot, it was already full of official vehicles: the coroner's van, the forensic identification truck, and several police vehicles, both marked and unmarked. The trailhead was cordoned off with yellow tape. A uniformed officer he didn't recognize was on guard, but when Green showed his badge wallet, he had no trouble signing in and going beyond.

As he strode along the gravel trail, he wondered where Hannah and her partner were and who Brian Sullivan had assigned to lead the investigation. It was a hot June morning with the temperature already climbing toward thirty degrees, and he knew the body would be putrid. He caught the first whiff of that dreaded stench even before he reached the turnoff, where more yellow tape and another officer marked the narrow path. He slipped on the foot covers the officer provided and steeled himself as he waded into the deep bush along the path Ident had already marked. Branches closed in around him, scratching his legs and clawing at his face. No one would have ventured in here willingly, not from this direction, anyway. But the map on his phone revealed that there were other entry points into the park, from the river and from the waterfront community of Crystal Beach. Where Edward McAuley lived.

A light breeze carried the carrion stench, along with the low murmur of voices, and soon up ahead he spotted the white canopy shielding the actual crime scene. A pair of bunny-suited Ident officers were snapping pictures inside, and a cluster of plainclothes officers hovered outside the tape. He heard the Scottish burr of Dr. Alexander MacPhail before he spotted the pathologist's tall, angular form bent over the ground, dictating while an Ident officer photographed. Green could only hear snippets, but enough to confirm his fears.

"Rigor come and gone long ago," MacPhail said, his voice still ragged and cigar-wrecked but now tremulous with age. "Insect and animal activity advanced. Bag those flies and maggots, will you, lads? They've been dining out for quite some time." MacPhail groaned as he lowered himself onto his hands and knees. "I'm too old for this, lads. Victim is on his side, no obvious bleeding or injuries except for a couple of bloody great cracks on his head. One nearly took his ear off. I'll have more for you once you get him to the comfort of my table." He reached for a hand to help him struggle to his feet. "He's all yours. I'll see him first thing in the morning."

With that the aging pathologist turned, stumbled, and headed along the exit path, with an entourage of assistants and students in tow. Green was about to intercept him when a hand fell on his shoulder.

"What are you doing here?"

He turned to see Brian Sullivan, who was trying hard not to scowl.

Green smiled sheepishly. "You know me. I can't resist a mysterious death."

"Uh-huh. A certain first responder wouldn't have anything to do with it?"

"You should have told me." Green searched through the crowd of officers. "Is she here?"

"They assigned her to one of the entrances farther away."

"How is she?"

Sullivan gave him a sharp look. "You know she wouldn't want you to talk about her like this. Like a worried father."

"I know, but I am a worried father."

Sullivan grinned. "Yeah, well, you can deal directly with her on that. And good luck."

"So ..." Green nodded to the burial site, now being methodically gridded and searched by the Ident team. Yellow markers were already scattered around the clearing. The old investigative juices began to flow as he speculated about what they marked. "What do we have?"

"Not much yet. It's a white male, approximately thirty-five to fifty years old, wrapped in an old tarp."

"Is it Edward McAuley?"

"Hannah got a look before she called it in. There's a lot of animal activity and putrefaction, but she thinks so."

"Fuck. How does she seem?"

Sullivan gave him a baleful look. "Like I said, ask her. I'm not getting in the middle between you and Hannah. That's one reason I didn't call you. I left my armour at home."

Green sighed. "Fine. Can you at least tell me who you've assigned to lead?"

"Gibbsie." Sullivan tossed the name off casually as he gazed into the trees, but Green grasped the subtext. Detective Sergeant Bob Gibbs was a competent investigator but also a newly minted sergeant, which meant Sullivan would be keeping close tabs. Equally important, he had come of age under Green and admired him deeply. He would not stonewall.

Green was tempted to say thank you but decided to match the tone. "Good."

"Don't put him in the middle either."

"I won't. I'll go ask Hannah myself."

"I didn't mean with her. I meant with our boss, Fanel."

Green made a show of scanning the crowd. "I don't see him around here."

"Of course not."

"God forbid." Green chuckled and clapped Sullivan on the shoulder. He was about to leave when he caught sight of a young man hovering near the edge of the perimeter, watching him. His skin was an unhealthy green tinge.

He inclined his head toward him. "One of yours?"

"Yeah, just up from general assignment for the summer. Josh Kanner. But I should probably send him somewhere else before he pukes all over the crime scene. This is his first homicide."

"I can tell. God, they make them young these days."

"No younger than we were."

"Feels like a lifetime ago." He sighed and turned away from the scene. "Hannah is at the trailhead, you said?"

"The one by the river. Turn right when you hit the trail."

Green had walked for almost fifteen minutes and was beginning to think Sullivan had sent him on a wild goose chase when he heard the crackling of radios and spotted a pair of cruisers through the trees. Behind them was the vague silhouette of rooftops. Yellow police tape was strung across the trail as it led past a cul-de-sac. Hannah was standing in the middle, looking small and vulnerable in her bulked-up gear. No match for a killer, he thought, but banished the idea as soon as it drifted into his head.

When she'd come into his life as a sixteen-year-old, spitting and cursing, he'd learned there was a lot of power packed into the waiflike frame. And since then she'd added the discipline of jujitsu to the street-fighting skills she'd brought with her.

As he crunched up the gravel path, she stiffened and turned toward the sound. Relief crossed her face, quickly replaced by a scowl that didn't quite make up for the pallor of her cheeks. "I wondered how long it would take you to show up."

He held up his hands in mock surrender. "Guilty. You know I can't resist a good mystery. Not a couple of drug dealers shooting each other up in a parking lot, but a body buried out here in the middle of nowhere."

"Discovered by a dog that started to dig the body up. And other animals had already made a mess of the scene."

"Ident's going to love that." He paused. "Brian says you think it's Edward McAuley."

She hesitated and dropped her gaze. For an instant her lip quivered. "It's pretty decayed, but yeah."

Glancing through the trees at the rooftops, he mentally retraced the route he had walked. "Through the woods, it's probably less than a kilometre to his house."

She still stared at the ground. "I know."

"The pathologist said the body's been there a while."

Now she looked up at him, her expression bleak. "Maybe even since the day he went missing. The dog walker said there was an injured dog. I mean, her dog found a bloody leash, and that's why she went into the woods, to look for the injured dog, and instead ..." She took a deep breath and swayed on her feet. Green knew she was fighting the gruesome image that had popped into her mind. An image that would stay with her forever. You never forget your first putrid, decomposing body.

Spontaneously, he reached out to take her arm. She quivered beneath his touch. "The head was a mess, Dad. Split open. Blood and hair and brains all over."

"I know," he managed, wanting to weep. "I know, honey."

That seemed to give her strength. She straightened and took a few deep breaths. "I told them they had to look for the dog — I mean, its body — with the remains, and check what it died of."

He cocked his head. "What are you thinking?"

"I don't know, Dad. But he went off with the dog that night, and he told his wife he left it tied up outside the Humane Society, but it wasn't there, and it's never been found. The next morning he packs a bag, tells his wife he's going on a business trip, and takes his car to the airport."

"According to his mother, the person who left the car at the airport was not Edward McAuley. The wife isn't sure."

"So …" He could almost see her mind racing as she tried to make sense of the pieces. "So what are you saying, Dad? That the wife is lying? That she made up the whole story about the car and the business trip? That she killed him?"

Her eyes had grown wide. He shook his head quickly. "We're a long way from making that kind of leap. We have a couple of pieces of information from two different sources, but big gaps in the timeline. Lots of things could have happened. His wife could be right that he left that morning and went to the airport. The mother could be wrong. Or she could be right, but someone else killed him sometime after he left his house that morning. Sergeant Gibbs is in charge of the investigation. The first step is to confirm identity, cause, and time of death. Forensics will get what they can from the scene, the body, and the tarp. Gibbs will go into cellphone, internet, and bank records. He'll track McAuley's movements that day, interview colleagues, family, friends, neighbours."

"But the dog is connected somehow, I know it! And it makes sense that —"

In the distance, Green could hear someone coming down the trail. "Bob Gibbs is a thorough guy," he said loudly to cut her off. "You can trust him. Tell him all the things you've learned and let him run with it. He and Brian Sullivan will put the pieces together."

The footsteps grew closer. As she searched his face, some of the old spark returned to her eyes. "Is that what you're going to do?"

He chuckled and risked giving her a hug. For a brief moment she let him before pulling free. "My old friends are welcome to bend my ear any time," he whispered. "That goes for you, too."

Josh Kanner appeared around the bend. He had lost some of his green hue and smiled when he spotted Hannah.

"Josh!" To Green's surprise, Hannah looked flustered. Her previous pallor vanished. "What are you doing here?"

"I … uh … They sent me to take your statement." Josh took a deep breath, turned to Green, and inclined his head in a small bow. "Inspector Green, Josh Kanner. It's an honour to meet you."

Behind him, Hannah rolled her eyes. Green suppressed a laugh. No acceptable alternative to the handshake had really caught on, but at least the man hadn't tried to kiss his ring. He sensed Josh was about to pepper him with questions, so he moved to head him off. "Welcome to Major Crimes, Josh. There's a lot to do in the first few hours of a murder inquiry, so I'll leave you two to it."

CHAPTER NINE

Green lasted two days before he phoned Sullivan and casually invited him to meet at the Pump again after work. It was a hot, sultry afternoon in late June, and Green managed to snag the last available umbrella on the patio.

"Two drinks in less than two weeks!" Sullivan exclaimed as he dropped into the chair opposite, puffing and perspiring from the walk up Elgin Street. "Should I be worried about you?"

"This job is driving me to it."

"Yeah, well, don't think you're going to pry any information out of me on the McAuley murder. Inspector Fanel has already warned me off."

Green took a sip of the crisp Beau's Lug Tread in front of him. "Furthest thing from my mind. Now that we've got that out of the way, so it is McAuley?"

Sullivan signalled to a distant server bearing a tray of beers. The man nodded before heading in the opposite direction. "Jesus, Mary, and Joseph, a man could die of thirst around here!" He leaned over to pick up Green's beer. As he chugged, he nodded. When he came up for air, he sighed with pleasure. "We're still waiting on the entomologist's analysis, but from the amount of decomposition, it looks like he's been dead three to four weeks. That makes it roughly the time the wife says she last saw him. The last time anyone saw him, as it turns out. At least the colleagues, family, and friends we've interviewed so far."

"Bank and phone activity?"

"Still working on the warrants. There's money in a few different banks, not all of which his wife knew about."

"Hiding assets from her?"

"Maybe he was trying to hide from creditors. It's early days, Mike. We just got the dental confirmation. DNA will take forever, but dental is good enough for now. Plus he's the right size and age."

"What did my old pal MacPhail find out?"

"He doesn't do the actual posts anymore. 'Getting too old for all that mucking about,'" Sullivan said in MacPhail's booming Scottish brogue.

"More likely he can't keep his hands steady."

"Or even stand up for that long. He's mostly retired, but he likes to attend the scene to keeps his hand in."

"Hannah said it looked like McAuley was hit on the head."

Sullivan grimaced. "Yeah, with something with a sharp edge. The photos are not a pretty sight. Poor kid, how's she doing?"

"Oh, you know Hannah. She bites my head off when I ask."

Sullivan's beer arrived. His eyes shining, he paused to take a long, deep drink. Green watched him with a twinge of alarm. Sullivan had always been careful with alcohol, having watched his own father smash a swath of drunken chaos through his family while Brian and his siblings were growing up. Was he now losing his grip on his self-restraint?

"So did they find the murder weapon?" he asked to refocus Sullivan's attention.

"Not yet. Nothing at the murder scene. No shovel either. Ident figures from the cut marks in the soil that the killer used a regular garden spade to bury the body. Luckily, it was spring and that ground gets flooded in the spring, so it was still soft. Still, there were lots of rocks and roots, so it would take some strength to dig the hole."

"And to strike a blow hard enough to kill him. Was the body moved there?"

"Too degraded to be sure, but MacPhail's colleague, Anwar Sadiq, thinks he died on scene or shortly before. The arms and legs were folded to fit in the hole, tough to do once rigor sets in."

Green tried to picture the scenario. Had McAuley walked through the bush into that remote clearing under his own steam, and if so, why? He was supposed to be going on a business trip. Had he arranged to meet someone there, like a secret lover? Or had he been followed on a walk and attacked once there was little chance of witnesses stumbling on them in the middle of the murder? Had McAuley screamed, or had the first blow knocked him out? Had the killer come armed with a weapon or grabbed whatever was at hand? A rock, a thick branch. Or …

"Did Dr. Sadiq have any theories on the murder weapon? Could it have been the shovel?"

"Definitely. Swung repeatedly. One of the blows was the flat side and fractured the skull. Others were the sharp edge of the blade that cut open the head."

"How many blows?"

"Four."

"So either our killer was very angry or determined to make sure he was dead. Any defensive wounds?"

Sullivan nodded. "A couple of cuts and abrasions to his arms, but not much. It looks like he was taken by surprise."

"Poor bastard. Scary last moment. I wonder if he had the chance to scream for help."

"We've been conducting door-to-door at all the nearby houses and asking all the trail users who show up. We have a general appeal out to anyone who knows anything. So far nothing useful, but it's not a busy trail."

Green drained the last of his beer. People were beginning to arrive for happy hour, celebrating the end of the workday with large, frosty pitchers. Green was tempted to order another but didn't want to encourage Sullivan to join him. He lowered his voice to avoid eavesdroppers. "All right, so most likely scenario, our killer either followed him or invited him to the trail, probably at night or in the early morning when few people were around. But he had a shovel with him and presumably a tarp. Why? Because he already planned to kill McAuley and bury the body?"

"Or he was burying something else — stolen goods or drugs, maybe? And McAuley stumbled upon him."

Green turned the idea over in his mind. It still didn't explain why McAuley was there in the first place. "Was anything else found at the scene? Or buried with him?"

"Nope. No wallet, no keys, just the clothes he was wearing and the tarp. The killer took away his shovel."

"Wait a minute. The dog."

"What about it?"

"A leash was found. Was the dog's body found, too?"

Sullivan shook his head. "Ident has the leash, which the wife identified as their dog's. But there's no sign of the dog or the remains of a dog in the vicinity, and we searched quite far afield to collect the remains scattered by coyotes and crows. None of them belonged to a dog."

For the third time, Hannah's finger hovered over her father's phone number. She wanted to hear his voice but hated to let him into her struggle. She'd always pretended to be tough, smart, and up for anything, not Daddy's little girl who needed protection. But the past two days she'd barely slept or eaten, and she'd gone through her shifts like a zombie. She couldn't get the McAuley case out of her mind. The bloody head, the dangling ear.

Before that, the 911 call from Philip Walker, reporting screams. Ted and Kristina at the door playing the perfect couple. Her own failure to get Kristina to talk and Rick saying they could just as easily charge her with assault.

Had they missed something? Had *she* missed something? She'd known abused kids. Her best friend at her alternative high school had spent half her nights on the street to avoid the terrors at home. She knew how cleverly they hid the truth and the shame, especially from cops and social workers. They pretended they lived in homes they could barely dream of, just to avoid descending into something worse. Were abused women any different?

She was still fighting with herself, finger over the button, when her phone rang in her hand, startling her so much she almost dropped it. She glanced at the call display. Philip Walker. As if he'd read her mind.

Philip sounded upset. "I hope you don't mind my calling you, Constable. I know you're not part of the investigation team, but those detectives are so ... I don't know ... officious with their notebooks and their questions. Not like you. I feel as if I know you, and you know the whole story, and I can trust you."

"What is it, Phil?"

"A detective came by yesterday to talk to me about the McAuleys and my 911 call. A Detective Kanner. Do you know him?"

Hannah groaned. "I know him a bit. Why? What did he do?"

"It's not what he did, it's his manner. He seemed to be pushing to get something important for his report. He asked me about their relationship. What I'd seen, what I'd heard, what kind of man Ted was and what Kristina was like. He kept pressing me, writing every word I said down. I'm afraid I may have given him the wrong impression."

"About what?"

"Well, mostly about her. He was especially interested in her." He gave a nervous laugh. "My guard was down, I admit. I like a glass of wine in the garden in the afternoon, and the last few days have been difficult. I mean, thinking about Ted and wondering if I should have done something more to help her. So I had started a second glass by the time Detective Kanner came around."

Hannah prayed for patience, not her best suit. Let the story unfold, her father was always telling her. "What happened?"

"I told him about the fights I'd heard over the years. He asked if I'd seen him hit her or shove her, if I'd seen any bruises. I had to say just on her neck that one time. Ted was usually very calm. She was the one screaming. And her little boy, when he was having a meltdown."

"It sounds like you just told the truth like you saw it, Phil. Don't worry about it. The police will be interviewing all the neighbours plus Mr. McAuley's work colleagues and friends. And Detective Kanner will be reviewing his interviews with the senior officers. So they'll get the full picture."

"I know, but I said more. He asked about the day Ted disappeared and the night before, about what time his red Mercedes was there. I didn't notice what time his car got back home."

"But it was there in the morning?"

"I think he stayed somewhere else for the night. I saw the car the next morning, and then it left again. But I remembered their fight the night before. It was a huge fight. I had my windows open because it was a warm night, and they have such bright security lights that you can see everything. When the screaming started, I went outside. I wanted to see for myself and make sure I heard everything this time."

He paused as if to collect his thoughts, and Hannah held her breath. "I stood in the bushes by the end of my drive. I heard Ted in the house shouting, 'That's it, I've had enough of this worthless piece of shit!' and Kristina shouting, 'No, Ted, no! Don't!' He swore at her, said the thing was nothing but trouble and they all cared more about it than they did about him. Kristina is crying, 'Don't hurt her,' and he says, 'I'll give you something to cry about.' He came out the door with the dog under his arm, and suddenly he lowered his voice, like he knew people could hear. He said something, and she said, 'Don't you dare'. He got in the car, she ran down the driveway in her nightgown and struck the hood of the car. Then she screamed clear as can be, 'I hate you. You hurt Toto, I swear I'll kill you.' He just took off, leaving her on the driveway. She was in a panic, and I was about to go to her when their daughter came out and persuaded her to come back in the house. Justine was begging her to shut up. Kristina said, 'He's going the wrong way. Why is he going that way?' And Justine said, 'Probably just going around the block.

Dad would never hurt the dog, he's just trying to get to you.'"

Hannah pictured the scene playing out on the darkened driveway. Ugly, raw, and all too human. "You told Detective Kanner all this?"

Philip groaned. "I didn't want to at first. I didn't want to get Kristina in trouble. But he kept asking and asking me to clarify details, so it just came out. I'm not the kind of person who can lie, especially to the police. I know how awful it sounded. But people say things like that, like 'I'll kill you,' when they're angry, but they never mean it."

"Totally. I'm sure Detective Kanner knows that."

"But then he wanted to know all about the dog and how Ted treated it. I felt like I was digging myself deeper and deeper into that hole. Ted never liked Toto. He's a neat freak, and he hated the fur, the mess in the yard, and the muddy paw prints all over their perfect white house. I never saw him walk the dog or even pet it. Toto was Kristina's baby through and through. Kristina's and the kids'. Their little boy played with her all the time. Apparently the child's therapist recommended a dog as an emotional support animal, and Kristina was so happy Toto was bringing him out of himself. Even Justine walked her. She was a bit high-strung and skittish, but she was a lovely little dog with the gentlest eyes. You'd have to be pretty nasty to hurt such an innocent little animal."

"Do you think that's what Ted did?"

"I don't know, but the dog has never been found. And there's another thing. Detective Kanner had me so rattled

I forgot to mention it. After the fight that night, I saw someone walking along the riverbank behind my house to Ted's."

Hannah's senses grew alert. "Who?"

"I can't be sure. They weren't using a flashlight. Sometimes neighbours go down to the river to see the stars, which are beautiful out over the water. But it was a man, walking with more purpose. I thought … to be honest, I thought it might be Ted."

It took Hannah a couple of hours to decide what to do. She toyed with the idea of approaching Josh directly to find out how he planned to write up the interview, and to give him this new tidbit, but their relationship wasn't exactly cosy. In the end she realized it was Bob Gibbs himself she had to talk to.

She and Gibbs had never been best buds, but she had been hearing about him from her father ever since he was a shy rookie detective afraid of his own shadow. She'd heard about his stumbles, his successes, his romance with fellow detective Sue Peters, and his recent promotion to sergeant in charge of a team. Her father used to complain that Gibbs couldn't even scare a street kid, let alone a hardened criminal, and she was counting on that when she phoned to meet him after her shift.

He was sitting at his desk in his small office, scrolling through his computer, when she arrived. She'd changed into civvies and untied her hair to let its neon green streak show. She had ditched all her body piercings when she applied to the police, so this neon streak was all that was left of her rebel past.

His greeting was stiff and proper, but she relaxed when she saw the twinkle in his eye. "It's about the McAuley case," she began after he'd asked her how she was enjoying police work.

"I figured that."

"You know I was on the domestic call that came in a few weeks ago?"

"Yeah, I read the report. And talked to Rick Geneva." He smiled a little. "I also know you were in touch with Meredith Johnson in Missing Persons."

She nodded and tried to sound casual. "I was just following up."

He waited.

"I … I wasn't too sure about Rick's — our — conclusion, because I didn't … well, the wife refused to talk to me alone. When the husband disappeared, I was concerned we missed something. Neighbours gave conflicting reports."

"They usually do."

"Anyway …" She faltered. His quiet eyes made her feel like a kid, and she was beginning to understand why, despite his shyness, her father had believed in him. "One of those neighbours, Philip Walker, phoned me this afternoon. He was the one who made the initial 911 call, and he always believed there was something going on behind closed doors in that house."

"I'm aware of his concerns. I've read the detective's report."

"That's partly why I'm here. Mr. Walker worried he gave the wrong impression to that detective. He was trying to stick to the facts, exactly what he saw and heard —"

"That's what he's supposed to do."

"He said the detective kept pushing for yes-or-no answers, but there are so many other little things." She had rehearsed the list and ticked it off on her fingers. "The closed blinds, the wife wearing a caftan, her hardly ever going out, the daughter never home, the little boy's tantrums.... I know he's on the spectrum, but couldn't he also be living in fear?"

"These are questions for an expert. I'll be consulting with the violence against women people."

She unclenched her fists a little. "Okay. I mean, that's good. A lot of this stuff is hidden. Often the husband controls by fear, and no one else sees it." She flushed. "Sorry, I don't mean to tell you your job."

His eyes twinkled again. "You're like your father."

She grinned. "Both pains in the ass? So here's the thing. Philip Walker is afraid you won't realize how nasty the husband was in the privacy of their home. Yes, Mrs. McAuley screamed at him, but she was frustrated and stressed. How many people say 'I'm going to kill you' when they're mad? But they don't mean it. She was scared to death about her little dog. She loves that dog, and so does her son. She was afraid he was going to hurt it. I'm guessing that's a threat he's held over her before. What Philip Walker witnessed that night was a totally freaked-out woman in fear for her pet's life. Maybe because she knew what he was capable of."

"It's possible. We're still in the preliminary stages of gathering information."

"Has anyone else reported he had a nasty side?"

He gave her a long, disapproving look. She knew she was pushing it, but what the hell. That had never stopped her before. Finally, he shrugged. "In the courtroom, he's a tough negotiator. Several women on the losing side of a case called him ruthless. But that's his job. We're only just getting to his friends and colleagues, but so far most of his neighbours, except Mr. Walker, say he was friendly and helpful, and it was the wife who was the difficult one."

"But that's how abusive men operate! Charming and friendly to everyone else, so their wife looks like the crazy one."

"We're keeping an open mind, Hannah. Don't worry." He pushed his chair back and stood up. "Thanks for coming, and if anything else …"

She pressed on. "Then there's the dog. Dogs don't know how to lie. That dog didn't like Ted McAuley. More than that, she was afraid of him. Why?"

"Lots of reasons. Some dogs are afraid of garbage cans."

Hannah thought of Modo, the dog who had come into her father's life at the same time as her. She felt a certain kinship with Modo, a dog so abused and traumatized, it had taken years to coax her out of her shell.

"I know, but if he beat it or harmed it, that would be a serious red flag. And if he killed it to punish her —"

"We're still looking for the dog. We don't know what happened, but we haven't found the body. We have an appeal out to the public for the dog as well."

He was standing by his open door now. Hannah rushed on. "There's one other thing Mr. Walker forgot to mention. Might not be relevant, but …" She filled him in on the mysterious night visitor. "We don't know what he was doing or where he went, but Walker thought it might have been Ted. And as part of the comings and goings of that night —"

A door opened down the hall. Gibbs had been listening intently, but now his gaze flicked nervously toward the man who was striding through the squad room. Hannah watched as he disappeared into the office that had once been her father's. *Uh-oh.*

Gibbs stepped out of his office, hiding her from view. "Thanks for all this, Hannah. We'll follow up."

She took her cue, muttered goodbye, and scurried through the squad room to the opposite exit.

CHAPTER TEN

Green studied the email that had popped up on his computer. He'd been making a rapid check of his messages before tackling the huge PDF file that had been sent to him from on high. It was an FYI only, but he had to at least pretend he had read it. New protocols to add to the constantly shifting guidelines for virtual and in-person appearances.

The email was from Ramon Ramirez at RR Contracting. He'd never had any dealings with RR Contracting. The name rang a faint bell, but he couldn't recall from where. Some long-ago case, perhaps? As he read, it slowly came back to him.

> *Hello Inspector Green,*
> *I don't know if you remember me but nine*
> *years ago you help me with my son Luis.*
> *He was hanging around with a gang that*
> *shot a drug dealer in an apartment build-*
> *ing near our house. He didn't know it was*
> *going to happen. He was seventeen and*
> *scared to go to jail and have a record. But*

you help him. You were a father, you said,
and you could see he was a good kid who
just join in a bad group. Because of you,
my son is good now. He finish his school
and is working in my company. I know
you are a fair man. Now I need help for
my daughter Kristina. I know you visit her
last week. But now her husband is killed
and I am scared the new detective don't
believe her. Maybe it is better I explain on
the phone. I hope you call me and maybe
help her like my son.

Much appreciate, Ramon Ramirez

Ramon had left his contact information in his signature line. RR Contracting had an address in Carleton Place, a bedroom town just west of Ottawa's outer suburbs.

It was all coming back to him now, and he cursed himself for not making the connection earlier, but Kristina McAuley's maiden name had not been in any of the reports he read. He remembered Ramon Ramirez as a hard-working refugee who'd fled El Salvador on foot with his wife and three small children. Like so many immigrants, he was grateful to be in Canada and wanted a better life for his children, one of whom died during the journey. He had struggled to speak and read English, but he was made of tough stuff and fought hard for his children.

Green remembered his son as a skinny beanpole who pumped iron and worked hard on his swagger, which he'd needed in the rough neighbourhood where they lived. He'd been lonely and lost in a sea of adolescent pressures, but he had not been guilty of pulling the trigger or of luring the victim into the trap. He had just been there, scared to join in and even more scared to leave.

Green wasn't surprised to get the email. He knew firsthand that most immigrants who fled oppressive regimes, including his own father, were frightened and suspicious of police, who'd historically never been on their side. Ramon had had a hard time trusting in the investigative and legal process that had scooped his son into its clutches. And now, here they were again. Of course! It was the son he'd seen driving away from Kristina's house that day.

He considered phoning Brian Sullivan. He had already stuck his nose into this investigation far more than he should. Ramon didn't know that he was no longer in charge of Criminal Investigations. Sullivan had also worked on the Luis Ramirez case, and he was quite capable of turning on the Irish charm. He'd grown up on a farm, and in many ways, his hardscrabble Catholic childhood made him a better fit than Green, nerdy son of Jewish Holocaust survivors raised in the crumbling inner-city tenements of Lowertown.

But he couldn't resist the pull of the case. He owed the man at least the courtesy of a phone call, he told himself. Maybe he could tease out the source of Ramon's fears about police bias more easily than a scary, six-foot-two ex-linebacker, no matter how much Irish charm Sullivan poured on.

All he had to do was make the call, and afterward he would hand over any information he gleaned to Major Crimes.

The man who answered the call sounded guarded, presumably because Ottawa Police had popped up on his call display. The accent was still strong, but the voice was deeper and hoarser than Green remembered.

"Mr. Ramirez, Inspector Green here."

"Inspector!" The guardedness vanished. "Thank you. I am happy you call."

"I should tell you, I'm not on the Edward McAuley case. I'm not in charge of that department anymore."

There was a pause. A groan. "You know the case?"

"I know of it. I'm sorry for your daughter's loss." He winced at the canned platitude.

"The detective think she kill him! My daughter is afraid. She have no money, no friends, a little boy who need help, and now she worry she go to jail! You remember how happy she was. Now her life is ruined!"

He hadn't met Kristina in person nine years earlier, but he remembered she had been the pride of the family and a poster child for the Canadian immigrant dream. She was the oldest child, the daughter who had married well, and all hopes had been pinned on her after their older son had died in a refugee camp in Mexico. That was one of the reasons he'd felt sympathy for the family. His own father had lost children in the Holocaust.

"Tell me about her."

"It's my fault," Ramon said. "I got her the job. I was working for Ted McAuley's father — he own a construction company, and I was carpenter, but I have my own business now." He broke off in a fit of coughing. Years of construction dust and paint fumes or something worse, Green wondered. Eventually, he dragged air into his lungs. "Sorry. Mr. McAuley was a rich man building lots of houses, and Kristina was a smart girl. She finish high school, and she want to go to college someday but college costs money, so I ask Mr. McAuley if there is a job. She work in his office and make bookings, send out invoices. That's where she meet Ted. He was a law student, and he was working there for a summer job. Mr. McAuley was proud of his son, handsome, smart, going to be successful. But ..." He paused as if trying to put his concerns into English words.

"There were problems?" Green asked gently.

"I didn't see. Kristina was crazy in love, he was everything she dream about. She would have a good life. My wife was nervous about it. He's not our kind, she said. He's white, he's got an education, his family will look down on her. On us. But he's Catholic, I said. She will go in his world. The Canadian world."

Green had heard this hope over and over from immigrants aspiring to be full members of Canadian society, to shed their immigrant roots and pass for white. It might work on the outside, but inside a marriage, it could lead to a sense of indebtedness. A classic power imbalance.

Ramon coughed again, and his voice dropped. "I tell you something, but don't repeat. Kristina was ashame.

My wife, too. Kristina got pregnant that summer. Just finished high school and now pregnant. Ted still in law school and he not want the baby. Mrs. McAuley say Kristina trick her son. My wife say who trick who? So the two mothers, they talk together and agree. No abortion, no shame. A quiet wedding and a little house in Kanata that Mr. McAuley pay for and I build. And so it started. A wife Ted didn't want, a crying baby, a house far from the university. I hear them fighting when I am working on the house. I hear her crying. I see her get tired and sad, and very ashame. He say it's her fault, he keep his part and now she have to do hers."

"What was her part?"

"I don't know everything. She is too ashame to talk to me. But she have to keep the baby quiet so he can study, make the dinners he likes, make the house clean, other things ... a wife does. My wife help her, say don't worry, when he is making lots of money, they will hire cleaners and babysitters. But Ted never did. He bought himself a bigger house, and a fancy car, and a boat...."

Green was getting the picture of a prize asshole who was uncaring and condescending, but was he also abusive? "Ramon, did he ever hurt her?"

Ramon said nothing. Green waited. "Ramon, this is important. Some of the neighbours said they thought so."

"This is what the other policeman said. That maybe he pushed her too far this time. But Kristina would never do that. For eighteen years she try to keep him happy. She has nothing without him. Her kids have nothing."

Green waited again. So far, Ramon hadn't answered the question. Ramon rushed on. "He wear two faces, one for outside in the world, another one for inside his walls. But that one is the real one, and someone saw it. You look at the people he cheated —"

"Cheated?"

"In the courts, with the law. The clients and the other lawyers, he walk on them. Everyone says he's a good lawyer because he wins. But someone loses, right or wrong. That's where you have to look."

"He's a fucking barracuda!" Lenny Feinstein exclaimed. "But it'll cost you a couple of beers."

Green groaned. Lenny was a former provincial Crown attorney whom Green had known for over twenty-five years. He'd honed his colourful, straight-shooting style over years of hanging out with cops, surly youth, and serious bad guys before escaping to the less chaotic and more lucrative courts of civil litigation. Green figured he had probably clashed swords with Ted McAuley several times.

Green had checked through the court dockets to see if McAuley had been involved in any contentious cases in the past few years, but nothing stood out among the dry, highly procedurized documents submitted to the courts. However, he knew most of the real fighting would have taken place outside the courts. He had hoped for a quick, off-the-record phone conversation with Lenny, but the lawyer had jumped at the chance for a beer at his favourite local pub, Darcy McGee's. A stone's throw from both the courthouse and Parliament Hill, the heritage pub was awash in the gossip and conspiracies of generations of lawyers and junior government staffers.

Darcy McGee's was a warren of small, semiprivate alcoves perfect for trading confidences and dirt, and Green found Lenny wedged in one at the back, already on his second beer. Another habit he'd picked up over his years in the criminal trenches. His expensive suit and silk tie did not hide the cruel beating of those years. His pouchy face was the colour of raw beef, and his eyes were webs of red. But the wide, bucktoothed grin was still the same when Green placed two beers on the table.

"Good man!" he said, rubbing his hands. "So you enjoying your twilight years in the dead zone?" he asked once Green had settled opposite him. The room echoed with the indecipherable din of a dozen conversations, making their privacy assured.

Green winced. *Twilight years?* "Not as much as you, obviously."

"There's lots of life after the bad guys and the crooks. You should think about retiring. How many years you got in?"

"Getting there. But I'd miss all the paperwork."

Lenny laughed. "Seriously. There's good money in the private sector for a guy with your skills. You could set up your own private investigations firm. Hell, I'd hire you in a heartbeat."

"This court gig is not so bad, and it won't last forever."

Lenny leaned across the table. "So what are you doing poking around in the Ted McAuley case? You miss it, don't you? You can't stand that a juicy murder has dropped in Major Crimes's lap, and you're stuck on the outside looking in."

"That's it, Lenny." Green sipped his beer. He had no intention of telling Lenny about Hannah's involvement or Ramon Ramirez's phone call. It would get all over town. "I figured you'd know better than most what kind of guy he was and who he might have pissed off."

"It would be a long list. Like I said, a barracuda. In court. He hated to lose, and he'd pull out all the legal stops. Never illegal, though. He always seemed to know exactly where the line was. But God help you if you had a shaky witness or a hole in your case. He'd charge through it like General Patton's army. He'd slice and dice that witness up so fast, they wouldn't even see the knife. Just feel the pain afterward."

"So not only might opposing clients and lawyers hate him, but also witnesses he'd humiliated along the way."

"Yeah, but that's the curious thing about Ted. It was just business, an act, and most people knew it. Even those poor fuckers he left bleeding on the floor, they admired him. He was Jekyll and Hyde, he put Lawrence Olivier to shame. On the job, merciless. Off the job, just a regular guy. He'd even apologize. He'd say, 'If you'd prepared better or had a better offer, I wouldn't have to slaughter you.'"

A group of young people, probably government gophers, pushed by, shrieking with laughter. Green hesitated and lowered his voice. "So which is the real Ted McAuley? Jekyll or Hyde?"

With a final deep swig, Lenny emptied his glass and gave a satisfied burp. He moved to get up. "Another?"

Green glanced at his watch. He'd promised to pick up Aviva from her day program, so another beer was out of the question. Besides, if he carried on with these off-the-record, off-the-premises pub meetings much longer, he'd have to buy a whole new suit.

He shook his head. "Love to, but my kid awaits."

Disappointed, Lenny sat back down. "Who's the real Ted McAuley? I think both. I think he could be nice as pie if he's winning, but God help you if you got on his bad side."

It was almost ten o'clock before Green could call Sullivan. Aviva was asleep, and Tony was up in his room, doing God knows what on his computer. The kid was bright and good-hearted, but a whirlwind, and they worked hard to fill his days with activities to wear him out and keep him challenged. At twelve, he was still a boy, but the teenage dangers lurked just around the corner. Green had been there himself, and as a cop he knew all the things that could go wrong. At times he was tempted to tie the boy up in the cellar until he was eighteen. Thank God for Sharon's wisdom.

Sharon was still out at her book club. She juggled a busy, stressful job as a psychiatric head nurse with the demands of an active family on the move, and book club was her one indulgence. Often she complained she was too tired to go, but in the end, the camaraderie of good friends always invigorated her.

The house was peaceful as he poured himself a finger of Scotch straight-up and sank into his easy chair. Modo struggled to her feet and lumbered over to drop all one hundred pounds of furry mutt on his feet. He winced as he wriggled them free.

"You got a minute?" he asked when Sullivan answered.

"The house burning down?"

Green chuckled. "No, but I want to fill you in on some stuff I heard today. Background on McAuley that might be useful to the investigation."

"You heard?"

"Yeah, well ... technically the first thing fell into my lap." He spent the next ten minutes reporting on his meeting with Lenny Feinstein and his phone conversation with Kristina McAuley's father. He was relieved that Sullivan didn't unleash his famous Irish temper but instead asked questions in a focused monotone.

"Luis Ramirez," he said in surprise. "Small world. The case rings a bell. A small-time street dealer, if I recall."

"Yeah, but scared straight by that drug execution."

"You're sure about that?"

It was Green's turn to be surprised. "No, I'm not. I've been out of the loop for four years, remember? You could check."

"I will. We ran a preliminary check on the whole family, and nothing popped up, but that charge was when he was a YO. If he's still active, he's staying well below our radar." He paused. "Thanks for the tip."

In the silence, Green chafed. "I'm stepping out of this now, Brian —"

"Sure you are."

Green ignored that. "But if there are ways I can help, I'd like to. Between you and me, I think Hannah is stressed, and I want to help her. Seeing your first body is never easy."

"You survived. We all survived."

"I know, but ..."

Sullivan softened. "Do you want me to keep an eye on her?"

"Oh, no, she'd kill you. No, just ... I don't know what I want you to do."

"Keep you informed on the case?"

Green laughed. "Would I ask you to do that? But if I learn anything, or you learn anything that impacts her, can we keep those lines open? Off the record?"

Sullivan didn't answer, but Green knew his friend. They'd worked cases side by side for years. Sullivan would find a way.

The door opened, and he signed off from Sullivan as Sharon slipped quietly in, all shiny-eyed, pink-cheeked, and smelling of wine. Modo thumped her tail but like him made no effort to get up. *We're all getting old*, he thought.

"I see the fort is still standing," she said, giving him a kiss. "What have you been plotting with Brian?"

"The McAuley case that Hannah was involved in. I had some background for him. Talked to a colleague."

She snuggled on the sofa beside him and rubbed Modo with her foot.

"Do you think a person can really be two people?" he said. "I don't mean something fancy like dissociative identity disorder. I mean present one face to some people and quite another to others?"

"Of course they can. At work I'm the model of patience, understanding, and support. I'm sweetness and light itself."

"You are?"

She shoved him. "I have to be. I couldn't be effective if I wasn't. But at home I can let my hair down. I can relax and yell at you when you're being dumb, stomp out and slam the door when I've had enough of you all. That's how I keep my balance."

"Nice to know I'm basically ballast."

"You have your uses."

He chuckled and reflected on her point. "But you're still the same you. Just the patient you and the exasperated you. Everyone has their good and bad sides. But you'd never do something completely out of character, something really cruel like beat up your kids, or" — he leaned down to pat Modo — "kick the dog."

"Neither would you. We all have our moral centre, our lines in the sand, if you like. Unless we're really desperate, and then you know even better than me that anything is possible." She eyed him thoughtfully. "Of course, some people's moral centre is a lot further to the extreme than others'. Where's this coming from? Edward McAuley? Or his wife?"

"I'm trying to get a handle on him." He turned her observation over in his mind. "But you raise a good point. I don't know a damn thing about his wife."

CHAPTER ELEVEN

Josh Kanner wasn't too thrilled with his assignment. He was happy that Sergeant Gibbs had included him as part of the search team, especially after his clumsy handling of Philip Walker, but he wished he were inside the house, not stuck outside searching the grounds. All the important clues to Edward McAuley's murder would be inside his house, and he wanted to get his own read on the grieving widow. All he'd managed was a quick glimpse in the front hall when Gibbs introduced his team. The woman looked like a zombie as she took the warrant, barely looked at it, and with a wave of her hand, told them to do whatever they wanted.

He doubted she looked like much at the best of times, but her hair was unwashed and uncombed, her clothes baggy, and her eyes like empty black pools. A small boy was glued to her side, and she seemed more concerned about him than the fact her house was being turned upside down.

Out front, Josh took stock of his task as he pulled on his nitrile gloves. There was an oversized two-car garage, a boat, a Lexus, and a shed at the back. Slim pickings for finding any worthwhile evidence to contribute to the investigation. Armed with his camera and notebook, he started at the front of the house, poking his stick through the gardens in search of anything odd. The grass needed mowing and the weeds had gained a serious foothold in the flower beds, but some yellow flowers still peeked through.

Nothing.

The garage was nearly empty; he'd never seen a place so clean. A canoe and kayak were suspended from the rafters, four bikes were hung on the back wall, and a collection of preschool ride toys were bunched in one corner. A wall unit at the back contained at least a dozen pairs of skis, as well as skates and snowshoes. He worked his way around the room, photographing and documenting, determined to prove he could be a thorough, objective investigator and not just a token nod to diversity. It was the same old story; despite having professional parents and a comfortable, middle-class childhood, he could never quite escape the colour of his skin. Not white like his dad, not brown like his mom. He didn't know who'd ratted him out to Gibbs about the Philip Walker interview, but it was not going to happen again.

The boat was a beauty. Josh had only been in a speedboat once in his life. How cool it would be to race this baby down the middle of the Ottawa River, engine screaming and wind roaring in his ears. He sat in the cockpit a moment, imagining, until the rumbling of a truck brought him back. He climbed down just as the flatbed tow truck arrived to haul the Lexus away. The driver backed into the drive, hitched up the front wheels, and was just beginning to pull the car up when the front door flew open.

"What are you doing!"

He turned to see a teenage girl flying down the walkway. She was dressed in next to nothing, her sleek, muscular body rippling as she moved. She sported multiple tattoos on her shoulders and down her cleavage.

He tamped down a stirring of interest to focus on objectivity. *Details, Kanner. Details.* Female aged approximately fifteen to eighteen, five foot ten, one hundred and forty pounds. One half of her hair was bleached pink to match her lips, and sparkling fake eyelashes made her dark eyes look huge. The toenails on her bare feet also glittered pink and black.

"What are you doing with the car?" she demanded.

"Who are you?"

"Justine McAuley. Who the fuck are you?"

The daughter. What a stroke of luck — a chance to size up one of the players in the case. "I'm Detective Kanner. We're impounding the car for analysis."

"Analysis of what?"

"Forensics. It's routine."

Behind them, the door opened and another detective emerged with an evidence bin full of papers, which he carried to the police van. Justine faced Josh down in the driveway. Her eyelashes fascinated him.

"You can't take away the car. It's the only one we have. Mom needs it for my brother's appointments."

"She'll get it back."

"When?"

He shrugged. This girl sure could push. "As soon as we're finished with it."

She scowled. "I don't know what you think you'll find. The murder weapon? It's a plain old car. Dad hardly ever drove it because there was dog fur all over it."

"Who does drive it besides your mother?"

"Uncle Louie sometimes. Just to run errands for my mother."

"Who's Uncle Louie?"

"Mom's brother. He helps her around here when work is slow." She looked around the overgrown yard. "You'd never know it."

Behind them, chains clanked as the tow truck driver secured the wheels on the flatbed. Justine looked sulky as she watched.

"Anyone else?"

She glanced back at him and seemed to size him up for the first time. A faint smile crept across her face, and her eyelashes fluttered. "Me, sometimes. When *she* lets me. I just got my G2 licence a month ago. She let me take my first solo trip last week, all the way to the corner store, yippee. Now I'll have to wait ages before I can drive it again."

Wow, aren't you the grieving daughter, he thought, relieved when the tow truck driver approached to ask him to sign off on the paperwork. They watched as the truck drove cautiously away. As it disappeared around the corner, it narrowly missed a pickup truck careening toward them, white with *RR Contracting* on its door. It slewed into the driveway and screeched to a halt. A man leaped out, his face red with fury. He took a few ragged breaths before he found his voice.

"Where they take the Lexus?" he snapped at Justine.

"Papito, the cops are taking everything! The car, Dad's computer, all his files and papers, even Mom's papers!"

The man turned his outrage on Josh. "Why are you doing this? My daughter didn't kill anyone!" His fists were balled, and he looked ready to go ten rounds. He was large, and although his hair was like steel wool and his face had more crags than the Grand Canyon, he was still built like a barrel. Josh tensed.

"Detective Josh Kanner of the Ottawa Police, sir. What's your name?"

"Ramon Ramirez."

RR Contracting, Josh thought. *Here's the boss himself.* He snapped a photo and recorded his name.

"What are you doing?" Ramon demanded with alarm. "I am Kristina's father. She call me."

"Just routine, Mr. Ramirez. This search is entirely routine, part of standard procedure in a murder inquiry."

"A waste of time to look in this house. Look at his work. At the neighbours. They don't like him."

"We will be talking to everybody."

Ramon waved his hand in disgust and turned his back to address his granddaughter. "Where is your mother? Is she all right?"

"She's being her usual hopeless self, Papito. There's nothing in the fridge, the house is a mess, but she doesn't care. She only cares about Peter."

"Don't talk about your mother like that." He gripped her shoulder and steered her toward the house.

"But it's true! No wonder Dad got so frustrated with her."

"Shush! She have a shock." He pushed her through the door and out of earshot.

Josh wished he could hear the rest of the conversation, but he scribbled it down word for word in his notebook. Even this might earn him some brownie points.

He headed along the side of the house toward the back, following a well-trampled path marred by gravel spills. He poked in the shrubbery as he went. Nothing, zero, nada. He stopped short when he came upon the gorgeous river vista up ahead. *Wow. What I wouldn't do for a few million bucks.* The gardens and grass at the back were unkempt, but the large stone patio stretching the width of the house looked brand new and immaculate. He did a quick check of the hedges, gardens, and shoreline before turning his attention to the wooden shed at the edge of the yard. It also looked new, and although there was a padlock hanging on the door, it was unlocked.

He cracked open the door and switched on the overhead light to reveal a perfectly organized space with a lawnmower, snow blower, bags of mulch and soil stacked in a corner, and a shelving unit loaded with gardening supplies. Long-handled gardening tools hung in a neat row on the wall.

Josh took photos and careful notes, starting in one corner and working his way around the room. Everything was neat and rust-free. There was not a speck of dirt or dried grass on the plywood floor. *Who keeps their shed like an operating room?* He paused when he came to a folded pile of tarps on the shelf. One looked exactly like the one used to wrap McAuley's body. He made a mental note to tell Gibbs before moving on to the garden tools on the wall. Two rakes, a hoe, a broom ...

He stopped at the spade. It was whistle-clean. More than clean — it was so shiny, he could almost see his reflection. Brand new? He peered at it closely. No, there were tiny traces of debris visible in the crack between the blade and the shaft. This spade had been scrubbed clean.

Bingo.

CHAPTER TWELVE

Hannah climbed off her motorcycle and took the photo out of her bag. She was getting weary and beginning to think this was a huge waste of time. This was the third day she'd been out on the road, and the list of vets seemed just as long now as when she'd started. Six vets today alone, with two more visits before she had to boot it back to Ottawa for her late-evening shift.

She had skipped all the vets within the Ottawa city limits, figuring that someone wanting to get a dog treated without raising questions would not go to a local. Kristina McAuley had flooded social media and plastered Toto's face on the hydro poles near her house. If whoever took her was smart, and if Toto was still alive — a big *if* — they would have taken the dog to a vet farther out in the country, where people had better things to do than scroll constantly through Instagram.

She knew there was a good chance Toto was dead and had been since the day Ted McAuley took her away, because the dude who'd taken a spade to McAuley's head probably wouldn't blink an eye at doing the same to a dog. She was a liability. Not only might she yap and draw attention to him, but someone might also recognize her. But Toto's body had not turned up, not at the murder scene or anywhere else within the park where the cadaver dogs had searched.

That small piece of the puzzle had niggled at Hannah, especially late at night when she was staring at her bedroom ceiling, trying not to see McAuley's bloody head. It was a loose end that begged to be tied up because no one else seemed to care, and it gave her something to do. She had begun in the town of Arnprior to the west and worked her way in a large arc toward the south and east. If, at the end of her long list of vets, it turned out to be a waste of time, at least she'd have had some nice rides in the country among the cornfields and pastures of dozing cows.

Kemptville was a town about sixty kilometres south of Ottawa, rapidly entering the big leagues with a cluster of modern big-box stores. The vet hospital was a shiny new building with large glass windows. As she walked into the waiting room, a couple of dogs surged forward on their leashes, and the receptionist looked up expectantly. Hannah had her spiel down pat after three days, and she laid the worry and confusion on thick as she placed the photo of Toto, pulled from Kristina's Facebook post, down on the counter.

"Hello, can you help me? Have you seen my dog? Her name's Toto, and she's been missing for four weeks. I've looked everywhere, and I've been going to all the vets and shelters in the area. I was staying with a friend at a farm near Merrickville, and she got spooked by a horse and ran off. I'm afraid she might have been hit by a car. Did anyone bring this little dog in with an injury?"

The receptionist studied the photo and started to shake her head. Hannah cut her off. "Could you ask around in the back?"

"Well …" the receptionist began doubtfully.

"Please! She's such a cute dog, and she's so friendly that someone might keep her if they found her. But I'm dying without her."

The receptionist, whose name tag said Meg, took the photo into the back but returned a few minutes later. "Sorry. Did you try the other vets in town?"

"Yes. And Smiths Falls and Perth and Merrickville."

Behind her, one of the dog owners stood up and came to look at the photo. She was a large woman with jowls to match her dog's. "Wait a sec. I think I saw this dog. Four weeks ago, right? Yeah, I was in for Buddy's shot, and this man brought the dog in. It was covered in dried blood, and the vet took it right into the back."

Hannah's heart leaped. The day Ted supposedly disappeared was exactly four weeks ago. "Did you get his name? Where he lived?"

"No, Buddy got his shot, and we left before they came out. The man didn't call it Toto, though."

"What did he look like?"

"Young fella. Maybe midtwenties? Skinny, shaved head, one of those silly little beards."

"From around here?"

"I didn't recognize him, but we're getting a lot of city people moving out here these days."

Hannah glanced at Meg. "But the vet should remember, anyway."

"Oh, it wasn't the regular vet," the woman added. "It was Jane Leitin. She only does a couple of evenings a week here. Most of her practice is big animals up in Pakenham."

Hannah groaned. Pakenham was out in the boonies, farther west than the circle she had drawn. She turned back to the receptionist. "But she would have opened a file, right? Four weeks ago? Can you check?"

"Without the name of either the dog or the owner …"

"Can't you search by date? All the dogs seen around June second to fifth?"

Meg looked dismayed. She glanced at the waiting room, where another dog and a cat had just arrived. "I'm afraid I don't have the time …"

"Please? I can wait." Hannah allowed a quaver into her voice. "I can't stand the thought of never seeing her again!"

Meg frowned, shook her head, and reached for the photo. "Leave it with me. I'll see what I can do when things quiet down a bit."

"Thank you so much!"

"I can't promise anything. But write your name and number on the back, and I'll get back to you in a couple of days."

In fact, Hannah's phone rang the next evening while she and Rick were parked at a gas station on Carling

Avenue, catching up on paperwork while waiting for a call. She didn't recognize the number and almost didn't answer, but at the last moment, she changed her mind. She had sent out a lot of feelers and left at least a dozen copies of the photo in the past few days. Maybe one had hit the jackpot.

"Hello," said an unfamiliar woman's voice. "Hannah Pollack? It's Jane Leitin here. You were inquiring about the injured Havanese I treated a few weeks ago?"

"Dr. Leitin! Yes, thank you for getting back to me. Hold on." Hannah opened the cruiser door and stepped out, peering back at Rick. "Sorry, got to take this. Personal stuff."

That ought to keep him quiet, she thought with a grin as she strolled away. "Yes, it's my dog. At least I think it's my dog. I lost her while I was visiting nearby. Can you tell me if she's okay?"

"She should be, if she's given the care I recommended. But the owner didn't say anything about her being a stray. He knew her name —"

"What was it?"

"Puck."

What kind of dumb name is that for a dog, Hannah thought. "As in hockey?"

"That could be. He was a young man. I was thinking more Shakespeare, but I suspect my age is showing."

"But what about the owner? What was his name and address?"

"I have it here, but I'm not sure I should … I have no reason to think this dog was stolen."

"But it's the dog in the picture, right?"

"It's certainly similar, but many Havanese look like that."

"And she was injured? No collar, no tags?"

"She had a collar with a tag — the kind you get in a pet store — that had *Puck* on it and a phone number."

Hannah's heart sank.

"But it did look brand new."

"How was she injured?"

"He said she was hit by a car. But ..." Doubt crept into the vet's voice. "The injury was a day or so old, and it was rather strange for a car accident. Out in the country, I see a lot of those. Usually a dog that size, struck by a vehicle, would have multiple lacerations and broken bones, if it survived at all. This dog had only a hairline skull fracture, a torn ear, and a lot of bleeding, which had stopped. Possibly from being struck by the bumper and thrown clear, but it seemed more like a single blow to the head."

Hannah covered her mouth in horror. Poor little thing. "Oh, my baby!" she wailed.

"Yes. Odd. The man was a rather odd duck himself. Fussy, particular, he wanted the instructions repeated several times so he could write them down word for word in his datebook. A well-used datebook, I might add, crammed with bits of paper. Very odd for someone of his generation. But he did seem to care about the dog. He bought her some food and treats, as well as all the meds and supplies I prescribed. Not one complaint about the cost."

"All the same, if it isn't his dog, he has stolen it. If you'll give me his name and address, I'd like to see for myself."

"How about I contact him and tell him you want to see the dog to make sure it's not your dog. That will seem strange, but you can handle that however you like."

Hannah thought fast. "There is a simple answer to this. If she's mine, she'll answer to Toto. If not, my mistake and I'll keep looking."

There was a pause. "Fine. Under the circumstances I'll give you his name and address. But I'll contact him first —"

"Please don't. If he's trying to pass her off as his, he'll hide her!"

Hannah dragged herself out of bed the next day and hit the road again as soon as she could. It was Canada Day, and she was still doing late-evening shifts, which meant she'd be hopping. Much to everyone's disappointment, the big concert and fireworks on Parliament Hill had been cancelled again this year, and Public Health officials were warning against overcrowding, but restaurants and bars were open, as well as some street shows. She'd probably be busy breaking up rowdies, untangling traffic jams, and responding to pickpockets.

Google was playing games and refusing to find the address, 5 MacPherson Lane, on the map, but she knew Google sometimes got mixed up on back-country roads and sent people to nonexistent houses in the middle of cornfields.

Google did, however, cough up a MacPherson Road in the general Kemptville area, so at noon, after five hours' sleep, she was cruising south on Highway 416, jacked up on espresso and Red Bull. The traffic was light out of town, but she kept an eagle eye out for her Ontario Provincial Police brothers hiding behind the pillars of the overpasses.

MacPherson Road was a narrow back-country road that sliced through mixed farms and woodlands west of Kemptville. It claimed to be paved, but she had to weave in and out between potholes like a slalom racer. Her motorcycle was new to her — a present to herself for getting recruited — and she still enjoyed the throbbing of the engine beneath her, the rumble of the tires on the road, and the wind in her face. It was a small bike by serious bike standards, but it suited her size, and it was quick and agile. Maybe someday she'd get a Harley for long road trips. It would be worth it to see the horror on her dad's face.

Houses were scattered along the road, and she counted down the house numbers on the blue signs outside each as she passed, but none were remotely close to number 5. At number 211, MacPherson Road ended in a T-junction with another road. Turning around, she slowly retraced her route. The word *lane* implied a very small road, possibly just twin tracks with a grass strip down the centre leading off from the larger road. She scrutinized the bush on either side for a small track, perhaps with a sign hidden in the overgrowth.

Most of the tracks were little more than rutted tractor paths leading to farmhouses or back fields. After about two kilometres, however, she came upon a one-lane dirt road leading into the forest. It had no name, but a handmade wooden arrow with the faded name *MacPherson* painted on it was hammered to a tree at the entrance. She nosed her bike onto the dirt lane and entered the thickly overgrown forest. The lane was in rough shape. Tree limbs lay across it, and ruts and furrows sliced through it.

"This is a waste of time," she muttered. "This road hasn't been used in forever." At the biggest downed limb, she left her bike and proceeded on foot through the absolute silence of the forest. Mosquitoes whined in her ears. She walked about ten minutes, flailing her arms and wondering what the hell she was doing. She was about to give up when she glimpsed open space up ahead. Sun lit the clearing and glittered off the water beyond. The contours of a roofline emerged through the trees, and soon she found herself staring at the sagging ruin of a log cabin. Just beyond it, the soft eddies of a river swirled along the shore.

She peered at the map on her phone. This was the Rideau River, smaller and gentler than the Ottawa, but legendary in its own right. From its meandering, weedy shore, it was hard to imagine that it had once bustled with boats and barges connecting the two mighty rivers to the north and south.

A dilapidated barbeque and two splintering Muskoka chairs sat on the wooden deck, and an old aluminum boat lay face down among the reeds by the shore. The door was secured with a rusty padlock that held firm at her tug. She circled the cottage and peered through the windows. Inside was a simple sofa, a bed, a couple of lamps, and a small kitchenette, about as basic as you could get. The smell of must and rotting wood was strong.

Nobody has lived here in a dog's age, she thought. *For sure not a fussy young man and his stolen Havanese.*

Disgusted, she walked back up the lane, climbed on her bike, and headed back up to the main road. As she drew near, she saw her exit was blocked by a mud-splattered Dodge Ram. Leaning against the truck with his arms folded, watching her approach, was a man with broad shoulders, a beer gut, and a face like thunder. She took quick stock. Should she accelerate around the truck and escape? Or should she assume he was harmless, despite the scowl? Maybe he could even help.

"What are you doing on my property?" he asked in a brusque, roughened voice when she turned off her engine.

She pasted a smile on her face and nodded over her shoulder. "That your place back there?"

"Well, it's not yours."

"I'm trying to find MacPherson Lane."

"No such place. Not 'round here, anyway."

She frowned and fished the paper out of her pocket. "Drew Austin. This is the address he gave me."

The man shoved himself away from the truck and came forward. She tensed, ready to fight, but the expression on his face was more curious than hostile, and he held out his hand for the paper. Dirt crusted his hands and fingernails. He stood so close she could smell him. Hay, manure, and sour sweat.

As he studied the paper, his brow wrinkled. "He's pulling your leg."

"Do you know him?"

"Never heard of him. But there's no such address."

She sighed. The sun baked her back, and sweat trickled down her forehead below her helmet. *An entire half day wasted!* She tried another approach. "Do you know a young man who lives around here, skinny, kind of short, midtwenties with a shaved head and a scrawny beard? He gave this as his address."

For an instant, a shadow passed across his face, quickly erased. He grunted and looked up and down the road as if expecting the dude to pop out from the bushes. "Not too many folks around here, mostly farms and bush and that. I know pretty near everybody that lives around here, and he's not one of them. So whatever bull he told you, he's lying."

She gritted her teeth. The more she investigated, the more she was certain she was on to something. *One last try, Pollack.* She reached into her bag for the photo of Toto. "He stole my dog. Have you seen this little dog anywhere around here? She's about a foot tall and ten pounds."

He had blue eyes set deep in his tanned face, and now they narrowed in sympathy. "A dog like that, it wouldn't last a night out here with the coyotes. I don't even leave my barn cats out at night."

She felt a small niggle of hysteria building. Exhaustion, frustration, and fear. Poor little Toto. To come all this way, to have survived near death, only to be a coyote's dinner. "I have to find her. She's been hurt, and this Austin dude told the vet he lived around here. I don't know where else to look!"

The man was gazing down the lane, a frown slowly gathering on his face. "Scrawny beard, you say?"

She sucked in her breath. "Yes. Why?"

"There was a fella last summer. He rented that old camp for a month. I told him it was a dump, but he didn't care. He said he was a student, writing a thesis or something, and he needed a quiet place on the cheap. And I mean real cheap. I wouldn't put my mother-in-law in that place. But he stayed the whole month. I hardly saw him."

"What was his name? Drew Austin?"

"No. It was one of them hippie names. Sedge. Yeah. Sedge something."

"Do you have an address? The lease maybe?"

The man laughed. "Lease? It was cash, no paperwork, and I didn't ask questions. Only a fool would stay there."

"Do you remember anything about him? Where he was from? What school he was at?"

"Some university. All I remember is he was studying a weird duck of some kind. Don't know what kind of job you can get with that."

"Did he leave anything behind in the cabin? Something that might help me trace him?"

MacPherson shook his head slowly back and forth. "He left piles and piles of papers, whatever he was writing, but I burned it all this winter. It was handy for the wood stove."

She scribbled her name and cell number on a piece of paper. "Look, if you remember anything else, give me a call. Please. And thank you, Mr. ...?"

"MacPherson. Dan MacPherson." He grinned. "Yeah, like the road. Like I said, I know pretty near everyone around and am probably related to most of them." He waved the paper at her. "I hope you find your dog, Hannah. Sorry I wasn't more help."

"You were, Dan. I've got a name, sort of. Sedge. How many of those can there be, studying weird ducks at a university nearby?"

CHAPTER THIRTEEN

When Green turned the corner onto his street, he spotted a familiar blue motorcycle parked at the curb and Hannah sitting on his front stoop. She smiled when she saw him and submitted to a hug.

"You have a key. Why didn't you go inside?"

"I'm enjoying the sun. Fresh air — you should try it sometime."

He laughed. "Who's home?"

"We've got the place to ourselves. Join me for a drink? Iced tea for me."

"Sure. But in the backyard, on a decent chair."

She was curiously silent as they were settling on the patio. "I thought you'd be on duty downtown," he began.

Hannah shook her head. "Tonight. Probably in the Market."

"Oh, boy. That's usually crazy on Canada Day. Hopefully not this year."

She said nothing, just fidgeted and inspected her drink.

"What's up, sweetheart?"

"Don't take my head off. I've gone out on a limb again about the McAuley case."

He sipped his iced tea and waited while she squinted into the trees at the bottom of the garden. A red bird Green had come to recognize as a cardinal was perched on a branch, singing its clear, plaintive call, but Hannah seemed oblivious.

"I've spent my off-hours driving around the countryside looking for the missing dog. I think I found her."

He kept a poker face as she described her visits to vets and the lead that eventually led her to a rundown cottage on the Rideau River. As the number of procedural irregularities mounted and she ventured farther and farther out onto that limb, he wondered how he could keep her out of serious trouble. But secretly, he was proud of her. She had an investigator's instincts and the fearlessness needed to brush aside the rules. At the end of her story, she glanced up at him nervously.

"Am I in deep shit?"

He put on a stern face. "You know the answer to that. Why did you do this, Hannah?"

"Because I think the dog is key, and no one is paying attention to it."

"You don't know that. You don't know what Gibbs and his team are doing."

"Okay, but have they found out all this stuff? I know there's still a lot of ifs…. This dog may not be Toto, because the breed often looks similar. The man who rented the cottage may not be the same man who brought the dog in to the vet. But there are enough red flags to look into it further. The vet said the dog had one blow to the head, and the owner gave a false name and an address that technically doesn't exist." She must have seen the doubt on his face, because she glared at him. "I found Sedge! That's a weird enough name that we can track him down through the universities. He studies ducks. How many guys like that can there be?"

He nodded slowly. "Okay. The next step is to tell Gibbs. He needs to fit this new information into his inquiry."

"Fine, but before I do that ... like I said, there are still questions. I'd like to find this Sedge dude and confirm the dog is Toto." He was shaking his head. "Dad, please help me do this! If I'm going to mess up my career and get more black marks, I want to make sure it's worth it!"

"Hannah, you're a fourth-class constable. You can't use your position to make inquiries at the universities."

"But *you* can." She leaned forward. "Dad, it's a simple inquiry. It's what you've done all your career."

Her intensity and determination reminded him so much of his younger self, before the rules, paperwork, and procedural roadblocks — not to mention time itself — had ground him down. He was debating what to tell her without killing her enthusiasm for the job when in the distance he heard a car door slam and Aviva's excited chatter. "Hannah's here!"

"Leave it with me," he said, draining his beer. "I have to think about it."

He spent the evening as well as part of the night thinking about it, going around and around, trying to think of a way to keep Hannah out of it without lying to his good friends. By six in the morning, he knew there was no way.

The morning began with wild wind and a torrential downpour that brought traffic on the Queensway to a halt. Despite the rain and the early hour, Brian Sullivan was already waiting for him when he arrived at the Elgin Street Diner. The diner was as busy as restrictions allowed, and he sat at a corner table, freshly shaved and shiny-eyed, looking ready for the day.

"That courthouse gig is making you soft," he exclaimed as Green slumped in, rain dripping from his umbrella. "I've got a briefing with Bob Gibbs in an hour."

Feeling seedy by comparison, Green shook out his raincoat and sagged into a chair. The waitress materialized immediately with a full pot of coffee and took their orders for the standard breakfast special.

"Good timing then," Green said. "I'll cut to the chase. I need you to keep this under your hat. I'm trying to rein her in, because I'm afraid she's not going to last a year at OPS. I wouldn't have, even back in our early loosey-goosey days, if it hadn't been for Adam Jules pulling me off the streets and into detective work. That would never happen today."

"What gibberish are we talking about? Hannah?"

Green nodded and sipped his coffee, scalding his tongue. "What she did is not illegal. Misleading, yes, and she did obtain information under false pretences, but who of us hasn't? She did it on her own time, she dressed in civvies, and she never identified herself as a police officer, but she did give her real name and her real cellphone number."

Sullivan's eyes narrowed. "What did she do?"

"She tried to track down the McAuleys' missing dog."

"How?"

"A peripheral investigation." He sketched Hannah's theory and her trips into the country. "She thinks no one is looking for the dog."

Their breakfast platters arrived, and the aroma of sausage, spicy home fries, and fried eggs wafted over them. Sullivan took a minute to dig into his. "We have looked all over for that damn dog. And before us, Kristina McAuley did."

"Yes, but not out in Kemptville. And that's where Hannah thinks she found it, and a lead on the person who took it. That's the reason I'm telling you. Because if the dog is Toto, and if this person has her, then it's no longer a peripheral investigation. It's absolutely smack in the middle of it."

Sullivan had been shovelling his egg into his mouth. Now he stopped in mid-chew and slowly set his fork down. "Who's the person?"

"We have a first name — Sedge — and a physical description: midtwenties, slim build, shaved head, and beard. Plus we have a couple of pieces of background.

He's a university student studying ducks of some sort."

"Ducks." Sullivan's brow wrinkled in puzzlement. "How the hell would a kid studying ducks get in the middle of this?"

"The cottage where he was researching was on the Rideau River, Hannah said. Marshy and reedy, perfect for ducks." He paused. "As is Shirley's Bay."

Sullivan's brow cleared. "Okay. So we've got a guy studying ducks at some university whose name is Sedge."

Green nodded. "I think this needs to be part of the official investigation." He pushed a sausage around on his plate and tried to sound casual. "Has the name Sedge come up in your inquiries at all?"

Sullivan shook his head. "But we'll get on it ASAP, starting with Edward McAuley's computer and phone. Gibbs has an officer combing through emails and messages."

"Anything interesting showing up?"

Sullivan smiled. "You want an update on the case, do you?"

"I gave you Sedge."

Sullivan grunted. Green could see him wavering. The off-the-record brainstorming felt like old times, and he suspected Sullivan missed those days as much as he did. "So far we don't have much," Sullivan said eventually, signalling for a coffee refill. "We found no information related to travel plans on his computer. No inquiries with travel agents, no online bookings, not even any online searches in his search history. There were searches about credit cards, banks, and loans, stuff suggesting he was looking for a way out of debt. Searches about boats on Kijiji and Autotrader sites. Even real estate searches."

"You think he was planning to move out?"

"More likely trying to downsize to something more affordable. But he never contacted a real estate agent and never asked for an appraisal of his house. His wife says he never discussed it with her."

"But if he was planning to leave her, he wouldn't."

"He also visited porn sites. Lots of them."

Green's ears perked up. "Kinky stuff?"

"Some. But if we arrested every guy who likes to watch a bit of rough stuff, we'd overflow the jails. I'd say more likely he was looking for some harmless outlet for his frustrations about his debts, his wife who had other priorities than him, and maybe even his high-stakes job."

"Any evidence he looked elsewhere for his outlet besides porn? Maybe had secret hookups in the woods near home?"

"So far no evidence of that. No unusual messages or phone calls. He doesn't appear to have a secret life. No time for it."

"What does his wife say? Does he like it rough with her?"

Sullivan gave him a baleful look. "Gibbs hasn't gotten that personal with the grieving widow just yet, Mike."

"Of course not." Green couldn't picture Gibbs ever getting up the nerve to broach the subject. "Anything else useful you want to share?"

"Yeah." Sullivan gave a sly smile as he mopped up the last of his egg with a slice of toast. "We found the murder weapon."

Green nearly dropped his coffee cup. "What? Where?"

"Ted's garden spade. We found it in the shed in his backyard, in plain sight."

"It's been confirmed?"

"Pretty much. MacPhail says the wounds to his head are consistent with its shape — both the flat side of the blade and the sharp edge that made the gash." He paused, his eyes twinkling. "The blade was scrubbed clean, but good old luminol showed minute traces of blood in the crack where the blade attaches to the handle. The killer did their best, but we should be able to get DNA."

"That's great news. Any prints on it?"

"It's a high-quality one with a wooden shaft, so nothing recoverable there. Some smudges on the grip, but only one usable print near the edge. Ident had trouble getting good prints on McAuley from his house, but they've got a probable match on that print to him. Not surprising, since his records show he bought that shovel himself two years ago at Lee Valley Tools."

"And you found it just sitting in his shed?"

Sullivan grinned. "Yup. Hanging on the wall right between a rake and a hoe, where you'd expect it to be."

"Jeez, that means the killer took the risk of coming to the house — into the backyard, no less — and returning it."

"So it seems."

"That's crazy! Why would they do that?"

"Presumably they didn't expect us to ID it as the murder weapon, and they didn't want anyone to notice a spade was missing."

"Would Kristina McAuley have noticed? Did she see it was missing?"

"She claims she never touches those tools and rarely goes into that shed. She couldn't even ID the tarp the body was wrapped in."

"Did anyone — neighbours, family — see anyone going in or out of the shed? Either taking the shovel out or returning it?"

"Both Kristina's brother and father have been in and out of the backyard all month, building a patio. They had lots of chances to go into the shed." He pursed his lips in thought. "But the next-door neighbour did spot someone walking along the riverbank later that evening in the direction of the McAuley house."

"Someone?"

"A man. He actually thought it was McAuley himself. But it was dark."

Green sat back, his thoughts racing. "Why the hell would McAuley be sneaking back to his own house?"

"I don't know, Mike. It's just one of the mysteries of this case, along with what Ted McAuley was doing in the woods in the first place. But listen, I've got to go. Thanks for the Sedge tip. We'll take it from here." He gestured to his empty plate. "This is on you, right?"

***

When Sullivan walked in the front door of police head-quarters, he was greeted by a querulous voice raised in frustration. A woman was braced against the security screen, shaking her walker.

"I don't want an underling. I want to speak to the head of the detectives."

When the officer on the front desk spotted Sullivan, he opened his mouth, and Sullivan silenced him with a quick shake of his head.

"Tell him Joan McAuley is here, and I have information about my son's murderer."

Sullivan had been about to slip into the elevator, but he snapped around. "Mrs. McAuley?"

She manoeuvred her walker to face him. Her body shook and her face was red with fury, but it was her eyes that struck him. Above her mask, they were deep blue pools of grief.

"I'm sorry for your loss. I'm Staff Sergeant Brian Sullivan."

"Are you the boss?"

He nodded gently. "I guess I am. Let's go —"

"Don't put me off. I'm the mother, but no one listens to me. I know who killed Ted, and I want that on record."

"Absolutely." He laid his hand on her forearm to steer her out of the cavernous, open front lobby. "Let's find some place more comfortable."

Not budging, she peered at him. "Have you found out who killed him?"

"The investigation is in its early —"

She batted his hand away. "I thought not. So let me save you some time."

It took some coaxing, but he eventually settled her in an interview room with a cup of coffee and signalled to Gibbs to join them.

"I told that Missing Persons detective from the very beginning, you must look at Kristina and her family. They want to be rid of him."

"I assure you we're considering all possibilities. Do you have some specific information that would help our investigation?"

"I do. A few days before he died, Ted told me he'd discovered Kristina had opened a secret bank account in her maiden name. For five months she had been stealing the money Ted gave her to run the household and putting it into this account. Ted told me when he discovered the account, he took the money out and shut it down. A week later, he's dead." She sat back, her voice quivering. "She was stealing from him. Planning to leave him."

Gibbs was sitting quietly, but Sullivan knew his mind was racing. They were in the early stages of looking into his financial records, and this was news to both of them.

"We'll be examining the family finances," Gibbs said, "so this is very helpful. But it's a big leap from leaving him to killing him."

"Because he ruined her little plan! So she had to come up with another. Mind you, I don't credit her planning all this by herself. Pathetic creature hasn't the nerve. It's that family of hers. They're all thick as thieves, and it's the parents with the cunning and the backbone. They've been up to no good for years, borrowing money from my husband and then from Ted, always needing more and more. For what? That's what you should be looking into!"

"What details can you give us about this bank account? Amount? Name of bank?"

"I don't know specifics. Ted has always tried to shield me. But I can tell you he was very, very angry. He felt betrayed, and when someone wrongs my son, well ..." She broke off, tears of outrage rising in her eyes.

Sullivan couldn't resist it. He leaned in, trying to sound gentle. "What happens when someone wrongs your son?"

But she had pulled herself back from the brink. Gathering her purse, she began to struggle to her feet. "I've given you the facts. The rest is up to you."

CHAPTER FOURTEEN

Hannah eyed the call display on her cellphone with a sinking feeling. This was the third time Kristina had called in less than twenty-four hours. It was seven in the morning, and she had woken with the intention of going to the beach before starting a string of nights. But the damn phone number was calling to her.

Kristina must be desperate to call at the inconsiderate hour of seven in the morning. The poor woman was grieving, broke, and essentially without friends because of the incessant needs of her son. Finally, Hannah pressed the button to answer the call.

"Oh, thank God!" Kristina sounded near the end of her rope, where she often was, Hannah realized.

She steeled herself. "Kristina, I'm not part of the investigating team. You have to discuss things with them, or with Victim Services. Have they been in touch?"

"Yes, they're very kind, but they can't do anything!"

"Neither can I."

"But I don't have anybody. Nobody's on my side."

"What about your family? Your parents, your brother?"

There was a pause. A groan. "I can't talk to them about any of this. They don't understand. They think my life was a perfect dream and I should have been happy."

"But now that your husband is dead, I'm sure they'll want to help you. At least your mother. I know she tries to help out."

"No, I don't dare —" She broke off.

In spite of herself, Hannah felt herself being drawn into the woman's drama. "Don't dare what?"

"I didn't mean that. I mean my mother comes from a different place. A different culture, where wives … She always talks of the hardships she and my father endured. That people in Latin America endure every day." She seemed to flounder. "Thanks to their efforts, I am in Canada. I should be grateful for their sacrifices. I don't want them to feel that's not enough. They already worry enough about the rest of our family still stuck down there. That's real suffering."

Hannah thought about her grandfather who had endured unspeakable tragedy in the Holocaust. Her father had spent his whole life trying to make up for that, trying to bring him joy and shield him from all the bumps along the way.

"I get that. I really do. Why don't you talk to your neighbour, Phil Walker? He seemed concerned about you."

"God, no!" Kristina nearly spat out the words. "He disliked Ted from the beginning, and I know he'd say I'm lucky to be out of it."

"I doubt that. He lost his spouse, too."

"No, no. He knows too much. He tattled to the police and made things worse, when it was none of his business."

A curious thing to say, Hannah thought, *but I'm not getting involved*. "All right, what about another neighbour? Or a friend?"

"I've had no time for friends. Running this house the way Ted liked it, taking care of my son …" Her voice broke. "I'm scared. I'm alone, and I don't know what the police are doing."

"Then talk to Sergeant Gibbs."

"They found the shovel! They came with a search warrant, and they went through my whole house like I was the enemy. I had to keep Peter quiet in the kitchen. They searched the shed and found a shovel. They demanded to know if I could identify it as Ted's. I told them I never go near the shed. But Ted hardly ever did any gardening, and the shed isn't locked, so anyone could have put it there. They asked if I'd seen anyone near the shed in the days after his disappearance. I said no, but I don't spend my days looking out the window. They don't understand Peter is a 24-7 job! They didn't look impressed, and that Sergeant Gibbs wasn't impressed that I didn't recognize the tarp either. I know they think I did it."

Hannah tried to find words to stem the panic. "They're just doing their job, Kristina. Trust me, the search of your house is standard procedure. They're looking into his life for clues. And they'll be exploring leads at his work, too."

"Then why don't they tell me? I feel like the walls are closing in, Hannah!"

"Did the police ask if you know anyone called Sedge?"

"What? Sedge? Who's that?"

Fuck, Hannah thought, backpedalling. "Just one of those leads. I don't know anything more."

"But … is he a colleague? A client of Ted's?"

"I don't know."

"How did they find out about him? Do they think he killed Ted?"

"I'm not at liberty to say. But can I ask you … your dog, Toto, are there any leads on her?"

"Toto?" Kristina seemed confused by the abrupt change of topic. "No. Peter is beside himself. I bought him a stuffed Havanese online, but it's not the same."

"Does she ever slip out of her collar? My dog does sometimes, when she's being stubborn."

"Yes, sometimes. I make it as tight as I can, but sometimes when she's really frightened, she backs up and wiggles free. Why?" Kristina's voice rose. "You think she broke free and is running loose?"

Hannah said nothing but felt a rush of excitement as the pieces of her theory began to take shape.

"Why are you asking about Toto? Do you know something? Does it have anything to do with this guy Sedge? Did he hurt Toto?" The questions spilled out of her in a panicked rush.

"There's nothing to suggest that." Hannah paused, debating what to reveal. "If anything, he may be trying to take care of her."

"How?" Kristina screeched. "Where is she? Where is this man?"

Fuck, Hannah thought again. *Now I really have gone a step too far.* Before she got sucked in any deeper, she muttered, "Listen, I gotta go," and hung up.

Her hands were shaking as she poured herself a cup of coffee, her thoughts in turmoil. She'd vowed she'd stay clear of Kristina. And yet here she was, sucked in again. The dog, Sedge, the step too far. What had she done, and how could she put it right again?

Finally, setting her half-finished coffee on the counter, she grabbed her keys, wallet, and helmet, and headed out of the apartment. If she were lucky, she'd catch her dad before he went to work.

Her parents' house was only a short bike ride away, and she slalomed expertly through leafy residential streets filled with dog walkers, commuter cyclists, and children going to day camp. With a mixture of relief and trepidation, she spotted her father's Subaru in the driveway as she rounded the final corner. He emerged from the house just as she was pulling off her helmet.

"Hey you," he said with surprise as he approached to give her a hug.

She backed away. Now or never, before she had time to second-guess herself. "Dad, I might have screwed up," she blurted, realizing she had no idea what she was going to say.

He took her arm. "Want to come inside?"

She shook her head but allowed him to steer her to the front stoop. Once seated, she hugged her knees to her chest.

BARBARA FRADKIN

"What happened?" he asked quietly, his jaw set in a grim line.

"I may have revealed confidential information about the case. The McAuley case."

"To whom?"

"Kristina McAuley."

His jaw grew tighter. "What did you tell her?"

"I mentioned the name Sedge. I asked her —"

"You what?"

"I thought the Major Crimes guys would already have asked her about him. I knew you'd told them about him, and it made sense they'd ask her if she knew him."

"No, they did not! They didn't want to tip her off. The less she knows, the better."

She began to tremble. "I'm sorry. I thought —"

"It wasn't your job to think anything! I told you to stay out of it. To stay away from Kristina McAuley."

"She called me. Three times."

"You don't have to answer! You don't have to talk to her."

"I know. But I'm involved, Dad. She trusts me."

"She's using you!"

Hannah recoiled. "That's a terrible thing to say."

"But it's true. When you've been a cop long enough, you learn you get used all the time. You're nobody's friend. People need things, and they're out to protect themselves first and foremost."

"But she has no one. And I don't think she's the killer."

"We don't know if she's the killer. That's the point! And she could be using you for all sorts of other reasons, maybe not even consciously. She's using you for sympathy, for support, and to get information out of you."

She had no answer for that. He could be right. While she was absorbing the feeling of humiliation, he said nothing, but she could almost see the steam coming from his ears.

"For what it's worth," she ventured, "the name Sedge seemed to come as a complete surprise to her."

He grunted. "So she says."

"She wanted to know if he'd killed her husband, so I told her no, I thought he was taking care of her dog."

Green froze. "Wait a minute. You told her this man Sedge has the dog?"

"She's so worried about it, I thought it would help."

"Jesus fucking Christ, Hannah! This is a murder inquiry. We don't know how all these people are connected." He shot to his feet. "I've got to alert Sullivan."

"But I don't think Sedge —"

"You don't know anything! And you're a fucking liability! From now on, stay out of it. And don't take another call from anyone about the case — ever!"

Green barrelled into the Major Crimes squad room twenty minutes later, having broken every speed limit along the way. He glanced quickly at Fanel's door, relieved to see the inspector wasn't in yet.

"Staff Sergeant Sullivan in?" he snapped at a detective who looked barely out of high school.

"Incident room." The kid pointed down the hall. "They're about to start a briefing."

Green swept through the doors into the incident room, stopping short just inside as the memories hit him. The clutter, the piles of paper, the smart board, and the banks of computers. All around the room were photos of the crime scene, lists of itemized evidence, and copies of witness statements. He knew the chaos was deceptive: there were officers assigned to manage every aspect of the investigation, from computerized records management to evidence tracking, guaranteeing that nothing would fall through the cracks and torpedo the case in court.

The room would soon be filled with officers giving updates and receiving assignments, but right now it was still fairly empty. One officer was already at the computer, inputting information into the Major Case Management system. Another was bent over a pile of witness statements, making notes. Gibbs was at the front of the room by the smart board, conferring with Sullivan. Both men turned in surprise as Green approached.

"Brian, I'm glad I caught you before the briefing. Can I have a word?"

Sullivan frowned at him. The other officers in the room looked up, their curiosity aroused by this unorthodox intrusion. "I've only got a minute," Sullivan said. "Is it about the McAuley case?"

When Green nodded, he gestured to the door. "Let's go in my office. Bob, you too."

Once inside, Sullivan shut the door firmly behind them and turned to Green. His eyebrows arched.

Green held nothing back as he briefed them on Hannah's latest transgressions. "I make no excuses for her. She's shown appalling judgment and, believe me, I came down on her hard. But she's a kid. She doesn't have our years of experience. I hope she's got the message to stay out of it now. Up until now, what she's done has been peripheral to the investigation and, in fact, helpful. But this time — revealing the existence of Sedge to the victim's wife and even telling her the man has her dog —"

Even Sullivan's deadpan control slipped. He clutched his head. "Fuck, Mike, that's a very dangerous leak!"

"I know. She has no excuse. She felt sorry for the victim and wanted to help."

"This so-called victim is far from in the clear in his death. Just so you know how bad this is, a neighbour across the street who was up with a newborn saw Kristina McAuley come out of her house at one a.m. on the night her husband disappeared. She got into her car and drove off in one hell of a hurry. When we questioned her on that, she said she went to find her dog at the Humane Society, where her husband had texted her he was taking it. No one can vouch for that. The daughter says she was asleep and didn't hear her mother go out or come back."

"So assuming he was killed that very night when he went off with the dog ..." Green began.

Sullivan nodded. "She's very much in the frame for it. And we have another neighbour who heard her screaming only hours earlier that she'd kill him."

"As well, sir …" Gibbs spoke for the first time, deferential as always. "We've just come into some information that may have a bearing on her motive."

Green looked from one to the other, sensing a subtle closing of the ranks. "What?"

"It still needs to be verified," Sullivan said. "Suffice to say, she's not looking good."

Green fought back his impatience and thought about other cases in which a wife murdered her husband. Statistics varied depending on definitions, but in the majority of cases, there was a history of abuse. "So the motive would be to escape the abuse?"

"Which she continues to deny," Sullivan said. "Strongly. As does everyone else. But just to add some spice, Ted McAuley also had a million-dollar life insurance policy of which she's the beneficiary. That, along with the sale of the house and other assets, could make for a nice chunk of change for her."

Green played with that scenario. "The house is heavily mortgaged, right? It still seems a stretch to ditch a husband with high earning power when you've got a child with expensive medical needs, just to get your hands on a million dollars and change. Unless there was abuse."

"The killing may have been in a moment of intense rage, which we know she experienced."

"But bringing a shovel and a tarp suggests planning."

"I know," said Sullivan, stretching his legs and heading toward the door. "That's why we're still looking. Collecting pieces."

"Who else are you looking at?"

"Mike …"

Green held up his hands. "Fine. I'm just thinking — the obvious suspects. Her father, her brother, maybe even her mother."

"Possibly. I'm not sure a middle-aged woman could deliver the fatal blow, let alone dig the hole. I know she does some hands-on labour at the construction office, moving boxes and stuff."

Green nodded. "And she does housework for Kristina. I wouldn't underestimate a woman like that."

"But what would be the motive for any of them?" Gibbs interjected. "The same applies to them as to Kristina. Why kill the cash cow?"

"The most obvious answer is the same: abuse. Have you looked into it?"

Sullivan and Gibbs exchanged looks, and Sullivan sighed. "Same old Mike, even when you're not in charge. When you're supposed to be up the street at the court-house, bossing other people around."

Giving a sheepish grin, Green waited.

"Of course we're looking into it," Sullivan snapped, "and of course they're all in the frame. You know the family. The father is tough and strong from all those years in construction, and he's suspicious as hell of us. He'd do anything to protect his family."

"Living under a terror regime does that to you."

"Oh, for fuck's sake, I know that. The brother's the same, and they could even be in it all together. But our problem is we don't have an exact time of death. So it's hard to track people's movements. Even if we assume the person who drove the Mercedes to the airport the next day was not Edward McAuley, they need to account for their whereabouts for a period of more than twelve hours. And none of them is being very co-operative with police."

"I can help with that. We have a history."

"No, you can't. You know damn well you can't."

Green stared down Sullivan for a few seconds, hoping for a sign of co-operation, but Sullivan's blue eyes were cold and unflinching. "Okay. I get it. What about other enemies? Colleagues or adversaries?"

Sullivan's eyes softened. "We've not turned up anything credible. Especially for a rage killing in the middle of the night."

"If that's what it was."

Sullivan laid a hand on the door handle. "Mike, leave it to us. We've got a briefing to get to."

Green shrugged in mock capitulation. He knew he'd pried far more out of them than he deserved. "Fine. But the offer of help stands if you need it, even if it's behind the scenes. I don't want to muscle in on your investigation, guys. I'm just offering an extra pair of ears. It's a complicated case. One of the most complicated I've seen in years. And Hannah is all tied up in knots over it."

CHAPTER FIFTEEN

Hannah barely noticed the passing streets as she rode back to her apartment. Her whole body was shaking. She'd never seen her father so angry, not even when she'd done some seriously crazy stuff as a teenager. She'd never known him to swear at her. They both had a temper, and arguments did blow up over silly things, but never like this.

She had seriously messed up. As soon as she'd mentioned Sedge to Kristina, she knew she'd gone too far, but it was too late to take it back. It was a dumb mistake she shouldn't have made. It showed she was way too involved in this case. Her nerves were raw and her sleep still wrecked by the images she couldn't get out of her mind. The case had hold of her and wouldn't let her go. It had shot her judgment to hell. She would just have to wait and see what came down on her head when her dad told Brian. Brian didn't scare her. He was a big, cuddly teddy bear who'd always seen past the black makeup and the studs and chains of the nihilistic kid she'd tried to be.

Deep down, she was also smarting from her father's accusation that Kristina was using her. She was no pushover. She'd knocked about on the streets enough to have pretty good radar for con artists. Kristina was frightened, defensive, and lonely, but she didn't seem deceptive, and the idea that she was capable of smashing a shovel over her husband's head didn't fit.

When Hannah got home, she was too restless to sit still and too wound up to eat. She had to do something to salvage the day. Before Kristina's phone call, she had planned to go to the beach in Gatineau Park and lie around listening to music, but that was out of the question. She needed to move. Maybe a jog instead. Jogging always allowed her to lose herself and set all her worries aside.

At eight o'clock, it was still misty and humid from yesterday's rain. She ran through her favourite routes in her mind, rejecting them all before the perfect idea came to her. The gravel path through Shirley's Bay was an ideal jogging trail: flat, peaceful, and far from the traffic and noise of the city. Maybe out there, revisiting the scene of the crime, she would find some closure.

She put on her jogging outfit and set out along Carling Avenue past the public beach, the waterfront park, the sailing club, and the exclusive enclave where the McAuleys lived. Out into the scrubby fields and forest of the greenbelt, still glistening from yesterday's rain. She was already feeling calmer by the time she turned in to the muddy parking lot. It was barely eight thirty, and there were only three other cars in the lot. After gearing up and doing her stretches, she hit the trail, deliberately hugging the eastern path that led past the crime scene. The yellow tape and barriers were gone, all trace of the tragedy erased. She fought a surge of anxiety by focusing on her breathing, and peace gradually stole over her.

She passed a man using a long lens to photograph something in a distant tree, and farther on she overtook a woman walking her small terrier. The little dog yapped in surprise. She ran on, thinking about the woman and her dog. Dog walkers had their routines. They often walked at the same time every morning and followed a similar route. They might even meet the same people and notice the same things.

Her thoughts drifted to Lillian Chang. Lillian had given Rick her statement about what she'd seen and heard that morning when she discovered the body, and Hannah assumed the Major Crimes detectives had followed up with their own interviews. She also figured they'd probably asked her if she walked the trail often and if she'd noticed anything unusual or anyone acting strangely on the day Ted was presumed murdered. They might have asked if she'd seen a little black-and-white dog running loose. But would they have returned to ask her if she'd seen a skinny young man with a scraggly beard? He studied birds, so maybe he came here. If her theory was correct, this was where he'd found Toto.

Her father would kill her if he knew she was even thinking about the case, and yet someone should follow up with Lillian. She was still dancing around the idea when she spotted a familiar black dog up ahead, bounding in and out of the bush, and standing next to him, focusing her binoculars in the trees, was the woman herself. Gold!

"Mrs. Chang!"

Lillian lowered her binoculars, surprised and puzzled. The dog rushed up to check her out.

"Constable Pollack," Hannah said. "From … well …"

"Oh yes, how are you?"

"I've been thinking about you," Hannah said, stopping at her side. "Wondering how you were doing. That was quite a shock."

"It was. It's taking me quite a bit to get over it. This used to be my favourite trail, and I was afraid I wouldn't be able to face it again."

"I understand. I'm glad you're able to."

"I forced myself. It's still disquieting, and I only walk on this part of the trail. I don't go over to the …" She trailed off and waved her hand toward the crime scene.

"It's a beautiful spot," Hannah said, "especially if you love birds. Did you come here regularly?"

"Most mornings, since I retired. I love the early mornings the best. That's when the birds are out and there are fewer people, so Titan gets to run free." She put her hand to her mouth. "Oh dear, I guess I shouldn't tell you that."

Hannah smiled. "Don't worry, it's not my jurisdiction. I guess there are a lot of birdwatchers out here in the mornings."

"A few, but serious birders come out even earlier than me. Dawn is the prime time, so at the height of the summer solstice, they can be prowling around before five in the morning!"

Hannah went out on a limb. "I wonder if you've seen a friend of mine. I've lost touch with him, and I'm a bit worried. Skinny dude about my age with a shaved head and a beard."

Lillian was peering at her doubtfully. "Possibly."

"He studies birds at the university, so I'm wondering if he spends time here."

"More likely at the Crown preserve, which is just west of here. It has limited access, but a serious student could get access through the Ottawa Duck Club. Although actually …" She paused. "There is one young man I've run into a few times. Usually he's out much earlier than me, and he spends most of his time down on the shoreline part of the trail. Your friend, you say?"

She sounded skeptical, and Hannah flushed. "Well, not exactly my friend, more like a family connection, but we've been worried about him. So I'm keeping an eye open for him. Did this man mention his name?"

"No. I used to see him more often, but come to think of it, I haven't seen him in a few weeks. He's a serious birder. Binoculars, fancy camera, guidebook, notebook, even a recorder. He'd record his observations and also bird calls." She pulled a face. "He'd get upset at me for letting Titan off the leash, said it disturbs the ducks, so I do put him on a leash whenever we're on the shoreline part. The young man had a polite, gentle way about him that didn't scare the birds, but he's odd. He obviously cares a great deal about nature, especially those little ducks he was studying, but not so fond of people."

"What kind of little ducks?"

"Hooded Mergansers. He's been monitoring a breeding pair down near the mouth of the little creek, checking their nest and keeping track of the chicks. I gather it's to find out what the unpredictable flooding and droughts in recent years are doing to their habitat."

Green had barely been back at his own desk for an hour when his cellphone rang. To his surprise, it was Hannah. He had come down hard on her and expected her to be licking her wounds and seething with defiance for a few days. Although he regretted the swear words, his overreaction had been born out of genuine concern for her. The McAuley case had shaken her more than she recognized, blinding her to reason and good judgment, and her reckless behaviour was putting not only the case and her career in jeopardy, but also possibly her safety. He knew what was driving her; he'd been there himself.

Was this call a sign that she'd come to her senses?

With a deep breath, he answered. The excitement in her voice dispelled any hope of contrition.

"Dad, I know I messed up, but I've got something! Just listen and don't kill me. It's too important to keep to myself."

He listened as she described running into Lillian Chang on the Shirley's Bay trail — literally and totally by accident, she assured him — and in the course of asking her how she was doing, they'd talked about a young bird-watcher who frequented the park in the early hours of the morning because he was studying a species of little duck. Lillian's description matched Sedge.

"Did you mention his name?" Green said sharply.

"No, Dad. I learned that lesson. I didn't even mention the case. I just tried to find out as much as I could. She said he's a bit weird but gentle and a real animal lover."

Once he'd relaxed, Green felt the stirrings of excitement himself. "I'll pass it on. We really need to talk to him."

"I have a theory, Dad. What if Toto was there when Ted McAuley was killed? And somehow she was injured, because there was blood on her leash and on her head. Ted was hit with a shovel, right? What if the killer hit her, too? Maybe Toto was barking at him or trying to bite him to protect Ted, and the killer wanted to shut her up. But the dog wriggled out of her collar — Kristina says she can do that if she freaks out — and ran away into the woods. When Sedge comes down there in the early morning, he finds the dog injured and scared, and he decides to keep her."

"Why?"

"I don't know, Dad. Maybe he thought she'd been abandoned or abused. Lots of stray dogs end up in shelters, where they get put down. Maybe that's why he kept her."

"Even with all the posters and social media appeals?"

"Like I said, Lillian said he was weird. In his own little world. He decided to save this little dog, so he took her far away where people might not recognize her. I know he cared for her, because the vet said he paid the bill even though he was nearly broke, and he recorded the vet's instructions carefully."

"What makes you think he was broke?"

"You should see the place he rented last summer. It was the cheapest of the cheap."

Green was silent as he mulled over the theory.

"Think about it, Dad! The theory makes sense!"

He had to agree it fit a lot of the pieces together. But it was equally plausible that Sedge himself was the killer and that after luring Ted into the remote woods, he'd taken the dog with him to get her some medical help. The only thing missing was the connection between them.

And the motive.

He told Hannah he would pass the information on to the team and made her promise to stay out of it from now on. "If anything more lands in your lap like this" — he tried to keep the sarcasm out of his voice — "you let me know and steer clear." They ended the call on reasonably cordial terms. The thaw was slight, but it was an improvement.

He caught Brian Sullivan on the phone just as the briefing was breaking up. To his relief, Sullivan was in a buoyant mood. The briefing must have gone well. He listened without interrupting or uttering a single protest while Green summarized Hannah's latest discovery.

"Just so you know, I didn't investigate anything, and neither did she. This piece of information came from a random encounter."

"Uh-huh. She just happened to be jogging way the hell out in Shirley's Bay?"

The same question had occurred to him, but he'd refrained from asking. If Hannah was going to lie, better he didn't know. "It's a nice, flat path and the surroundings are peaceful. Maybe she was trying to clear her head."

A grunt. "Okay. It's a useful piece of information, and Gibbs will get one of his guys on it right away. They talked to a lot of trail users and birders afterward, asking if they'd seen or heard anything. No dice."

"This guy has apparently disappeared. The witness hasn't seen him in a few weeks."

"Which is suspicious in itself."

"Unless he was spooked because he heard something or even witnessed something. He could have been there at the exact time of the murder."

"Or he could be the killer. If he saw something, why wouldn't he come forward?"

Green shrugged. "Afraid of getting involved? Who knows?"

"This isn't some mob or gang hit where witnesses get eliminated. Finding him is top priority."

Green tossed the question out as casually as he could. "Any progress ID'ing him?"

Sullivan chuckled. "Really, Mike? Yes, we got a name and a photo and a last known address from Carleton University, where he's doing his Ph.D. on the ecological impact of climate change on bird populations along the Rideau and Ottawa Rivers. Water birds, that is."

"Hooded Mergansers, to be specific."

"Yeah. Shy little things, so he'd have to be patient. His full name is Drew Sedgwick, and he's twenty-five."

"Have you interviewed him yet?"

"We haven't located him. His last known address was a basement sublet in Bells Corners, but it ran out at the end of June. None of the neighbours have seen him in a few weeks, in fact, since around the time of the murder. But he wasn't the talkative type. He kept to himself. Kind of like his little duck."

"What about at the university? Friends, profs?"

"Jeez, not everybody is a super detective, Mike. We only just ID'ed the guy. But that's what the team will focus on today."

"Good." Green paused. He was dying to ask Sullivan to keep him posted, but knew that would be pushing it. "It's coming together."

"Something is coming. No idea what the fuck it is yet, however."

"Yeah, well … you know where to reach me. If you want a beer or something."

CHAPTER SIXTEEN

Josh Kanner spent the morning getting the runaround. It seemed like no one was working in the whole freaking university! Administrative and secretarial staff was gone, and departments were shut down. Half the biology professors were on holiday and the other half were off doing field research. He had finally been connected to someone in the registrar's office who was able to confirm that Drew Sedgwick was a doctoral student in the ecology and conservation section of the biology department, but phone calls to his adviser netted him a voice mail message that he was away in Georgian Bay. He tried a few other professors with similar results until a human being finally answered, a young woman with a faint Scandinavian lilt to her voice.

"Sorry," she said, "there's almost nobody here. Just me, and I only answered because I'm expecting a call."

"I'd like to speak to Drew Sedgwick. Is he there?"

"Sedge? No. I haven't seen him in a few weeks. He's probably out in the field. That's where most of us are right now. Data collection. It's the height of the fledgling season."

"Do you know where?"

"Not specifically. In Shirley's Bay, I think."

"Do you have a phone number for him? Or an email?"

"No, he is not in my group. I don't know him well."

Josh sighed. "Can you give me the name of someone who does know him? A colleague or friend?"

There was silence. "Is he in trouble?"

"What makes you ask that?"

"Well … you're the police … and he's odd."

Why does everyone keep using that word? "How?"

"He doesn't mix, he doesn't look at your face. He's a bit … OCD?" She said the term like she wasn't sure what it meant. "It makes him a good scientist. He can spend hours in the field, sitting, watching, waiting. His records are very detailed."

Interesting, but none of it got him any closer to finding the dude. "Always alone?"

"Most of the time. But there was one student he did talk to. They shared sightings and observations. He's working out in Shirley's Bay, too. Maybe he can tell you more." She stopped and Josh waited. "Would you like me to find his name?"

"Please."

Five minutes later, Josh thanked her and hung up, armed with a name and cell number. "Yeah, I know him," Gaetan Desmarais said when Josh reached him. "We have the same prof, and our research is all part of the prof's book on climate change and shorebird decline. But I don't know where he is. I haven't seen him since he left Ottawa."

"When was that?"

"Beginning of June? I figured he'd gone to check out some nesting sites on the Rideau River where he was working last summer. He's a loner, does his own thing."

"Can we meet somewhere for coffee? I'd like to get a read on him."

"What's he done?"

"He hasn't done anything. I think he may have information that could help us."

There was silence on the line.

"I just want to talk to him."

"Is this about that murder in Shirley's Bay?"

"I …" Josh backpedalled. "I can't say. Can you spare fifteen minutes?"

"I'm actually out in Shirley's Bay right now in the Crown preserve. I have to grab this time frame, but I can meet you in the parking lot by the river."

It was a warm, muggy summer day, and the parking lot was still awash in puddles from yesterday's rain. Josh cursed. His expensive Nikes were going to take a beating. At the far end of the muddy expanse, a young man was leaning against a fencepost, dressed in a camouflage rain jacket, mud-caked rubber boots, and a wide-brimmed hat. A large backpack was slung over one shoulder and binoculars over another. His eyes were dancing with excitement as Josh squelched through the puddles toward him.

"I've been thinking about it since I talked to you. Something was definitely off with Sedge the last time I talked to him. We were supposed to make recordings on a nest about to hatch, then all of a sudden he bails. Phones me up and says you do that part, I want to check out something else on the Rideau. That's not really weird, because there's a bird sanctuary on the Rideau where he was working last year, but he sounded … I don't know, spooked. Plus he forgot a seminar we were supposed to give, totally didn't show up."

Josh tried to scrape the mud off his shoes against the railing. "Exactly when was this phone call?"

"Beginning of June? The third or fourth?"

"Have you got his phone number?"

Gaetan nodded and fished his phone out of his pants pocket. While Josh copied the number down, Gaetan eyed him sharply. "This is about the murder, isn't it?"

"Did he talk at all about visiting Shirley's Bay? The trail, I mean, not this preserve."

Gaetan chuckled. "He wasn't much for talking about anything if it wasn't ducks. But he did go there often in the spring when the forest was more flooded. There was a little creek he was interested in. We went there a couple of times."

"Did he talk about meeting anyone else? Seeing anything that worried him?"

Gaetan eyed Josh's shoes with a smile but refrained from comment. "Well, not worried, but I think there was a woman — well, more a girl — and I think that's why he kept going there."

Keeping his eyes on his notebook, Josh tried to hide his excitement. "What can you tell me about her?"

He shrugged. "Not much. She used to jog on the trail in the morning before she went to school." He squinted into the woods as he tried to think. "He was embarrassed to talk about her. I teased him, because you had to know Sedge to know how funny it was. Him and a girl. Any girl. But he did say they talked about universities. She was thinking of going to Queen's so she could get away from home, and she asked him about athletic scholarships."

"Did you meet her?"

He shook his head. "I saw her once from a distance, that's all."

"Can you describe her?"

"Like any teenage girl. Dressed in a skimpy jogging outfit. She looked buff. Powerful legs."

"Hair colour?"

"She was wearing a baseball cap."

"Height? Weight?"

Gaetan rolled his eyes. "I'm no good at this. Taller than him. Maybe five-ten? Legs went on forever."

"Did Sedge mention her name?" Gaetan was shaking his head. "Anything else that stands out?"

"Oh, wait. Sedge said she had a dog she used to walk there sometimes. It was one of those little black-and-white mop things that growled at him. The girl said it was afraid of men."

Hannah was startled to see the name pop up on her call display. She'd sworn off the case and for the past couple of days had been keeping her mind on her proper job. But how could she resist this? It might be another clue dropping right in her lap.

"Dr. Leitin," she answered cheerily. "Hello."

"Hello. Did you ever find your little dog?"

"No, I didn't. Why?"

"I think I may have found her, or if not, another Havanese that looks just like her and has a healed wound on her head."

Hannah sucked in her breath. "Where?"

"She's in a foster home near Spencerville. A farmer spotted her hanging around his barn, but the poor little girl kept running away. They started putting food out, and eventually his wife was able to coax her in."

"How is she? Is she hurt?"

"No. The farmer has her. We have a rescue down here that finds homes for abandoned pets, first in foster homes, and if appropriate, adoption. I work with them to provide vet care." She laughed lightly. Hannah had never met her but pictured a country woman with broad shoulders and strong hands.

"I know," Dr. Leitin continued. "I've got my fingers in a lot of pies and end up putting hundreds of kilometres on my truck every week."

"I'm so happy she's found. Thank you for taking care of her." Hannah did a quick calculation. Spencerville was less than an hour's drive, so she could be there and back well before her night shift. "Give me the farmer's name and address, and I'll get down there right away."

"It's not a hundred percent certain it's your dog."

"But I'll know. And if she responds to her name …"

The vet's voice dropped. "The thing is, Hannah, while we were running a check to see if anyone had reported her missing, we came upon the postings for Toto, listed missing in Ottawa over a month ago by a Kristina McAuley. Whose husband was recently found murdered."

Words stuck in Hannah's throat. "Oh."

"So who are you really, Hannah?"

Hannah straightened her shoulders. "I'm Constable Hannah Pollack of the Ottawa Police."

"Then why the deception? Are you undercover?"

"No, no. It's just …" Fuck, she'd really walked into this one. She thought fast. "I'm the patrol officer who was involved in the case at the beginning, but I'm not one of the investigators. The dog has not been a priority in the investigation, but I was worried about it. So I decided to look for it on my own time."

"I see." She didn't sound convinced. "So what do you suggest? That I phone Kristina McAuley and tell her her dog has turned up?"

Bad idea, Hannah thought. "The dog is actually part of the police investigation at this point. I'll have to run it by the senior investigator, but before I do, I'd like to make sure it's her dog. Can you let me know where she is?"

Dr. Leitin took some time answering. "That seems fair enough. But I'll meet you, and I'd like to see some official ID."

"No problem. Thank you." Hannah was already dashing through her apartment, grabbing her jacket and tossing her keys and police badge wallet into an overnight bag that she hoped was big enough to fit the dog.

The cruise down the nearly empty four-lane highway to Spencerville took her less than an hour, and soon she was driving through the quaint little town toward the address she'd been given. While she drove, she second-guessed her decision not to alert her father but promised herself that the minute the dog was positively identified, she would.

Her GPS led her to a typical Eastern Ontario farm nestled in rolling fields of corn and hay. A dozen cows were clustered near a barn, and tall trees sheltered the century-old red-brick home. A few tractors and vehicles were parked in the yard, among them a muddy pickup. As Hannah was slaloming up the lane through the potholes, the truck door opened and a woman hopped down.

Jane Leitin was not at all what she expected. Judging from the spiky white hair and wrinkles, she was at least seventy and barely tipped the scales at a hundred pounds. Her bare arms looked like twigs, easily snapped by a strong wind, and how she wrestled with sick cows and horses, Hannah couldn't imagine.

But her voice was confident and her movements strong as she strode over to greet Hannah. "Call me Jane. Sorry for the suspicion," she said as she looked at the badge wallet. "Havanese are an expensive breed much in demand these days. Let's go inside. Pat is keeping her in the house in case she tries to run away."

The ripe stench of farm animals and manure carried inside and mingled with the smell of herbs and onions. The farmer's wife greeted them and led them toward a sunroom at the back that was cluttered with everything from shovels and snowshoes to old bikes. A little black-and-white dog jumped off a mattress and ran to the corner, her tail between her legs.

"She's pretty skittish, but once she gets more comfortable, we'll give her a proper bath and let her out into the main house with us." Pat crouched in the middle of the room and snapped her fingers toward the dog. "Right now, Lyall can't even get near her."

"I wonder why," Hannah said.

"Many abused dogs are afraid of men," the vet said. "They're big and loud."

"And often they're the abuser," Pat added.

"But she was okay with Sedge, wasn't she?" Hannah asked. "The man who's been taking care of her."

Pat shrugged. "Well, something happened."

Beneath the dirt, the dog certainly looked like the one she'd seen in Kristina McAuley's arms. Remembering how her stepmother had handled their dog when she first arrived, Hannah knelt down on the floor near the door. She didn't reach out or signal the dog in any way. "Toto," she called softly. "Come."

There was no mistaking it. The dog's head shot up, she turned, gave Hannah a puzzled look, and then trotted cautiously toward her.

"Okay," Jane said. "That settles one question."

Hannah ran her hand gently over the dog's ears. "But not another. Where she's been and where Sedge is now."

"She may have just run away," Pat said. "She's easily frightened, and if the man wasn't her real owner, she wouldn't have been very attached to him."

Hannah cradled the little dog as she tried to think what to do. She couldn't ignore her duty any longer. She had to call this in, because the investigative team needed to know. But she knew their first priority would be to find Sedge, and the frightened little dog might get lost in the scramble.

"The police will want to speak to him," she said. "Did anyone around here see him? Or see where Toto was staying?"

"I did ask around when we were trying to find out if she was lost or abandoned," Pat said. "A couple of people had spotted her in the area, mostly down by the river on the other side of the highway. She hasn't been lost too long, because she's still well nourished. In need of a good scrub, but it's not like she's been weeks in the bush."

"What river? The Rideau?"

"The South Nation. Much smaller than the Rideau. It runs right through the village. Toto was seen along the river outside of town."

"But no one spotted her with an owner?"

"Nope. And she arrived at my barn without collar or tags."

"And I've searched for a microchip," Jane added. "None."

The dog had begun to squirm in Hannah's arms, so she set her down. Her mind was racing ahead, plotting next steps. If she notified her father or the team, they would either order her back to town with the dog or more likely descend on the village themselves. But she was already here. It wouldn't hurt to gather as much information as she could while waiting for them to arrive. Even if her father killed her.

"Where exactly on the river was she spotted?"

"Northeast shore, over the highway. Look for the house on the corner." Pat grimaced. "How the poor little thing got across that busy highway, I don't even want to think. There's not much out there but country houses, farm fields, and bush."

"Are there any ducks in the river?"

Both women stared at her like she'd grown an extra head. "Umm …" Pat began. "On the northeast side for sure. It's prone to spring flooding. But she's much too small to catch ducks."

"No, it's not that." Hannah laughed as she scooped up the dog and headed for the door. "Are there forms to be signed?"

"Wait!" Jane said as they went outside. "You're not planning to transport her on your bike, are you?"

"I brought an overnight bag that I can strap down. She'll fit in easily and it can be left partly open."

Both women looked horrified. "No! She might panic and jump out on the highway. I have a small carrier in the truck. It can be strapped on the back and will keep her secure."

Together they helped get Toto leashed and settled in the carrier. Before she pulled on her helmet, Hannah handed her card to both women, who seemed reluctant to let the little dog go. "Be very careful with her," Pat said, wiggling her fingers through the mesh. "She's been through trauma, and she's very scared."

"I know," Hannah said. The dog's eyes did look huge as she peered out. "I will be. And thank you very much for all you did."

She headed back down the lane and turned onto the road that led through the village. Out of sight, she paused to text her father. The text would avoid an actual conversation, but she needed to at least lay some groundwork to appease him.

Dad, found the dog. Please contact me.

Of course, if she was driving, she wouldn't hear his call, but this might buy her some forgiveness. She drove past the mill and over the river, which wandered out of town into overgrown brush, and then took the road over the highway. On the other side, she took a random couple of side roads to stay close to the river, crossed over a bridge, and ultimately arrived on a junction. At the house on the corner, she stopped and took Toto out of her carrier. An elderly man was riding his lawn tractor on his vast, green lawn, oblivious to her approach, but when she walked in front of him, he stopped and turned off his engine. His surprise gave way to a smile.

"Oh, that little fella yours?"

"No," she replied, "but I know whose she is. Was it you that saw her the other day?"

"Yep, down that road over there. I was fishing off the bridge. She ran away into the bush when I spoke to her."

"I'm trying to track down the owner. A skinny dude, midtwenties, beard, shaved head. Have you seen anyone like that around here?"

He scratched his head. "I don't get out much. Into town now and again for supplies, but that's about it."

"He might have been renting a place, like a cabin by the river. He was studying ducks."

He started to shrug but then stopped. "Yeah. Could be him. You can't hardly live in the place. Roof probably leaks, and every spring it gets flooded out. But it used to be a waterfront bunkie for the farm down the road a ways. The farm's empty now. Some developer bought it last year. But I seen a truck there. And yeah, I heard a dog."

"Where's this farm?" Hannah was already scanning the woods at the bottom of his yard. She listened with growing excitement as the man explained the directions. A remote waterfront bunkie that was almost falling down. It sounded like Sedge's kind of place.

CHAPTER SEVENTEEN

Josh Kanner could hardly wait for the briefing in the morning, and he listened on pins and needles as the others gave their reports. He was disappointed that he hadn't actually found Sedge and that all his calls to the phone number Gaetan had given him had gone unanswered. "Customer unavailable." But he did have a pretty big mother of a bombshell to drop despite that.

First came the updates from the Ident Unit. DNA analysis of the blood sample from the shovel was just in, confirming it was Ted McAuley's blood. Next came the Lexus. Multiple fingerprints had been lifted from both the inside and outside, and prints had been taken from all family members for elimination purposes. So far, matches had been made to Kristina McAuley and her son and daughter, as well as her brother. It appeared all three adults had recently driven the vehicle.

No surprise, Josh thought. It was Kristina's car, and Justine had just got her licence. Ted was hardly going to let her drive the two-hundred-thousand-dollar Merc. The brother was a bit of a surprise but not grounds for suspicion. He was working and helping her out around the place.

Next, the Ident officer moved on to the analysis of the transfer evidence recovered from the tires and the interior. All the dirt and debris had been sent for analysis, much of it not yet complete. But no dirt or blood had been found in the car, and the dirt in the tire treads was consistent with the neighbourhood streets. So far there was nothing linking the Lexus to the murder.

But the Mercedes was a different story, the officer said triumphantly. All the identifiable fingerprints were Ted's, although those on the steering wheel and door handle were smudged. The car's exterior was polished, and the interior had been recently detailed, which made the minute traces of dirt all the more noticeable, both on the floor in the back and on the carpet on the driver's side. This debris, the Ident officer finished with a smile, was consistent with samples of soil and forest mulch taken from the crime scene.

"Which means," Sullivan said, "that someone who was at the crime scene drove that car and transported something from the crime scene in the back. I'd be willing to bet a whole keg of beer that it was the shovel. Since Ted was probably already dead, it looks like the killer was driving the Mercedes when it was spotted by Philip Walker that morning, likely returning the shovel to the shed before taking the car to the airport."

"Pretty ballsy," Josh said. He'd been quiet all through the briefing but felt it was now time to be noticed.

"It has tinted windows, but I agree," Sullivan said. "That car is so remarkable that neighbours would re-member it, and the killer could easily have been noticed. We also know that besides returning the shovel, the kill-er might have gone inside to get Ted's overnight bag. Not too many people could have done that."

A small fragment of information niggled at the edge of Josh's memory, but before he could capture it, a woman beside him piped up.

"Kristina's brother was there working that day, and her mother picked up some laundry in the morning."

Josh felt a flash of annoyance at the competition but said nothing. Samina Khan was another minority hire, and female. He'd better watch his step.

"Good point, Sam," Gibbs said. "We need to nail the timelines down." He nodded to the woman. "Any updates on the Ramirezes? Alibis? Suspicious activity?"

The woman leaned forward eagerly. "Luis lives with his parents, and they alibi each other. All three of them were in all night from seven p.m. until about ten a.m., when the mother went out."

Gibbs grimaced. "Anyone else confirm they were home? Neighbours? Friends?"

Samina talked without consulting her notes, as if the entire case was in her head. "Not so far, but one of their neighbours provided useful background. The Ramirezes are quiet and private but well liked in the community. They do minor house repairs for every-one, and they don't charge, and Luis helps the seniors with yardwork and snow removal. Also for free. But their relationship with Ted McAuley is unclear. Both Luis and Ramon told me Ted was a great guy, generous to them and very good to Kristina. You couldn't find a more stand-up guy, they said. But the neighbour I talked to said they were always complaining about Ted. Apparently Ramon's business was his own in name only. In reality, McAuley Enterprises — Ted's father, and later Ted — owned it, and all their business was funnelled through them."

"Did you ask the Ramirezes about that?"

"Yes, Sarge. The father's very proud. He acted insulted when I asked. He said McAuley is their biggest client, but they run an independent company."

"Sounds like it could be a tax dodge for both of them. See what else you can learn about the Ramirez finances, and pay close attention to any links between McAuley and Ramirez finances." Gibbs scrawled some notes on the smart board and stepped back to study the lines of inquiry. "Did the Ramirez neighbours say anything about the abuse angle?"

Samina shook her head. "The neighbours don't see much of Kristina or the kids. She didn't visit her family's home much."

"A falling-out?"

"No, but supposedly Ted disapproved of her family and resented any time she gave them. They visited her house when he wasn't around."

Staff Sergeant Sullivan had been listening quietly, his chair tilted back and his gaze on the ceiling. "Why did he disapprove?" he asked without moving.

"He was very tight with his money, and he thought they were freeloaders. That's what Luis told this neighbour when he was drunk, then denied it when he sobered up."

Gibbs glanced at Sullivan, who nodded and closed his eyes. "This Luis sounds like he might be the loose cannon in the family," Gibbs said. "Who's managing the money? What are the Ramirezes spending it on? Is Luis still connected to drugs? That's an important line of inquiry. Then there's the hints of possible domestic abuse but no record of calls for assistance or contacts with shelters. Kristina doesn't seem to have any close friends she confided in either." He held up a hand when Samina opened her mouth to interject. "I know most of these cases are underground and never get reported, but someone, somewhere, should know something. Dig. That's another major line of inquiry."

As Gibbs studied the notes on the smart board, looking for the next step, Josh chafed like a horse in the starting gate. It was Staff Sergeant Sullivan who noticed. He'd opened his icy blue eyes again. They settled on Josh, and he arched one eyebrow. "Kanner, you got something to add?"

"Yes, Staff. About Sedge. Drew Sedgwick."

Gibbs snapped to attention. "Right! What is it, Josh? Did you find him?"

"No, Sarge, but I talked to two colleagues, and he dropped out of sight almost exactly the same time as the murder. No one at the university has seen him since the beginning of June." He filled them in on his conversation with Gaetan Desmarais. "Gaetan said he sounded … I think he used the word 'spooked.'"

"About what?"

"He didn't know."

Gibbs looked frustrated. "Then keep —"

"But there's more, Sarge." Josh paused, trying to slow down his racing heart. Everyone's eyes were on him, and he loved the feeling of power. "Gaetan said he used to meet a girl jogging on the Shirley's Bay trail in the early mornings."

"Name? Description?"

Josh shook his head. "He didn't get a good look, but she wanted to get away from her family and was planning to apply to university out of town next year. And …" He smiled. Paused. "She sometimes walked a little black-and-white dog."

Like he'd hoped, the room erupted in a buzz of excitement. Finally, a crack in the case! A possible link made between two separate pieces of the puzzle.

"Finding Sedge is now our top priority," Gibbs said. "Next step is to interview the daughter."

"I'd like to do it, Sarge."

Gibbs and Sullivan exchanged looks. Josh could see the doubt in their eyes. That fucking interview with Walker was coming back to haunt him! "I made the discovery, Sarge. And I'm the only one who knows anything about Sedge."

"It's a sensitive interview, Josh," said Gibbs. "She's a minor, so her mother has to be present, which may be a problem given her attitude." He paused. "Besides that, she's the bereaved daughter."

"I *have* met her," Josh said. "She may be seventeen, but she seems tough. And not all that bereaved."

"That doesn't mean she isn't."

"I can do sensitive, Sarge."

A ripple of laughter spread through the room. Josh flushed. "I can."

"You'd have to watch her reaction every step of the way, too. That's a lot to juggle."

"Then send two of us. But let me run with this, Sarge."

Sullivan was still leaning against the wall, his long legs crossed and his face without expression. Josh watched Gibbs glance at him and saw the faint smile twitch the staff sergeant's lips. He felt a rush of hope.

"Fine," said Gibbs. "You can lead. But I'll be at your back, watching every move."

CHAPTER EIGHTEEN

Hannah found the property easily enough. The empty, boarded-up farmhouse sat at the top of the slope, shaded by sprawling trees and overrun with hay and wildflowers. A couple of barns and machine sheds also sat empty, except for an ancient, rusty tractor. Deer flies buzzed in the heat of the July sun. She parked her motorcycle out of sight behind a barn and opened the carrier. Toto cowered inside, wide-eyed.

"It's okay, Toto," she whispered. "Don't be scared. We're going for a walk. Do you want a walk?"

The dog perked up at the word, and Hannah lifted her carefully out and placed her on the ground, keeping a tight hold on her leash. Toto sniffed around excitedly, her tail wagging. Together they circled the house, and Hannah peered in the one open window. The inside was empty and looked like no one had lived there for ages. There were no vehicles anywhere in sight; if Sedge was here, he had not parked his car up here.

As they rounded the last corner, Toto grew impatient and tried to tug her down a track cutting through the field. The track was rutted with thick tire marks carved into the hardened mud. She followed it until it branched off onto a much narrower path that led straight down the slope. Without hesitation, Toto took the narrower path. Hannah had a sudden qualm. The dog knew where she was going, and she was excited. What if Sedge was down there? What if he was dangerous? What did anyone know about him except that he'd ended up in possession of a dog last seen with a man on the night of his murder?

She stopped to take stock. She was in civvies, with no use-of-force options. No Glock, no Taser, not even a baton. She had a small motorcycle tool kit, but it contained nothing useful to subdue a full-grown man. Her martial arts skills would have to do.

For a minute she considered going back to the city to report this to her father and the investigative team. That's what she should do. But Toto was getting even more agitated and pulled her forward almost frantically. For such a little dog, she was really strong.

Up ahead, the path disappeared into the trees. Maybe she could improvise a stick for a weapon. In the woods, the air grew more humid and the mosquitoes swarmed with delight. The dirt path was indented with the traces of many footprints. She peered at them more closely. They looked fresh to her, as if someone had been up and down this path many times recently. Her heart pounded in her throat, and she gripped the leash tightly as she reached for a piece of deadwood at the edge of the path. She tested its strength and snapped off a sturdy three-foot piece that she could use as a weapon.

Toto led the way down the slope, panting. Overhead, birds flitted from tree to tree, and shafts of sunlight shot through the canopy. Soon, the ground grew spongy as the forest gave way to grass and reeds. Up ahead, the South Nation River sparkled as it drifted lazily by.

Toto was whining now, her ears flattened and her nose sifting the air. *Something is spooking her*, Hannah thought. Perched almost at the water's edge was a dilapidated cabin in even worse shape than the one off MacPherson Road. The dock had broken loose from its moorings and lay upended against the riverbank, half buried in yellow and white water lilies.

Crap for swimming, she thought, *but I bet the ducks love it.*

She crept toward the cabin, all her senses on high alert. There was no sign of Sedge. No sound from inside the cabin. *I need to know whether he's staying here*, she thought. Gripping her club, she began to circle the cabin. Toto planted her feet and refused to budge, her fear so contagious that the hair rose on the back of Hannah's neck.

Exasperated, she scooped the dog into her free arm and carried on around the outside of the cabin. On the other side was a small, mossy clearing where a plastic table and a broken lawn chair sat in front of a rudimentary firepit. Logs and kindling were piled nearby. The light breeze off the river was fetid with rot. She checked the ashes, which were cold and damp. She tried to remember the last time it had rained. Three days ago?

Toto was thrashing about in her arms, so Hannah put her down and headed for the cabin door. If Sedge was inside, he already knew she was here, so she might as well look. Maybe there were clues to where he was and what he was up to.

The interior was a single room with a homemade bunk bed in the corner and a battered pine table with two chairs in the middle. The walls were hung with life jackets, paddles, and fishing gear. A bucket, camp stove, some clean dishes, and a few cans of food were piled on the plywood counter along one wall, and a propane camp lantern sat on the table. Talk about roughing it!

Hannah inspected the food curiously. Canned fish, beans, tomato sauce, and a bowl of peppers, wilted and nibbled by animals. Everything was neat, but mouse droppings littered the counter, and the stench of decay was strong. Someone had been living here, but maybe not in the last few days. Toto was by now glued to her leg and, as she approached the table, the dog fled underneath. Papers were scattered carelessly across its surface, some printed, some photocopied, and others handwritten. She poked through them carefully with her stick, aware there might be important fingerprints that could be Sedge's.

They were all about ducks, moisture levels, and plant growth. Jotted recordings in shorthand that meant nothing to her, dates, articles on rain models, nesting dates, ducks, ducks, ducks.

There was, however, no sign of the datebook crammed with notes that Lillian Chang and Dr. Leitin had mentioned. She examined the rest of the room. On the bottom bunk lay a sleeping bag and beside it some clothes hanging on pegs. On the floor was an open backpack with its contents tossed on the floor. She sifted through them as well. Guy stuff: T-shirts, jeans, boxers, sweaters, most of them clean but frayed. It reminded her of kids on the street, surviving on what they scrounged at Value Village.

She gazed around the room, trying to gather impressions. What would her father make of it? What would he think of the man? Clearly not a dude with a trust fund to keep him afloat, but somehow he'd latched on to a passion for ducks. She wondered about his family, his parents, and where he'd grown up. She backed away, puzzled by the vibe in the room. He was a simple man who didn't care about comfort or money but rather about the fate of innocent creatures. A man who, even without money, had paid for the treatment of a dog he barely knew.

Was this a man who would kill, and if so, why?

The room felt dark and lonely, so she started to go back outside to call her father when she noticed two stains on the stones outside the door. They looked smeared and scrubbed, but she recognized the colour: deep red, almost black. Cold dread crawled up her spine. As her eyes adjusted, she saw more drops, smears, and scuff marks in the leaves and moss. She followed the trail across the small clearing, past the woodshed toward the woods, where branches were torn and ferns trampled. Her pulse pounded in her ears.

Toto was growling and whining as she resisted every step. Finally, Hannah tied the panicked dog to a tree while she continued her search through the dense brush past raspberry bushes and prickly junipers. She could hear Toto whimpering, but she didn't stop. She had to know!

Up ahead, wedged between tree trunks, was a large pile of leaves and debris. Flies buzzed, and the smell of decay became overwhelming. She didn't even have to look. *Fuck*, she thought.

Fuck, fuck, fuck.

She pulled out her phone to call her dad.

Green shot along Highway 416 with his foot to the floor, hoping to beat the Ontario Provincial Police to the scene, although he knew it was futile. Even driving his staff car flat out, it was nearly an hour from his downtown office through Ottawa traffic to Spencerville. If Hannah had called them as she'd promised, the first responders from Leeds-Grenville OPP in Prescott would be there in fifteen minutes. He wasn't sure he'd have any clout with them to get past the perimeter tape.

But he'd give it his best shot. Prescott was a small border town across the St. Lawrence River from upstate New York. It served a mostly rural constituency, and its detachment was probably more used to handling minor border infractions, MVAs, and speeding tickets on the 401. They would have called in the real muscle, including Ident and Major Crimes, from OPP Regional Headquarters in Smiths Falls, at least forty-five minutes away. Green was confident he could beat those officers to it.

He had punched the coordinates into his GPS, and as he turned onto the final back road, he saw just two OPP Interceptors parked in the field behind an abandoned farm up ahead. The big guns had not yet arrived. He bumped down the track, bottoming his staff car on the deep ruts several times before pulling up beside them. Both Interceptors were empty, but as he set off down the path, careful to stay to the side, he heard the crackle of radios and the murmur of voices up ahead. Soon he spotted an officer stringing yellow tape through the trees.

The kid looked about twelve. Green was wearing his workday civilian clothes but had had the presence of mind to grab his uniform jacket as he was leaving the office. He hoped the inspector insignia would at least give the frontline officers pause.

Sure enough, the officer stopped abruptly and stared at him, his mouth open. "Sir?" he stammered, half order, half question.

Green brandished his badge wallet and introduced himself. "My officer is the one who called it in. Where's your SO?"

The officer pointed down the path into the woods. "She's down at the … the remains, sir. Sergeant Paulsen, sir." He moved to speak into his radio.

"It's okay," Green said, stepping around him. "I'll catch her down there."

The officer didn't object. Green suspected he'd never secured an active crime scene in his life. The procedures would have been drilled into him, but it was quite different to be out in the remote woods, surrounded by mosquitoes and acres of nothing but scrub. Possibly with a killer on the loose.

He picked his way down the trail, trying to disturb the path as little as possible. Who knew what thread of fibre might be clinging to a branch or what shoe tread was imprinted in the mud? He took in the smells and sounds as he drew near: the swampy forest loam, the muffled drone of voices, the whisper of the river, and the unmistakable whiff of human rot.

Arriving at the river, he peeked into the cabin, which was empty, but someone had clearly been living and working there. The dock looked precarious, but even he, who knew nothing about boats, could see the canoe had been used. It was overturned on shore, but dried weeds clung to its hull, and the muddy drag marks from the river were fresh. It had been tied to a tree with a sturdy knot.

Rounding the corner of the cabin, he came upon two women sitting on a log with their backs to him. One was obviously the sergeant from Leeds-Grenville County OPP. She was dressed in field uniform but had taken off her cap and was waving it to fend off the bugs. Her short, no-nonsense blond hair shone in the sun. At her feet was a little black-and-white dog. The other woman was Hannah, hunched over and hugging her knees. His heart quivered.

At the sight of him, the dog barked, startling both women. The sergeant leaped to her feet, ready for action.

"Dad!" Hannah cried, uncoiling herself and flinging herself into his arms. It was a brief hug, and he could feel her every muscle fighting for control. All too soon, she thrust herself away.

"Sorry. Sorry." She turned to the sergeant. "Sergeant Paulsen, this is my father. Michael — Inspector — Green."

Paulsen wasn't old, but she looked as if she'd spent too many hours behind the wheel of a patrol car, and both her chin and her stomach had begun to fold over her uniform. Green watched her wrestle with her poker face as she tried to decide how to respond.

She finally decided on a curt nod. "Inspector, this is a crime scene. I appreciate you want to support your daughter —"

Green held up his hands. "I'm not here to interfere. But this death may be connected to an ongoing case of ours, so I could be of assistance to the investigative team. I assume they're on their way?"

She nodded again. "That's what we're waiting for. The coroner will be here soon, along with more back-up. Meanwhile I've got a unit doing a search of the periphery."

"Have you looked at the body?"

"Only enough to confirm there was one. I uncovered a hand."

"A man, youngish?"

"I can't tell anything from a hand."

Green moved toward the woods behind the shed, where more yellow tape was visible. "You'd be surprised."

She stepped in front of him. "Sir. My instructions are to wait."

He began to skirt the scuff marks on the ground. "I don't know if my daughter told you, I know a thing or two about murder scenes, Sergeant."

"She did."

He eyed her. Every inch of him screamed with impatience, but he needed her on his side. "I had a quick look inside the cabin as I came by. It looks like someone was settled in there. Someone who kept few possessions, lots of notes, and who used the canoe."

"I didn't notice the canoe," Hannah said, "but I did notice the clothes and papers were a mess. I think Sedge was very orderly."

Green nodded. "I also saw binoculars and a bird book but no camera or laptop."

The sergeant's eyes narrowed. "The detectives and the Ident team will go through that room. If there's fingerprints or any sign to suggest it was searched, they'll determine that."

"There's blood just outside the door there." Hannah pointed to the steps.

Green followed the faint trail of blood from the steps across the clearing into the woods. At the woodshed, he paused. It was a ramshackle structure sliding sideways toward the ground, with more moss than shingles on the roof. Inside was a neatly stacked pile of firewood, so freshly split that the wood hadn't begun to turn grey, and tucked into the corner was an axe, gleaming new and clean except for a dark smear on its handle.

Another crime of opportunity.

Voices sounded behind him and grew louder as he squatted for a closer look at the smear. Male voices, noisy and excited. He straightened and turned just as three men and a woman rounded the cabin, all dressed in bunny suits from head to toe. The man in front stopped abruptly at the sight of Green.

"What the hell? Mike! What are you doing here?"

Green had been preparing himself for a pissing contest with the OPP Major Crimes detective, but behind the white cap and glasses, he recognized the craggy face of Sergeant Tim Vickers, an OPP legend who had worked with him on a joint provincial task force years earlier. The OPP had tried for years to promote him, but he'd always refused. He wanted to run cases, not push paper.

Green could relate to that. With a grin, he tipped his fist for a greeting. "Good to see you, Vick. This is my daughter Hannah. She's in the OPS now and discovered the body while following up on a lead. Unofficially."

The man's dark eyes crinkled as he cocked his head at Hannah. "This is the little spitfire that gave you all that trouble?"

"Still gives him trouble," Hannah shot back. The spark was back in her eyes, Green noted with relief.

Vickers laughed before turning back to Green. He nodded toward the woods, where the coroner was now bending over the ground and the Ident team was readying their camera. "So have you solved the case yet?"

"Give me another few minutes. I haven't even seen who it is. As soon as Ident and the coroner give us a description, I'll know if it's who I think it is. He's connected to our case up in Ottawa."

The officers stood in a silent ring outside the perimeter as the body was examined. Green didn't recognize the coroner but assumed it was a local doctor who took on the extra duty. He looked a little green as the officers brushed away the leaves to expose the body limb by limb, and he reached for a nearby tree to steady himself. The stench wafted up from the remains, along with the sickening hum of flies.

After a few minutes, the coroner wobbled away from the scene and paused to take a few deep breaths before joining them. "Well, he's very dead," he said. "I'm no expert, but I'd say at least two days. Rigor's come and gone. There's some … uh, animal activity. But Forensics will do their thing, and we'll figure out how to get him to —" He squinted in thought. "Probably Ottawa, for the post."

"Any ideas on cause of death?"

"There are half a dozen wounds — those are just the ones I can see — and quite a lot of bleeding. My guess, a blow to his head killed him."

Green leaned toward Vickers. "Get Forensics to check the axe in the shed. And also do a thorough ground search for his camera and lenses. He's a bird expert. He had an expensive camera, probably the most expensive thing he owned."

"There's a solar-powered charger in the cabin but no electronics," Hannah added. "No laptop or cellphone. What student doesn't have those?"

"Could it be a local who saw him with all his expensive equipment?" Vickers said. "Maybe they just intended a simple burglary, but the victim showed up."

"If it's who I think it is, that would be one hell of a coincidence," Green said.

Vickers's dark eyes fixed on him. "Mike, it's our case."

Green held up his hands. "Of course it is. I'm not even in the department anymore."

Vickers snorted. "Of course you're not." He cocked his eyebrow at Hannah. "You believe that?"

"Brian Sullivan is the one to talk to," Green said. "Sharing info would benefit both of you."

"Well, first things first."

One of the Ident officers stepped away from the body and came toward them, holding his iPad. "There's no cellphone or ID on him, but here are some preliminary photos. Enough for the team to start to ID him."

He handed the iPad to Vickers, who held it so Green could see it. Beside them, Hannah crowded in. Vickers flicked through the close-ups, bloodied, waxy grey, and just beginning to swell, but still human enough to see the shaved head, the skimpy beard, and the smooth, pale cheeks.

With the briefest of nods, Green pulled out his phone to call Sullivan.

CHAPTER NINETEEN

The house was quiet and the blinds drawn despite the warm sun spilling through the trees. It was midday, and the humidity was already creeping up. Josh sweated as he stood on the front doorstep beside the marble pillar, listening. Centring himself. This was a big moment for him. Gibbs was behind him, breathing down his neck but letting him take the lead.

The door chime rang through the house, followed by silence. He pressed again and spotted the blind twitch on the basement window. Nothing more.

"They know who we are, Sarge," Josh said, his finger poised for a third try. Gibbs leaned past him and stabbed the bell rapidly three times. The chimes reverberated. Josh felt a surge of annoyance. He would have done that if Gibbs hadn't been watching his every move.

"Get the fucking door!" came a screech from somewhere deep inside the house.

Josh was just trying to identify the voice when the door opened and a sweaty, dishevelled Kristina McAuley appeared, hastily pulling on a mask. Her eyes widened. "News?"

Josh shook his head. "We're working on several promising leads. We have a few more questions for you."

She stepped outside on the porch and shut the door behind her. "What?"

"Do you mind if we step inside?"

"Well ..." She flicked her gaze uneasily over her shoulder. "My son ..."

"It'll be more private."

With a sigh, she led them inside, where the heat and humidity were almost as bad. Didn't the big fancy house have AC? Josh wondered. There was a fan set up in the living room, blowing the hot air around, and Peter was sitting on the carpet, twirling the wheels of his truck. Kristina stroked his hair as she went by.

"You remember the nice policemen, don't you, sweetie?"

Peter shrank back. Unfazed, Kristina perched on the sofa and faced them. "What is it?"

Josh had the photo from Drew Sedgwick's driver's licence on his phone and held it out to her. "Do you recognize this man?"

"Is that the killer?"

"Have you ever seen this man before?"

She gave the photo a cursory look before shaking her head. "But I don't meet many people. I don't get out much. Who is he?"

"Please take a close look. Maybe you've seen him in the neighbourhood? Or on the trail? You told one of our officers you sometimes walk your son on the trail in Shirley's Bay."

She continued to shake her head. It looked genuine enough, and Josh gave Gibbs a quick glance. Above his mask, the sergeant's eyes gave nothing away. *Your call*, he seemed to say.

"Does the name Sedge mean anything to you? Or Drew Sedgwick?"

She looked surprised. A good act or the truth? "Sedge, yes. Constable Pollack asked about him. Is that him?"

"Your husband never mentioned him? Or your daughter?"

She looked alarmed. "My daughter? No. Does he live around here?"

"Can I show the photo to your son?"

She stiffened. "He — he wouldn't know."

"Sometimes kids remember things we don't realize." He looked at the boy, who acted like they didn't exist. Was he listening to every word?

"You won't get anything out of him. He doesn't talk."

"Maybe a nod or headshake?" He held out the phone to her. "Do you want to ask him? Just so I can tick that box?"

She pressed her lips tight but eventually took the phone and went to kneel beside her son. "Petie," she murmured, all sweetness. "Look at this pretty phone. Look at the picture on it."

Peter kept playing. Kristina held the phone closer. "Look at the funny man, Petie."

The boy paused, his eyes still on the truck. Josh watched for every twitch or flicker on the boy's face. For a long time he didn't move, but as Kristina wiggled the phone, his gaze flicked briefly toward it. No curiosity, no hint of recognition.

Kristina ruffled his hair and returned to the sofa. "He's very tense because you're here. But I'm pretty sure he didn't recognize him. Is this man … is he a suspect?"

"Is your daughter at home?"

She flushed. "Can't you tell me that at least? You come in here and you ask question after question, like I'm just another suspect. I'm not! I'm the widow, and you're telling me nothing!"

Josh hesitated. Beside him, he felt Gibbs ready to intervene. *Keep control*, he told himself. "I'm sorry, Kristina. I appreciate this is hard for you, and thank you for helping. I'm sorry I can't tell you more, but as soon as we have anything solid, we will let you know."

To his relief, Gibbs sat back. Josh waited a beat before repeating his request. Kristina glanced nervously toward a closed door in the hall. "I don't want her disturbed. She's sleeping. She's been training for a challenging bike race."

Josh remembered the twitching blind. "Please. You'll be present."

Heaving an irritated sigh, Kristina went to knock softly on the door. "Justine, the police have a couple of questions."

Silence.

"It won't take long. Can you come up, honey?"

"What questions?" came the angry retort.

"About a man. Who might have killed Dad."

Josh cursed inwardly and hurried over to the door. "Mrs. McAuley — Kristina — please let me handle the questions."

Kristina swung around, angry. "I won't have you harassing her!"

"I just want to talk to her. You'll hear every word." He wanted to ask her to keep quiet. If he had any hope of getting the truth out of Justine, he needed Mom to stay out of it, but before he could think of the right words, Gibbs butted in.

"We'll try not to upset her, Kristina," he said. "We're just trying to fill in a picture."

Kristina took several deep breaths, like she was stalling for time. "Kristina?" Gibbs prodded gently.

She blinked and flicked a glance at her son. "I don't want Peter upset. Justine can be …"

"Then let's talk to her outside," Josh said, wanting to take back the reins. He tried the door, which was locked.

Kristina grabbed his arm. "She likes her privacy."

"Justine!" he called. "It will only take a minute, and it would really help us with our investigation."

He heard a thump, followed by drawers opening and slamming shut. About a minute later, footsteps thudded on the stairs, the door flew open, and Justine emerged, her hair lank and loose over her shoulders and her face red from the heat. She was buttoning up a pair of shorts as she pushed past them.

"Justine, darling, don't —"

"I can handle it, Mother," the girl said as she slammed out the front door. Josh scrambled to follow and found her leaning against the pillar with her arms folded. "Sorry," she muttered. "We're getting on each other's nerves. It feels like everyone's watching." She waved her hand toward the street. "The neighbours, the media. People who have no business here drive by, like we're a circus show. I don't like people knowing our business. I can't even go out to school without everyone asking questions. And my mother's off the charts. Dad always handled everything."

Behind him, Gibbs had opened the door quietly and ushered Kristina outside just as Justine spoke. The mother looked about to blow a gasket.

"I know it's really rough, Kristina," Josh said to head the mother off. "Are you getting any help?"

Justine grunted. "Help? At a hundred and eighty bucks a pop? She even gave up the therapist she used to have."

"Justine!"

"Truth, Mother? But fuck it, that's not the cops' problem. Mother said you have a suspect?"

"We're just following up on some leads. Does the name Sedge mean anything to you?"

Her expression grew still. Shuttered. "Who's he?"

"His full name is Drew Sedgwick. Have you heard of him?"

Slowly, she shook her head back and forth.

"Are you sure? Maybe in the neighbourhood or on the Shirley's Bay trail?"

"I see lots of people on the trail, but I don't pay much attention to them. I'm in my own head when I jog."

Josh produced the photo on his phone. "Do you recognize this man?"

"Is that Sedge?"

Josh said nothing.

"Okay, fine. Don't answer. Cops. Honestly, where do you learn that poker face? My dad had it, too. Like don't show a thing about what you're thinking and then pounce. A good lawyer trick, he always said."

"So do you recognize him?"

She took the phone. "Don't think so."

"We have a witness who says he saw you two on the path a few times, talking to each other."

In the doorway, Kristina sucked in her breath to object, but Justine barrelled on. "Really? What witness?"

Again he said nothing, and this time a smile twitched on her lips. She peered at the phone. "Maybe. It's a terrible photo, but yeah, I might have bumped into him while I was jogging."

"I understand you are friends."

"Friends?" She snorted. "I don't think so. Is that what he says?"

"You talked about university. About athletics programs."

"Oh yeah. I remember. He said he was working on his dissertation, so we talked a bit about universities. No biggie. I hardly remember."

"Did you ever meet him anywhere else? His home? School?"

Kristina stirred again. "Justine, you don't have to answer that. He's fishing."

Justine ignored her. "No." She flicked her hand at the phone. "He was just a dork. He seemed lonely, liked to talk about his ducks. But if he's saying we are friends, that's all in his head."

Gibbs had been standing quietly to the side, leaving Josh to carry on, but now his cellphone rang. He stepped away to answer it and listened for a few seconds. "When? Where?" he demanded, then, "On our way."

After he hung up, he turned back to them. His own poker face was shot to hell, and his tone was grim. "That was the staff sergeant. We've got to go."

Green met them in Sullivan's office. It was late afternoon, and Inspector Fanel had gone home, which was a bonus. A few detectives were still scattered around the squad room, none of whom Green recognized, but if they were curious about Green's presence, they said nothing.

"So I guess we can scratch Sedgwick off our suspects list," Sullivan said once Green had filled them in on the details to date. "When did the coroner estimate time of death?"

"He's not an expert," Green said. "I doubt the poor guy's ever seen a decomposing murder victim before. But he thinks more than forty-eight hours and less than a week. Even in that shaded spot and insulated by forest debris, in a week the bloating would be more advanced."

Sullivan's eyes narrowed. "And when did Hannah mention Sedge to the family?"

"What?" Josh demanded. He'd been sitting so quietly in the corner of the office that Green had almost forgotten about him. Now he cursed inwardly. Hannah's screw-up would now be all over the squad room.

Sullivan, too, seemed to remember him belatedly. "Josh, thank you for your work this afternoon. Sergeant Gibbs can fill everyone in when we're done. This is a major new development, so we'll be holding a full briefing in the morning. That'll be all for now."

Josh didn't move. "But I'm the one working the Sedge angle. I know more —"

"And we'll need your full report ASAP. You can write it up now or at six in the morning."

Josh looked from one detective to another, lingering just long enough to register his objection, before rising and yanking open the door. He shut it with just enough force to rattle the plaques on Sullivan's wall but not enough to be insubordinate.

Green cocked his head at Sullivan. "A handful?"

Gibbs had not uttered a word, but now he flushed. "He's ambitious. Pushy. But ..."

"But what?"

"But Sue was, too, when she first came here."

Green smiled. "I remember."

"And you won her over. I think I can do that."

Green was not so sure. Gibbs was a gentle detective, thorough and careful, but Green had never known him to throw his weight around. The picture of him up against a headstrong, overconfident young detective running on testosterone and ambition did not inspire confidence.

But he kept his concern to himself. Josh was not his detective, and Sullivan would back Gibbs up. Few men were scarier than Sullivan when he drew himself to his full height.

"Then you might want to give him a job to keep him busy," Green said. "The OPP team is going to need a liaison. That gives him something to focus on."

Gibbs glanced at Sullivan, who was stone-faced.

"And impress on him that everything he heard in here is confidential."

"Point taken, Mike," Sullivan said curtly. "Now, getting back to my question — when did Hannah ask Kristina McAuley about Sedge?"

"Four days ago."

"And we have to assume Kristina could have told anyone in her family about him, probably asked if anyone knew him or had heard his name. Luis, Ramon, and the daughter."

"As long as we're including everybody," Gibbs said, "don't forget Kristina's mother."

Green hesitated. "I saw Sedge's body, and the axe. The axe was new and very sharp, but it would still take a lot of strength to inflict that much damage."

"Any resistance? Defensive wounds?"

"Like I said, the coroner is not a forensics expert and the focus was on extracting the body and gathering evidence. He said there were several blows, but we'll know more when the post is done. There was also some blood between the cabin and the woodshed. The OPP blood spatter and DNA people will tell us more in due course, including whether the killer got injured himself, but it looked to me like Sedge was first attacked just outside the cabin door, and then more blood was spilled in the clearing, and the final blows were struck just behind the woodshed. My guess ..." Green leaned forward, tamping down his excitement. This was his favourite part of the investigation — venturing, as Sullivan called it, "out into the wild blue yonder."

"This is off the top of my head," he continued, "and it's not even my case, but do you want to know my guess?"

Sullivan rolled his eyes. "By all means. We'll all take bets on how close you get. A hundred might do it."

Green grinned. "This is very preliminary, so ten tops. I think the killer was waiting outside the cabin door for him. Sedge was inside working. Something made him get up and go to the door. Maybe the killer knocked, or maybe the dog barked. Whatever the reason, he went outside, and the killer delivered the first blow. It wasn't enough. Maybe they missed their aim, or Sedge reacted in time. So they tried again, and Sedge started to run away. We'll know from the post if he fought back, but I think his instinct was to run. This is not a tough guy. Not athletic. And an axe is a scary thing."

Sullivan folded his arms, looking skeptical. "When they're desperate and fighting for their life, almost everyone fights."

Green nodded. "Which makes it less likely it's Kristina's mother. I can't picture her charging across the clearing swinging the axe and able to connect several times."

"Not Kristina either. More likely a man."

"I wouldn't rule Kristina out. She's a tall woman, and probably strong from carrying a small child around. And don't forget, the killer was desperate, too. This guy could expose them. But I have a further theory. I think the killer timed the attack for nighttime. This gave them the advantage. They had been outside in the dark for some time, first when they were walking down the path and then waiting outside the cabin. Their eyes would have adjusted to the dark, whereas Sedge … Have you ever used a propane lantern?"

"Oh, says you, wilderness camper extraordinaire."

Green held up his hand. "Hey! I learned a thing or two up in the Nahanni. Night in the country is very dark, and those lamps are very bright."

Sullivan straightened, and his expression changed from skeptical to thoughtful. "So you're saying Sedge came out the door and couldn't see a thing."

"Exactly. He was literally fighting blind. And I think that's why he was running away and why in the end he didn't stand a chance."

He looked at the two men. Gibbs was wide-eyed, and even Sullivan managed a doubtful nod. "Good theory, Mike. Now let's wait for the evidence."

CHAPTER TWENTY

The murder of their key person of interest set the squad room buzzing the next morning, and with the two deaths now linked, the energy during the briefing was palpable. Both killings were savage and opportunistic, hinting at a level of ruthless desperation that sent chills down the spines of the more experienced detectives. Josh felt the urgency, but he also felt the excitement.

Although the link between them as well as the motive was still unclear, no one argued with Gibbs's theory that Sedge was killed because of something he knew about the McAuley murder. Perhaps something he'd witnessed on his early-morning outing, or something he'd learned.

"We need to dig into any connection between these two men," Gibbs said as he scrawled the point on the smart board. "See if they ever met or had any communication. We don't have Sedge's phone or laptop yet — the OPP are still searching for them — but we have his phone number and email account. We can cross-check with Ted McAuley's laptop and phone records."

Gibbs paused to write five names on the board. "So far these are our main suspects. Kristina, her parents, brother, and daughter. We need to dig into any connection to Sedge and determine their activities in the past week, with specific emphasis on nighttime. The drive is about one hour each way, so we should assume an absence of nearly three hours. We already know the daughter had contact with him, but according to her, it was minimal. Ask her friends, show his picture around to them and the neighbours. Get me something more so I can get warrants for her phone and electronics."

"Sarge," came a voice from the front. Samina, Josh noticed. Always on the ball. "Won't the OPP be doing this?"

"We're working closely with the OPP. Right now they're concentrating on witnesses and tracing Sedge's movements and contacts down there, as well as analyzing the crime scene, while we concentrate on Sedge's activities up here. Our primary focus is Ted McAuley, but the answer to his death may lie in Sedge's. And vice versa. I've assigned Detective Kanner to act as OPP liaison so we can pool our information efficiently."

As eyes turned to him, Josh flushed with pride. Was it his imagination, or was there a flash of anger in Samina's look? Gibbs carried on outlining the lines of inquiry and assigning jobs. Finally, he studied his notes as if looking for gaps.

"So, new reports? Sam, updates on McAuley's bank or computer records?"

The woman was trying to keep a poker face, but she looked to Josh like she'd swallowed a canary. "Yes, Sarge.

Two things from his internet records. There's another device that sometimes connected to the McAuley home Wi-Fi account. I've ruled out all the cellphones and laptops in the household, including his wife's and daughter's. It's not unusual to have other devices link in, from visitors or even neighbours if they know your password. But so far I haven't found who it could be."

"How far back does it go?"

"The first connection I found was six months ago and the last link was May twenty-ninth. Five days before Ted's death."

"How often did this occur?"

"At least once a week. In the last week it was several times a day, always during the workweek. Never evenings or weekends."

Gibbs's eyes narrowed. "So when Ted was likely at work. Both Luis and Ramon Ramirez were doing work at the house over that time. Check —"

"I checked, Sarge," Samina interrupted. "It's not them. I've asked the immediate neighbours, too. No dice."

"Any other ideas?"

"Wel-ll …" She dragged the word out. "Something else has turned up that makes me wonder. The woman who's been looking through Ted's financial records turned up a couple of interesting things. First, that the Ramirezes owed Ted a lot of money, over twenty-five thousand dollars in personal loans on top of their mortgage. It looks like he's been lending them money for years, and they've had trouble keeping up with the payments. So a few months ago he cut them off, and since then they've basically been working for him for free to work off their debt."

Gibbs put into words what Josh was thinking. "Twenty-five grand is hardly motive for murder. They were family, after all."

"Yes, Sarge. But it does confirm why Ted disapproved of them. And also suggests a reason for resentment on their part."

Gibbs looked unconvinced. "Did you get any more info on the state of Ramirez's finances? Possible reasons for his lack of money? He seems to have had steady work from McAuley over the years."

"His finances are precarious. He's overdrawn at the bank, and Ted holds the mortgage on his house, which, by the way, he was threatening to foreclose on. Nothing formal yet, just a few letters of warning."

For the first time, Josh was intrigued. Here, possibly, was a man desperate enough.... What did he do with all this money? Josh had seen the father and the son. Their truck was old, their tools battered, and their work clothes worn thin. They didn't give the impression of being greedy, but they were proud. If Ted was squeezing them even further ...

"We're trying to track down what he spends his money on," Samina said. "So far it looks like lots of cash withdrawals."

Gibbs frowned unhappily. Josh suspected it was because it was a lead that didn't fit anywhere. Yet. "Okay, thank you, Sam," he said. "Was there any evidence of that extra account his mother reported?"

"I was getting to that. Yes, we found another account, in another bank entirely. I got the first trace of it on Ted's laptop. His search history showed he accessed this new bank about a month ago. We knew he was hiding accounts in different financial institutions, but this wasn't one of the established banks or brokerage firms. It was a small credit union. So we dug deeper. It turns out it's a small savings account opened six months ago, on December twenty-eighth, in … get this … Kemptville."

A murmur of excitement rippled through the crowd. Kemptville was a larger town not far from Spencerville. *What the hell does that mean?* Josh thought. *Sedge? Was he linked financially somehow?*

Samina was basking in her moment of glory. "It had irregular deposits, almost all less than a hundred dollars each, and all made in cash."

"In Kemptville?"

"A few, but mostly through ATMs in Ottawa."

"We need to check CCTV footage for those deposit locations and dates," Gibbs said, scrawling on the board. "How much money are we talking about in total?"

"The balance was just over three thousand dollars a month ago, when the last deposit was made."

"Any withdrawals?"

Samina nodded. "None until a month ago, when the money was all transferred out and the account was closed."

"A month ago. Around the time Ted died?"

"May twenty-eighth. A few days before, yes."

"Where was the money transferred to?"

"To Ted McAuley's main chequing account."

Her triumphant tone hung in the air. Josh sucked in his breath as he tried to make sense of the implications. Gibbs was leaning forward, intense and focused. "What was the name on the account?"

Samina smiled and gave a slow nod. Josh felt a twinge of envy. She and Gibbs were up to something, and she was playing this perfectly.

"Kristina Ramirez."

The room erupted. The sergeant looked like he'd scored a hat trick. "So the mother was right! Kristina was squirrelling away money in a secret account for the past six months, under her maiden name, and Ted found out about it. I'm willing to bet that unknown electronic device operating off the household Wi-Fi over the same time period was also Kristina's. Our house search didn't turn up any extra devices, but we were focusing on his things, not hers. We need another search warrant for her, and let's hope she hasn't gotten rid of it in the meantime." He put a big circle around Kristina's name. "She was up to something. Let's find out what and whether her family was involved. Maybe that's where their extra cash was going."

Josh waited impatiently while Gibbs made a few more assignments, none of which affected him. He had an idea, and he was trying to figure out how to sell it. Samina had the bank and internet angles all wrapped up, but data analysis wasn't his strength, anyway. He preferred to be out in the field, imagining scenarios. As the detectives filed out of the room, chatting and planning next steps, he moved toward the front of the room, where the sergeant stood gazing at the array of leads and theories on the wall.

"Sarge? I have a request to make."

Gibbs swung on him, looking distracted.

"I'd like to visit the Sedgwick crime scene. I know it's not our case, and I know the OPP will have been all over it, but I'd like my own impression."

"Have you discussed this with them?"

"I wanted your okay first."

Gibbs pursed his lips in thought. "What do you expect to learn?"

"I want to see distances, layout, type of terrain. I want to reenact the killer's movements."

"The OPP will do that."

"I know, but they don't know the players." He gestured to the suspects' names on the board. "I've met almost all these people."

"Okay, I'll clear it with Sergeant Vickers. And while you're down there, see what you can learn about this credit union account in Kemptville."

"Thanks, Sarge." He hovered. That reenactment had been a stroke of genius, but now came the key point. "And I'd like to take a patrol officer with me. Not just any patrol, but the one who was first on the scene."

Gibbs eyed him, expressionless. Why was it so hard to read the man's face? "Constable Pollack."

"Yeah. She also knows a lot about the case."

"I'll think about it."

CHAPTER TWENTY-ONE

Hannah gazed out the car window at the farm fields scrolling by on either side of the highway. They were driving south toward Spencerville, and the morning sun blazed through the windshield, already hinting at another hot day.

She should have been thrilled. She had been taken off her patrol schedule for the day and given the chance to keep exploring the mystery of Ted McAuley and Drew Sedgwick's deaths. To be connected to such a complex, high-profile case was a privilege most officers didn't get for years. If ever. She knew there would be grumblings among her friends in patrol. There would be mutterings of *favouritism* and *daddy's girl*. But she didn't care. You grab whatever chance is on offer, and you prove you belong there.

She wasn't even sure her father knew. The request had come down through channels from Bob Gibbs, and at first she'd thought Gibbs really valued her contribution. But she'd just learned it had all been Josh Kanner's idea.

And that was the problem.

Josh had his own agenda, his own reasons for wanting her along, and it had nothing to do with her competence. She was just a stepping stone. Once they'd hit the open highway, he'd put on a mixed playlist of hip hop and techno that grated on her nerves, and for half an hour barely a word had passed between them while she wrestled with how to handle him. But now, as they approached the bridge over the Rideau River, she made up her mind. She was a cop. He was a cop. They had an assignment to carry out. Period.

It had been two days since the discovery of Sedge's body, and Hannah had been struggling to put the images and the memories out of her mind while she returned to patrol. The little dog had been handed over to a vet to be checked out and cleaned up before being returned to Kristina. Hannah would have loved to see firsthand how Kristina reacted to the dog and to the news of her recovery, but instead another officer handled it. The official story was that the dog had been picked up as a stray in the country. No mention was made of Hannah's role or of the dog's connection to Sedge. She wasn't even sure Kristina knew Sedge was dead. The OPP had not released the name of the victim and had chosen to keep a lot of information under wraps. She'd been thanked for her help and sent on her way back to patrol.

Until now. She glanced across at Josh. He had cracked open his window, and the breeze ruffled his thick black hair. Damn, he was cute. He was casually dressed in chinos, sneakers, and a short-sleeved cotton shirt, everything colour-coordinated in rust and olive green to complement his skin. The guy knew style and didn't mind spending a few bucks, although being un-attached and pulling in a detective's salary, she supposed he could afford it. She felt scruffy in her faded jeans, T-shirt, and beat-up sandals.

As they passed over the river, she finally decided it was time to break the silence. "Can we turn this stuff off? I hate techno."

He turned to her, his expression hard to read behind his sunglasses. "Oh, sorry, I thought that would be your thing."

Was that a dig to remind her she was a kid? "Don't ever assume anything about me."

He lifted both hands off the steering wheel in mock surrender. "What would you like?"

"I'd like to talk about the case."

"Oh. I don't know much about it yet. The OPP hasn't let me in on much, but I don't think they've got too far. They're waiting for the post-mortem, which is being done today, so the sergeant in charge is actually going to Ottawa for that this afternoon. And they're waiting for Forensics, which is slow as molasses. They located his family — a sister who lives with her husband and kids in New Brunswick, and his father who's also in New Brunswick. That's where Sedge was from. They don't sound like they were close; they hadn't talked to Sedge in weeks. Not since Easter, his sister said. She's coming to make the formal ID and to make the arrangements. She doesn't know who his friends were. He was always a loner, loved wildlife, and liked to spend hours a day wandering the rivers and forests near Miramichi where they grew up."

"Same picture we've got up here. Any reason why he chose the Ottawa area? There are lots of universities on the East Coast."

"She said he wanted to work with a particular professor here. And he's loved ducks all his life." He shook his head. "Definitely a strange one."

She thought of the primitive cabins he had chosen to live in. "Yes, he didn't care much for luxury. Did Vickers say anything else? We don't want to go over old ground."

"They've been canvassing in the vicinity of Spencerville, asking the usual. Who saw him? Was there ever anyone else with him? Any other strangers spotted in the area? Anyone he hung out with in the village?"

She looked across at him doubtfully. "They think the killer might be local? Why?"

He shrugged. "Maybe a robbery gone bad?"

"That doesn't make any sense. He lived in a dump."

"Just ticking the boxes. Anyway, Vickers said hardly anyone in the village talked to him. Spencerville is too small to have many amenities, so he went to Kemptville for his groceries and gas, and he kept to himself. That cabin is pretty out of the way, and even the property rental guy never met him."

"So do you have a plan for today?"

"I was hoping you did."

232

"You're the one making the big bucks."

He laughed. "You're the one who tracked him down."

She waited.

"Fine," he said. "Just teasing. I want to start with the murder scene. I want a walk-through, to get my bearings."

"Those pretty clothes are going to get messy."

"These are in case I have to impress the OPP, okay?" He jerked his thumb over his shoulder to the backpack on the rear seat. "I've got my jeans and workboots in there. And I want to do my own canvass of the village. Kemptville, too, if we have time, since he shopped there. Maybe we'll have more luck than the OPP."

"You'll want to keep the chinos and the two-hundred-dollar shoes under wraps, then. This is cow manure country."

He was silent for a moment as he navigated typical Ontario scrub country of mixed forests, rolling farm fields, and empty land. As they passed a sign announcing the exit for Spencerville, he sighed.

"Give me a break, will you, Hannah? I'm just trying to do a good job. I honestly asked you along because of what you know about the case. And before you say I'm using you, I'm not."

"Furthest thing from my mind."

He jerked the car angrily onto the exit ramp and braked hard as they approached a T-junction. The manoeuvre spared him from answering. "Which way?"

"Do you want the village or the crime scene?"

"Crime scene first."

As she guided him through the series of back roads, Hannah took stock of the houses and farms. Sedge and his killer would have driven past all of these, probably arousing the curiosity of those watching the road from their windows and fields. She was sure the OPP had already interviewed them, but it was worth a try.

When they reached the farm where Sedge had stayed, she was relieved to see no sign of police vehicles or any tape restricting access to the path. Ident had obviously released the scene, so she and Josh should be able to tramp about unchallenged.

While Josh went behind the barn to change his clothes, she stood in the open field and scanned the rutted track, which was pockmarked with residue from police moulds. A deer fly began to buzz around her head, so she clamped her ball cap down and tried to ignore it. Over the past couple of days, she'd spent a lot of time wondering how the killer knew where to find Sedge. Even his university colleagues didn't know exactly where he was staying. Had he invited his killer here, or had they followed him?

Her curiosity grew as she explored possibilities. Who would he have invited, and why? Assuming the murders of Ted and Sedge were connected, the list of potential suspects was small: Kristina, her brother, father, and daughter. It seemed unlikely that Sedge had even met the father or brother. Why the hell would he invite them? The most likely person he'd invite was Justine. Supposedly, he had a crush on her. But what if it was about the dog? What if he'd finally decided to call

Kristina about the dog? That was as likely a scenario as him getting up the nerve to invite the girl he secretly liked.

But if that was the case, maybe Kristina had told her father or brother and sent one of them in her place. Would these tire marks tell the tale?

Hannah was so deep in her own head that she barely noticed Josh emerging from behind the barn, pulling a battered ball cap down on his head. The switch from classy city cop to country local was nearly complete. All he needed was three days' growth and a layer of dirt under his neatly clipped nails.

He was eyeing her warily, but she was too excited to give him grief. She gestured to the tire tracks. "Has the Lexus SUV been released back to Kristina yet?"

"I don't know. Ident takes a long time. There are lots of different analyses."

"You should check. Then we should tell the OPP to check these tracks against it, as well as the Ramirez vehicle."

"What are you thinking?"

She filled him in on her thoughts as she led the way down the narrow path. When he said nothing, she wondered if she'd made a mistake handing all her ideas over to him. Would he claim all the credit? But she wasn't even a detective, let alone assigned to the case. She was only here because he'd asked for her.

"The OPP took tire impressions. I'll tell Sergeant Gibbs we should follow up at our end." He paused and smiled at her. "Thanks."

They batted mosquitoes away as they descended closer to the river. The cabin stood quiet and serene, just as she'd first seen it. Inside, all Sedge's belongings had been removed, leaving an empty shell.

Josh poked around at the remaining dishes and food. "I know Sedge wasn't a guy for luxury, but this is one step above sleeping rough."

"Yeah, he didn't have much. Do you know if the OPP found his cellphone or laptop? Or his camera?"

He shook his head. "They searched the property the best they could, even brought in a metal detector, but the place is nothing but bush and swamp, most of it impossible to penetrate. And there's always the river."

He headed down to the dock, stood for a minute looking out into the lazy current, and then glanced at the canoe. "This was used recently."

"Well, he studied water and ducks, so it makes sense he'd go out in it."

He looked unconvinced. "Or the killer could have used it to dump the equipment somewhere out in the river. I bet they were afraid there was something on it that incriminated them. Emails, texts, or photos on his camera. The water would wreck them."

Her eyes widened as she remembered. "He had a datebook that he recorded everything in. Did the OPP find it in the cabin?"

He shook his head. "They didn't mention it."

"It would be a pretty big find. It was just a ratty old notebook, but he kept important records in it. If they took that, I think we can safely rule out a robbery gone wrong."

Josh walked over to the clearing. Half visible through the bush behind it was an area that had been cleared and scraped. The OPP had meticulously removed all the evidence markers, but a few wisps of yellow tape remained. She shivered at the memory. They stood at the edge of the clearing, sombre.

"Sergeant Gibbs believes the murder took place at night under cover of darkness."

Hannah nodded. "That was my father's theory."

He shot her a surprised glance. "That means the killer had to sneak down here, kill Sedge and bury him in debris, then search the house, all in darkness. And if he took the canoe out, that's even longer. Pitch darkness doesn't last long at this time of the year. At most six hours, at a time when most people are sound asleep. If Gibbs and your father are right, that's the time frame to check our suspects' whereabouts. It would help to know if the theory is correct."

She ran through the scenario in her mind's eye. "There is one thing we can check. It might not work, but ..." She turned and made her way back to the cabin. Inside, the propane lamp was still sitting on the table. She peered at it. He watched her, bemused, as she picked it up.

"I think the gas is on. You got a match?"

"Who carries those nowadays?" He walked over to the pine shelf where the pots and dishes were stored and groped along the back until he brandished a packet of matches in triumph.

She struck a match, held it to the lantern, and turned the switch back and forth. Nothing. She smiled as she blew out the match. "The propane was all used up. According to my father's theory, Sedge was working on his papers by the light of this lamp when the killer arrived. He went outside, leaving the light on. Either it burned out during the time the killer was disposing of the body, or they just left it on when they left."

"That's risky."

"A lot of what they did was risky. They might not have thought through everything. Or they didn't know how to turn this thing off."

"So … you figure this proves Sedge was killed at night."

"I think it strengthens the case."

"I'll buy that." Josh peered out the window at the river. "But I still think the killer took the canoe out to dump the electronics. That's much easier to do in daylight."

She shrugged. "Fine. Maybe it was early dawn by that time. Maybe Sedge liked to work late. But the killer would want to get away as fast as possible. Why not take the stuff with him?"

"Because then he'd have to stop to get rid of it. More risk that he'd be noticed, especially if it's almost dawn. Farmers get up really early."

"There's lots of stuff to ask the neighbours, then. Let's hope the OPP are on it." She turned in place, picturing Sedge bent over his notes, lost in thought. A wave of sadness washed over her. "Are we done here? Have you got what you need?"

He said he wanted one last look at the canoe and the fresh grooves leading to it, so she left him and started up the path. The memories were beginning to crowd in, so to distract herself, she ran through the scenario one last time, this time concentrating not on the murder or even the search of the cabin afterward, but on the moments when the killer went back up the path, perhaps exhausted and shaken by what they had done. Justifying it, trying to figure out how they were going to cover their tracks.

That's when the biggest hole in their theory leaped out at her. Tracks.

There had been no vehicle parked in the field the day Hannah discovered the body. Yet Sedge had to have a car, because there was no other way to reach this remote cabin, especially with all his gear and a dog in tow. One of these sets of tracks had to belong to Sedge's car. A rented car? Borrowed from a friend? That was a lead the Ottawa team should be tracking down.

But that car was no longer here. Who had taken it? The killer could not have, because they would also have needed a car to get here from Ottawa in the first place, and if they had driven off in Sedge's car, then their own would have been left.

Josh caught up with her just as she reached the field. A small battalion of deer flies had collected around his head, and he flailed in frustration. "I'm going to ask the OPP to deploy divers in the river," he said.

"Did the OPP say anything about the cars?" Seeing his baffled expression, she rushed on to explain her concern.

Josh put his hands on his hips and studied the rutted tracks and flattened grass. "That's a good point. If one of them had a motorcycle —"

"Sedge had a lot of equipment. A motorcycle is possible but not likely. I had a hard enough time carrying the dog."

"The killer could have come by motorcycle."

"And what? Stuck it in the back of Sedge's vehicle? That would only work if Sedge had a truck." She frowned and glanced around the empty field. "Motorcycles are damn heavy, even little ones like mine. They'd need some kind of ramp, at least."

"Which they could put in Sedge's truck. We need to find out if Sedge had a truck."

She smiled. "And I know exactly who to ask."

CHAPTER TWENTY-TWO

They found the elderly man sitting in the shade of his front veranda, watching the world go by. They hadn't passed a single car as they drove up, so Hannah figured an unfamiliar vehicle would catch his attention.

He straightened stiffly and came down the steps as Josh pulled into the drive.

"Hello again," Hannah called out as she climbed out of the car. "Remember me from the other day? I didn't introduce myself then. I'm Constable Pollack of the Ottawa Police, and this is Detective Kanner."

They met on the lawn and exchanged awkward nods. The man's pale blue eyes peered out at her from a maze of wrinkles. "You're the one who found him, right?"

"Yes, and Detective Kanner here has some follow-up questions."

Josh had his notebook out. Luckily, he still had his jeans and workboots on, matching those of the older man.

"The cops were already here asking questions. Twice. I don't know what more I can tell you."

Josh nodded. "I'm looking at a different angle of the case, so if you don't mind going over it again, sir ... What's your name?"

"Bert Collins."

"And what's the full address here?"

While Josh recorded the man's details, Hannah scanned the area. Bert Collins's property was at the top of a rise at the juncture of two roads, and from his farm he could see not only all the way down to the bridge over the South Nation River, but also along the river toward the property that Sedge had rented. The cabin itself wasn't visible through the trees, but in the distance the roofs of the abandoned farm poked up. Nothing stirred in the sunny heat but the deer flies.

"A nice spread you have here," Josh said.

"Our retirement dream, me and the wife. Moved down here from Ottawa twenty years ago when taxes were cheap, designed the house ourselves. It's just me now, and my son wants me to move to Toronto, but I got no use for that. I was born in the valley, and as long as I can keep it up, this is where I'll be."

"I can see why. It's very peaceful. I bet you know every vehicle that goes by."

"Pretty near." Bert grinned as he watched Josh take aim at a deer fly. "You folks want to come inside? These damn flies will eat us alive."

They followed him inside the modest bungalow. The place was cluttered with furniture that still retained a woman's touch, from the flowery covers on the sofa set to the painted ceramic canisters on the counter and the ruffled yellow curtains on the windows. The kitchen window overlooked the front yard and the road, Hannah noted with interest.

"I'll tell you what I told the other cops. About five nights ago I heard that little dog barking" — he pointed to Hannah — "the one you were asking about. Far away, but I could still hear it carrying on. Howling, yelping. And that got me up. I was wondering if I should go check on it, but then it stopped. I was just enjoying a wee dram" — his eyes twinkled as he affected a Scottish accent — "to help me back to sleep when a car drove by. From down that way, heading over toward the bridge."

Josh looked up from his notes. "What time was that?"

"At four thirty-eight. I know because I checked to see if I should go back to sleep."

"You're sure it came from there?"

"Well, there's not much down that road past that. Where else would it come from?"

"Did you see any vehicle go down that way earlier in the night?"

"Nope. But I'm asleep by nine thirty. Up at five thirty."

"So it was just the one vehicle? No other vehicles any time during the night or early morning?"

"Just the one. Others in the morning, of course. There's a few locals that commute to the city. Most of them go by around seven."

Josh looked excited. "Can you describe this vehicle?"

"Pickup, light colour. I can't tell you more. It was dark, and it looked like half the trucks around here."

"That's very helpful, Bert." Josh paused to study his notes.

Hannah had been listening quietly, thinking he wasn't doing a half-bad job, but now she grabbed her chance to jump in. "Have you ever seen that truck before?"

"Well, to be honest, I thought it was that young fella's truck. The one that died. He had a small pickup, probably white but now more rust than paint."

"Where did he park it?"

"Well, on the hill there, at the old farm." Bert hesitated. "I actually drove by there later that morning, still worrying about that dog, and the truck was gone. So I figured he'd gone. Maybe taken the dog to the vet. Surprised the heck out of me when I heard he was dead."

Josh was alert again. "Did you see any signs of activity around the property? Anyone on foot or in another vehicle?"

Bert's eyes twinkled again. "I don't spend all my time watching my neighbours, you know."

Josh waited, pencil poised, and the man's face fell. "Nope. Maybe one of the neighbours saw something more, but I wouldn't count on it."

Josh closed his notebook and headed back outside. "You've been a big help, Bert. Thank you for your time."

Bert stood on the veranda, watching them wistfully as they climbed back into the car. As Hannah studied the lines of sight one last time, she caught a glimpse of the river gliding under the bridge. She pointed. "Did you ever see a red canoe go by down there? Either that night or any other time?"

Bert frowned. "Nope."

"Sedge never took that red canoe out?"

"I fish off that bridge sometimes, never seen it. Don't even know if it floats. It's been there forever."

"Mike, I'm coming into the city this afternoon. Can we grab dinner somewhere?"

Green felt a quickening of excitement, followed by dismay when he glanced at his calendar. It was going to be a long, complicated day, spent stickhandling a court appearance by a known drug kingpin who'd already arranged the death of one witness and terrified several others. Green longed for a relaxing evening sharing a couple of beers and catching up with an old friend. Besides, he was dying to know why Vickers wanted to meet.

But tonight was Sharon's long shift at work, and he was in charge of dinner, homework, and all the unexpected domestic crises that invariably cropped up.

"I've got home duty, Vick, sorry. Rain cheque tomorrow?"

"Can't. I've got an audience with your old pal Alex MacPhail this afternoon to get the goods on Sedgwick's post-mortem. Can you spare half an hour for a beer before your house duty?"

Green winced. The drop-dead deadline for picking up Aviva from the sitter was five thirty. By then, both children would be starving. "If you can stand the company of a six-year-old and a twelve-year-old, come for dinner. Casual, burgers on the barbeque. It's a nice, warm evening. We can sit outside and talk afterward. I've even got a decent selection of beer."

Vickers chuckled. "You're the only guy I know with one foot on the retirement path and the other managing a six-year-old. Jesus! I'm tired just thinking about it."

Green bristled. Why was everyone suddenly mentioning the R-word? Vickers was at least five years older than him, and he was still in the traces. "Hey, I'm not heading out to pasture just yet. So what's the verdict? Six o'clock?"

Vickers arrived at two minutes after six and followed the sounds of laughter and chatter around to the backyard. Despite Green's promise of beer, he was carrying a bottle of Spanish red and an ice cream cake from Dairy Queen. Aviva and Tony danced with delight. They kept the conversation light during the dinner, but once the children disappeared inside to watch TV, Vickers poured them both another glass of wine. To Green's dismay, he looked as if he were settling in for a long, increasingly drunken evening of reminiscences.

He tried a not-so-subtle hint. "Are you still living out in Smiths Falls?"

"Nearby. We bought a property on Big Rideau Lake." Vickers winked. "Even I'm retirement-planning."

"That's what? An hour's drive?"

"Bit more." He chuckled. "Don't worry, I'm staying at my sister's tonight. She's not far from here." He leaned back in the patio chair, propped his feet on a stool, and shook his head. "Man, you and I have seen some strange cases."

Green tamped down his impatience. He wanted to hear what Vickers had to say, but he knew he had at most an hour before he had to get Aviva ready for bed.

"What did MacPhail have to say?"

"Sad thing. Three wounds from the axe; two to the head and one to the left shoulder, but none of them were fatal right away. He was still alive when he was buried, although almost certainly unconscious."

Green ran through the scene in his mind. The killer was clumsy or in a hurry. Did they know their victim was still alive? Did they care? Had they panicked and just wanted to get away? "So what was the cause of death?"

"Cerebral haemorrhage from the blow to the side of his head. But it would have been a slow bleed, maybe over three or four hours. He had some cannabis in his system, and we found a small stash in the cabin. Personal-use stuff."

"Enough to impair his reflexes?"

"Not likely."

"Estimated time of death?"

"More or less what we figured. We don't have the entomologist's report yet, but based on rigor at the time of discovery and decomposition, and given the warm temperatures and insulation, MacPhail figures three days before he was found."

"Day? Night? Any clues about that? It could give us a more exact time frame."

"He was dressed in jeans and tee, so he hadn't gone to bed. But he was a student, and you know what they're like. Gibbs told me your theory about being ambushed at night, and it makes sense. We're probably looking at somewhere between eleven p.m. Tuesday night and five a.m. Wednesday morning. Of course, no one's going to swear to that in court, but it gives us a range for checking alibis."

Green sipped his wine in silence, giving Vickers time to broach what was actually on his mind. All this information could have been passed on to Josh Kanner as the official liaison, or even directly to Gibbs. There was something else. Vickers fidgeted, topped up his glass, and watched two squirrels fighting over the bird feeder. Through the patio screen door, Green could hear Aviva screaming at her brother. Pumpkin time was nearing.

"There's more," he nudged finally.

Vickers pursed his lips. "I decided it would be wiser to pass this one to you rather than to Kanner. It's tricky. Violation of confidentiality is involved, and maybe conflict of interest. Sergeant Paulsen paid me an unofficial visit to pass on some information she was privy to, as supervising officer, that she thought had a bearing on the case. Maybe not so much my case as yours."

Green frowned at him. "You mean the McAuley homicide?"

Vickers nodded. "It's more background than actual evidence, but since the two cases are probably linked, I told her I'd figure out a way to tip the Ottawa team off. Outside official channels."

"Ah. You mean me. I'm supposed to dance around privacy violations and conflicts of interest?"

"Do you want this information or not?"

Green waited.

Vickers gazed into his glass. "There's a women's shelter in Burritts Rapids — that's a little village on the Rideau River, not far from Kemptville. The shelter is not a big place, only a few beds. Most of its clients are local, from the farms and villages in the area, but they sometimes get the overflow from bigger centres farther away, if there are no available beds in the Ottawa shelters, for example."

Green sucked in his breath, knowing what was coming.

"There's a lot of domestic violence in rural communities, where women are isolated and don't have a lot of escape options. During the pandemic, a lot of it was kept hidden behind closed doors because women didn't even have a safe way to call for help. But the pressure really built up in families, so Ottawa got hit with more calls this past winter than they could handle. In rural areas there are fewer outside resources available to women, so at this shelter in Burritts Rapids, an officer from the Prescott detachment sometimes acts as an unofficial resource to the shelter. Generally, there's no conflict between her role as support and her role as law enforcement officer. She's there to protect women and to help them with legal procedures and how the police can help. At the moment, the contact is a young constable who takes her role seriously. She's taken a special interest in the clients, especially those with children. When the Sedgwick murder occurred and it was clear it was

connected to the McAuley one, she went to Annette —
Sergeant Paulsen — with an ethical dilemma."

Vickers paused and cocked his head. "You knew this,
didn't you?"

"We all had a gut instinct something was going on,
but we could find no hospital or police reports, or re-
quests for help. So this ticks off one of our boxes. Did
the wife go?"

He nodded. "She did, with her son and daughter,
just after Christmas. They spent four days in the shelter, participating in counselling and learning about their
options."

Green held up his hand. "Okay, let me take it from
here. You've told me enough for us to pick it up from
here, without having to violate confidentiality any further. And without any further breach of trust."

CHAPTER TWENTY-THREE

"Brian, I've been thinking about the McAuley-Sedgwick connection. We assume the motive for killing Sedgwick was because he knew who killed McAuley, or at least the killer was afraid he knew something. But the motive for the McAuley homicide is much murkier."

"Is this going somewhere, Mike? It's after ten o'clock."

Green glanced at his watch. Vickers had finally stumbled off into an Uber, leaving Green alone in the backyard as the warm, velvety night slowly enveloped him. The murmur of distant traffic mingled with the rustle and chirp of the night creatures. He realized now that he should have left this call until the sober second thought of morning.

"Yeah, it's going somewhere," he replied irritably, "but I'll spare you the preamble. You guys had no luck finding any reports or evidence of abuse and no luck at the Ottawa shelters, right? But the pandemic changed lots of things. Social distancing and closures affected capacity in a lot of the local shelters. Have you checked farther afield? Maybe some of the smaller shelters in rural areas?"

Silence. Then, "Where the hell is this coming from?"

Green dodged that. "It makes sense, right? It's worth a shot."

"And I suppose you have an idea how to check them out? They're not going to tell us any more than the local ones do, and I've got no inside contacts out there."

"But there may be ways to get at it, maybe through correspondence on Kristina's phone or laptop? Through her search history or the GPS on the Lexus? There's also the therapist her daughter mentioned. There should be some trace of them in her records as well. I've been thinking about that secret bank account and the unknown device. I bet she was setting up an escape plan. That's what the domestic abuse help lines and shelter counsellors would have advised her. Find that mystery device and you may have your way in."

"Okay." Sullivan's tone was softer. "I'll discuss it with Gibbs first thing in the morning. He's got a young woman on his squad who's good with tech stuff. Being a woman would be a bonus, too."

"What, not Kanner?"

Sullivan chuckled. "Hardly. This will help to keep the peace in the squad room, too."

"All you need is a small chink to confirm the abuse theory, then I bet someone will talk. Her friends, his colleagues … This may be deeply hidden, but she has to have confided in someone."

"Well, it's possible her family knows and have been helping behind the scenes, maybe for years. They deny it, but —"

"Of course they would. This would be an internal family matter, and remember, they don't trust the police." A mosquito whined in Green's ear, and he batted it away absently as he considered Sullivan's idea. "What tipped you off?"

"The father has been borrowing money from McAuley for years and building up quite a debt, but it doesn't show in his lifestyle. He withdraws money in regular cash payments that vanish into thin air."

Green turned the information over thoughtfully. "But they don't show up in Kristina's secret bank account?"

"Not in such large amounts, although there may be other secret accounts."

"How long has this been going on?"

"As far as we can tell from Ted's records, ever since he inherited the company. We did wonder if McAuley Senior was into something illegal and the payments were bribes to ensure loyalty. But we've found nothing else suspicious, and short of getting our forensic accountants to plough through all the company records, we've got nothing to go on. And Ramon Ramirez won't tell us a thing."

"Any chance it could be money to purchase drugs? Have you checked out Luis Ramirez?"

"First thing we did. If he's dealing, he's keeping a really low profile. No one has any intel on him."

Green was silent, remembering the outrage and shame Ramon had displayed when he discovered his son was hanging out with the drug crowd. Remembering something else, too.

Sullivan broke into the silence. "What?"

"I have something I'd like to check out."

"Mike …"

Green ignored the warning tone. The door creaked behind him as Sharon opened it to let the dog out. She looked at him through the darkness and raised an eyebrow. Green shrugged, and she withdrew. "Leave this with me for now," he said, watching Modo hobble across the yard. "Here's something else to think about. If Kristina's secret bank account was part of her escape plan, it looks like her husband found out about it. He transferred all the money out and shut down the account. Didn't you tell me that was less than a week before he died?"

Sullivan spoke quietly. "In fact, it was the same day as the 911 call that Hannah took. I should have seen that connection before."

Hannah flung herself onto her back and stared at the patterns of light cast on the ceiling by the street lamp on the corner. It was 3:00 a.m., the blackest depths of night, and she'd been woken by yet another dream about the job. This time she was responding to an urgent 911 call, but she couldn't find the address. Each turn and new street took her deeper and deeper into a suburban maze where the houses had no numbers and the street lights cast pale, useless haloes on the pavement. The 911 call kept repeating, more and more frantic. Where was her partner? Why couldn't he read the goddamn map?

Someone was going to die and all because their computer GPS was down.

Her racing heart had finally woken her, and she'd gone to the kitchen for a glass of milk, resisting the urge to add a shot of Baileys. She'd spent most of her teens managing the struggles in her life with drugs and alcohol, and she knew how seductive but dangerous they were. She'd get through this with willpower.

She lay on her back, working her way through the dream. It didn't take a shrink to know what it was about: her failure as a cop. From the moment that first McAuley call came in, she had made one awful mistake after another. In her naïveté she had poked her nose into the family's fragile equilibrium, potentially putting Kristina at risk and, who knows, possibly precipitating the husband's murder. Then, with one colossal slip-up, she had revealed the existence of Sedge and probably signed his death warrant.

What else could it be? Why else would Sedge have been murdered if not for his connection to the McAuley family? He was a shy, harmless young man with a tender heart for animals and an obsessive passion for ducks. He did not deserve that terrifying end.

Her life had always been one long series of screwups. And just when she hoped she'd finally got herself on the right path, along comes the worst screw-up yet. She knew she should step back from the investigation completely, possibly even policing itself, before any more lives were lost. But the very thought made her angry. She was better than this. She had the brains and the instincts to do better — many of the breakthroughs in the case had been due to her — and it angered her to be defeated by her own clumsy missteps.

She could make this right. She *had* to make this right. There were still avenues to explore and leads to follow up that wouldn't put anyone at risk. The mystery of Sedge's truck, for example. His missing electronics. And most important of all, how the killer had found him.

How could she get herself back on the case? When Josh dropped her off at her apartment after the day in Spencerville, he'd said nothing about another trip. He hadn't even suggested they grab a bite to eat after the long day. He'd pulled up to the curb and turned to her with a smile.

"I bet that was a whole lot more fun than a day on patrol."

She'd said nothing, wondering whether that was a hint of a put-down.

He nudged further. "I guess detective work is in your blood."

Oh, here we go, she thought. *The lead-in to pump me about my father.* She shoved open the door. "If you have no curiosity, you are no use as a cop," she shot back just before she slammed the door.

Now she wondered if she'd been too hard on him. He hadn't made a pass at her, hadn't even hinted at a pass, and he hadn't mentioned her father at all until that last minute. But he had thought enough of her to suggest to Bob Gibbs that she go with him on his fishing expedition down to Spencerville.

As thanks, she'd given him little but grief. She'd had enough experiences with shit men that they were now all guilty until proven innocent, and the burden of proof was high.

All this kept her tossing and turning most of the night, but by the time her early-morning alarm went off, she had a plan. Her regular day shift would end early enough for her to jog, shower, and still be ready for an after-dinner drink at a pub. The heat of the day would have given way to the soft, oblique light of evening. Perfect for a patio.

She debated between a phone call and text before deciding on the latter. Text allowed her to be simple and direct. *Hey, just wondering if there's been any follow-up on our leads. Free for a drink at the Heart and Crown on Preston? Eight?*

Her phone chirped less than ten minutes later while she was unlocking her motorcycle. *How about Churchill's rooftop pub instead? Richmond Road.*

A tingle of excitement ran through her. That was fast. A good sign. He'd counteroffered, but she could live with that. Churchill's was a classier choice, anyway, and right near her apartment.

That evening, he was already there when she arrived — another good sign — and he'd chosen a quiet corner table overlooking the street. He smiled and stood up as she walked over. Good God, was there no end to the class?

"Have you eaten? I haven't, so I asked them to bring menus."

The silence felt awkward and uncertain as they both studied the menus. She ordered a burger and a pint of

Beau's, and when he ordered the same thing, she paused. Had he done that on purpose? Was he buttering her up? *Give it a rest, Pollack!*

When their beers arrived, he lifted his mug in a mock toast. "To a great investigative team."

She laughed. "Yeah, it was a fun day." She sipped. "Anything new on it?"

"You're dying to know, aren't you?"

"Hey, half those brilliant ideas were mine." She paused, her eyes on his. Amazing eyes, like a restless sea or a deep forest. *Down, girl.* "Yes. Patrol can be pretty boring."

"So is detective work a lot of the time, believe me. But there have been a couple of interesting developments. First off, on the vehicles. We've been able to identify the vehicle Sedge was using down in Spencerville. Another graduate student rented him his truck while he was away in Costa Rica. It's an old dump of a thing, so the price was right and it suited his needs. As Bert Collins said, mostly rust and mud, but underneath that, a 1996 Chevy Silverado. White."

"Have the OPP found it yet?"

He shook his head. "But here's where it gets interesting. Kristina McAuley's Lexus is still impounded, so she couldn't have driven it down to Spencerville, but her father lent her his vehicle to use in the meantime. And guess what it is?" He paused, his eyes dancing. "A white F-150."

"Wow! Did Ident take tire treads? Transfer material?"

He grinned at her. "That's the next step. It's a joint coordination with the OPP, but yeah, it would be super exciting to match the tire treads and soil samples from that vehicle to the farmer's field."

"Are you involved?"

"No, just the Ident teams." Their food arrived, and they took a minute to dig into their burgers. As he chewed, his expression sobered. "I haven't been doing much of interest right now. Following up on neighbourhood interviews and combing through tips. I wanted to go back down to Spencerville to talk to the locals like we discussed, but Gibbs says that's the OPP's turf. Sedge is not our case, and I shouldn't tread on their toes."

A couple arrived at the next table and settled down with a flurry of laughter and scraping chairs. Josh scowled and lowered his voice. "There's another line of inquiry that's just opened up, but I'm not part of that either. The sergeant got a tip to check out-of-town women's shelters, and he tracked down one in Burritts Rapids. That's a tiny village in the middle of the country just inside the Grenville catchment area. Anyway, he went down there this morning to meet with them personally to see what he could learn. I wanted to go, but instead he took the female detective in the squad."

"Well, that makes sense. Two male cops showing up to ask questions about one of their clients, especially if she's a suspect in her husband's death — that's not going to go down well. When women murder their husbands, it's most often because they have endured awful abuse and they fear for their lives, but that doesn't always get them much of a break in our court system, so they don't trust cops much."

He shrugged. "I know that. But I know the case. I've talked to the players. Sam's done nothing but work the computer behind the scenes, checking bank and electronic records. Besides, she's not the most sensitive person. The sergeant would be better off with you!"

She was startled and, to her embarrassment, her face reddened. "Maybe someday," she muttered. "How did they do?"

"As you'd expect, they got nowhere. Not even an admission that Kristina had been at the shelter, let alone the circumstances. The director was polite but firm. Confidentiality laws. No warrant, no info. She talked in generalities about the services they provide, but that was it. Counselling, financial advice, liaison with other helping agencies, assistance to develop a plan, blah, blah, blah. All public knowledge."

Hannah was barely listening anymore. Her thoughts raced ahead to other possibilities. Should she suggest that she and Josh try again together, or would she be better off approaching someone at the shelter on her own, without a man to rouse their defences?

"Did Sergeant Gibbs have a Plan B? How else to get the information?"

"From friends and neighbours, and from Kristina directly if he has to. I'll try to get myself assigned to go with him, but he'll probably take Sam again." He picked a couple of her sweet potato fries. "Sorry, are you finished with these?"

"Whatever. So no warrants? No court orders?"

He shook his head. "He thinks there aren't sufficient grounds, and, anyway, the optics suck. He says we want to work with these agencies, not come in with jackboots."

Subtlety almost always works better than jackboots, she thought, but said nothing as a plan slowly took shape in her mind. A plan that would go some way toward making things right.

CHAPTER TWENTY-FOUR

The morning sun was just washing the Ottawa River in pink when Hannah parked her bike around the corner and snuck up the street toward the McAuley house. Birds flitted from tree to tree in a chorus, but the only people out were dog walkers. She spotted the white truck in the driveway from a block away but waited until she was at Philip Walker's house, shielded by the thick cedar hedge, before she took pictures — several photos from the side and more from the back. She would have liked some of the front grill but didn't dare trespass on Philip's property. The truck was old but clean, with traces of rust around the wheel wells. The only distinguishing mark was a stylized black *RR* logo on the front doors, with *Contracting* in small letters.

Since she had a long day ahead, she could not afford to hang around, but she took a minute to study the house. As she expected, the blinds were drawn. The expensive boat was still at the side, but a couple of kayaks were missing. Sold? She wondered if the high-end bikes were also gone. The house looked peaceful. It was hard to believe two brutal murders had been linked to this luxurious home.

She tucked her phone away and hurried back to her motorcycle. Within less than ten minutes, she was on the open highway, heading out of town. She had the day off until the graveyard shift, and she planned to use it well. The trip to Burritts Rapids took just over half an hour, cruising through the crisp, early-morning sunlight. Nearly two hundred years ago, the village had sprung up around one of the locks on the Rideau River, and it straddled the river. In its prime, it had served the bustling river trade of barges and steamboats, but now it was mainly a countrified bedroom community for Ottawa.

Like with all emergency women's shelters, the exact address of the Burritts Rapids shelter was not public knowledge but was known to police. Hannah had dressed in casual civilian clothes and had not phoned ahead. She didn't plan to conceal her identity but hoped her lack of formality would soften resistance.

She parked her motorcycle down the street and sat watching the house for some time, choosing her moment and her line of approach. After fifteen minutes, a woman in her forties emerged, strode briskly to her car, and accelerated away like a woman on a mission. Like the boss.

Perfect, Hannah thought as she eased her motorcycle into gear.

The shelter was a rambling, two-storey clapboard house tucked into one of the back streets. A faded plaque at the gate labelled it a heritage structure originally built in 1872 as a hotel, but it had obviously gone through a lot since then. Flowers and vegetable gardens brightened up the outside, and the vibrant yellow door was welcoming, but Hannah noticed the stonework at the base was crumbling and the paint on the window trim peeling. Signs of an ongoing struggle for funding.

There was no one out front, although Hannah heard the chatter of children behind the fence and saw a couple of strollers parked by the front door. She took off her helmet, put on her mask, and headed up the front walk, scanning the surroundings for cameras or other security equipment. She could see none but was sure her every move was being scrutinized.

Sure enough, before she could ring the bell, the door opened and a young woman stepped outside. Her expression was neutral. "Can I help you?"

Hannah kept her notebook out of sight but flashed her badge wallet. "Hi, I'm Hannah Pollack of the Ottawa Police. What a peaceful place this is."

The woman eyed the motorcycle, and a faint frown flickered across her face. "What's this about?"

"I'm not here to cause trouble to you or to any of the residents. I'm trying to confirm …" Hannah paused and took a deep breath. "Have you got a few minutes? I want to tell you a story."

"Well, I'm not really the one to talk to. Our director deals with the police."

"Is she here?"

The young woman hesitated before shaking her head.

"I'll only take a bit of your time. Please. Maybe we could sit over there?"

The woman glanced reluctantly around the front yard. Gardens and children's toys took up most of the space, but in the corner by the fence, in the shade of a spreading maple tree, sat a pair of lawn chairs six feet apart. She led the way toward them, and Hannah smiled as she sat down and took off her mask.

"Thanks, I appreciate this. Can you tell me your name?"

"Holly. I don't have much time. What's this story?"

"I'm a rookie patrol officer. I've only been with the police service for five months. I didn't have the easiest childhood, I spent some time on the streets, and I had my share of run-ins with the law. It made me want to do better, to be a police officer who helped people instead of hassling them."

Holly was still perched on the edge of her chair, but at least she was listening.

"On patrol, I was partnered with this old-school cop who's putting in his time to retirement. He's seen it all. Don't get me wrong, he's good at his job, but it's mostly *deal with the call and move on*. Don't get involved, don't go looking for trouble. About six weeks ago, we got a report from a neighbour about a disturbance at a wealthy suburban house. When we got there, the husband met us at the door, all smiles, nothing to worry about, that neighbour overreacts, maybe because he just lost his wife, so go easy on him. The guy's a lawyer that my partner knows, so he doesn't push hard. The wife won't talk to us alone, but she confirms the husband's story. I broke something in the kitchen. Nothing to see here. No visible injuries, no cause for concern. My partner writes it up as unfounded and moves on, but something bugs me. Something in the woman's eyes, and in the fear the dog shows —"

Holly started. She hid it quickly, but Hannah suspected she knew where this was going.

"So I did some follow-up. Talked to neighbours and to the wife again without the husband present. I got nowhere, but I still had this knot in my gut. My best friend on the streets — her mother was killed by her stepfather. I had a gut feeling this woman was abused and was too trapped or terrified to do anything but endure. You know the drill. Maybe, if I try really hard and am really, really good, he won't hurt me next time. I think lots of people knew, including her family, but they protected him. He had all the status and money, how could it be that bad? And because of this secrecy, because of this denial, now two people are dead. One is the husband, and I don't lose too much sleep over that, but the second one, just a few days ago, was an innocent young man who loved animals and was doing his doctorate on birds not far from here."

Holly blinked. Her body went rigid as she tried not to react.

Hannah softened her voice. "I don't know who's responsible, but it's a terrible thing and I feel like I have to know what happened to him. I found his body. It will haunt me forever. The idea that if I'd pushed harder in the beginning, then maybe this abuse would have been stopped and this young man would not have ended up murdered."

Holly swallowed. "That body they found down in Spencerville … That's connected to …?"

"To the McAuley case? Yes. To whatever she and her kids went through. She was here, wasn't she?"

"I can't say."

"Okay, you don't have to say. I know she was here. I want to know if her husband found her here. If he came here and dragged her back home, and that's when she knew there was no escape."

"No, it wasn't —"

"Wasn't what?"

"Like that. She left of her own accord."

A crack in the wall! Hannah moved in fast. "She must have been threatened."

Holly shook her head. "Not that way. She decided it was best. Her little boy couldn't handle it; he cried and screamed for three days straight. He was scared for his dog — they had to leave the dog at home. He trashed the room, and when he started banging his head, something the mother said he hadn't done in months, she said they had to go back. I don't blame her, really. I've seen kids traumatized by abuse, but this kid was off the scale."

"I believe he's on the spectrum."

Holly was just warming up, all her doubts erased in her rush of feeling. "Maybe, but the counsellor we called in said she's seen this sometimes in very young kids, kids who can't talk yet, who've experienced prolonged abuse or terror. Refugee kids in war zones, for example. Anyway, we tried to persuade the mother to stay and get help for the little boy, but in the end …" She shrugged. "It's their call. They have to be ready, and sometimes we see women come back six, ten times before they finally make the permanent move. We helped her as best we could, discussed making an escape plan and set up follow-up counselling …"

A bell went off in Hannah's head. "Did you give her the name of a counsellor?"

"The one we always use. The appointments were virtual, but she has an office in Kemptville."

"Name?"

Holly pressed her lips tight and shook her head. "I better not. But she knows her stuff. The daughter was pushing her really hard, but the mother wasn't ready yet."

"Wait a minute, the daughter was here, too?"

"Yes, all three of them arrived the day after Christmas. The daughter tried to help with the little boy, and she was very angry when Mom gave in. She did not want to go back."

"So how did they go back? Did she call her husband? A taxi?"

Maybe realizing she'd gone too far, Holly whipped her head back and forth. She plucked a dandelion and began to shred the flower petals. "I've said enough. More than I should. She was a good mother. A kind woman."

"I don't doubt that, Holly. I've gotten to know her since this all started. I know how hard she's been trying."

"I should go." Holly shifted in her seat as if to flee, but instead she twirled the tattered dandelion. "This young student you mentioned, why was he killed?"

"We think he witnessed something or knew something about Mr. McAuley's death."

Holly picked a new dandelion. "But you don't know who killed Mr. McAuley?"

Sensing something was holding Holly back, Hannah risked a little nudge. "Do you?"

"No! But it could have been someone else, right?"

"Like who?"

Holly shook her head. She shredded the second dandelion as the story came out in reluctant bursts. One of the residents had witnessed something while she was out on a walk. When Kristina was leaving, the shelter offered to drive the family back to Ottawa, but she said she'd already arranged a lift. The next morning, a man drove into the village and stopped at the end of the street. Shelter staff were horrified because no one was supposed to know the address. The resident said Kristina and the man embraced. When the resident came back from her walk, she told the staff Kristina had a boyfriend. *That girl's playing with fire*, she said, *and it's going to blow up in her face.*

Hannah was on high alert. "She was sure it wasn't the husband?"

"Kristina didn't act like it was. The daughter was furious, because she didn't want to go home, but Kristina looked happy. Not at all afraid."

"Any idea who it was?"

"None of the staff saw him. The resident said he was youngish and dark-haired."

"Vehicle?"

"A pickup."

* * *

As Hannah walked back to her motorcycle, her head was spinning. This was big! Was there a boyfriend? Had the secret bank and device been part of a plan not to escape abuse but rather to start a new life with her lover?

She knew she should pass this information directly on to Josh. The homicide team needed to know this. But Kemptville was on her way home — well, not really — but only a few minutes' drive. Perhaps she could find out about Kristina's counsellor at the same time. The town only had a few thousand people, so how many counsellors could there be?

She fed a few search words into Google and came up with a short list, but only three were women, and one of them specialized in children and another in geriatrics. Her gut told her that most victims of spousal abuse would be uncomfortable confiding in a man.

Elena Markos listed herself as an M.S.W. specializing in family therapy and trauma counselling, which seemed perfect. Only a phone number was provided, but a little backdoor hunting yielded an address, which Hannah plugged into her GPS before setting off.

The address turned out to be in the middle of a modern retail business park, cheek by jowl with a Canadian Tire, Giant Tiger, and Tim Hortons. It was an unobtrusive door on a windowless brick wall around the corner from a wellness centre advertising massage and beauty treatments. There was no name or business plaque on the black door, only a simple doorbell and a mailbox beside the door. Hannah looked inside the mailbox, but it contained nothing but faded flyers. *This must be the place*, she thought, and pressed the bell. No answer. She looked up. There were windows on the second floor, which she assumed were business and administrative offices. Elena Markos must be in one of those, but she sure kept a low profile.

She rang again and pressed her ear to the door, but there was no sound from within. Frustrated, she walked around the corner to the wellness centre. As she entered, a wall of conflicting scents hit her: nail polish, remover, and floral perfumes. A woman behind Plexiglas in the corner was having a pedicure, and another woman was sitting at the reception desk, working on the computer. She looked up with excitement as Hannah crossed the room.

Hannah had never been big on beauty treatments. She trimmed her own long hair with a pair of kitchen shears and dyed it whatever colour suited her mood over the bathroom sink. It used to be goth black, but as her mood lightened, so did her hair colour. Right now, it was mostly her natural honey brown with a secret streak of neon green. Her nails were short and plain, and her makeup was minimal. She'd gone through a stage of piercing every possible part of her body but had given them all up except three studs in each ear.

The woman at reception, on the other hand, had never met a trend she didn't want to try. She had swirling tattoos all down both arms and around her wrists, nails that glittered with multicoloured fake stones, black eyelashes at least an inch long, and a see-through mask that showed off the reddest lipstick Hannah had ever seen. She was a walking rainbow.

Hannah could see her sizing her up, counting dollar signs. The name tag on her hot-pink uniform said Tasha.

"Hello!" Those red lips parted in a big smile, revealing a red smear on her teeth. "You're new here. What can I do for you today?"

Hannah glanced around at the array of beauty products. Creams, polishes, every kind of makeup and fake hair extension. She did a quick calculation on how to get the woman's co-operation and decided, in the interest of detective work, she'd better submit to a manicure.

Tasha seated her at one of the booths along the wall and picked up one of her hands. "Oh my," she murmured.

"Yeah, well …" Hannah shrugged. "It's been a while."

"We can work with this," Tasha said brightly. She waved to a wall of polishes behind her. "What colour do you want?"

Hannah thought fast. She could just see the guys in the squad room if she turned up with sequins. "Maybe taupe?"

Tasha studied her and then plucked a bottle from the shelf. "How about smoky green? To bring out your eyes."

As Tasha worked, they chatted about Kemptville and Tasha's business, which was just sputtering back to life after the pandemic restrictions. "Have you just moved here?" Tasha asked her.

"No, I … I'm looking for Elena Markos, the therapist, but there's no answer at her address."

"Oh! Well …" Tasha eyed her shrewdly. "She's by appointment only, I think. She works, like, different places."

"Bummer." Hannah sighed. "I got her address from someone I know. I think she came to see her here. She said it was by a wellness centre."

"Yeah, well, that would be her."

"She sees women, right? Women who … are in trouble?"

"I suppose."

"Have you ever talked to her? Is she nice?"

Tasha scrubbed briskly. "I have nothing to do with her. She rents space upstairs, I rent this space. That's all."

"But you've seen … See, I'm worried about my friend. I don't know if she stopped getting help or even if she came here at all. But you see the women who … I mean —" Hannah took her free hand out of the soaking solution, dried it off, and fished her phone out of her pocket. She thumbed through photos. "Here. She might have come here with her kids."

Tasha frowned. "This is not something I'm comfortable with. Like, I don't even know you."

"I know, I know. I'm sorry. But I thought since they would park right outside, you might notice. I just want to know that she's safe. That she's getting help." She dropped her voice. "Please. We women have to stick up for each other." She held out the photo of Kristina. "Just look, will you? Tell me if you've seen her."

Tasha peered at the phone reluctantly. "Maybe. I don't know."

Hannah thumbed to a photo of the little boy. "This is her kid. He's three."

Tasha was shaking her head, so Hannah switched to Justine. Recognition flashed across Tasha's face. "This one, yeah. I've seen her a few times."

"Well, they would have been together."

"I don't think so. Not recently, anyway. I only ever saw her by herself. Actually, I saw her last week. She parked right out front like you said and went around the corner."

Hannah hid her excitement. "What car did she drive?"

"Pickup, light coloured."

"By herself? Or was someone with her?"

Tasha looked up from her task to give Hannah a suspicious look. "She got in the driver's seat, but there might have been someone with her. I couldn't tell for sure because of the sun's glare. Now, put your hand back in the solution if you really want me to save these nails. Or are you just here to pump me for information?"

Hannah laughed and dropped the interrogation. She had what she'd come for. Far more than she'd hoped for, in fact. And when she left the centre an hour later, with her glossy new green nails, she stood in the parking lot and noticed the businesses in the strip mall across the way. A fresh food store, a pet store, and, tucked into the corner of the strip, a credit union.

CHAPTER TWENTY-FIVE

On the ride back to Ottawa, Hannah debated what to do with the information she'd acquired. It was all unofficial, and probably unethical. She had not concealed her identity from the woman at the shelter, but she had definitely misled Tasha. Which was not really a crime but might make Tasha mad as hell and unlikely to co-operate with the cop who followed up.

She had half a dozen more questions she wanted to ask and ideas she wanted to explore. She didn't want to be stopped in her tracks by an official order or reprimand. To be able to get those answers, she needed to continue flying under the radar. She was dying to run her ideas by her father and mine his experience, but she knew even he would forbid her from continuing.

Josh might be her best option, and he seemed willing to include her in the investigation. She knew he had his own agenda, but who cared? So did she.

Back home, she was just changing into her jogging clothes and wondering how to contact Josh when he phoned. "Telepathy," she said, quelling a small thrill that ran through her. "I was just about to call you. I have news."

"So it *was* you."

"What?"

"A very pissed off director of Amity Shelter in Burritts Rapids phoned the boss this afternoon. Not my boss, but the big boss, Staff Sergeant Sullivan. She said one of his detectives had shown up unannounced, without clearing it with her, and taken advantage of one of her junior staff. That staffer knew she'd disclosed too much confidential material and confessed to the director."

"Did she have the detective's name?"

"No, the staffer didn't remember it. Too flustered. But she described you to a T."

Hannah felt a quiver. "Did you tell Sullivan it was me?"

"Are you kidding? And drop myself into it, too? But I think he knows. I expect you'll be getting a call soon. I'm not sure from who, but this is a heads-up."

Hannah thought fast. What would Brian Sullivan do? He'd known her for years and had been her rock when things were really rough with her father. There was a love and a loyalty there, not just to her but also to her father.

The silence lengthened. Finally, Josh broke it. "So? Did you learn anything interesting?"

Irritation piqued her. Her career was potentially in crisis, and he had thoughts only for the case. "Plenty. But I don't know how to tell you without both of us getting into deeper trouble."

"Well ..." He floundered, as she hoped he would. "I can follow up on whatever you tell me and get confirmation on my own."

"Oh, come on. They'll know it came from me."

"But you can't just sit on it. It's important to the case!"

Her phone buzzed, signalling another call. *Oh, shit.* Her father.

"Listen, Josh, I gotta go. We'll talk later."

Not ready to face him, she let her father's call go to voice mail and then listened to the message. *I'm on my way over. Don't go anywhere.*

Part of her was tempted to run downstairs and escape on her bike. Trying to stay one step ahead of trouble had been the story of her life, but she knew it wouldn't work in the long run. It never had.

So she fetched two Cokes from the fridge, grabbed a bag of chips, and waited for the buzzer.

When he strode in the door, his face was like a thundercloud. "First question. Did you do it?"

She held out a Coke, which he ignored. She shrugged, popped open her own, and strolled over to the couch, feigning calm and buying herself time. Once she was settled with her feet propped up, she looked at him.

"Yes."

He paced in a circle, swearing. "When are you going to learn to follow the rules?"

"When did you?"

"Don't make this about me. I've been a detective for more than twenty-five years. Experience is something you build. Credibility is something you earn. You are going to get yourself tossed out on your ear before your probation is up!"

"Did Brian Sullivan report me to my sergeant?"

"I don't know what Brian is going to do. First he has to patch things up with the shelter. We build trust in this job, Hannah, and with abused women, that trust is very fragile. He'll have to pretend you were an over-zealous rookie who only wanted to help. And you know what that will cost him. You know he hates any kind of deception."

"I am sorry about that. I didn't think it would blow up in his face."

He was still pacing, her tiny apartment no match for his fury. "What *did* you think, Hannah? Did you think about the consequences at all? To the investigation? To the court case? In this job, above all, you have to think ahead to what might be the result of your action. I'd have thought you learned that after the Sedge debacle."

She felt stung. She worked hard to keep her face calm and the sudden threat of tears hidden. She didn't dare look at him and waited until she trusted her voice. "It's because of Sedge that I'm doing this, Dad. I have to find out what happened. To know if I caused … if what I did …" She gripped her Coke can to control her shaking. "I've been in on this case since the beginning. From that first 911 call, when I knew she'd been abused and no one wanted to believe it. And I was right! Kristina McAuley did go to that shelter, she did start an escape plan, but she returned home because her son was having melt-downs. She gave up everything to keep him calm. She sacrificed her safety and her happiness so that her son could have the security of his routine."

He snatched up his drink and dropped into the chair opposite. He was as rigid and cold as a stone, but he was listening.

"But it turned out that she may have been wrong! The therapist she saw at the shelter thought the little boy's problems might have been caused by trauma, not autism. I'm no expert, so I don't know if that's possible, but somebody needs to talk to that therapist. I tracked down her name and her address — Elena Markos in Kemptville —"

He stiffened. "Please tell me you didn't speak with her, too?"

"No, she's available by phone only."

"She won't talk about a patient, anyway."

"But she might talk in hypotheticals, Dad. About the effects of prolonged trauma on small children."

Her father's eyes had narrowed thoughtfully. Hannah felt a rush of relief. If she could divert his natural instincts toward the puzzle of the case, he might be an ally instead of a furious father.

"It may affect how Kristina felt about the abuse," she added. "And I did learn a couple of useful things about her from the shelter."

She was about to embark on the possible boyfriend angle, but he was shaking his head. "Hannah, please. The investigative team knows what it's doing. Yes, they need to gather information, but they also have to build a case that stands up in court. Brian will go out on a limb for you, and if we're lucky, he may still be able to get some co-operation out of the shelter director."

"But —"

"Tell him what you know! Apologize to him, and for God's sake, stay the hell out of it!"

Her father had barely left the building when a motorcycle rumbled outside her window. When she peered out, she spotted Josh astride his Harley. He squinted into the setting sun as she came out the front door.

"I waited until your father left. Is he very pissed?"

She shrugged.

"Want to grab your bike and go for a ride?"

She glanced at the time on her phone. "I've got the graveyard shift. And I haven't eaten anything but potato chips since breakfast."

"So what are we waiting for? Grab your helmet and we'll take my bike."

It felt strange to be a passenger pressed up against Josh's warm back. She could feel the ripple of his muscles through his shirt as he leaned into the turns. His Harley throbbed with power, making her Honda feel like little more than a moped.

He pulled up outside the Clocktower Pub in Westboro, and they joined the throng of locals enjoying the late rays of summer sun on the patio. Bright red umbrellas lent a cheerful air. He picked a table in the corner.

"How did it go with your dad?"

"He'll forgive me."

"Did … did my name come up?"

She fixed him with a stony glare. Just when she thought maybe he was cute enough to date, he showed his true colours. "Your ass is safe."

He flushed. "Look, I just meant —"

"I know exactly what you meant. And I don't want to talk about it."

To make sure he got the point, she picked up her menu and was startled when he laughed.

"You've got green nails."

She spread her hand to study the nails. They really were kind of cool. Maybe if she added a black diagonal stripe ... "What we do for the job."

"Are you going to tell me anything that happened today?"

"I haven't decided."

He leaned forward and lowered his voice. "I told you stuff about the investigation that was in confidence. I thought you'd like to know, since you helped me the other day. But I didn't expect you to run with it and start investigating on your own!"

When she opened her mouth to protest, he held up a hand. "You didn't warn me, you left me exposed if they figure out I told you that stuff."

"I'm pretty sure they already know. At least my father does. He's pretty tight with Brian Sullivan."

He sat back in his chair. "Fuck."

"Nothing is going to happen. Brian Sullivan is going to handle it. Somehow."

"Okay, but you owe me. At least the courtesy of telling me what you learned."

The server breezed up, cutting off all conversation. Josh ordered beer and a steak sandwich. She hesitated. After that blowout with her dad, she could really use a beer, but she'd soon be sharing a patrol car with Rick for ten hours. As a consolation prize, she ordered mussels and fries with an iced tea.

"I don't think I owe you anything, Josh," she said once the server left. "We both made our own choices, and now we have to live with the fallout. That was my father's lecture for the day. But I will tell you, because …" She paused, and a slow smile stole across her face. "What I learned is gold."

She filled him in on Kristina's brief stay at the shelter and the mysterious boyfriend who picked her up. Young and dark-haired, Holly had said, which wasn't much to go on but suggested a whole other line of inquiry. Their food arrived, and she dug eagerly into her mussels, breaking up her story to take frequent bites.

"And the final discovery, while having these done," she said, flashing her nails, "was that Kristina may not have kept going to the therapist in Kemptville, but Justine did. And she came and went in a light-coloured pickup, possibly white."

Josh blinked. He chewed another french fry. "An awful lot of white pickups."

"At least two. The one Sedge drove and the one Kristina's father lent to her. I imagine that's the one Justine was driving."

"Unless Sedge picked her up."

Hannah considered that with surprise. It seemed a stretch. He would have had to drive all the way into Ottawa to pick her up and then back again to take her home. That was a lot of devotion, even for a dude with a serious crush.

"We don't know that they weren't in touch," Josh was saying. "We only have Justine's word for it, and she has good reason for denying it now that he's dead."

He toyed with his fries. "The OPP has some forensics back from the scene. The tire treads in the farm field above Sedge's cabin? They're all from the same tire brand and size — a light truck tire, a low-end Motomaster from Canadian Tire, worn to the point of bald, with lots of chips in them. Easy to ID."

"All the same truck?"

"That's what they think. Unless there's another truck with the same tire brand, size, and wear."

She frowned. "Sedge's truck?"

"Probably. The truck is twenty-five years old. They're trying to contact the truck owner to confirm, but he's in the Costa Rican cloud forest."

She turned this idea over. "So Sedge's was the only truck parked there."

"It's not definitive, of course. The ground could have been too dry for other prints."

"I thought about that. It rained three days before I found the body, so probably just before he died. The ground should have been wet."

He shrugged. "Maybe the killer parked on the road-side or in the grass. But there's something else. Forensics took soil samples from the tires of the Ramirez truck. That took a bit of paperwork and freaked out Kristina, but we gave her the usual 'to eliminate the truck from our inquiries' bullshit."

"And?"

"No joy. There was lots of trace dirt in the tires, but none matched that field. It's baby steps, but …"

"Leading nowhere." She turned the puzzle over in her head. How had the killer gotten to and from the murder scene? "Have the OPP found Sedge's truck?"

"Not yet. They're patrolling all the roads and even sent a drone overhead. But the country is a big place. People ditch unwanted things like fridges and bathtubs in the bush all the time."

She mopped up the last of the broth from her mussels while she considered the possibilities. As her blood sugar recovered, she began to feel better. He was beginning to look cute again, too. "Do you think you can wangle another trip down to Spencerville?"

"Probably. Why?"

"And can you get me invited along again?"

He met her gaze. "That might be pushing it. I want to have a future in this job. Going up against the staff sergeant and your father —"

She tamped down a snarky retort. *Maturity, Pollack.* "I don't want to go behind their backs. I'll be along because of what I know."

"Which is?"

She scowled. "The trucks business bugs the hell out of me. I keep thinking it might be the key. I'm off at seven a.m. tomorrow and the day after. Before we go, get a photo of Sedge's truck, or at least one of the exact year, model, and colour. I took some of the Ramirez truck. We're going on a hunt."

CHAPTER TWENTY-SIX

When they turned onto the road leading to Bert Collins's house, they spotted a cluster of OPP vehicles and trailers parked on the roadside near the bridge over the South Nation River. Hannah craned her neck and saw officers standing by the water's edge, surrounded by gear.

"I wonder what that's about."

Josh took his eyes off the road briefly. "Do you see a Zodiac or divers?"

"No, but there's a lot of bush in the way."

"We can check it out on our way back," he said as they headed up the hill toward Bert's place. They had called ahead to make sure he was there and found him standing on the veranda waiting for them with cups and a pot of coffee on the little wicker table. He wore a large straw hat against the deer flies.

"Want some?" he asked. "It's a fresh pot."

Hannah accepted with relief. After a full overnight shift, she had caught a quick nap in the cruiser but woke feeling like a limp rag. She had not been up for much small talk on the drive but had stayed awake long enough to ask how he'd worked his magic to get her invited along.

"Sergeant Gibbs was fine with it," Josh had said. "I'm guessing Sullivan didn't tell him about your shelter visit. He just said …" He trailed off.

"What?"

"Well, just that we make a good team."

"What did he mean by that?"

He shrugged. "He's a man of few words."

She had been mulling that over, wondering if there was locker room gossip about them, when her eyelids drifted shut, only to reopen when they exited the highway.

Now she chugged half the cup of Bert's coffee at one gulp, hoping to revive. It was weak and too sweet, but what the hell, it was caffeine. The three of them settled in the wicker chairs on the veranda.

"Have you remembered anything else about Drew Sedgwick or unusual vehicles since we spoke last?" Josh was asking. "Especially about the light truck you saw that night?"

Bert shook his head. Josh took out his phone and thumbed through some 1996 Silverados he'd taken off Autotrader. Hannah found her photos of the Ramirez truck and handed her phone to Josh.

"Do you recognize either of these vehicles?" Josh asked.

Bert took the phones into the shade of the veranda roof. "Hard to say. Pickup trucks look a lot alike from a distance, eh?"

"Is either of them the one you saw in the early hours of July third?"

Bert tapped Josh's phone. "Well, that looks like the kind of truck Sedge had. I've seen it lots of times. Not this exact truck; his was rusty and dirtier. Those fields get pretty muddy when it rains. But I think it's the one I saw that morning." He peered at the Ramirez truck on Hannah's phone. "Oh, well.... No, I don't think so."

"Have you seen that one any time in the past month? Visiting Sedge, maybe?"

Bert shook his head. "I never saw anybody visit Sedge."

Hannah came to stand beside him. "You notice it has a black logo on the door. *RR Contracting*. That would have been visible as it drove past your place."

Bert sighed. "It was still pretty dark. I don't think it was that one, but I couldn't swear to it in court. I know you guys need that. Sorry."

Josh retrieved the phones and stood up. "It's okay, Bert, don't worry. This is very helpful. Thanks for meeting us."

"No problem." Bert looked a little dismayed that they were leaving so soon.

Hannah paused and nodded toward the cluster of vehicles down by the bridge. "Do you know what that's about?"

Bert brightened. "Searching the river. Been there for two days. First they towed away that red canoe, and yesterday they brought in the divers." He squinted at the bridge. "I hope they're not looking for another body. Folks around here are getting a bit jumpy."

"No, nothing like that," Josh said. "There's no risk to the public. I'm sure the OPP has assured the community of that."

As they walked back to the car, Josh grunted. "Well, that was worth a try, but it didn't get us much further ahead."

"I think it did. He was leaning toward Sedge's truck. I think if it had been the Ramirez truck, he'd have noticed the *RR*. At four thirty-eight on the morning of July third, it was already lightening up."

"Like he said, 'leaning toward' won't cut it in a court of law."

She slammed the car door without replying. Did he have to point out the obvious, like she'd slept through the entire course on evidence? Like she hadn't listened to her father at endless dinner discussions? Instead, she turned her attention to the OPP officers scattered along the riverbank. Two Zodiacs had pulled up on the reedy shore, and several divers were clambering out. As they drove closer, she recognized a familiar figure in khakis and golf shirt.

"Oh look, there's Sergeant Vickers. Pull over."

Josh steered the car over behind the last OPP Interceptor, and they climbed out. Several officers moved to block them, but Vickers's face lit up at the sight of Hannah.

"What are you doing here?"

She gestured to Josh. "Helping out, Sergeant. You know Josh Kanner?"

Vickers looked from one to the other as if sizing up the relationship. "Kanner, how did you hear about this?"

"We were following up a lead and spotted your operation. Any luck with the hunt?"

Hannah eyed the stack of evidence bins on the grass and strolled over to see what they'd found. Much of it was so caked in mud that it was unrecognizable, but in one of the bins was an expensive-looking camera with a telephoto lens.

"You found his camera!"

Vickers looked about to reprimand her but thought better of it. He and Josh joined her. "We found *a* camera. We don't yet know if it was his." He turned to Josh. "When we get it cleaned up, I'll send you guys photos and specs of it — serial number if we can find one — and you can show it to his university colleagues."

"Maybe the photos inside will help," Josh said, "if the memory card isn't ruined."

"The camera is waterproof, so the tech guys should be able to get something."

Hannah bent over to peer at the camera. She knew almost nothing about cameras, but even she could see it had a lot of settings and adjustments. Not a camera for your average point-and-shoot tourist. "So whoever got rid of the camera, they didn't know it was waterproof. I bet they were trying to get rid of evidence."

"Yup," Vickers said. "Makes me think it probably is Sedgwick's. The water was not too deep, so if you lost an expensive camera overboard, you'd probably try to retrieve it."

Josh scanned upstream, where another Zodiac bobbed in the water. "Any luck finding his laptop or phone?"

Vickers shook his head. "We've been on this river two days, covered it for a kilometre on either side of the cabin with sonar and divers. It's amazing the crap people dump in the water. We found a whole washing machine down there! Bikes, tires, beer bottles, you name it. But no devices. They're heavy, so they're not going to drift far in the current. We found the camera only a hundred yards from the cabin. I think our man was in a hurry to get away, so he didn't go far to ditch the stuff. Especially if it was dark."

Josh had pulled on a nitrile glove and was poking at the camera carefully. "No corrosion or bleaching."

Vickers peered over his shoulder. "Yeah, it hasn't been down there long. And Hannah's right. Unless we assume Sedgwick was killed for his obscure research findings on ducks, I think the killer was afraid there was something incriminating on it. Same reason we're not going to find the laptop or phone. They'll be smashed into a thousand pieces and buried in the garbage."

Hannah was studying the camera, which was large and probably heavy. The killer had to go back up the path to the truck on foot, carrying the laptop and God knows what else. He had rummaged through Sedge's backpack and left only the clothes.

"Did you find any other personal items like his wallet?" she asked. "Or a datebook?"

Vickers nodded to another evidence bin with a soggy black mass in it. "We think that bag may be his. It was weighted down with stones, so we'll get it to the lab and see what turns up."

"Any luck finding his truck?"

Vickers shook his head as he started back up the slope toward the vehicles. The sun was high overhead now, and even with the breeze ruffling the river, the heat was stifling. Deer flies zoomed in circles. "We've had patrols on every country road and lane around," Vickers said, waving them away. "We brought in helicopters, and we even sent drone cameras overhead. We've interviewed up the wazoo. Lots of people saw Sedge's truck coming and going, but none of them have seen it around since the murder. My guess is the killer ditched it farther away."

The puzzle of the two vehicles still bugged the hell out of Hannah, but before she could voice her concern, Josh spoke.

"Do you mind if we poke around ourselves? Since we're down here?"

Vickers climbed into his car. "Knock yourselves out."

They cruised around the countryside, speaking to locals on nearby properties and on the streets of Spencerville. They scanned the parking lots and roadsides for dirty white trucks, but after three hours they headed home, tired, hungry, and discouraged.

And without a single lead.

* * *

"Do you want to meet my father?" The words were out of her mouth almost before she thought them. She and Josh had just passed by her parents' street on the way to her apartment, and she felt a sudden pang. Her father would figure out the next step. He would see the answer to the riddle. She glanced at the car clock. He should be home by now. Gone were the long hours and reheated dinners now that he worked in the courthouse. Now he acted like he couldn't wait for the clock to strike five.

Josh shot her a surprised look. "Really?"

A wave of conflicting emotions washed over her. She knew how much it would mean to him, but did she really want to do this? Was it too forward? Was it crossing the line, and could she push him back over the line if she needed to?

She shrugged. "Well, you invited me along. One good deed deserves another."

She guided him around the block, and seconds later they pulled up at the curb outside the house. Sharon's car was not there, but at the sight of her father's, she felt a twinge of trepidation. How was she going to explain this?

They found her father in the backyard, trying to repair the barbeque. If he was surprised, he hid it well. But then, he'd had years of practice.

She knew her dad's reputation was larger than life in the inner circles of Criminal Investigations, but in person he was nondescript. The perfect statistical mean, Sharon called him. Medium height, medium build, medium brown hair now shot through with strands of grey. He'd always looked younger than his age thanks to the freckles that were only now beginning to fade. Even his eyes were neither brown nor blue but some murky in-between like hers. Smoky green, the manicurist in Kemptville had called them, which was nicer than puke green, her father's term.

Unlike many cops, he'd never acquired an aura of power and authority. Nobody stopped talking when he walked into a room. In fact, he was proud of the fact he could stand there for five minutes before anyone noticed him. It was his greatest asset, he'd told her once. This ability to go unnoticed and underestimated, until it was too late.

Now this supposed detective wizard was swearing over the barbeque, shirtless, barefoot, dressed only in shorts. When Hannah introduced Josh, he gave nothing away. Another trademark.

"You kids want to join us for supper? I've got salmon on offer if you can fix this thing."

"Uh, well …" She was already regretting her rash impulse. Dinner was definitely crossing the line. "Josh has to go. He was just dropping me off."

Green raised his eyebrows. "Oh?"

"We were down in Spencerville for the day, sir," Josh said, "following up on some leads."

"Were you?"

"Your daughter has a good head for investigation. But I guess I know where that comes from."

"Well, don't let me keep you," Green said as he bent back over the grill. "Hannah, you'll stay for dinner?"

It sounded more like an order than a question. When she returned from seeing Josh off, he turned on her. "What is all this?"

She avoided his eyes. "Thank you."

"For what? Getting rid of him?"

"No. For keeping my name out of the shelter mess. You and Brian."

He eyed her steadily. "That was all Brian. I didn't ask him to. So here you are, still in the thick of the investigation. How tightly have you got that kid wrapped around your little finger?"

For a moment, she smarted. But then she laughed. "Fair enough. But he's using me, too."

"I know." They walked through the house to the kitchen. "What's your poison, beer or white wine?"

The house was eerily quiet. Normally there was a background level of din from the TV, Tony's music, or sibling squabbling. Modo struggled to her feet and came forward to say hello, her tail thumping.

Hannah scratched her ears. "Where is everyone?"

"Sharon took Aviva to the splash pool, and Tony is out in the park, doing I don't know what." He brandished two bottles. Regretfully, she shook her head.

"Working tonight, so I better not. But pour cranberry juice into a wineglass so I can pretend."

"You lead a charmed life, you know," he said as he hooked two glasses and opened the fridge.

"Making up for lost time, maybe?"

He stopped short and turned to look at her. For a moment, he said nothing. Remembering, maybe? "Right."

She watched in silence as he poured his wine and her juice. "You've got something on your mind," he said as he headed back outside. A statement, not a question.

"I don't know why I brought Josh to meet you. I want you to know that."

"You like him?"

She swirled her fake wine, enjoying the crisp burst of cranberry on her tongue. "I can't decide."

"That's always the most dangerous."

"I can't get a good read on him. But whatever his motives, he's smart and he's not half bad as a detective. We think alike that way."

"Don't forget. He's a detective. And you're a probationary patrol officer."

She scowled at him. "I don't want to talk about this. It's not why I'm here. I'm here to pick your brain."

He laughed. "Ah."

"About the riddle of the two white trucks."

They finished both their drinks while he tinkered with the barbeque and she filled him in on the mystery of the extra truck. "No matter how I run the scenario over in my head, I keep coming up against the same stone wall. The cabin is in the middle of nowhere, at least five kilometres from the village, and even the village is in the middle of nowhere. It's eighty kilometres from Ottawa, and the only way to get there is by car. So if our killer is from Ottawa, they had to bring their own wheels, which means two vehicles were parked in the field. When they left, they could only take one, and it seems like they took Sedge's truck."

"And left their own sitting in plain view in the field?"

"It was still dark then."

"But why take Sedge's? Why that extra risk?"

She'd puzzled over that during the long drive home and thought the answer that finally came to her was genius. "Most likely so everyone would think Sedge had gone away, so they wouldn't look for him at the cabin and discover the body. From what we know, hardly anyone knew exactly where he was staying, even his colleagues, so when people finally did notice he was missing, they'd have no idea where to look for him without the truck."

"Okay." Her father was smiling, not giving an inch. *Surely he sees where this is going*, she thought with exasperation.

"But they still had to pick up their own car to drive back to Ottawa," she said. "Which means they ditched Sedge's truck nearby and went back for their own car. OPP have searched everywhere within a reasonable distance, and they've even got divers in the river, but no sign of the truck. Josh and I searched all the little roads again and talked to locals. Nothing. There's only so far the killer could walk back from."

"This is assuming two things. That the killer wasn't local —"

"Dad, that makes no sense! What motive can a local person possibly have? The police found his camera; that's the only expensive thing he owned, and the killer threw it in the river. No, this is tied to the dog. And to Ted McAuley's murder."

As he fiddled with the gas line, he smiled at some private joke. She scowled. "What's my second assumption?"

"That the killer walked back."

She turned the idea over. Her head was spinning. Not enough sleep or food. "Josh and I did wonder if the killer had driven a motorcycle and put it in the back of Sedge's truck." She shook her head slowly. "But neither the brother nor the father have a motorcycle. Josh checked. And I know there was none at the McAuley house. Besides, they're really heavy to lift and really noisy. I bet even in the middle of the night, my witness on the nearby property would have heard it."

"Something to ask him. A motorcycle is only one possibility."

Through her fatigue, she groped her way toward an elusive idea that had been nagging at her: that the killer had used another way to get to the cabin. "I did wonder about the canoe. Someone had taken it out since the rain the day before the murder. I wondered if the killer parked their own car somewhere farther down the river, took the canoe, and paddled up to the cabin. Then they left the canoe there and took Sedge's truck back to where they left their car. But it seems too crazy. Too far-fetched. They would have had to scope it all out ahead so they knew where to find a canoe with a launching site and a safe place to hide their own car." She shook her head. "Too many ifs."

Her father had lost his annoying smirk. He stood with his wrench in his hands, and his eyes had a faraway look, which meant he was thinking. "They could have brought their own canoe. But you're right, too many ifs. Even if the killer used a canoe, a bright-red canoe going down the river? Risky even at night. This is the country. Way too many nosy Parkers. But what if he had a bicycle?"

"What? You mean the killer biked all the way from Ottawa? Eighty kilometres? At night?"

He laughed. "No. But a bike fits easily inside most SUVs and trucks. And on a bike he could cover a much greater distance and hide Sedge's truck farther away." He paused as he laid down the wrench and turned on the gas. When the flame caught, he grinned. "Look at that! Before Sharon came home, too. You might also want to consider the killer had an —"

A door slammed in the house, followed by Aviva's excited shriek. "Hannah's here!" Two seconds later she burst out the back door. "Daddy, we're starving!"

And all chance for further discussion came to an abrupt end.

CHAPTER TWENTY-SEVEN

Once again, when the bedtime ritual was over and peace had settled on the house, Green found himself unable to sleep. Sharon had gone to bed early, leaving him and the dog to the stillness of the living room. Modo was snoring softly at his feet. He distracted himself with the news and then sat in the semidarkness, unable to turn off his roaming thoughts. Like Hannah, the case had its grip on him.

In retrospect, he was glad he'd been interrupted before finishing the suggestion he was putting to Hannah. *You might also want to consider the killer had an accomplice.* As always, his insatiably curious mind had been driving him forward during that conversation, but it would have been unwise. Hannah did not need more reasons to investigate. She needed to put the case aside and leave it to those who knew what they were doing. It was bad enough that he'd planted the idea of a bicycle in her head.

But the possibility of an accomplice had been in his mind ever since Sullivan had mentioned the mysterious cash payments disappearing from Ramon Ramirez's bank account. Had Ramon been secretly funnelling money to Kristina for years to help her prepare a way out? The money in her own secret account was certainly not enough, but perhaps Ramon had set up another account farther from the clutches of Ted McAuley. Ramon would have enjoyed the delicious irony of using Ted's own money against him.

Or perhaps his son Luis really was in the drug trade, in which case it would not be wise to tip off Ramon that the police were aware of the missing money.

Green had spent a day trying to decide how to handle it. His recollections of Ramon and Luis came into sharper focus as he replayed his involvement with them all those years ago. Luis had been a follower, full of insecurity and eager to bask in the reflected glory of the Big Man. Green had thought him naive, impulsive, and not too bright. But he'd only been seventeen, so he had plenty of time to mature. Ramon, on the other hand, had been tough and shrewd. Life had hardened him, but it had also made him fiercely loyal and protective. He'd been so proud and relieved to be in Canada, a peaceful, law-abiding country where his children could grow up without fear or threat. He believed the Canadian dream; if you worked hard and obeyed the law, you'd be rewarded with a good life.

Green remembered Ramon's outrage when he'd learned Luis was involved with a drug gang. Against the police, the family had closed ranks and formed a united front to protect him, but within the privacy of his own home, Ramon had meted out his own swift form of justice, probably with a belt. A punishment that probably did more to turn Luis around than the protracted song and dance of the Canadian courts would have.

But had Luis just become smarter and more secretive in his dealings? Or were those cash payments for another purpose altogether? To help another of his children in need.

Green had bumped up against Ramon's protective side nine years ago. Ramon had a strong sense of right and wrong, but his experiences in Latin America, first in El Salvador and later during his long trek through Mexico toward freedom, had robbed him of trust in those who decided right and wrong. In the final reckoning, only family could be trusted. Only family mattered, and Green knew he'd fight tooth and nail to protect his family.

The question was — how far would he go?

Sitting in the dark, Green didn't like the answer that came to him. As midnight approached, he leaned forward to give Modo a poke. "Time for our midnight walk, old girl."

The dog raised her head and blinked at him slowly, as if in disbelief. It was the same ritual every night, and every night she gave him the same look. Only when he produced a treat did she struggle to her feet and hobble after him to the front door, where he snapped on her leash.

Walking Modo through the quiet late-night streets always cleared his head. Worries seemed to recede, and sometimes answers floated down from the vast, empty sky.

Only family mattered. A passing remark made by Ramon nine years ago drifted into his memory. It was a toehold, a way to pose the question without tripping an alarm bell in Ramon's head. He remembered Ramon had been trying to sponsor his brother and his family to immigrate to Canada but had run into a snag because one of the brother's children had a serious medical condition. Heart, maybe.

He composed numerous emails in his head as he walked, and by the time he arrived home, he had pared it down to two simple sentences. He found Ramon's email in his inbox and typed out the single line. *Ramon, how is your brother's family? Are they still in El Salvador?*

He left his cellphone number below his signature and then headed off to bed.

By the time Hannah rolled out of bed the next day, the afternoon sun was pouring through her bedroom window. She felt leaden. These graveyard shifts were going to kill her, especially if she continued sleuthing during the day. She stumbled out to Equator, her favourite indie coffee shop, and ordered a four-shot latte and chocolate chip muffin. Sitting in the shade on the patio, she considered her next move. Her string of night shifts was over, and four long days off stretched ahead of her. Jogging, grocery shopping, maybe a pub night out with friends.

What friends? The truth was, her lifestyle up till now had been too screwed-up for lasting friendships.

At sixteen, in full rebellion and one short step from the streets of Vancouver's Downtown Eastside, she had instead hitchhiked across the country and landed on the doorstep of a complete stranger. Her father. She had ricocheted between alternative school, street culture, and profound depression for several years, forging friendships out of shared misery and rage. Finally enrolling in university, she had found a chasm of life experience separated her from her vacuous, fresh-faced classmates, and now that she'd chosen policing, the thin bonds she had managed to form with them were snapping under the strain of disbelief. In their criminology classes, cops didn't rate much sympathy.

She had to find new friends. There were a couple of promising young female recruits, and the woman down the hall wanted to jog with her. *Patience*, she told herself. *Your new life has just begun.*

She pushed aside the fleeting thought of Josh Kanner. Workplace affairs were usually a bad idea. When they ended badly, you had to live with the gossip and the accidental meetings. He was cute and fun and useful, but what did she actually know about him? He had an aura of privilege about him, from his Harley and his chinos to his cocky confidence.

She turned instead to the puzzle of the case. A bike, her father had suggested: easy to transport, faster than walking, and capable of covering over twenty kilometres in any direction, which expanded the search area a lot.

The McAuleys had bicycles. She recalled that on an earlier visit she had spotted a few hanging on the garage wall, gleaming and expensive-looking. Only the best for Ted McAuley. She wondered if they were still there or if Kristina had sold them for much-needed cash. Only one way to find out.

She brought her dishes inside and walked back home to get her motorcycle. Carling Avenue was a torrent of afternoon cars, but the moment she turned in to the Crystal Beach neighbourhood, cool, leafy serenity enveloped her. As usual, she parked up the street and approached on foot, trying to figure out a plan. Should she ask Phil Walker or go directly to Kristina?

The dilemma was answered for her when she spotted Phil working in his rose garden. He looked up and waved a greeting, so Hannah veered over to talk to him.

"How's the case going?" he asked.

"I'm not in the loop, but these things take time."

"I heard there was another murder. Connected, they say."

"Oh? Who're they?"

Phil reddened. "Sorry. I shouldn't gossip. It's just that we're all a bit on edge around here. The police came to take Kristina's father's truck, and he was very upset. Very vocal."

"What did he say?"

"He blamed Ted's mother. Old Lady McAuley, he called her. People like her have the police in their pocket, he said. Accused the officers of racism because he was Latino. He said he needed it for work, which wasn't exactly true. It was sitting in Kristina's driveway for over a week. They just brought her Lexus back today, along with his truck."

"How did she get around while they were gone? Bicycle? Kayak?"

Phil laughed. "Not kayak. Peter is frightened of the water. But she did get around on her bicycle. It has a kid's trailer, and she takes him out frequently for long rides."

"Still, it's a long way to the nearest grocery store, isn't it? All the way up to Bells Corners on a busy road?"

A door slammed next door, and Hannah glanced over but could see nothing through the thick hedge.

"Yes, we're not ideally located for a car-free existence," Phil was saying. "I don't know where she shops, to be honest. I've offered to pick things up for her, but she ..." He stared at his fingers, picking dirt off. "She avoids me."

"Still?"

Phil nodded. "I think she's worried about what I think. Maybe that I know more about her private life than she'd like. The family kept to themselves, pretty much, including her brother and father. Not a trusting bunch." He shrugged. "I suppose that's to be expected, given where they came from."

Hannah wanted to get back to the bicycles. Faint rustlings nearby unnerved her, but a moment later a squirrel popped out of the hedge. "I wonder if she had to sell any of her bikes to pay for things until the estate is settled. Do you know?"

He looked startled by the question out of the blue. "She wants to sell the big boat. I heard that from one of the neighbours who's interested. But it's tied up in the estate. She sold the canoe and one of the kayaks, but she and Justine still have their bikes. Justine uses hers all the time to get to work."

"Oh, she's working?"

"Summer job. Two, in fact. She's gone much of the time."

"Where?"

"One is a city lifeguard. The other one is helping her grandfather renovate houses. She says it keeps her mind off things."

"How's the family doing?"

He flushed and bent down to pick some dead leaves from a rose bush. *Choosing his words*, Hannah thought. "Well, Kristina doesn't confide in me, although I've tried to help, but I've overheard some tense moments. I guess that's to be expected. The father and brother have been there quite a bit to help her prepare the house for sale once the estate is released, and sometimes tempers flare. Justine and Kristina are at each other over little things, and the father hasn't much patience for that." He paused and cocked his head. "But as odd as it sounds, the house seems more peaceful now than it used to. I think it's because the little boy is a bit better. I don't hear the tantrums and meltdowns as much."

"That's good. Maybe it's because the dog is back."

Phil looked thoughtfully toward the McAuley house. "Maybe. I wondered if it's because Ted is gone."

Movement behind the hedge caught Hannah's eye, and this time when she glanced over she saw a person duck from view. She hurried over and parted the branches just in time to see Kristina disappear through the front door.

"Sharon, what do you know about children with autism?"

Sharon looked up in surprise from the potato she was peeling. A thick black curl fell over one eye, and she blew it back. "That's random."

Hannah laughed wryly. "The McAuley murder. I can't seem to shake it."

Sharon set the knife down and leaned against the counter. "The first case often grabs you the hardest. Your first close-up peek at the messy pain of people's lives."

Hannah bristled. She'd come to love Sharon, but the woman was a psychiatric nurse and sometimes couldn't resist the urge to psychoanalyze. "I've seen the messy pain of people's lives. Lots of times."

"Of course you have. I'm sorry, that sounded patronizing. It wasn't meant to be. I meant, your first peek at how complicated your job can be."

"My first time screwing up so royally."

"And it won't be your last. Your father still screws up regularly. In your work, you learn as you go along." She scooped the potatoes into a pot of water. "I'm in the mood for a beer out back. Let me get these potatoes on while you grab two beers from the fridge. Unless you'd rather have lemonade."

Hannah laughed and fetched two Beau's from the fridge. Outside, she was just savouring the peace and beauty of her stepmother's garden when Sharon appeared. Gardening was Sharon's escape from the hassles and exhaustion of her work, and she had coaxed beauty from even the most remote, inhospitable corners of the yard. Now she took a deep breath and sighed as she sank into her chair.

"So what's this about children with autism?"

"What do you know about the McAuley homicide case?"

"A little. But you can fill me in on the relevant parts."

"The McAuleys' three-year-old son supposedly has autism, although they're still on a waiting list for an official diagnosis. He's withdrawn, doesn't talk, has tantrums and meltdowns over minor things, and freaks out in new situations."

Sharon sipped her beer without comment. She had always had a calm, centred vibe that Hannah had grown to appreciate. The diametric opposite of her real mother. Sharon was the perfect rock for the excitable, passionate brood she took care of.

"Does that sound like autism to you?"

"It ticks the boxes. But I'm no expert in autism. I've always worked with adults." She smiled at Hannah. "Neither of us should be trying to make a diagnosis as complicated and fraught with unknowns as serious childhood disorders."

"What causes it?"

"Well, that's one of the fraught with unknowns. The number of cases is increasing every year, from a disorder that was almost unheard of seventy years ago to about one in sixty kids today. Part of it is greater awareness and wider diagnosis. No two kids on the autism spectrum look the same, and there's no blood test or brain imaging to confirm it. It's a collection of behaviours, some of which can seem like variations of regular behaviour, and others fit into other disorders."

Hannah frowned. "Are you saying it might not even be real?"

Sharon looked startled. "Oh, no, it's real. It can be devastating for kids and their families. And I do see them as adults. There *are* unique features that, seen together, point to autism. And researchers are finding genetic links. Families with one autistic child are much more likely to have others. They have identified key genes — I don't know the details — but every day we're learning more."

"But ... you said some of the behaviours could fit other disorders. Could it be caused by stress?"

Sharon's eyes narrowed. "You mean, like the stress in the McAuley household? Is that where this is going?"

Hannah shrugged. "Yeah."

"Stress would normally cause anxiety, stomach problems, maybe nightmares and fears, trouble sleeping or being left alone. I doubt very much it would cause the behaviours you describe all by itself."

"But what about if there was abuse in the home?"

Sharon's eyes lit up. "Ah! That's different. A child witnessing abuse is traumatized. That violence and level of threat to his mother, who's the most important thing in his life, would be terrifying. As well, often if there is violence against the mother, the child is also physically abused. In either case, if the abuse goes on for a long time, the child could become severely disturbed. Sometimes they act out — violent outbursts and aggressive behaviour, other times they turn inward on themselves. I see the effects lasting even into adulthood, in major depression, withdrawal, dissociative disorders, phobias, addictions, major problems with trust and relationships. And the younger the child, the deeper the damage." She reached out to touch Hannah's hand. "But this is all theoretical, Hannah. We're not experts. And you don't know this is what's happened to this little boy."

When Green descended the stairs after getting Aviva settled in bed, he found Sharon loading the dishwasher.

"Hannah dropped in this afternoon."

His brows shot up.

"She's still gnawing at this case, like a dog with a bone. Now she's trying to psychoanalyze the son. She's trying to connect his behaviour problems to domestic abuse."

"Could that be possible?"

"I have no idea. And more to the point, it's not our job. There are experts who train for years to tease apart these issues, and I'll bet even they might not all agree. Welcome to psychiatry. I tried to tell her to leave it to the experts, but I'm not sure she listened."

"She's got too much personal stake in the game. She's getting way too deep into the case."

She turned on him and put her hands on her hips. He recognized the scolding set of her jaw. "She wouldn't if you didn't keep encouraging it. By suggesting new theories like the bike, for example."

He smiled sheepishly. "Yeah, I probably shouldn't have done that. I did tell Brian and Gibbsie about it this morning, so hopefully they'll get on it."

"Here, make yourself useful," she said, thrusting a pot in his hand. "Admit it, you *like* it. It's a murder case, and a fascinating one at that. How many years has it been since you were part of a case like that?"

He put the pot in the sink and turned on the tap. He had to raise his voice over the hiss of running water. "I look at what Vick is doing and I feel over the hill. And a couple of people have mentioned the R-word. Can you imagine?"

"Can you retire?"

"Not yet, but theoretically, soon. But it's something you plan for by laying the groundwork for the next step."

"And what would that be?"

He shrugged. "Consulting. Teaching. Or private investigations. Some guys even consult back to the police service they left. But I don't want to do any of that. I don't want to be a behind-the-scenes guy, advising, training, or helping draft policy. That's not what I'm good at."

"But your years of experience make your advice valuable."

He made a face as he began to scrub the pot. "But it's not running a case. Vick is running a case."

She looked at him, her rich brown eyes troubled. "Do you think you're done at OPS? Do you think they'll never let you back into Criminal Investigations?"

"I think they want me to wait it out in some Siberia until I retire. Or die of boredom."

"Is there an Option Three?"

"There is." He put the pot on the draining board and turned to face her. "There are other police services. Secondments, or cross-appointments."

"To what?"

"To the Ontario Provincial Police or the RCMP."

She was silent as she began to wipe down the table. It would mean leaving Ottawa, and he knew she was probably thinking about the implications for her job and the kids' schools.

"Or even going overseas," he added.

She stopped, her sponge in midair. "Where?"

He shrugged. "Africa? Southeast Asia? There are countries looking for expertise in setting up modern investigation protocols."

"You've been thinking about this for a while, haven't you?"

"It could be an adventure for all of us, and just think what you could do in the mental health field. The pandemic has hit those countries hard."

A slow smile spread across her face. "It's a crazy idea, Mike."

"Maybe it's time in our life that we did something crazy."

CHAPTER TWENTY-EIGHT

Hannah had three more days off before her next day shift, and she planned to use every minute. She was beginning to form a theory of what had happened in the McAuley-Sedgwick murders, and it scared the hell out of her. She wanted to test her theory and find more proof before she shared it with anyone.

She set her motorcycle on the highway bright and early the next morning, with lunch and a change of clothes in her pack. She also had a detailed map of the twenty-kilometre radius around Sedge's cabin, printed from Google Satellite View, which showed all the back roads, private lanes, and cattle tracks, as well as farm buildings and car lots.

One of the high-end bicycles she'd seen in the McAuley garage had been a mountain bike capable of travelling off the beaten track. It would take an experienced, fit cyclist to cover twenty kilometres over rough paths in the dark, but Hannah figured whoever had done this had grit and desperation on their side.

The proof of her theory, at least of that part of it, would be Sedge's truck. The OPP had not found it. It could be in dense woods, invisible to air searches, or it could be tucked into the end of a little-used track. But the OPP had done a thorough search and had put the word out to all the locals. Surely, any farmer who noticed a strange truck sitting on their property would report it. The locals were on edge with a mixture of fear and excitement at the thought of a killer on the loose. Stuff like this didn't happen often in Grenville County.

Hide in plain sight. The phrase kept drifting through her mind, tantalizing in its simplicity. Where would you hide a rusty old truck in plain sight? In a busy mall parking lot? The closest parking lots of any size were in Prescott, which the OPP had covered thoroughly. The towns of Kemptville and Smiths Falls seemed too far away.

In a junkyard or vehicle disposal yard? These were tightly regulated and had to register incoming vehicles, which made them traceable. OPP would likely have that covered, but if she came across an unofficial one, she'd check it out.

It was 10:05 a.m. when she reached the outskirts of her search area. She had drawn out a route on her enlarged map, beginning at the northernmost road. She drove down countless laneways, paying special attention to rundown or derelict properties while ignoring the well-manicured ones. Anyone who paid that much attention to their property would surely notice a dilapidated truck.

She followed dirt tracks into the bush, drove along endless, arrow-straight back roads through farmland, and passed dozens of farm compounds with vehicles of every shape cluttering the front yards. Each time, she slowed to study them. There were pickups of all makes and colours, including a couple of rusty white Silverados, but none had the right licence plate.

Farm dogs barked or chased her, especially if she slowed down, and whenever she saw anyone outside, she stopped to ask them if they'd seen an abandoned white truck. None of them had. The OPP had put out a public notice, but no OPP officer had dropped by to check in person.

As she worked her way south to Spencerville, she began to feel discouraged. Four hours had passed without a lead. Maybe this was a wild goose chase. What had begun as a glorious summer adventure in the country had become a hot, dusty chore. She was caked in grit and sweat. She stopped for lunch on the roadside and gulped eagerly at her water. Nearby, a farmer was adjusting the irrigation system on his green velvet field. She walked over to ask the question for the tenth time.

He laughed. "Not on my place. Most of us know pretty near every truck in the area, right, and we've all been keeping an eye out. Have you been driving all over the county?"

"Pretty much."

He sobered and scratched his head. "There's a couple old abandoned places with barns you could fit a tank into. You try the old Jenkins place off Murphy Road, farther east?"

She shook her head. "I haven't checked that area yet."

"Well, if I wanted to hide something, I'd park it up there. No one's lived there for years, don't even know who owns it now. Worthless piece of land. Part of it is swamp and wetland that the government won't let you touch, and the rest is cedar scrub. Old Cyril Jenkins tried to make a living fixing up and selling anything with four wheels, but like his property, most of it wasn't worth fixing. So when he died, the stuff just stayed there. All of us used to play there as kids."

Hannah's spirits lifted. She got directions — *turn left at the T, go down a mile, no, maybe two, till you pass the apple orchard, and you'll see a big white shed, turn right and it's just up the road a mile or so, look for the auto repair sign* — and climbed back on her bike.

It took a few missed turns. Who knew what an apple orchard looked like? But she finally spotted a wide track through flattened grass and wildflowers. In the distance, in a jumble of outbuildings, she could see a red-brick century home with a collapsed porch roof and gaping holes for windows. Vines grew up the sides and along the roof. The yard was overrun with weeds and brush, and in another decade nature would reclaim the land completely. But for now the clutter of junk was still visible.

There were tire tracks where the tall grass had been flattened. Her hopes soared. Someone had driven down this recently. The farmer said kids came here to play and probably to scavenge junk, so it might mean nothing, but it was her best lead yet.

She nosed her bike into the lane and followed the tracks toward the house. As she drew nearer, the junk took shape: frames of old cars stripped of doors and wheels, rusted-out trucks, a huge jumble of tires in the corner by the main barn, a green fridge, a bathtub, and spiky, unidentifiable farm equipment. Most of it was covered with vines and weeds, but some of the vehicles looked intact.

She parked her motorcycle and began to search on foot, fighting her way through the prickly bush. One truck caught her eye, but when she peered inside, it had no interior seats or steering wheel. The grass was trampled by visitors, probably animals as well as local kids. But one path stood out, wider and double, leading toward an old barn. She hurried over. The door was hung slightly ajar on broken hinges, and she forced it back to get inside.

She gasped aloud. Inside was a wooden buggy, an old car from the gangster movie era, and a rusty white Silver-ado. Hannah rushed to look inside. It was intact — steering wheel, seats, and even a bottle of engine oil tucked in beside the door. It had no licence plates, but it had all four tires.

Equally important, it was probably less than fifteen kilometres from Sedge's cabin.

Shaking with excitement, Hannah pulled out her phone. One flickering bar. She slipped back outside and angled it until there were two bars. Her finger hovered over her call list as she considered whom to phone. Finally, she pushed Josh's number. It went to voice mail. Frustrated, she hung up and was halfway through a text when doubt crept it. She hadn't heard from him for a couple of days: no updates or invitations to help out. She had no idea what progress they'd made on the case. Was he punishing her for not letting him stay to dinner at her father's?

Fine. Who needed him? Why should he get all the credit for her discoveries? She had her own inside track; she could go straight over his head to Gibbs. For a moment she relished the thought of Josh's chagrin and regret. But that would only prove his point that she was a privileged little daddy's girl who got ahead on connections. *Like it or not, that's who you are, Pollack. Maybe you should go straight to Daddy, who gave you the tip in the first place.*

She heard the distant rumble of a vehicle coming down the road. It seemed to slow, its tires growling on the gravel, then stopped with its engine idling loudly. She ducked down and peeked toward the road but could see nothing but a plume of dust drifting across the field. Maybe it was behind the copse of trees near the laneway entrance. She listened but heard nothing but the throaty idle of the engine and the rustle of the breeze through the grass. The barn door moaned, and she jumped. In an effort to avoid detection, she scurried back inside and pulled it shut, realizing too late that her motorcycle sat in full view in the yard, gleaming in the sun.

Fuck.

She waited without moving, clutching her useless phone. Should she risk going outside to call her father? What the hell could he do from his office in Ottawa? Just as she was dithering, the engine revved and the vehicle took off, spitting dust and gravel in its wake.

God, I'm getting paranoid. It could be nothing. How could the killer possibly know she was here? Had they followed her? That made no sense, because she'd been driving around for hours. It was more likely a curious local wondering who was hanging around this old dump.

She waited another five minutes, but the vehicle did not come back. She cracked open the door to look outside. The fields were serene and empty. Keeping her head down, she hurried back to her bike and started it as quietly as she could. She eased down the grassy track and stopped at the road to scan her surroundings. Fields stretched as far as she could see. Empty.

Now she felt foolish and angry with herself for not trying to get a better look at the vehicle. It probably was a local, but what if it wasn't? What if it was the killer, and he'd been stalking her or lying in wait for her? An experienced cop would have seized the opportunity to sneak through the grass to get its licence plate. Maybe that would have been the piece of information that solved the case!

Instead, she had cowered in the barn, too spooked even to phone.

She nudged her bike onto the road and set off to retrace her route to the main highway. The road was straight and deserted, so she opened the bike up, anxious to get away from the area and report what she'd learned.

Up ahead, she saw a clump of trees and beyond it the white storage shed that had been her landmark coming in. *Turn left at that building*, she thought. She had just started to slow down to pass the trees when a flash of metal caught the corner of her eye. Not enough time to react, or even to think, before that flash of metal launched from behind the shed into the road in front of her.

Instinctively, she slammed on the brakes and swerved left, her tires chattering uselessly across the gravel road. She only had time to think *Oh fuck* before the bike pitched down the embankment and hurtled toward the trees.

CHAPTER TWENTY-NINE

Green finished his last meeting of the day, a post-mortem on the first day of the drug lord's trial, which had thankfully gone without a hitch, and now he had time to think about Hannah. What was she up to? She had dropped by the evening before to talk to Sharon about autism, which suggested she had some theory percolating, but she had left before he got home. He hadn't spoken to her since the evening when he'd suggested Sedge's killer might have used a bicycle in his getaway. In retrospect, a bad suggestion. God knows what she'd do once that idea started churning in her brain, too.

Even worse, he knew she had three more days off. If she continued mucking about in the case all that time, she could do a lot of damage to the official investigation.

Once he'd worked up a sufficient head of worry, he phoned her. It went straight to voice mail. He left a vague message and sent a text. *Can you call to discuss the case?* That ought to pique her interest.

Half an hour later, she still hadn't replied; in fact, the text hadn't even been read. What the hell was the girl up

BARBARA FRADKIN

to, and was she deliberately avoiding him? Maybe it was time for some damage control.

He phoned Sullivan. "Brian, thanks for keeping a lid on Hannah's latest shenanigans. I hope you were able to patch things up at the shelter."

"We're working on it."

Despite Sullivan's terse tone, Green carried on breezily. "Any luck getting information from the director?"

Sullivan paused, and Green sensed him wavering. "I talked to her today. She wouldn't confirm anything, but her protests were pretty pro forma. I think she'll co-operate once the subpoena is in hand."

"What about the possible boyfriend angle? Any leads on that?"

"Not yet. We're trying to see if we can access the emails deleted from the mystery device. They may be stored on the web server for as long as sixty days, and we're still in that time frame."

"Any candidates?"

Sullivan chuckled. "Everyone says the woman had no free time for an affair. But we found out her husband had installed a location tracker on her phone that also could read her texts without her knowledge."

Green mulled over this new revelation. Ted McAuley didn't trust his wife. Many abusive husbands controlled and spied on their wives even without cause, but had he suspected she had a lover? And that was the reason for the secret bank account? How long had the tracker been on the phone, and had Kristina discovered it? Most of these apps were undetectable.

He had a chilling thought. If Ted knew her location, he knew she'd gone to a shelter. That would have escalated his violence.

"That raises the risk," Green said. "Can the tracker access her emails, too?"

"No. But according to neighbours, she did take her son on picnics and long bike rides on the Greenbelt pathways. She could have met someone on those rides, and while the little boy napped under a tree, they could have got up to some fun without the husband knowing."

Bikes. Damn. "There's something I should tell you on that subject. Hannah is still fretting about this case, and a few days ago we had a conversation we probably shouldn't have. She was wondering where and how Sedge's truck disappeared." He embarked on the convoluted explanation of the two trucks–one-driver problem. "I mentioned the killer could have used a bicycle to get to and from the hiding place. A bike makes no noise and could go undetected in the night, and it's much better than walking."

"Mike, Mike." Sullivan chuckled, and Green could almost see him shaking his head in resignation. "I know Vickers and his team are looking all over hell's half acre for that truck. I'll get Kanner to mention it to him."

"You might want to do that soon. I'm afraid Hannah may be off on this hunt right now. She's ignoring me because she knows I'll be mad."

"Speaking of mad," Sullivan said, "Kristina's father is hopping. We seized his truck so we could check tire treads and transfer evidence, and he nearly took our officer's head off. That's raising a few eyebrows on the team that the guy has something to hide."

Green said nothing. Ramon hadn't yet replied to his oblique inquiry about his brother. Despite its innocuous tone, had that spooked him? He knew he should let Sullivan know, but the unanswered question bothered him. After he hung up, he pulled up the email and reread it. Should he email again? Phone? Or simply hand his suspicions over to Sullivan.

In the end, he phoned, but after four rings, the call disconnected with the message *Call declined.* Yes, the man was certainly angry. Green sent a text. *It's Inspector Green. I'm going to call again. Please answer.*

This time, on the second ring, Ramon picked up. His voice sounded wary. "Yes?"

"What's going on, Ramon?"

The wary tone roughened. "You ask me that? The police harass my daughter, search her house, take away our vehicles — *my* truck — like we're the enemy? Her husband is dead!"

"This is all routine, Ramon. We look at everything."

"I ask your help. I thought you help! But you are no different."

Green changed tack. "How is your brother? Is he in Canada now?"

"Why you ask that?"

He could have mumbled some vague expression of concern but knew Ramon would see through that. "Because Ted McAuley gave you a lot of money over the years. Have you been sending money to your brother?"

"Gave? No. Ted gives nothing for nothing. I am working hard for that money, but when I can't pay enough, he say he will take my house." Ramon seemed to hear himself. "But I not *kill* him for that!"

"So was it for your brother?"

"Is it against the law that a man try to help his brother? You have no idea what his life is like down there."

Green did have an idea. His father had spent two years in a displaced persons camp after the war. Over the years, he'd heard other stories about refugee camps, protection money, and bribes needed to stay safe, not to mention the cost of basic food. "No, it's not against the law, and you are not in trouble."

"You Canadians don't want his daughter, so we try to fix her. Many doctors and operations, but ..." Ramon's voice grew ragged.

Green's phone buzzed, signalling an incoming call. Sergeant Vickers. Reluctant to cut Ramon off at this crucial juncture, he sent the call to voice mail. "I am sorry, Ramon. I hope they find a solution. Where are they living?"

"Mexico City. There is a hospital. But I have no money now —"

Vickers called again. Green cursed but couldn't ignore it again. "Ramon, I'm sorry, I have another call. But we will talk again." He wanted to say more, to offer some feeble hope, but Vickers's call had scattered his thoughts. He disconnected to make the switch.

"Vick! Where's the fire?"

"Have you heard from your daughter?"

Something in his cold, urgent tone sent Green's anxiety soaring. "She's not answering her texts. Why?"

"I'm standing on the bridge over the South Nation River not far from Sedge's cabin. We've just pulled a blue Honda motorcycle out of the water. A passing car spotted it half submerged. Licence plate …" He rattled off a number, but Green was no longer listening. He was frozen with dread.

"Is Hannah there?" he managed.

"According to Motor Vehicles, that bike is registered to her. Is that correct?"

"That's correct." Green went onto autopilot. "Is there … any …?"

"No, there's no sign of her. Patrol and paramedics are on scene. I'm just on my way to the site now."

"I'll meet you there."

For the second time in a week, Green broke all speed limits getting to the accident scene. He spent the entire time on the phone between Sharon and Vickers. After telling Sharon about the accident and asking her whether she'd had word from Hannah, he badgered both her and Vickers constantly for updates.

When he arrived at the accident scene, the first thing he saw was Hannah's motorcycle, lying on its side in the mud and reeds of the riverbank. A couple of officers in protective gear were bent over it, and another in a wetsuit was in the water. Green's breath stopped, and tears rose to his eyes. He fought them back and forced calm as he assessed the scene. The roadside was lined with OPP vehicles, trailers, and equipment, an EMS vehicle was parked on the grass, and officers were scattered about, searching the area. A Zodiac was hovering offshore. It looked like chaos, but Green knew everyone had a job to do. There would be collision investigators, duty officers, emergency response teams, and detectives.

He slewed to a stop beyond the bridge and leaped out. Vickers detached himself from a knot of officers and held up a hand to intercept him as he plunged down the embankment toward the bike.

"We haven't touched anything yet, Mike. Not till the accident guys have finished processing the scene."

"But is there any sign of her? Footprints? Blood?"

Vickers shook his head. "But we've got teams searching the area, and it's early days."

Green clenched his jaw to stop the trembling. "Can you tell what happened?"

Vickers turned to gesture toward the road. "There are skid marks on the shoulder coming down the hill just before the bridge." He pointed to some yellow evidence markers in the gravel. "We think she lost control. The bike sustained some damage." He led the way down toward the bike. Up close, Green could see the scratches and dents, the broken fender, and the crushed front wheel. "It looks like she hit something head-on with some force. There's some wood debris in the tire."

Green glanced around the grassy slope. "There are no trees around."

"No, but there's a wooden post on the guardrail by the bridge. It looks damaged, too. We'll know more when we get the samples to the lab."

Green tore his eyes away from the broken motorcycle and walked back up to the bridge. His legs felt like rubber, but he forced himself to study the scene. Despite their attempts to protect the area, the grassy slope from the bridge to the river's edge was trampled, but faint tire tracks were still evident. Vickers was right; the guard post was gouged, although still upright. Something niggled at the back of his mind.

He knew the laws of physics. It didn't make sense that the bike had hit a guard post and continued down to the riverbank. If she had come down the hill, lost control, and struck the guard post, she would have catapulted forward over the handlebars and tumbled down the slope. The river wasn't far below.

It didn't bear thinking about.

Vickers seemed to read his mind. He laid a hand on his arm and steered him away. "Let's go to my car, and I'll bring you up to speed on what we're doing."

Inside the car, Vickers turned on the engine, cranked up the air conditioning, and poured Green a cup of coffee from a thermos. "I wish I had something stronger to offer."

Green took a sip of the sharp, biting black coffee. "It's okay. I need my wits."

"We're not jumping to any conclusions, Mike. We've got divers in the river, yes, but we've also got ERT combing the woods, officers checking all the roads and nearby farms, we've deployed our drone, and K9 is on its way. We'll find her. When did you last hear from her?"

"Not for a couple of days, but that's normal. She didn't answer my call or text today."

"What time was that?"

"Just a couple of hours ago. But she came to the house last night to talk to Sharon, and I don't think she'd drive down here after that."

"Which means this happened sometime today."

Green bobbed his head up and down. "That's good. It means she hasn't been lying around out here somewhere all night." His hand trembled, and he set the coffee cup down hastily on the dash. "Any clues on the motorcycle? Backpack, notebook, cellphone?"

Vickers shook his head. "Only her emergency repair and first-aid kit."

"So she might still have her cellphone. She might call." He pulled out his phone and stared at the screen. Nothing. Feeling useless, he dialed her number. Voice mail.

"That's helpful, though," Vickers said. "It might help us locate her. Give me the number." Once he'd relayed the number to the Com Centre, he sat back and studied Green. "What was she doing here, Mike?"

"She got a bee in her bonnet about Sedgwick's truck. She was probably trying to find it."

"Oh, and we weren't?"

"I know, but she had a theory about a bicycle." He sketched out Hannah's theory, thinking how ludicrous it sounded now that he explained it out loud. But Vickers looked thoughtful.

"That truck has been sticking in my craw, too. We can canvass farther afield, and we'll put out a public appeal in the area. Circulate her photo. We'll find her."

Green felt panic lurking. He put his hand on the door handle. "I've got to do something. I can't just hang around here waiting for reports."

"Fair enough. We've got a lot of avenues we're exploring. Maybe you can get on the phone and dig around back in Ottawa to find out who she might have talked to, who might know she was coming down here. Any of our suspects, for example."

Green's eyes narrowed. He stared at Vickers, his heart racing. "You're thinking what? That this wasn't an accident? That she was driven off the road?"

Vickers shrugged, maddeningly deadpan. "Just keeping our options open, Mike."

"Is there any evidence …?" Green flung open the door and strode over to the road. There were skid marks on the shoulder but none on the asphalt and no traces of debris around the post. And the damn guard post was still upright.

Vickers came to stand beside him. "Forensics will take the scene and the bike apart. Just exploring all possibilities, Mike. The killer we're chasing is pretty ruthless. And desperate."

CHAPTER THIRTY

G reen paced around for an hour, hanging on each update from the search manager and the collision investigators, as well as peppering Gibbs, Kanner, Sullivan, and Sharon with questions. Kanner knew nothing about Hannah's latest theory to find the truck but told him he and Hannah had already combed most of the area within five kilometres of Sedge's cabin. It has to be farther afield, he said. The young man sounded ready to jump in his car and come down to join the search, but Green put him off. The last thing Vickers and the OPP team needed was one more Ottawa cop getting in the way.

Sullivan was a rock. "We'll find her, Mike. There's lots of dense bush around there, so it may take time, but it's not remote. There are farms and roads all around. The minute she stumbles upon one of those, help won't be far away."

"But what if she's injured and can't move? What if she's unconscious?"

"That's what ERT is for, and the K9 Unit. They know what they're doing."

"Vickers thinks it might not be an accident. He thinks the killer might have targeted her."

"But how would he know where to find her?"

"I don't know, Brian. Maybe he was tailing her. But if he was, he may have taken her away. What if he's holding her somewhere? Or … worse."

"Let's take this one step at a time, Mike. Not jump to conclusions."

How like Sullivan, Green thought. *One plodding step at a time.* "We have to figure out who this bastard is!" he shot back as he watched some officers unload ATVs from a trailer. "Are you any closer to an answer?"

"We've got our short list."

Green took a deep breath to settle his temper. "Can you check their whereabouts right now? Find out if they can account for their movements today? I can't leave here."

There was silence for a moment. Through his mounting impatience, Green heard the search team calling Hannah's name deep in the woods. He watched the Zodiac as it motored slowly downstream, its sonar tuned for every underwater obstacle. His breath quickened. *Fuck, fuck, fuck.*

"Absolutely. I'll do it personally," Sullivan replied, pulling him back.

After Sullivan signed off, Vickers came over to speak to him. "This is a waiting game for now, Mike. I'm going to grab the guys some food in Prescott. You want to come with me?" Green started to shake his head.

"Prescott is not far. We'll be back in half an hour. Or you can go to Kemptville."

Kemptville! Green sprang to life. The therapist! Hannah had been asking Sharon about the little boy's autism and the possibility of post-traumatic stress. Had she gone back to talk to the therapist? Had she stumbled into the heart of the story and inadvertently tipped the killer off? How else would the killer know she was a threat, and what she was up to?

Green stood outside the nondescript black door and stared up at the second-floor windows. There had been no answer to the bell and no flick of blinds upstairs, so he hammered on the door with his fist.

"Police! Open up!"

Nothing, except a couple of curious shoppers stopping to watch. He returned to his car and dialed the therapist's number. He was certain he had the right address, and he was damned if she thought she could avoid him. He wasn't expecting her to answer, so when her voice mail kicked in, he was prepared.

"Ms. Markos, it's Inspector Michael Green of the Ottawa Police. I am outside your office in Kemptville and urgently need to talk to you. Two people have been murdered and now a police officer is in serious danger. Either call me immediately, or meet me here."

He left his phone number and sat in his car, waiting. No call came, and after a few minutes of building frustration, he spotted a young woman with blue hair locking up a nearby beauty salon. He strolled over and showed his badge.

"Good evening. I'm trying to locate Elena Markos, the therapist. Have you seen her around today?"

The woman looked wary. "Why?"

"It's in connection with an ongoing incident involving one of her clients."

"She's not around very often, and she keeps to herself."

"This is urgent. Have you noticed anything in the past day or two? Any of her clients acting unusual, or anyone else?"

The woman started to shake her head but stopped. "Well, there was this young woman. She came into my salon a few days ago saying she wanted her nails done, but really she wanted to talk about Elena. And her clients." Her expression grew worried. "I probably told her more than I should about the girl who came. Afterward, I got worried because, like, I know Elena handles domestic violence, so I did tell Elena about it. She went ballistic on me." The woman's brow furrowed above her impossibly long eyelashes. "I ... I hope I didn't make it worse."

A car turned in to the parking lot. The woman jerked her head up, and her eyes widened. "That's her now, I'd better get out of here before she sees me talking to you." She unlocked her door and ducked back inside.

Green turned to see an aging Honda driving slowly past the line of cars in the parking lot. Through the windshield he could make out the sombre face of a young woman. He signalled to her, and she stopped some distance away, rolled down her window, and looked him up and down. He had expected an officious, matronly type, but Elena Markos looked young, despite the severe bun at the nape of her neck and her lack of makeup. She had honey-coloured skin and a round face with large, thick-framed glasses. Behind them, her dark eyes were wary. He realized that, wearing civilian clothes and driving his own Subaru, he didn't look like a police officer.

He held out his badge wallet as he approached. "Ms. Markos, Inspector Green. Thank you for coming. Should we talk in my car, or would you prefer Tim Hortons?"

Her gaze flicked from him to his car, as if she were weighing the pros and cons. "This may be a very brief conversation. What's it about?"

"It's about Police Constable Hannah Pollack. Has she been in contact with you in the past couple of days?"

"About what?"

"It's a straightforward question."

"Fine. No."

"Has anyone else asked you about her? Or did you discuss her with anyone?"

Elena glanced at the salon. "What my clients and I discuss is confidential."

Green felt what little patience he had left starting to fray. "I know you were seeing Kristina McAuley and her family, so let's not pretend. Constable Pollack was working on her husband's murder investigation, and now she is missing. Possibly the victim of foul play. So this is going to be a longer conversation than you might hope. Would you prefer to continue it down at the Ottawa Police Station?"

Elena's eyes flickered at the mention of foul play before regaining their stony stare. Social workers, like cops, practised the art of not reacting. "I just don't see how I can help you. I've never heard of Constable Pollack, and any other conversations that may or may not have occurred with any of my clients are protected by privacy laws, as I'm sure you're aware, Inspector. You need a subpoena."

The crowd of curious shoppers was growing, standing by their cars. "Do you really want to have this conversation in the parking lot?"

"Unless you show me a subpoena, I don't intend to have this conversation at all."

When Green approached so he could lower his voice, she flinched. "Did you have any inkling that murders were being planned?"

"I have no idea what you're talking about."

"Ted McAuley? Drew Sedgwick? Both dead."

She shrank back, and he could see her eyes had grown wide behind the glasses. "I can't — I can't talk to you without a subpoena, which protects both you and me."

"I'll get you your subpoena, but right now we have no time. This very instant, Constable Pollack may be dying." His voice quavered, and he fought to regain control. "If you know someone is in imminent danger, you can — should — warn them. It overrides confidentiality.

You can be held responsible, and if you don't co-operate, I will personally make sure you are!"

She blinked rapidly, as if trying to sort through her legal obligations, which were far murkier than Green had implied. "I can tell you this much. No, I had no inkling."

He pressed his advantage. "Didn't you think, when the second victim turned up dead, that maybe your client presented an imminent danger?"

She shook her head, nostrils flaring. "I haven't spoken —" She broke off as if reconsidering. "Seen them — any of them — since before that young man died."

"But didn't you think … wasn't there any hint in their discussions with you that he might be in danger? An innocent young Ph.D. candidate who was just study-ing ducks is dead."

"No. I wasn't seeing all of them by the end. The mother found it too difficult, but the daughter was de-riving some benefit."

"Why did the mother drop out?"

Elena was recovering her footing, and she pursed her lips. "Those details go far beyond imminent risk. But I can assure you, if either of them had mentioned anything about the young man or —" She frowned as if remembering something.

"What?"

"I can't imagine either of them being that cold-blooded."

"What did they say?"

She shot him a reproachful look. Frustrated, he circled around for another approach. "Did you tell either of them that the little boy's behaviour could have been caused by extreme, prolonged abuse?"

"Seriously, Inspector, that discussion is also way beyond imminent danger."

"No, it's not. Because it provides a powerful motive for murder. If I thought my spouse had terrorized my child to the point of severe disturbance, then murder would be very much on my mind."

"But there were other solutions. That's what we discussed. An escape plan, a way to protect the children."

"And yet Kristina quit therapy instead. Did that not worry you?"

Colour rushed to her face. "Of course it worried me! It's one reason I kept seeing the daughter, hoping to keep the family engaged."

"Did Kristina talk to you about a boyfriend?"

Elena stared at him in surprise. He shrugged. "We have evidence there was another man. If so, his actions would not be covered by confidentiality at all. And he might be a crucial piece in what happened."

"I can't … those personal details are still protected."

"But what if he was an imminent threat? Maybe he saw himself as the saviour."

She whipped her head back and forth. "It never came up."

"Do you know who he is?"

"This is all I can tell you. We discussed plans. What supports the family had, ways to cope, ways to get further help for the children. I can assure you, I never, ever, thought there was any danger."

"But now, looking back, do you see a danger?"

She sucked her breath in. "I'm not a mind reader! I try to listen and offer guidance, but no one ever said, 'You know what, I think murder is a better idea.'" She clutched the steering wheel, trembling, all vestiges of the stony facade gone.

He dropped his voice. "But you're losing sleep over it now, aren't you?"

"Yes. Yes, I am. But I can't talk about it."

CHAPTER THIRTY-ONE

When Green arrived back at the accident scene, long fingers of twilight darkened the woods, and the river glistened black beneath a deep-lavender sky. Hannah's motorcycle had been removed, and OPP divers were securing the Zodiac and packing up their gear. In the distance, Green heard the thump-thump of a helicopter.

Only a scattering of vehicles remained along the shoulder, among them the Command Centre and Vickers's unmarked Interceptor. Green saw him down at the waterfront, conferring with two men. One was the duty inspector and the other was Brian Sullivan. Green fought a lump in his throat as he embraced his friend.

"I figured this was the place I needed to be," Sullivan said.

Green nodded mutely and glanced at Vickers. "Any news?"

"Not a lick. ERT has been tramping through the bush and along the roads all evening. We've got a helicopter doing sweeps, officers canvassing the area, and public alerts out in the media. The canine team has been working the area for hours without picking up a reliable track. Nothing along the road, through the bush, or along the riverbanks. Their conclusion? They think she's either in the water or she got into a vehicle. The Zodiac has covered the river a kilometre downstream, so …"

"He's abducted her."

"Or some passing local gave her a lift."

"Then why hasn't she called? Why hasn't anyone called?"

Vickers shrugged. "Disoriented? Frightened? I don't know, Mike. The point is, we don't think she's here anymore."

Green turned in a circle, fighting anxiety. He knew he should be relieved that she wasn't dead in a ditch nearby. Maybe she was using her wits to stay safe. But she'd be so scared.

It was Sullivan who spoke. "She's resourceful, Mike. And fit."

"Anything from her phone?"

"It's not emitting a signal, so the battery is dead," Vickers said. "She might have lost it in the crash, although we haven't found it."

"It was last used at two oh-nine p.m. today," Sullivan said. "She called Josh Kanner, but she didn't leave a message."

Green swung on him. "Kanner! What did he say? What was she up to?"

"He didn't know. He's as worried as we are and wanted to come down to help." When Green started to object, Sullivan held up his hand. "It might be worth it. He'd know the places they visited. Maybe they accidentally tipped off the killer."

Green's irritation flared. "The killer is not from here, for fuck's sake. He's from Ottawa. Where was that call made from?"

"On the road somewhere north of here."

"We got the cell tower coordinates. It's in back country," Vickers said. "But we'll check it out tomorrow morning."

Green gaped. The mosquitoes had begun to swarm, but he barely felt them. "Tomorrow morning? Why not tonight? K9, heat sensors, night goggles; they can all operate in the dark! And by tomorrow the scent might be too old for the dogs."

When Vickers hesitated, the duty inspector stepped in. "First thing in the morning, the scent will still be fine. We only have the general area; we don't have a ground zero for the search. We don't even know if she stopped there or was just driving through. We've got officers patrolling the roads, stopping vehicles, and going door-to-door in the area. If we get any sightings or useful intel tonight, we'll call K9 back out." He turned to climb up the slope. "Meanwhile let's get some rest and regroup at six a.m."

Green stood on the riverbank, watching the vehicles start up and drive away. Darkness had settled in, matching his despair. Beside him, Sullivan stood quietly. Green raised his arms in defeat. "I don't want to leave. This is the last place … What if she's hiding, waiting for dark?"

"She's not here, Mike. The dog would have found her. Have you eaten at all?"

Green shook his head. "I had other things on my mind. Did you find out about our suspects?"

"There's an Irish pub in Kemptville. Let's grab a bite, and we can talk about it."

It wasn't a fancy place, but it was classic Sullivan: blackened wooden beams, wide plank floors, and a huge stone fireplace. Once they were settled at a corner table with beers and a platter of wings, Sullivan sat back and began his report.

"I've got people looking into the activities of our key players today, and they gave me some updates on my way here. We're looking at an approximate time frame of one to five p.m. Unfortunately, the family has closed ranks. Kristina says her father and brother were both working at her place, repairing some flood damage in the basement. They alibi each other, but since it was indoors, none of the neighbours can corroborate it. According to Dad and Bro, Kristina was there most of the time; she just went out for groceries. Took her son."

The smell of the wings made Green nauseated, but he forced himself to eat one. "How long was she gone?"

"An hour and a half, tops. From one thirty to three."

"Can anyone else confirm those times?"

"The neighbours weren't paying attention."

"Whoever did this needed two hours minimum, more likely three. Any less and it would be too tight. And they'd have to know exactly where Hannah was in order to intercept her."

Sullivan sucked his fingers noisily and gestured to the platter. "Come on, eat more. You have to get some food to that brain."

Gingerly, Green picked up another wing and began to nibble. "What about Kristina's mother? Her daughter, Justine?"

"The mother says she was at the company office all day, but we have no corroboration. Ramon and Luis say Justine was at work all day."

"But as you say, this is family. They're going to protect each other." He sat thinking. As the food began to revive his energy, his spirits lifted. *Now or never.*

"I talked to the father this afternoon."

Sullivan stared at him, his fork suspended. "Why?"

"Following up on the cash disappearing from his account."

With a heavy sigh, Sullivan laid down his fork. Green shrugged. "I had a hunch, which turned out to be right. Ramirez was sending support money to his brother down in Mexico, probably in the form of Mexican cash."

Sullivan was still stone-faced. "It was a lot of money."

"There were significant medical expenses and other things. It makes sense. It fits what I know about the man."

"Was this conversation in person? Are you saying you're the man's alibi?"

"No, it was by cellphone. So yeah, he could have been anywhere, including driving through the back roads of Grenville County."

Sullivan brightened. "But we can trace the location of the call. So that's a help. We're closing in, Mike!"

Green sipped his beer gloomily. "But it still doesn't tell us what happened to Hannah. I leaned on the therapist earlier. She clung to her rulebook like a life raft until I threatened her with duty to warn. Then she confirmed the family did see her for therapy regarding the abuse, and they discussed escape plans. However, Kristina dropped out and the therapist continued with the daughter."

Sullivan arched his eyebrows. "Really? That's unusual."

Green nodded. "Up until just before Sedgwick died. She was hoping to persuade the mother to come back. Anyway, she said she saw no danger signs and didn't see either of the women as capable of murder. But something rattled her when I pressed her on the little boy's problems. I think she's holding back. I wouldn't be surprised if right now she's consulting her professional college for advice."

Sullivan chewed another wing, frowning thoughtfully. "Is she experienced? Would she even recognize a danger?"

"She's young, kind of full of herself, obviously committed to abused women, so she's sympathetic to their side. But I think she did react to something at the gut level. I asked her about a possible boyfriend. She wouldn't confirm it, but reading between the lines, there was something." He leaned forward. "We need to confirm this boyfriend, Brian. We need to know if we have another viable suspect or if we're chasing a blank theory."

"Okay, I'll get Gibbs to —"

"No. I want to do it. I want to look Kristina in the eye, see her reactions for myself, and break her silence wide open. She's stonewalled us long enough. If I have to, I'll use Hannah. I'm a parent desperate for my child's safety. I'll get her, Brian."

"Mike, you can't. You know you can't."

"I can! I know this case, too. I know the players, and Kristina knows me. I can reach her." As Sullivan kept shaking his head, Green began to tremble. "Damn it, Brian, I'm not sitting around on the sidelines watching them drag the river and send tracking dogs through the bush, while the killer might still be out there —"

"Besides the fact you'd be putting the case at risk, you need to be down there, ready to help her as soon as they find her. We don't know what she's been through, but she'll need her dad. Let me handle this." Sullivan leaned forward, his blue eyes soft. "I love her, too, you know."

Green hunkered down in his car across the street and two houses down from the McAuley house. He knew his aging silver Subaru did not scream cop car, and he wanted to be able to watch the house without attracting too much attention. It was a quiet street. There had been a flurry of doors slamming and engines revving as residents set off for work in the morning, but now, at nine o'clock, the street had settled into peace.

He'd been there since six o'clock. He wanted to catch Sullivan the minute he arrived, and he hadn't known what time that would be. He himself had given up trying to sleep and had been up since four, pacing and ruminating until he decided he could reasonably wake up

Vickers. He'd touched base with him, the duty inspector, and the search manager, all of whom were back out in the search area, but they had nothing new to report. There had been no sightings of Hannah and no useful tips from locals.

It had been a warm, calm night, which was some comfort, but they were all keeping a wary eye on the storm working its way up from New York State, threatening gusty winds and possible hail, as well as a plunge in temperature later in the day. Wind and rain would make it challenging for the dogs to find the track, even without the time delay.

He was anxious to get down to the search site, but first he had to find out what Sullivan pried out of Kristina. Identifying the killer was key to finding out what had happened to Hannah.

The McAuley house was quiet and shuttered when he arrived. There was a Ramirez company truck in the driveway. At eight o'clock, the front door opened and Justine emerged, dressed in jogging clothes with the little black-and-white dog on a leash. They strolled down the street with the dog sniffing at every bush and disappeared around the bend in the direction of the Shirley's Bay trail.

At eight thirty, Sullivan's staff car drove slowly down the street, as if he were searching for the house number. Green slid down in his seat and trained his binoculars to watch Sullivan turn in to the McAuley drive and park behind the truck, effectively blocking its escape. Kristina took a long time to answer the door, possibly assuming he was a pesky reporter, and she confronted him with anger and defiance on her face before reluctantly stepping back to let him in.

Shortly afterward, the front door of the neighbour's house opened, and a man came out. His gaze flicked briefly over Green's Subaru, which was parked almost directly across the street, before turning instead to the staff car in Kristina's drive. He frowned, pulled on a jacket against the morning chill, and crept over to peer through the cedar hedge. Then, shaking his head in dissatisfaction, he moved back along the hedge until he was close to the side wall of her house.

Ah, the nosy neighbour, Green thought. No wonder they were upset with him. He waited, with one eye on the neighbour and the other on the McAuleys' front door, for at least ten minutes before he spotted Justine coming back up the street. She froze when she saw Sullivan's car, so obviously a police car despite its lack of markings. She paused, backed up a few steps, and then turned to hurry down the street and around the bend out of sight, hauling the little dog behind her.

Well, that's interesting, Green thought. It might mean nothing other than the whole family was spooked by the idea of cops. The nosy neighbour was also curious, for he'd left his eavesdropping post and had stepped forward to watch her scurry away. Green kept his head low.

There was no further drama until the front door opened again and Sullivan emerged. Green used his binoculars to try to catch a glimpse of Kristina, but she slammed the door so fast, he saw nothing but the whip of her arm. Sullivan stopped on the doorstep to look at the door before heading back to his car. He backed up the car, drove past Green, and parked up the street. He wore a half smile as he walked back toward Green.

"I suppose I should be glad you didn't crash the interview," he said as he folded his large frame into the passenger seat.

Green managed a thin smile in return. "It's a long time since I've done a stakeout. Learned some interesting things. Nosy neighbour has an unhealthy interest in Kristina McAuley's activities, and the teenage daughter freaked out at the sight of your car."

Sullivan looked thoughtful. "So she wasn't home during my interview. I wondered if she was eavesdropping." He gestured to Green's thermos sitting in his cup holder. "Aw, did you bring me coffee?"

Green poured him the remaining drops, and Sullivan made a face as he sipped. "Let's go grab some coffee made today and I'll fill you in."

"Wait." Green nodded to the McAuley house. "I want to see what she does now that you've poked a stick in the nest." He turned in his seat. "*Nu?*"

"*Nu* nothing. She's a tough one. At first she acted offended. She was raised to believe in her marriage vows and would never be unfaithful. She asked if I was Catholic and if marriage vows meant so little to me. I tried to play that a bit, how hard it would be, but if I found someone who loved me and treated me well … Then she progressed to outraged. Like when would she even have the time, she's got a disturbed child to care for, a whole household to run, and a husband to keep happy. So I told her we knew about the abuse. At first she denied it, but eventually she got mad. 'Then do you think, after all I've been through, I'd want another man in my life? I just wanted out. I never wanted my husband dead, but now that it's over, I just want some peace so I can help my children heal. That's all that matters to me now.'"

Green looked at him thoughtfully. "Heal. An interesting word."

Sullivan nodded. "I was beginning to think we were barking up the wrong tree, but I pushed her one last time. I told her we had two separate confirmations of another man in her life. A dark-haired man who drives a white truck. And wow, she panicked. 'It's a lie!'; she demanded to know who had told us that, and where had this man been seen. I didn't answer, of course, but —"

At that moment, a white truck appeared around the corner, passed them, and pulled into the McAuley drive behind the Ramirez truck. A dark-haired man climbed out of the cab and headed up the walk.

"Well, well," Sullivan muttered.

Green craned his neck. Barely visible through the shrubbery on the walk was the logo of the second truck. *RR Contracting*. He sucked in his breath. There were two Ramirez trucks, not one! He should have known.

Kristina yanked the door open, pulled the man inside, and flung herself into his arms.

"It's not a boyfriend," Green said. "It's the brother."

CHAPTER THIRTY-TWO

Hannah drifted slowly to consciousness, aware first of musty cold and then of throbbing pain. Everything screamed, as if her whole body had been pummelled, and when she tried to move, more pain shot like a hot knife through her right leg and shoulder. She took a deep, cautious breath, forcing the pain down enough to think. Her head ached, and her brain felt like sludge.

What the hell?

She twisted her head to squint at the pale grey light that filtered through … what? Leaves? Trees, as motionless and breathless as the dawn. In the stillness, birds twittered and blurry shapes darted from tree to tree. She reached down to feel her body, and her fingers met prickly needles. A balsam branch lay over her body. Had she done that?

Her mind swirled. The trees spun, and she shut her eyes to fight the nausea. Breathed deeply and tried to make sense of it all. A black mist descended, and she drifted on waves of pain and nausea. When she woke again, the sky had lightened to blue, and wind was buffeting the trees. Flashes of sunlight seared her eyes. Every inch of her howled with pain. But she remembered.

Bits and pieces, disjointed memories that she tried to knit together. She remembered dragging herself through the woods, her leg useless and her shoulder numb, knowing she had to escape. Had to hide. Was it hours? Days? Nothing but roots and rocks and tree branches that clawed at her. Stopping whenever the knives of pain were too sharp. Plunging her face into a trickle of stream to drink and ease the throbbing. Resting her head on a mossy rock, listening. There was no sound but the forest, no more heavy breathing and cracking branches now. She had escaped.

But to where?

Darkness, mosquitoes. Wrestling with a balsam branch to create a shield. Dizziness. Blackness. Sleep.

Now she pushed the balsam branch away and probed her body with fumbling fingers. Her right arm was numb. No bones protruded, but she suspected it was broken. She rubbed it carefully to get the blood flow back. Her right leg would not obey her, and her jeans were stiff and crusty. Her panic spiked. Would she lose her leg? Was it bleeding?

She had to find help. A road, a farmhouse. But all around, she saw nothing but a wall of trees. She listened. Beyond the chirp of birds and the distant croak of frogs, she heard the growl of an engine. Her heart thudded. The killer, or a farmer out in his truck?

She had to get closer to check it out. If she stayed out here, she would die. She could hear no dogs barking, no sound of searchers calling. Was anyone looking for her? Did they even know she was missing? Through her brain fog, she remembered she'd told nobody about her plans. Like an idiot, wanting to claim all the glory of solving the case. No one would miss her because she didn't have to work for another two days.

Long enough to die.

Survival training drifted back to her slowly. She had to fix her leg so that it didn't move or bleed. She had to secure her arm. She dragged herself through the bush on her stomach, groping for tools, until her fingers closed on a straight, sturdy branch.

She lost track of the time it took her to fashion a splint and wrap it tightly to her leg with vines. The wind was whipping the trees now, cold and damp. Her head was pounding with the effort, and her vision was blurring. When the splint was secure, she slumped back, panting in exhaustion. Slept. Woke to the sound of an engine closer than before. She strung more vines around her neck and shoulder as a sling and slowly began to haul herself along the ground in the direction of the sound. It was her only hope.

Green left Sullivan to stickhandle the warrant and seizure of both Ramirez trucks while he set off toward Spencerville to check the progress of the search team. Fear for Hannah's safety coursed through him like a cold dread, but he no longer felt so helpless. Cracks were forming in the family wall of secrecy, and with them some light on the puzzle.

It *was* a family conspiracy. There was no boyfriend, no extraneous players, just a fiercely protective family closing ranks around one of their own.

Some of the team had been continuing the search along the reedy shorelines and dense woods around the accident scene, while others had spread out along the network of nearby roads. So far, no trace of Hannah had been found. The teams kept their expressions neutral and their words noncommittal, but Green knew what they were thinking. Hannah was not calling for help or actively working for her rescue. The reason did not bear thinking about.

Vickers met him at the site of the accident, where the collision reconstruction team was busy with survey equipment and measuring tape. "We're working on confirming something," he said, handing Green a fresh cup of coffee and leading him over to the team.

"The pattern doesn't add up, even before we look at the forensics from the motorcycle," the collision investigator explained. "There's no gouge in the gravel where the bike supposedly hit the guard post. There is no debris from the motorcycle at the point of impact. There are no tire marks on the asphalt prior to going on the shoulder. Nothing to indicate she swerved, braked, or lost control. She would have had to drive directly toward the post without trying to avoid it. But it's a straight, open road, and the day was sunny and clear. And ..." the investigator gestured to the damaged guard post, "this is not at the same height as the tire."

"What the hell?" Green exclaimed.

"Yup," Vickers said. "And then there's the forensics just in from the motorcycle, still preliminary, mind you, but Ident wanted us to know. The debris in the tires did not come from this site. It's mud, grass, and forest loam. And the bits of wood embedded in the fender and tire are bark. She collided with a tree."

Green sucked in his breath. "She crashed somewhere else, and the killer moved it here!"

Vickers was looking thoughtful. "That motorcycle weighs four hundred pounds. A lot of bike to move."

"But somebody did it," Green snapped impatiently. His mind was already racing over the implications, thinking of the Ramirez men, both powerfully built from years of construction, and of Ramon, who'd fight to death to protect his family.

Vickers was already heading toward his car. "We'll keep processing this scene because it's obviously a secondary crime scene, but the duty inspector is moving the search effort up to the last known location of her cellphone."

Green felt a chill in the wind, and he glanced ner-vously up at the sky, where clouds were churning. He headed back toward his car. "Let's go then. That storm is going to hit any time."

As he followed Vickers's Interceptor through a series of back roads, he turned on his radio. The storm was already cutting a swath through the St. Lawrence Seaway corridor just to the southwest, bringing thunder, lightning, and hail the size of marbles. It was expected to hit the Ottawa region within the hour.

The duty inspector had set up the Command Centre at the intersection of two county roads, close to the signal tower. Assorted police vehicles already lined the road, and officers were patrolling the shoulders on foot, looking for signs of a collision. The ERT and K9 teams were not visible, and Green hoped they were already in the bush, doing a grid search.

Green pulled in behind Vickers, and the two of them were just walking toward the Command trailer when the duty inspector stepped out of it, waving his phone excitedly.

"Listen to this! A farmer west of Spencerville just called in to say he saw the public appeal about Hannah, and he recognized her. He said she dropped by his place yesterday afternoon, asking if he'd seen a white truck. She figured someone was trying to hide it. He told her about an old abandoned homestead that used to be owned by a junk dealer and auto repair guy called Jenkins."

Green's hope soared. "Where?"

Vickers was already flipping through his phone, checking property listings.

"The farmer gave us directions," the inspector said. "I've got a guy trying to locate it on the sat map inside."

At that moment, the Command door burst open and the officer looked out. "Got it! Not far from here." He rattled off some coordinates.

Green was already on the move. "Let's go!"

"You're going nowhere," the inspector snapped. "We don't know what we're dealing with. They could be holed up there. Could even be a hostage situation."

Green thought quickly. "Three of our five main suspects were in Ottawa as of nine thirty this morning. The only ones I didn't personally see are Kristina's father and mother, who's a long shot. So odds are the killer is long gone from this Jenkins place."

"'Odds are' isn't good enough. I'll get an ERT team together and make a plan."

Green chafed as the inspector called the ERT commander inside and worked out a plan. It took ten minutes while the wind whipped the trees and the sky grew more bruised and angry. Finally, the cavalcade departed, with ERT taking the lead and Vickers and Green taking up the rear. The duty inspector had given them radios along with strict orders to stay far from the action.

The Jenkins farm was a jumble of derelict buildings and rusting junk. There was no sign of people or functioning vehicles on the property, but Green's hopes rose at the sight of fresh tire tracks in the trampled grass leading from the road. He could barely contain himself as the ERT units fanned out and approached the compound. From a distance, he saw them moving from building to building. The inspector stood at Vickers's side, their radios crackling in the wind with each negative report.

Until, finally, "Bingo. White truck located in red equipment barn. Old model Silverado."

"Drew Sedgwick's truck," Vickers said. "Any sign of human presence?"

"Negative, Sarge. But we'll do a full search of the premises."

Green's heart sank. So close, yet nowhere. He turned in a circle, staring down the deserted road in both directions. *Hannah, where are you? What's happened to you? And why the hell didn't you call in if you found the truck?* He began to walk along the road, studying the ground on either side. If she had found the truck, and the killer had spotted her, he might have ambushed her somewhere along the road. But not just anywhere. Forensics had found forest loam in the tires. Here, there was nothing but fields.

His phone rang, startling him. Sullivan. He snatched it up. "Anything?"

"We only got one of the Ramirez trucks, at the Ramirez home. The other one is missing."

"Who's got it?"

"I don't know." Sullivan's voice came through, muffled by the wind. "We're getting no answer from anyone in the family. No one is answering their phones or doorbells."

Green turned his back on the wind. "My hunch is we're looking for Ramon or Luis."

"Why?"

"Strength. Have you had eyes on either of them recently?"

"Nope. Not since we left this morning. My visit to Kristina seems to have sent them all into hiding. I'm working on warrants to bust the doors down."

"Fuck, fuck, fuck!" Green exclaimed. "We should have put that brother under surveillance right away. Or apprehended the whole lying bunch of them!"

At that moment, the first pellets of hail struck the ground at his feet.

CHAPTER THIRTY-THREE

Hannah's progress was infinitely slow. As she dragged herself along the ground, using her uninjured leg to push and her uninjured arm to pull, each small obstacle — a fallen tree or mossy rock — seemed insurmountable. *Jeez, a snail could make better time.* Worried that she'd lost her bearings and strayed off course, she listened for sounds of the road. Nothing. *Not exactly a four-lane highway, that's for sure.*

Exhausted, she rested and assessed her make-shift splint. If she made some sort of crutch, could she manage to stand up and make better time?

She found another sturdy branch with a fork near one end, broke off four feet, and hauled herself upright against a tree. Pain spasms raced through her and black spots dimmed her vision. Wavering and gritting her teeth, she waited for the dizziness to pass. When she tested the crutch, she found that if she leaned hard to her good side, she could hop and hobble forward, but her balance teetered and pain knifed through her leg. A second crutch would help, but her injured arm would never support it.

Overhead, the clouds were billowing in, swollen and bruised, and gusts of chilly wind tore at the trees. *Just great.* A storm was coming. She had no time to waste. She swung and hopped a meandering path through the woods, grabbing at tree branches to keep from falling. Somewhere up ahead, an engine rumbled, and tires hissed on the gravel. Much closer this time. She forced herself to hurry. So near! Could she make it in time? And what if it was the killer, back for another look?

She flinched as something stung her cheek, cold and hard. *Hail! Half my body doesn't work, my head is exploding, I'm lost, and I've got a killer on my ass. But that's not enough?*

Why the hell hadn't she looked for her cellphone yesterday after the accident? She'd barely been able to think. She just remembered tumbling and spinning, the smell of balsam and the prickle against her cheek, the jarring stabs of pain as her body hit. Aware of terror, of heavy breathing and someone trampling through the grass, the all-consuming urge to get away.

A whimper escaped her lips as the approaching engine passed by and faded away again. But not before she glimpsed a pale flash through the trees ahead. A truck? An SUV? The road must be barely a hundred feet ahead!

She hopped and lunged and slithered as the hail slicked the forest floor, and soon she burst out of the forest into a weed-choked ditch. Beyond the ditch lay a gravel road, straight and deserted. She crouched in the ditch, wondering if she should stay in hiding and wait for another vehicle. From this point she could see them before they saw her and decide if they were friend or not.

Forest loam, Green thought. That was what the Forensics team had scraped from the motorcycle tires. Not just gravel, but debris from a forest. He stood on the road and looked in both directions, squinting against the hail. Fields of scrubby pasture stretched into the distance on either side, interspersed with the occasional swath of green crops and bordering trees.

I need to find a real forest, he thought. After leaving Jenkins's farm, Hannah would have driven west toward the main road that led to the highway. The killer must have followed her and waited for the perfect spot to ambush her.

He returned to his car and headed slowly west, keeping a sharp eye out for any suspicious signs. As he drove, he phoned Vickers.

"We have a situation," he told him, shouting over the noise of the hail hammering on the roof. "We don't have eyes on any of the suspects, and one of the Ramirez trucks is missing. Brian was only able to seize one of them. It looks like his early-morning visit stirred them all up. I don't know what they're up to, but it's safe to say our suspect is on the loose. We need officers patrolling these roads."

"He'd be a fool to walk into a hornet's nest of cops."

"A fool, or desperate."

Vickers grunted. "I'll pass that on to the DI. Where are you?"

"I'm driving west, following a hunch. Get the dog and ERT ready to search. I'll keep you posted." Green rounded a bend and spotted a line of trees up ahead on the left. As he drew nearer, the forest took shape, dense and thick, stretching down the slope and far ahead. He slowed to study the gravel shoulder and the edging of grass and cattails that gave way to the forest beyond. He was almost upon it before he saw a white storage shed tucked into a small clearing on the opposite side. Beside it was a gravel drive, hidden from the road.

His pulse leaped. The perfect ambush! He drove past, pulled onto the shoulder, and jogged back across the road, careful to avoid disturbing the ground. The hail sent up little puffs of dust as it pelted the ground, and he pulled his collar up against the chill.

With a detective's eye honed by years of experience, he studied the ground. The hail was rapidly obliterating the tracks, but he could still see churned-up gravel and multiple skid marks that slid sideways before veering off the road. Fighting the urge to plunge into the grass, he took out his phone, knowing he had to capture what little evidence was left, and took a few quick snaps of the tracks leading into the ditch. Beyond the ditch, the grass and shrubs were flattened in a swath leading into the woods. Turf was churned up, and branches were broken in the headlong rush toward a tall, thick oak with a deep gash in its trunk.

Abandoning all attempt to preserve the scene, Green crashed through the underbrush to the tree. "Hannah! Hannah!"

No response. He flailed frantically around, sweeping aside branches and screaming her name. Nothing but the hiss and pop of hail. Grabbing the radio, he called in.

The OPP teams arrived sporadically over the next ten minutes as they withdrew from their original searches and regrouped. Green chafed, knowing that with each passing moment, the track would get harder for the dog to pick up. Rather than disturbing possible scent tracks, he ran along the roadside in both directions, frantically calling Hannah's name, to be met once again with nothing but the drumming of hail.

The search manager took stock of the new terrain, which was densely forested and tangled with underbrush. The area was bounded by the river on one end and the gravel road on the other. The officer grimaced. "Must be two to three square kilometres of impenetrable crap here, and that's not counting the hay fields farther up. A person could be lying injured five feet away and you wouldn't see them. But ..." He pointed to the trampled forest floor. "We have a clear starting point, so we'll get K9 right on it."

"Is there still time for the dog? In this weather?"

The dog, a German Shepherd with long, lean legs and pricked ears, was pulling on the lead, eager to get to work. Her handler grinned. "She thinks so."

Green watched as the dog scouted in ever-widening circles. She seemed to pick up a scent, follow it for while, pause and pick up another scent, and raise her head as if puzzled. The handler, following behind on the eight-foot lead, watched her behaviour closely as he guided her in a wider circle, around and back.

"She's picking up tracks," he said, "but there's a lot of criss-crossing. I think there may be two people, so it's confusing her."

Two people. Green's gut tightened. Hannah, and her assailant, who must be searching for her.

He grasped at straws. "We know the assailant had to get the motorcycle out and take it to the staged accident scene at the bridge. Could that be what the dog is detecting?"

The handler shrugged. "Yeah, she may be on the assailant's scent. I'll circle her farther out, and if your daughter has left a track, we should cross it."

Green held his breath as he watched the dog and her team disappear into the bush. As much as he wanted to join them, he didn't want to add to the confusion. The rest of the search team stayed back as well and used the time to search the underbrush for evidence. The wind had eased, and the hail was dying to a sputter, but a cold drizzle dripped down Green's neck. Finally, the radios crackled with a shout of triumph, and everyone cheered as they hurried in the direction of the call. When they reached the K9 team, the dog was moving confidently, excitedly, her nose to the ground in a tight, zigzagging pattern. No more stopping or doubling back. The handler gave a thumbs-up, and the whole team exchanged grins as they followed.

Hope swelled in Green's chest. She was alive! And she was on the move.

"She's heading away from the road," said the ERT officer in front of him. He was a beefy, barrel-chested man with a shaved head. "She's not trying to get help."

"Maybe she's trying to escape," his skinnier partner said.

The two of them paused to study the ground. To Green, it looked like a tangled, soggy mess of green and brown debris, but they squatted down and pointed to the broken shoots and overturned moss.

"Looks like she'd dragging something," Beefy said. "I think maybe she's injured, dragging herself along the ground."

Green's hope died. *Please, God. Please be wrong.* He squinted. "Do you see blood?"

"Impossible to say, with this hail and all." He looked up ahead, where the dog was still making slow but steady progress around fallen trees and over slippery rocks. "But if she's that injured and heading away from help, we better pick up the pace."

Hannah huddled in the ditch beside the road, growing stiff and cold. The icy damp seeped through her jeans, and her leg began to seize up. *This plan isn't going to work*, she thought. *No one comes along here. I have to get up on the road and look for help, either a busier road or a farmhouse.*

She had no idea where she was or what direction she should go, how much distance she'd covered since yesterday, or even whether she'd been going in circles. Was this the same road she'd been on or somewhere else entirely?

She forced her muscles to obey as she dragged herself up onto the road. Beneath her, her good leg shook with exhaustion as she propped herself up on it with her crutch. Teetering, she looked up and down the road and scanned the fields on the other side for any sign of help. A house in the distance, a farmer on his tractor. But there was nothing. Far across the field, she could see some grain silos, but she'd never reach them before collapsing in exhaustion. She'd be better off on the road.

Her head pounded and her limbs shook with cold and fatigue. The hail had turned to a relentless drizzle that soaked her to the core. Slowly, she began to hop along the road, gritting her teeth and fighting the urge to wail in despair. Surely someone would come along. If she just kept going, this road would lead somewhere.

She'd managed no more than fifty feet before she stopped to drape herself over her crutch, gasping for breath. Dimly through the noise, she heard the growl of tires on gravel approaching from behind. Relief rushed in as she struggled to turn around. A pickup was crawling along, its windshield wipers flapping. Hannah moved into the road and propped herself on one leg to wave it down with her crutch. Surely it would see her.

As it drew nearer, it slowed as if to stop. It was close enough now that she could see a single driver at the wheel and the colour of the truck. White. Then suddenly its tires spat gravel as it accelerated directly at her. Her brain registered this with dizzy disbelief an instant before she flung herself off the road and tumbled into the ditch. The truck barrelled past and skidded to a stop down the road.

Adrenalin shot through her, obliterating pain, and before the truck had even stopped, she was dragging herself frantically into the brush. She heard the truck door open and footsteps crunch on the gravel, swift and light as the driver raced back toward her.

I can't outrun them, Hannah thought, casting about for shelter. She spotted a wide, sturdy tree trunk and rolled over and over to hide behind it. She didn't dare peek around it but heard panting, cursing, and branches cracking as the killer came straight for her.

Hannah stifled her own breathing and, in a surge of rage, gripped her walking stick and prepared to fight.

The dog paused to bury her nose in the damp loam at the base of a fir tree. She snuffled and swung back and forth as if exploring. The handler stopped her and squatted to examine the ground. He lifted a loose branch shaped like a fan and dense with tiny green needles. The others crowded around.

"This is freshly broken off," he said. "It looks like she may have rested here for a bit and covered herself for camouflage."

Green felt a flood of hope. She was still alive and using her wits. "Any blood?"

The handler probed the soggy leaves with careful fingers. "Nothing obvious, but with this rain, it's hard to tell."

"Let's mark it for Ident and move on," Green said, forgetting he wasn't in charge.

Vickers chuckled and pointed to one of the officers. "What he said."

From up the slope came the faint hiss of a distant car, the only one that had passed since they arrived. Green noted the distance with dismay. Had Hannah lost track of the road or was she afraid?

The handler ordered the dog to search, and she set off again, tracking a meandering path that angled away from the road. The rest of them stumbled and groped their way through the dense underbrush, some wondering aloud where the hell she was going.

After some time, the dog paused again at a trickling stream and raised her head to sniff the air. Then, instead of continuing down the slope, she changed direction and began to track a slow, painstaking path up the slope.

The dog is heading for the road, Green thought. *Did Hannah change direction, or did the dog catch a scent in the air? Are we close?* As the rest of them continued to tramp along the track, he broke off and headed directly up the slope. Slipping and sliding, he splashed through streams and over rocks as fast as he could, shoving branches out of his way and fighting to stay afoot. His jeans were caked with mud and his shoes squelched, but none of that mattered. Only reaching the road as soon as he could mattered. Once on the road, he'd be able to see long distances more easily.

His heart was hammering and his lungs were on fire. When he stopped to gulp in air, he heard the roar of an engine and the scattershot of gravel. Up ahead, the forest canopy thinned. He plunged forward, fighting thick, shoulder-high weeds, clambered up the ditch, and burst out onto the gravel road. He looked wildly in both directions, about to call Hannah's name when he saw a truck parked askew at the edge of the road, its driver's door hanging open. From inside came the thin, lost wail of a child.

Groping for his gun, he broke into a run.

The forest was alive, branches cracking, boughs vibrating, as her pursuer flailed through the underbrush in search of her. Stifling ragged sobs, Hannah pressed herself against the tree trunk and gripped her crutch in her one good hand. Waiting. She had one chance — one Hail Mary swing — before she'd be overpowered.

The panting grew closer, the ground seemed to tremble beneath the footsteps, and then two legs dressed in blue jeans and neon orange sneakers appeared around the base of the tree. Hannah waited a split second to be sure of her aim and swung the stick overhead with all her strength, adding a martial arts roar to give her power.

The killer screamed and stumbled back in shock, tripping over a root and landing hard on their back. The shovel in their hand went flying. Hannah scrambled to regain her own balance against the tree and gripped her stick for another swing. Her assailant struggled to their hands and knees and groped in the underbrush for the shovel.

"Don't even think about it!" Hannah roared with as much fury as she could muster. The assailant closed their hand on the shovel and swung around. Hannah gasped and almost dropped her stick.

"You!"

Kristina staggered to her feet and faced her like a caged bear, wielding the shovel. Panting. She took a step forward.

"Kristina, don't. Don't make this worse."

"My children need me. I can't go to jail." Her voice quavered, hopeless and full of despair.

Hannah grasped at straws. "Kristina, you can't hide from this. There are cops everywhere. But if you stop now, the courts will understand."

Kristina's eyes filled with tears. They fell silently as she shook her head. "No, they won't. I can't ever change what happened."

"You can change what you do now. I know you don't want to kill me. You want this killing to stop."

"But …" She faltered. "I have to protect my children. They will have nobody."

"Kristina, look at me." Hannah forced herself to wait while the woman kept shaking her head. In the distance, very faintly, she heard the crackling of police radios. She barely dared to hope. "You know I'm on your side. I tried to help you. The courts will understand that you were desperate, trapped. He was a monster."

"They won't understand!" Kristina cried. "They never do. This is all my fault. That nice young man, why did he have to …?" She began to sob. "I didn't want to kill him, but I didn't know what else to do." She hung her head, and the shovel drooped to the ground in her hand.

Hannah wished she could reach it, but she was shivering all over and could barely stand. She heard a crunch on the gravel road, and through the underbrush she caught a glimpse of her father. His gun was drawn, but he was motionless.

Through Kristina's soft sobs came the wail of her son.

Abruptly, her father parted the bushes and stepped forward. "It's okay," he said quietly. "It's over. Kristina, put the shovel down and come to me. Your son needs you."

As he closed his hand on Kristina's wrist, Hannah felt her legs give out, and she slid soundlessly to the ground.

CHAPTER THIRTY-FOUR

Hannah was comfortably ensconced on a chaise longue in the backyard with her leg propped on a pillow and her arm in a proper professional sling. Green had brought her a tray with her dinner and cold lemonade and now stood watching her as she struggled to wield the fork with her left hand.

"You don't have to hover, you know."

"I know. I just want to make sure …"

"Make sure what? That I'm real?"

He managed a thin smile. He wasn't sure who was more traumatized by her near-death confrontation with a killer. After three days in hospital, she'd been released into his care. The first day home, she'd slept almost the whole day in a special bed set up in the sunroom, but by the end of the second day, he'd found her trying to manoeuvre herself into the wheelchair so she could look at something other than the four walls.

"I made a lot of rookie mistakes," she muttered now.

"A few. But because of you the case is solved, the killer is in custody, and no more lives were lost."

"Do you think it will stick? That admission she made about killing Sedge? You heard it, too, right?"

He pulled a chair over to sit beside her. He'd promised himself he wouldn't talk about the case, only about silly, cheerful things. But he knew her. She was too much like him.

"I heard it, but no, it's not going to stick. Her husband's law firm has already retained the best defence attorney in Ontario."

Hannah snorted. "That shows you what they really thought of their law buddy Ted. Who?"

"Nina Novak. She's already shut her client down. The word is she's going to push hard on the abuse angle and extreme provocation for the husband's death and deny all involvement in Sedge's death. She's going to claim that her client's comments about that death were made under duress and subject to multiple interpretations. That there is no concrete evidence linking Kristina to Sedge's death."

"But what about the truck? There has to be forensics on the truck."

He nodded. "There were tools in the truck bed, yes — rope, chains, a ramp, winch —"

"So that's how she moved my bike."

"Probably, but the family is saying that's ordinary equipment they carry around all the time. There was also wood and grass debris in the truck bed that Ident hopes to match to your bike, so we may still get her on that. But her lawyer says it's a company truck that several people had access to, including all our other suspects."

"But she tried to run me down. She came after me with a shovel!"

"She was scared, didn't recognize you. You were a filthy, bloody sight. And you attacked her, remember."

Hannah rolled her eyes. "She was way the hell out in the middle of freaking nowhere, almost a hundred kilometres from her house, and just happened to come across the one cop who was unravelling the case?"

"Believe me, I've seen Nina Novak eviscerate the most solid witnesses and turn the whole case on its head."

"No. Kristina fully intended to kill me, Dad. She ambushed me and drove my bike off the road, then she hunted all over the place for me. It was blind luck I was able to hide. I was barely conscious."

"And Novak is going to use that, too. She'll ask if you ever actually saw her client driving that truck or hunting for you afterward."

Hannah dropped her gaze. She had given up on the fork and was picking at her food with her fingers. Now she abandoned even that. "No, it happened too fast. And afterward I was confused and in pain. I see where this is going."

"All is not lost, honey. If we can put the motorcycle in the truck bed, we'll have some threads to hang a case on."

She looked up at him through bleak eyes. Her face still bore the bruises and abrasions of the crash, adding to the melancholy look. "Like you said, all the suspects had access to that truck."

"The guys are also going to work really hard to find her fingerprints and DNA on the motorcycle so we can pin her directly to it. That would be hard to discount."

"I don't understand why she moved my motorcycle in the first place. That was risky. It took time, and someone could have come by and seen her moving it."

"That puzzled me, too." He cracked open a beer and poured it into a glass. Hannah was watching the amber liquid with longing, and he smiled with sympathy. "Maybe tomorrow. When you're off the heavy-duty meds."

She scowled. "Fine. I can tell you have a theory."

"A theory. We'll never know, because they sure as hell won't tell us, but I think she wanted to direct attention away from the area. Remember, she'd gone to great trouble to hide Sedge's truck, and the ambush site was only a kilometre away. She knew cops would pull out all the stops searching for a fellow officer, and we would wonder why you were even up there. She knew we'd turn over every rock in the vicinity looking for you. By moving the bike closer to Sedge's murder site, she figured the cops would concentrate their efforts there. And it almost worked! If not for the farmer who phoned in the tip about the old Jenkins place, we might not have searched as far away as that."

He paused and sipped his beer, avoiding her eyes, hesitating to explain the next part of his theory.

Hannah was eyeing him with eagle eyes. "But I was a loose end, wasn't I? I wasn't killed in the crash the way she'd hoped, and as long as I was alive, I could bring her whole cover-up crashing down."

He said nothing.

"That's why she came back the next day, despite all the risks, despite having to bring her son with her. She had to get rid of the loose end." She bit her lip, and he saw a shudder ripple through her. "That's what the shovel was for."

He spread his hands in a gesture of defeat. "We'll never know what she planned."

"*I* know. Looking into her eyes, seeing the desperation and the fierce focus in that moment, I saw my own death."

He leaned forward to squeeze her hand and held on as much for his sake as hers. "But she didn't do it. You turned her back from the brink. You. By reminding her of who you were and who she was."

She took a shaky breath and flicked her good hand toward his beer. "Dad, let me have just one little sip of that, will you? Or better yet, some of that single malt you have stashed in the cupboard."

He stood up. "It's against doctor's orders."

"Yes, it is."

He laughed and headed for the house.

Hannah was alone in the house the next afternoon when the doorbell rang. Sharon had set her up with a bedside tray of snacks and drinks and arranged for Tony to come straight home from school to make sure she had everything she needed. She smiled at the memory of her carefree, skateboarding little brother agreeing to take on such a solemn task. Time would tell whether he remembered it when all his friends headed off to the park.

Modo let out a half-hearted bark and lumbered toward the front door. Hannah ignored the bell. Her father had been adamant that she not answer the phone or the doorbell when she was alone. "What's the big deal?" she'd asked, trying to sound cavalier. The truth was, she was fighting serious terror. Nightmares, flashbacks, anxiety attacks. She was trying to combat them by reassuring herself that the threat was over. Kristina was in jail. Her father and brother were being investigated as possible accessories after the fact. No one would dare come after her.

"So what's your worry?" she'd demanded, and her father had just shrugged.

"Humour me," he'd said.

The doorbell rang again. Modo managed a more enthusiastic bark. Silence. Footsteps on the gravel path, a shadow crossing the backyard. Her adrenalin spiked as she shrank back in her bed, trying to be invisible. Then hands cupped the sunroom patio door, and a face peered in.

Oh, for fuck's sake.

His eyes locked on hers. "Can I come in?" he shouted.

Was it locked? Her father had double-locked everything. "If you can open it." Her heart was still pounding, but now the terror slowed to relief. Even joy.

He rattled the door, fiddled with the catch, and slid it open. "Not much protection," he said as he walked in. His dark green eyes reflected worry and relief as he sized her up. "You look better than I expected."

Sorry to disappoint you was on the tip of her tongue, but she held it back. That tender look suited him. While she was searching for a safe response through the minefield of her thoughts, he came to her side and gestured to the empty table.

"Can I get you anything?"

"Do you know how to make coffee?"

The tender look dissolved in a grin, which suited him even better. "Point the way."

She collected her wits as she listened to him moving around the kitchen, opening and closing cupboards, sliding open drawers, clattering cutlery, and running the water. She was glad for the extra minutes as she fought her wild bedhead into a ponytail and tugged her baggy T-shirt down. Eventually he came back with a tray bearing two coffees and a plate of cookies.

"Those might be two months old," she said.

He shrugged and handed her a cup. "It's the thought that counts." He pulled a chair closer and sat back in it. "That was quite an adventure. How are you doing?"

"Honestly?" She fought a lump in her throat. "Not great. Getting there."

"Why didn't you take me with you?"

"You were at work."

"I would have figured out a way. Why didn't you at least tell me what you were up to?"

"It's complicated."

He flushed and looked down at his coffee cup then squinted out the back door. "I was so worried — no, scared — when you went missing. When your motorcycle turned up in the river."

"Yeah. I was, too."

"Of course you were. Sorry." He looked sheepish. "Should I go?"

She was startled. "No, of course not. I'm glad to see you. These four walls get pretty claustrophobic."

He pointed to the wheelchair. "Do you want to go out in the backyard? Are you allowed?"

"Allowed? Not in my vocabulary." She grabbed the overhead bar to pull herself up. "Take me away!"

Once settled in the shade of the backyard, she shut her eyes and took a deep, peaceful breath. It was a sultry July afternoon, with wisps of cirrus clouds against the hazy sky and not a puff of breeze. High up in a maple, their resident cardinal sang its clear, bell-like tune. Josh said nothing, like he was waiting for permission. "Talk," she said.

"Do you want me to tell you about my trip to the beach? My pickup game of soccer with some of the guys?"

She opened her eyes. "About the case."

"Right." He paused and then seemed to throw caution to the winds. "Well, we've got Kristina in custody on a detention order. Her children have gone to live with her parents. We're working on shoring up the case, because she's got a kick-ass lawyer who's already applied for a bail hearing. It's next week."

"Any new evidence?"

He nodded, relaxing into his role. "We haven't located Sedge's phone and laptop, and I don't think we ever will, but the OPP have recovered his emails and texts from the Carleton University server. He wasn't on social media, but Justine was in his contacts, and he'd sent her a couple of messages in May. Stuff like *Nice to talk to you* and *Here's the link to Queen's athletics*, and the last one a couple of days before her father's death: *I'll be on the trail tomorrow, hope to see you.* She sent a thanks for the Queen's link but didn't reply to the others."

Hannah smiled wryly. "She was way out of his league."

"And ..." It was his turn to smile, a great big grin of triumph. "The OPP have recovered the photos from Sedge's camera. We think we have McAuley's killer on camera."

She sat bolt upright, barely noticing the pain that shot through her arm. "What?"

He nodded. "All the photos are date-stamped. Most of them are ducks, nests, eggs, or rivers. Hundreds of them. A few of Justine, too, taken from a distance on the Shirley's Bay trail in the three weeks before her father's murder. Most taken around six a.m."

"Wow, she's an early riser!"

"Yeah, well, runners can be intense. And don't forget, she'd have to shower and get to school afterward."

"So what about the killer?"

"Okay. So on June second, the night McAuley died, Sedge pulled an all-nighter. There's photos starting from eight p.m., just around dusk, of shorelines, close-ups of water plants, flooded woods, holes in trees, and, of course, ducks. A boat going by in the bay, several of a dog off-leash swimming."

"What dog?"

"Too far away to tell, but it's probably not relevant. This was down at the Ottawa River, at least half a K from the crime scene."

"But a dog means an owner, and an owner means a possible witness."

He smiled at her. "Yeah, we're following up on it, but it was hours earlier in the night. What's really important are the photos he took around midnight. He was in the woods by then, sometimes walking and sometimes standing, photographing night life. A porcupine, owls, a fox, a coyote, even a beaver chewing on a branch."

"Videos?"

"A few. But mostly stills, shot with a wide-aperture, high-ISO, and telephoto lens, according to the tech guys at the OPP. There was a half moon that night, so there was enough light to capture quite a lot of detail with his high-end camera."

She found she was holding her breath as she mentally urged him on. "And?"

"It is still hard to distinguish facial features, but at eleven fifty-one there was a photo of someone walking through the woods, carrying something. Sedge must have increased the zoom because, in the next shot two minutes later, you can see the person is carrying something bulky under one arm and something long and thin in the other. The tech people cleaned up the image enough to ID Ted McAuley with a shovel in his hand."

She gasped. "So *he* brought the shovel!"

"And the tarp. That's what he was sneaking back to get when Phil Walker spotted him on the riverbank. The next photo is of him digging with the shovel and another one of the little dog tied to a tree."

"That's what I thought! Ted McAuley was going to kill and bury the dog."

"It looked that way. Sedge switched to video after that, and you can hear the dog barking furiously. The next few minutes are messed up — blurry, swirling images of trees and ground, like Sedge was trying to get closer, maybe to see what was going on. But then the video picks up another figure in the corner of the frame, running through the woods." He paused and twisted his empty coffee cup in his hands. "At one point you can see the shovel swing through the air toward the dog. The dog gives one howl and stops barking. Sedge swears. The video starts jumping around, like Sedge is running. He's panting for breath, and then there's this godawful scream. 'Noooo!' Sedge stops in his tracks. We think he forgot the video was on, because it was tilted all crazy and mostly filming treetops. There's a lot of screams and Sedge says, 'Holy Mother!' and the camera swings like he's turning around. We think he started to run away, but the video stops." Josh took a deep breath. "That's it. The next photo is not until six days later. Ducks again, location the South Nation River."

"So he not only rescued the dog, but he actually witnessed the murder!"

Josh nodded. "Tech has broken the footage down to examine it frame by frame and enhanced it every which way, but unfortunately few frames actually capture the killer, and it's never full face-on. There is one where it looks like the dog is running away. Maybe it ran after Sedge."

She found she was trembling at the vivid picture Josh had painted. Such an eruption of rage and destruction in the peaceful forest night. "Why the hell didn't Sedge come forward? It was weeks before that body was found!"

"Maybe he was afraid he'd been seen and the killer would come after him."

"Even so ... What about an anonymous tip about the body?"

He shrugged. "We'll never know. He was an odd person, timid and antisocial. But at least we know what happened. Ted was going to kill the dog. Kristina must have followed him — maybe she saw him sneak back to take the shovel and tarp from the shed, and she was afraid of what he'd do. When he struck the first blow to the dog, she lost it, grabbed the shovel from him, and ... finished him off."

Hannah pictured the scenario and remembered Kristina's desperate face as she'd confronted her. "Poor woman, pushed to the brink by a brutal husband who was about to destroy the one thing that brought both her and her son joy."

He nodded. "This will shore up the defence. Abuse, provocation, state of mind." He bent his head and poked the ground. "Maybe that's the way it should be."

CHAPTER THIRTY-FIVE

On a routine day, bail court was normally packed as dozens of accused, their lawyers, and their families revolved through its doors, but pandemic restrictions had severely reduced its capacity, with many appearances done by video link. On the day of Kristina McAuley's bail hearing, however, it was filled to its limit. Some people, including other lawyers, were there just to watch the legendary Nina Novak tear the Crown to shreds; others to get a glimpse of the rich wife turned double murderer; and still others from women's groups to provide solidarity.

Green spotted Kristina's father and brother, and between them her daughter, Justine, all sitting in a rigid row near the front. Ramon glanced back but seemed to look right through him. He looked haunted and the brother defiant, but behind her mask, Justine's expression was difficult to read. Her face was the colour of putty and her whole body quivered.

Green chose a seat just behind with a clear view of them as well as the defence table. From that vantage point, he scanned the room, wondering how many genuine friends of Kristina's had come, but it was impossible to tell. Perhaps none. When Kristina was led into the room, silence fell and all eyes turned toward her. Handcuffed and dressed in an orange jumpsuit, she looked the picture of defeat. She kept her eyes lowered and acknowledged no one as she took her seat behind the Plexiglas barrier of the prisoners' bench. Nina, in a nice piece of theatre, approached to press her palm to the Plexiglas and give Kristina a gentle nod.

The formal process, dry as dust, droned on. Although in this case the onus was on the defence to show Kristina did not present a risk, the Crown attorneys were taking no chances with Nina Novak on the opposing bench. They spent a long time expounding on the charges and describing the assault on Hannah. Nina also took her time, giving a soft, measured plea for release with strict conditions and surety. "The accused is a loving, committed mother and a law-abiding citizen with an impeccable record and strong family support. She has a three-year-old son with serious medical and mental health challenges who needs her care."

Blah, blah, blah, Green thought. He knew the plea was largely for the benefit of the media and the public, setting the stage for Kristina's tragic story. The eventual outcome of the hearing was beyond dispute; no court in their right mind would release a woman accused of two murders and two subsequent assaults on a police officer.

Throughout it all, Kristina sat with her head bowed and her handcuffed hands clasped in her lap. When the bail judge rendered his decision, she flinched, but Nina did not bat an eye. Green watched the family carefully. Both father and brother surged forward as if to reach out to Kristina, and the anguish was plain on their faces. Tears welled in the father's eyes. But Justine sat like a stone, her face and body rigid as she fought for control.

When Kristina stood to be led away, she looked over and lifted her eyes for an instant. Her gaze locked on Justine's before she turned to leave the court. Around him, the spectators were beginning to stand up, talking excitedly and speculating on next steps, but Green had eyes only for Justine. She was so pale, he almost felt he could see through her. Her fingers clutched at her grandfather's arm. Green leaned closer.

"I can't do this," she murmured. "She says I can, but I can't take care of him. Not —"

Ramon shot a quick look at Green and clamped his hand over hers so tightly that his knuckles turned white. "You can! We will do it together! Always."

Justine was shaking her head, tears spilling.

"Don't talk. You will! You promised." Still gripping her arm, he began to pull her toward the aisle, out of hearing and soon out of sight.

Green played the scene over and over in his mind as he returned to his office. It was such a brief exchange, lasting less than fifteen seconds, yet in the silences between the words lay an ocean of meaning. *I can't take care of him. She says I can, but ...* And Ramon's answer, *You promised.*

And most powerful of all, the words left unspoken in Kristina's last look.

Scraps of memory fell into place, and nagging questions suddenly made sense. Back in his office, he phoned Sullivan. "Any chance I can have a peek at those photos Sedgwick took on the night of the McAuley murder?"

"Why?"

"Just … reassuring myself."

Silence. "Mike, what's up?"

"Maybe nothing. I'll fill you in once I've seen them."

"I'm in back-to-back meetings, but Mike, if you've got anything that's going to screw up our case, I need to know."

"And you will."

"Fine. Four o'clock. Fuck, you're making me crazy."

At five thirty, Green arrived home to find Hannah in the backyard with a bowl of fresh cherries and a glass of white wine. Another glass and a half-empty bottle sat on the table at her elbow. He brought his own glass out.

"Kanner's been here again?" he said, sitting beside her and helping himself to a cherry.

The trace of a smile lingered on her lips, but she shrugged. "He's company. It's either him or the squirrels."

"Kristina's bail hearing was today. Denied."

"Josh filled me in."

He chewed the cherry. Kanner was a good kid. Cocky and ambitious, but underneath it, he had substance. Green had peeked at his file, and it was unblemished and impressive. Was he going to break Hannah's heart, or was she going to break his? Green knew any man who caught and held Hannah's interest would have to live a bit on the edge, just wild and dangerous enough to keep up with her but solid enough to keep her safe. Was Kanner that guy?

He had no idea. Relationships that looked perfect on the surface could be rotten at their core.

"Are you just going to sit there and eat my cherries, or are you going to tell me?"

"I looked at the photos Sedgwick took that night."

She blinked, obviously not expecting that twist. "And?"

"I think the murder scenario the guys came up with is accurate. McAuley's murder was not premeditated. It was an act of sudden, overwhelming rage."

"So?"

"But it's damn hard to be certain it was Kristina who swung the shovel."

"Josh says you can tell it's a woman from the voice and the shape."

"Yes, it's a woman."

Hannah stared at him a long time. "You're saying it was Justine?"

"I'm saying I don't know. The team has cleaned up the images the best they can, picked them apart almost pixel by pixel, compared body shapes, profiles, even clothing. Sullivan thinks they have enough. But both women are tall. Kristina is heavier, but the clothing was bulky. Both women sometimes put their hair up in ponytails. They're related, so they have the same nose. The jacket shown in the photos has disappeared, almost certainly thrown out because it was covered in blood." He paused. "And there are more holes. How did Kristina find Sedge?"

"I think she spotted him in the parking lot in Kemptville." Hannah's voice quivered. "I've wracked my brains about that, Dad. Is Sedge's death my fault? I tipped Kristina off that he had her dog, and I think she realized he must have been there when she killed her husband. That's why Sedge fled the scene that night and why he dropped out of sight. And it's why she got rid of the camera."

He took a slow sip of wine. "But it was Justine who kept going to the therapist in Kemptville. Justine who would have seen him in the parking lot and could have followed him back to the cabin."

Hannah frowned. "But she could have told her mother, especially after I mentioned Sedge to Kristina. Dad, there's absolutely no doubt it was Kristina that tried to kill me. We do know that."

"Yes. Tidying up. But I think there's more to this story. Ted McAuley's murder was a desperate act of rage, whereas Sedge's was carefully planned and coolly executed, right down to hiding his truck in the perfect spot. I think the two of them know what happened. I think Kristina's known since the day I showed her the video from the airport parking lot. The look that passed between them in the courtroom spoke volumes."

"What video?"

"The CCTV of the driver of the car. Kristina identified it as her husband, but we know now that he was already dead, so she lied. But her expression was odd. Puzzled, even afraid."

"Dad." Hannah rolled her eyes. "Maybe she was afraid because she realized she was on camera."

He shook his head. "When Sedge witnessed the murder, why didn't he come forward?"

She gazed into her glass and said nothing. When she finally looked up at him, he saw she had made the connection. "Okay, yeah, he liked Justine. And maybe he thought Ted deserved it for what he was doing to a defenceless little dog."

"True. Anyway, I think the whole family knew, and they've closed ranks to protect each other. For whatever reason, Kristina has chosen to take the fall. What were her exact words when she confronted you in the woods the other day?"

Hannah took a deep breath. "They're seared into my brain. 'I have to protect my children. They will have nobody.'"

Green nodded. "Exactly. Her children. She's their mother. She would put them before herself. And I think she probably felt responsible because she hadn't left that awful man. It was her fault her son had been damaged by him, perhaps irreparably. Her fault that the whole family was trapped in a nightmare that she didn't have the courage to break. That, unfortunately, is the guilt that many abused women carry."

"Even though the bastard really responsible for the nightmare is the abuser."

He nodded. "And don't forget, Justine grew up under that same reign of terror. Seventeen years of terror can do a lot of damage. Maybe that's why Elena Markos wanted to keep treating her."

Hannah twirled her wine in her glass. Took a deep, shaky breath. "When I was on the street, I had a friend. She'd lived with that. She had these triggers, when she'd just lose it, like she was trying to bust free from something inside herself."

He was silent, afraid to break the fragile thread of connection. Hannah let him in so rarely.

After an instant, Hannah herself drew back. "So she stepped in to take the blame, to protect her daughter when she couldn't before."

"I think that's very possible."

"Do you think she'll plead guilty then? To make sure her daughter stays safe?"

He straightened, on firmer emotional ground now. "Not after she's hired Nina Novak. She's going for full acquittal. I think the whole family plans to keep quiet and force the Crown to prove its case, and as we've both pointed out, it's pretty shaky as long as everyone sticks to their story. Nina Novak may drive a tank through it."

"Which means no one pays for McAuley's murder."

He kept his face deadpan. He'd always done his job, but in all the homicide cases he'd worked, there were some victims he'd mourned less than others. "Possibly not."

She grunted as if her thoughts echoed his. But then her expression gradually grew sad. "But no one pays for Sedge's murder either. That's … that's on me."

He fought a sudden wave of sorrow, knowing he could never take that away from her. "Maybe not in court," he said eventually. "The OPP still has a lot of forensics to analyze on that case, so it's still possible. But judging from Justine's behaviour in the courtroom today, I'm not sure she'll be able to keep up the family charade, anyway. If she's responsible for even one of the murders, I think she'll break. It's a hell of a lot harder to live with blood on your hands than you think, and for a seventeen-year-old who killed her own father, it may be a cost too great to bear."

Seeing Hannah's stricken expression, he reached over to lift the empty wineglass gently from her hand. "I know, honey. There were a lot of victims in this case, and regardless of whether anyone is actually held accountable in court, that's only a small part of the price they will pay."

ACKNOWLEDGEMENTS

Writing this novel during the pandemic has been a challenge. When I started the first draft, the pandemic didn't exist. Shortly thereafter, it existed but should be resolved in a month or two. And finally, as I neared the end of the book, it looked as if it might never be resolved. I decided it had to be included; as possibly the most important single event in modern history, I couldn't pretend it didn't exist. But what would the future look like? How much detail was too much? Up until the final copy editing, the manuscript was being edited to include the latest guess what the pandemic would look like by the fall the book came out. My apologies if I guessed wrong.

Besides presenting challenges to the story, the pandemic cramped my research efforts. In-person discussions, as well as visits to the courthouse, the OPP offices, and various restaurants were out of the question, and I had to make do with internet research, which yields a pale imitation of real-life experiences. If I made mistakes in police or court procedure and detail, blame it on Covid. It has a lot to answer for this year.

But numerous people pitched in to help me get my facts straight, and their help is much appreciated. I want to thank Ottawa Police Superintendent Don Sweet (retired) for addressing everything from forensics to court procedure, and Kim Cooper, owner of Best Friends Dog Training School and founding member of the Ottawa Valley Search and Rescue Dog Association, for her expertise on K9 searches. Tim Desjardins, Gerhard Bruins, and my friend Ben Mancini from the Ottawa Duck Club answered my questions about ducks and Shirley's Bay. Keri Lewis, executive director of Interval House, provided helpful input regarding women's shelters, and my good friends Alex Wexler and Lily Cox, both social workers, answered questions about legal issues. Iden Ford provided expert advice on camera equipment. Thanks to all of you, and a very special thank-you to Mark Cartwright of the Ottawa Police Services (retired) for continuing to read every Inspector Green manuscript and providing valuable input, as well as correcting my errors in police procedure. Any remaining errors, whether accidental or intentional, are mine alone.

Throughout the writing process, from the first draft to the book on the shelf, many people helped to make *The Devil to Pay* the best it could be. I owe a big debt of gratitude to the continued support of my close friends and fellow writers in the Ladies Killing Circle: Sue Pike, Linda Wiken, and Mary Jane Maffini. As well, a big thank-you to my editor Allister Thompson for his astute and gentle feedback, Laura Boyle for the beautiful cover design, and the rest of the Dundurn team for playing such an important role behind the scenes and for continuing to support my work and that of other Canadian writers. And last but not least, thank you to readers for making the journey worthwhile.

ABOUT THE AUTHOR

Barbara Fradkin was born in Montreal and worked for more than twenty-five years as a child psychologist before retiring in order to devote more time to her first passion, writing. She is also the author of the Amanda Doucette Mysteries and the Cedric O'Toole series, and her short stories have appeared in mystery magazines and anthologies such as the New Canadian Noir series and the Ladies Killing Circle series. She is a two-time winner in *Storyteller Magazine*'s annual Great Canadian Short Story Contest, as well as a four-time nominee for the Crime Writers of Canada Award for Best Short Story. Her Inspector Green series has garnered an impressive four Best Novel nominations and two wins from the Crime Writers of Canada. She has three children and two dogs, and in whatever spare time she can find, she loves outdoor activities like travelling, skiing, and kayaking, as well as reading, of course.

THE
DEVIL
TO
PAY

Inspector Green Mysteries

Do or Die
Once Upon a Time
Mist Walker
Fifth Son
Honour Among Men
Dream Chasers
This Thing of Darkness
Beautiful Lie the Dead
The Whisper of Legends
None So Blind
The Devil to Pay

BARBARA FRADKIN

THE DEVIL TO PAY

AN INSPECTOR GREEN MYSTERY

DUNDURN
PRESS

Publisher and acquiring editor: Scott Fraser | Editor: Allister Thompson
Cover designer: Sophie Paas-Lang
Cover image: shutterstock.com/Daniel Carson Fung
Printer: Marquis Book Printing Inc.

Library and Archives Canada Cataloguing in Publication

Title: The devil to pay / Barbara Fradkin.
Names: Fradkin, Barbara, 1947- author.
Series: Fradkin, Barbara Fraser, 1947- Inspector Green mystery.
Description: Series statement: An Inspector Green mystery
Identifiers: Canadiana (print) 20210244836 | Canadiana (ebook) 20210244844 |
    ISBN 9781459743847 (softcover) | ISBN 9781459743854 (PDF) | ISBN 9781459743861 (EPUB)
Classification: LCC PS8561.R23 D49 2021 | DDC C813/.6—dc23

We acknowledge the support of the Canada Council for the Arts and the Ontario Arts Council for our publishing program. We also acknowledge the financial support of the Government of Ontario, through the Ontario Book Publishing Tax Credit and Ontario Creates, and the Government of Canada.

Care has been taken to trace the ownership of copyright material used in this book. The author and the publisher welcome any information enabling them to rectify any references or credits in subsequent editions.

The publisher is not responsible for websites or their content unless they are owned by the publisher.

Printed and bound in Canada.

Dundurn Press
1382 Queen Street East
Toronto, Ontario, Canada M4L 1C9
dundurn.com, @dundurnpress

For the women in my life